SICK THINGS

Sick Things

AN ANTHOLOGY OF EXTREME CREATURE HORROR

EDITOR: CHERYL MULLENAX

COMET PRESS NEW YORK

SICK THINGS

A COMET PRESS BOOK

Sick Things copyright © Comet Press, 2010
"Devils" copyright © Randy Chandler, 2010
"Threshold" copyright © Fred Venturini, 2010
"This Is My Body" copyright © Lawrence Conquest, 2010
"Hunger Pangs" copyright © Matt Kurtz, 2010
"Fly on the Wall" copyright © Stephanie Bedwell-Grime, 2010
"Legacy of the Last Invader" copyright © M. Shaw, 2010
"Acceptable Losses" copyright © Simon Wood, 2006
"An Unfortunate Incident at the Slaughterhouse" copyright © Harper Hull, 2010
"Rotsworth" copyright © Kurt Bachard, 2010
"Evil, Bent, and Candy-Sweet" copyright © Tim Curran, 2010
"Heat" copyright © Daniel I. Russell, 2010
"The Neglected" copyright © Sean Logan, 2010
"Betty and the Cambion" copyright © Ralph Greco, Jr., 2008
"Jimmy Sticks and the Outlaw Critter of Doom" copyright © Michael Boatman, 2010
"Ranching the Sleore" © copyright Aaron Polson, 2010
"Paper Angels on Fire" © copyright John Shirley, 2010
"The Special Son" copyright © Jeffrey Hale, 2010

"Acceptable Losses" first appeared in Dark Wisdom magazine, Spring '06

ISBN: 978-0-9820979-7-7

Comet Press website: www.cometpress.us

FIRST COMET PRESS TRADE PAPERBACK EDITION, JUNE 2010

TABLE OF CONTENTS

DEVILS by Randy Chandler   7

THRESHOLD by Fred Venturini   19

THIS IS MY BODY by Lawrence Conquest   25

HUNGER PANGS by Matt Kurtz   35

FLY ON THE WALL by Stephanie Bedwell-Grime   57

LEGACY OF THE LAST INVADER by M. Shaw   68

ACCEPTABLE LOSSES by Simon Wood   85

AN UNFORTUNATE INCIDENT AT THE SLAUGHTERHOUSE by Harper Hull   94

ROTSWORTH by Kurt Bachard   103

EVIL, BENT, AND CANDY-SWEET by Tim Curran   110

HEAT by Daniel I. Russell   120

THE NEGLECTED by Sean Logan   131

BETTY AND THE CAMBION by Ralph Greco, Jr.   144

JIMMY STICKS AND THE OUTLAW CRITTER OF DOOM by Michael Boatman   155

RANCHING THE SLEORE by Aaron Polson   170

PAPER ANGELS ON FIRE by John Shirley   187

THE SPECIAL SON by Jeffrey Hale   198

ABOUT THE AUTHORS   220

DEVILS
Randy Chandler

The damned room. Where it all happened. Where it's still happening. The room that isn't really a room, but what exactly it is, Jeze just doesn't know. *That* room. Four walls or six or more, owing to the fertile darkness, volume of blood spilled and temper of the times. A *living* room, the beating heart of a phantom house. The damned room that haunts Jeze's waking life and gives her nightmares actual teeth and claws.

"Why does that place scare you so much?" Jeze's shrink always wants to know. Never satisfied with first answers, he prods for unsacred revelations.

Her answer is always the same: "Because when I die I'll be stuck haunting that place. Forever."

"In a sense, you're stuck there now, aren't you?"

Clever bastard. "Clever bastard," she says. Sometimes words come to her from back there in that room, back where the tree of death grows on roots exposed and sickly white like naked bodies. Where roots *are* naked bodies.

"Well, aren't you?" His teeth are white as maggots. His eyes dead as roadkill.

"No I'm not. It's for dead souls, not for me. Not yet."

"Talk about your creatures. What was it you called them?"

"Too dangerous. They don't like being probed."

"You're protecting me from them, then?"

She shrugs. "If you like."

"But you called them something. Descriptive."

"Check your notes. I'm sure it's there."

"Ah. Here it is."

"You're such a putz."

"'Dark guardians' you called them. But you never made clear what they guard."

"Because I can never be sure. If they're keeping me in check or keeping others out. I don't know *what else* they want with me. What they might have planned."

"I can help you figure that out. If you let me."

Saying nothing, she avoids looking into the doctor's dead eyes.

He goes on: "Or . . . you can keep your life and your career on hold, sit and spin, and get absolutely nowhere."

She feels herself going now, slipping off into shadow, gooseflesh aquiver, sliding into the desperation of self-mockery: *Be still my trip-hammer heart.*

◆ ◆ ◆

Even before you got there, you knew it was going to be bad. But by then it was too late to turn back. So there you went, the almost-famous filmmaker/documentarian in hot pursuit of the bloody slice-of-darkside-life that would win essential funding and eventual respect of critics and art-house audiences everywhere. Working title: *Blood Cult.*

Tyler had warned you about these creepy people. The Lost City Luciferians. He told you you'd be nuts to go unescorted with them to a secret location to film their forbidden ceremony. But of course you had to do it. Just you and your handheld movie camera getting right up in reality's face. Rolling. Balls-out tits-atilt *rolling,* shooting for all you were worth. All the marbles. The whole shooting match and shebang. Shoot clichés and kill them dead.

When they put the bag over your head, you turned the camera on yourself and became part of the story. It was only later, when you were *in the room,* that you realized you *were* the story.

You had no inkling then that what you were looking for was God. But the moment you entered the room you knew you had stumbled undoubtedly into the realm of the Devil.

◆ ◆ ◆

"Call me Ishmael." That was what the cadaverous cocksucker actually said, and you framed his horse face in warty close-up, while behind you, others were making preparations, laying out steel edges and ancient crucibles. You didn't stay on his emaciated face long. The massive black tree in the center of the room drew itself into the viewfinder. A tree you could only think of as *Biblical.* It towered over the room, its soaring upper black branches forming a cathedral-like ceiling for the otherwise ceiling-less room.

Though you couldn't see them, you had the sudden unmistakable impression that catlike creatures had draped themselves over favored branches and were waiting to make great springing leaps down onto these pitiful humans who had little idea of the deep evil they were toying with. You weren't equipped to see them either but you caught their dreadful scent and it nearly sickened you.

No, these things were not feline. There was *nothing* natural about these creatures.

An insistent thought insinuated itself: *demon tree.*

Then a porcine man wearing thick sideburns and a white jumpsuit showed up and assumed a ceremonious position with his back to the tree.

Fat Elvis, you thought and laughed inwardly. You zoomed in on his face and froze there as Fat Elvis curled his lips and began to chant in lisping southern-fried Latin. Ishmael appeared at his side and slipped a knife in his hammy fingers. "Thank you," said Fat Elvis, "very much."

Now a skinny woman with a smoked-leather face and big hair teased into hedgehog spikes glossy with a slick hairspray sheen sauntered in from stage right, dragging along a small white pregnant dog in a pink tutu on a jeweled leash.

Fat Elvis smiled at the woman (or maybe at the preggers little dog) and took command of the leash. Skinny Minny scowled and exited with an uneasy backward look at the gleaming knife.

The air grew thick and oily, and you could feel those lurking creatures wanting to rip and rend the darkish air to get at the juicy blood-packed meat sacks (the pitiful humans) for a grand feast at the foot of their evil tree.

◆ ◆ ◆

"I seriously considered changing my name to Noira Dark and leaving the continent. Did I already tell you that, Doc? So those things would lose my spoor? You know: my scent, my trail, my droppings? Jeze Bellefleur becomes Noira Dark in the blink of an eye. You laugh but I did. Consider it. Not that it would've done any good. They were already on me like flies on shit, pardon my fucking French. No? Then white on rice. Black on boots. Any way you fucking slice it, I was stuck with those wicked bad things. If I'm making light it's only because it's all so dark and deadly serious. There's really no way to make light of cutting unborn babies out of a mother's belly—even if the mother is only a mongrel bitch. That sort of thing makes the demons hungry and pretty much guarantees that they'll be up your ass indefinitely. Or at least until the cows come home. Uh-oh, news flash: the cows aren't coming home because they're all in the slaughterhouse."

◆ ◆ ◆

You didn't dare dream of turning away. You kept the camera's unbiased eye on the action and watched in sick fascination as Fat Elvis lifted the mutt by the scruff of its neck and sliced its belly open and six bloody little squirming sacs came sliding out and went splat on the ground at the foot of the tree. Malnourished Ishmael began speaking in tongues, his voice growing louder and louder until he clamped his teeth, clammed up and convulsed.

He foamed at the mouth and fell over like a hundred-pound bag of shit.

Zooming close-up of the canine abortions, moving within blood-slimed sacs.

Wide out to get fat boy's bloody white jumpsuit and expressionless face. You were trembling so hard you were afraid you'd ruin the shot.

And then the real horrorshow began.

•   •   •

Doctor Dead Eyes doesn't know it but you are shooting your therapy sessions. Cute little nanny cam hidden inside a teddy bear with a pink bow round its neck, sitting next to the few get-well cards and the plastic vase of flowers (no glass allowed on the psych ward). These therapy scenes might make a good companion piece to the unedited snuff footage in your safety deposit box, or a decent DVD extra feature if you end up releasing the hardcore shock-the-monkeys movie.

"And even though you knew the cultists were into sacrifice," he says, petting his beloved beard, "you went anyway. For the sake of your art. In a sense, you were making a personal sacrifice for your art."

"Well yeah. That's why I went. Because they were serious about blood sacrifice. Animal, not human, but my plan was to get good footage of an animal blooding and then push them to reveal how close they might be to actually doing a human. I was convinced that's the way they were heading. Why mess around with sacrifice if you aren't willing to go whole hog. Or *whole human*. Right?"

•   •   •

The membranous air rippled and the walls shifted, expanded. She swung the camera slowly left, purposely counting walls as she made a 360 sweep. *Five* walls now, each corner forming the point of an implied pentagram. And Skinny Minny Shiny Spikes was on her knees, shoveling the aborted pups one by one into her bloody maw, chewing them until their little bones crunched, then sucking off their juices, and finally spitting out the mutilated remains. She wiped blood from her mouth with the back of her hand like a seasoned drunkard, then licked her fingertips with her grotesquely smacking gob.

The tree's exposed roots writhed, or seemed to, for roots that big don't writhe—unless they're not really roots.

This was the moment when filmmaker/documentarian Jeze Bellefleur lost whatever psychic protection her role as detached photographer afforded her, the moment when fear became palpable, a thing gnawing at her insides and turning her mind cold with brain shivers. But she kept shooting, daunted though she was. Vulnerable to the max and scared shitless.

"God help us," she whispered. "Please God."

A subterranean whisper: *Feed the tree.*

Then something unseen ripped Skinny Minny's head off her shoulders. Red rain gusted against the camera lens, then quickly diminished to a thin drizzle.

Jeze's impulse was to wipe clean the lens but she let it ride. Let things run. Run down.

Fat Elvis looked like he'd just dropped a load in his pants, and his jowls jiggled as his jaw dropped toward his chest. All shook up and looking to book. Exit, stage right.

From somewhere outside the room that wasn't a room, Ishmael cried, "O Lord!"

◆   ◆   ◆

"If I was Catholic, I would've joined a convent as soon as I figured out that the devils had followed me out of that room. I did spend a lot of time hiding out in random churches before I had to come here."

"And how did you figure out that they had followed you?"

"A talking dog told me. Black German Shepherd, fucking Nazi-looking mutt with spiked collar. Don't get your panties in a twist and go thinking Son of Sam's talking-dog bullshit. Those devils can slip into animals and they seem partial to big dogs. That's just the way it is. I don't make the rules or make this shit up."

"And what did the dog say?"

"He said, 'We are with you.'"

"That's all?"

"No. I said, 'Are you shitting me?' More to myself than to the dog. And the son of a bitch answered: 'When we shit your soul you will have no doubt of it.'"

As the devils frosted her face with their breath, a Biblical line snaked through Jeze's head: *By the envy of the Devil, death came into the world.* Fat Elvis had tripped over a root and was now on his knees, beseeching the Lord to save him, please Jesus, but she didn't see how the Devil could possibly envy the likes of this blubbering tub-of-guts with comical muttonchops and greasy hair.

◆   ◆   ◆

You have to be morally degraded to make a good nonfiction film. A good film document digs deep, pushes people—the subjects and audience—to the edge and then further to get at the terror throbbing at the center of every living thing. Like the time you were seventeen and shot your old man with your first real movie camera. Your first shot at a real doc. Docu-Dad. You sat him in a raggedy-ass folding lawn chair in front of the bleak cinderblock garage and made him do the one thing he never wanted to do. You made him talk about what he did in the war, particularly at a place the grunts called *Devil's Valley*. Before it was over, you'd reduced him to a trembling heap of bony meat and you had some fine gut-wrenching footage, a piece of unvarnished oral history of the Vietnam war, what he did to those fucking gooks and what they did to his buddies, to him. There's nothing better than war to bring out your inner demons. That was the hardcore truth of it. And you dug it out of the old man with the rusty knife of your ambition. How could he go on living after that clusterfuck of a war? "Well," he said, "sometimes you can feel God's presence by His absence." When it was done, you were so hyped that you went to your room and fingered yourself until you came like crazy, your delirious cries given cover by hard-rocking death metal banging out of your stereo.

To make a good documentary film, you have to be a coldhearted bitch. You develop a nose for that eternal terror at the center of things, at the very heart of life, and you'll go to any extreme to expose it and nail it to the wall, same as a hunter hangs the heads of his kills on his wall.

◆　◆　◆

Fat Elvis got off his knees and shed his jumpsuit. His flesh was fish-belly white with warty hairs sprouting in odd places. His dick was the color and size of a boiled shrimp. He muttered prayer-like inanities until he took the first bite of his own flesh, canines and incisors ripping out a big bloody chunk. Then he hummed unmusically as he proceeded to partake of more of the fatty flesh on his right arm, forearm first, then the flabby upper arm, wincing with pain that must've been beyond excruciating, but he went right on feasting on himself, and Jeze knew that he had a devil inside him, driving him to do it. Devil in the driver's seat, burning up the road. His humming rose in pitch as he exposed bone, and it became shrill and unnerving as he gnawed his ulna. When he passed out from blood loss or shock or from overeating or all three, Jeze danced around his body, shooting the carnage from every angle, hoping that the devils would be pleased that she was taking such care in filming their savage handiwork. Then Fat Elvis stopped breathing with a final snorting death rattle. And she thought she glimpsed him hauling dead ass up Ghost Road.

Then she shot Skinny Minny's headless body. Quick photographic study. (Her head had simply disappeared, as if swallowed up by one of the disembodied demons.) Her neck resembled the stump of an unfortunate young tree, and Jeze wondered if trees had souls of a sort. Skinny Minny's pitiful remains made her wonder if humans could actually have anything as sublime and potentially exalted as a soul.

But then something happened that sent spectral fingers slipping into the bottomless depth of Jeze's terror: The gore and goo inside Skinny's neck stump began to move and squish like thick strawberry jam and Jeze realized that one of the devils was fucking the stump.

Before she could flee, they started on her. They didn't stop until they'd fucked her half dead.

•   •   •

"Have you given any more thought to what these things you call devils, demons and dark guardians might actually be? What they represent?"

She gives him a cold stare. Then: "They don't represent anything, unless you want to see them as representatives of Satan. I think they were there—are here—on their own damned dime. Whether they're fallen angels or demons created out of the fires of hell, I can't say. But sometimes I do think fondly of them as my Bad Angels, my evil guardians. And when they have their way with me, I come so hard I go back to that room with the demon tree and they're doing me again like they did the first time. I told you about that, right?"

"Yes, you did. In explicit detail."

"Talking about it like that makes it more real. When it actually happens it's so freaking bizarre it's unreal. But trust me, it's real. They fuck me in orifices I didn't even know I had and then when they're done with their sick fun, they leave me bleeding from most of them and yet wanting more. It's not your standard love/hate deal. It's more like a love/fear thing. They scare the shit out of me but I can't stop wanting them to *fuck* the shit out of me. That's why I know I need help. I know I'm sick. Sick in my soul. My only hope is that I sink so deep into sin and degradation that I find a low road to God. That could happen, right? A salvation road could open up in front of me? Jesus never turned his back on whores. No fucking way. He liked to hang out with them. *These* bad boys put the *evil* in *devil*. But Jesus can save me if I can get his attention, right? Huh. I just had an insight, Doc. The only time I'm not scared out of my mind is when they're ravaging me or when they're slaughtering someone right in front of my eyes. It's the in-between times that terrify me and make me want to jump out of my skin. All that wicked anticipation, and I'm walking around with a mean hair-trigger and a come-button hard-on. It's enough to make a girl sex crazy with fear and wild for a devils gangbang."

"Have you considered talking with a clergyman?"

"Been there, done that. Big mistake. I still feel bad about what happened to that priest. The devils bent him over the altar and fucked him sideways and inside-out, literally tore him apart. Then they painted the big golden crucifix with the holy man's blood and shit. And me not even Catholic. Poor bastard. He's probably still in Purgatory, going, 'Jesus Christ, what the hell just happened?'"

She looks hard at him and sees that his dead eyes are already rotting. "I think we're done, Doc. You can discharge me. Today. Right now."

"You really think you're ready for that?" He tries to look concerned.

"We've gone as far as we can. There's no danger of your helping me. If you could, they would've already turned you into deviled ham. They *will not be exorcized*. No way. Not until Jesus comes. But talking to you has helped. I know what I need to do now."

"What?" Now he is genuinely interested, dead eyes reanimated.

"What I should've been doing all along. Whoring. And documenting the varieties of carnal sin. Turning tricks for slick dicks in my own flicks. In other words, I'll be killing time, the in-between times, while waiting for the devils to do me. Or for Jesus to save me, whichever comes first."

Doctor Dumbfounded drops his jaw.

Jeze laughs. "Hell, it's the perfect way to finance my film."

She leaves the hospital feeling only a tad disappointed that the devils didn't destroy her shrink. It would've made good teddy-bear cam footage but it also would've plopped her in the middle of a murder investigation and she has neither time nor energy for that sort of shit. She sees her future laid out before her, shining darkly, and deliciously terrifying.

◆　◆　◆

Fuck Pad Confessions. This is what she decides to call her new film project. Jeze Bellefleur will transform herself with the surefootedness of a seasoned shape-shifter into Jezebel the whore for the sake of her art and her salvation. By giving herself body and soul to the devils of perdition, she will become a living flesh-and-blood prayer for redemption in Christ the Savior. But first, she must talk to whores. Interview them on camera and get them to reveal their tricks of the trade, as well as their wounded souls, for certainly you couldn't peddle your ass, your cunt, your moneymaker without doing everlasting damage to your soul.

And Jezebel's Bad Angels seem drawn to damaged goods and human debris.

She landed a low-rent Southside apartment, had a mirror installed on the ceiling over a brass bed she'd found on Craigslist, and researched the subject of prostitution in books she ordered from Amazon. Berlin of the 1920s, the Weimar Sin City, captured her imagination. She lost herself in Berlin's pantheon of tricked-out tramps and backstreet sex goddesses. The Boot Girls,

Half-silks, Bone-shakers, Grasshoppers. Five O'clock Ladies, Dominas, Table Ladies, Phone Girls, and most interesting of all, the Woodchucks: physically repulsive hookers with deformities or missing limbs. She read up on all manner of perversions, sex magick (with intense emphasis on bodily fluids and mirror magic) and sexpot orgies of oddball occult orders. She more than warmed to her subject; she flushed with hormonal heat. When at last she felt ready to begin, she painted a pentagram on the carpet under the bed, dangled a crucifix from a gold chain around her neck and went out to lure her first street whore back to the fuck pad.

Magda was a short Mexican with tinkling bracelets, big dark eyes, bad skin and petite breasts. She was relieved that all she had to do was talk for the camera. Her accent was thick but her English was passable, and she knew how to tell a good tale. She relaxed as she talked, giving graphic details of how she played to the twisted lusts of flaming fetishists and serviced her most perverse johns, but then she went off on a mad tangent about the Chupacabra that had tried to kill her outside of Matamoros. She said the legendary goat-man beast had been after her for years and that it had killed her baby sister instead. She sometimes thought it was still stalking her here in the States. She worked herself into a state of fear and Jezebel sensed that Magda's terror aroused the devils to a fine frenzy.

Leaving the camera on the tripod rolling, Jezebel grabbed the handheld and started shooting with it too. She knew something was about to happen, something so bad it would be good. Or so good it would be horrible.

Magda was sitting on the side of the bed, legs crossed and showcasing nylons lined with ragged runs, smoking a cigarette and swinging her foot vigorously enough to create friction between her thighs. Jezebel did a languid zoom on her legs, then panned upward slowly, seductively to the small woman's lips sucking on the white filter and then venting smoke through her upturned nose and half-pursed lips. This was good. This was hot. Devils' breath turned the room sultry. Jezebel was getting wet. She was almost panting. Things were about to blow. Explode into demonic chaos.

A tear rolled down Magda's cheek. She no doubt knew now she was in the presence of something more powerful, far more evil, than her dreaded Chupacabra.

Jezebel had a sudden moment of weakness, of conscience, and thought she should warn the woman away, should shout *Run!* But then Magda whispered, "Diablo," and Jezebel just said, "Yes, God help you."

A fat tear tumbled from Magda's other eye, dropped and slid down her meager cleavage and disappeared into the cup of her lacy black bra. She shot a worried glance at the mirror above the bed, then she crushed out her cigarette in the plastic ashtray, crossed herself and whispered a prayer in Spanish, something about the Mother of God. A rosary appeared in her hand. As she began to feverishly finger the prayer beads, she all at once flung herself backward onto the bed. But Jezebel knew better, knew the devils had flung the sad little whore backward. Invisible talons sliced away Magda's scanty clothes.

Two sad-eyed angels, one tattooed in deep primary colors on each thigh, offered no protection against the demonic assault that was about to rip her out of this world and into a hell not of her own making, but of evil *other-worldly* making. Jezebel saw it coming, knew how it would end, just as her ancient namesake must've seen in advance the bad end her worship of Baal would bring down on her cursed head.

The devils were not going to stop with Magda.

Magda seemed to levitate three feet above the bed. She called out for Jesus to save her: "¡Jesús me ahorra!" To absolutely no avail. They wrenched her legs apart and snapped her in two like a chicken wishbone. The left leg detached itself from the pelvis, bone bursting through skin, and a cloudburst of blood showered the bed, the walls and the floor. The broken whore screamed just before her body slammed face-first into the wall. Her skull cracked with the sound of a cork popping out of a bottle of cheap-ass champagne.

That the devils hadn't taken time to gangbang Magda boded ill for Jezebel, that much she knew for sure. The dead hooker was nothing but an appetizer, a token offering as prelude to the meatier main course. What could Jezebel do but keep shooting? Shoot she did. The blood-spattered bed, the discarded leg, the mangled one-legged corpse of the poor chica who should've stayed in Ol' Meh-hee-co and married her bumpkin boyfriend Hor-hay. Where the hell was Hey-soos when you needed Him?

"Hey-soos Cristo!" Jezebel shouted. "Where the hell were you, huh? I mean, what the fuck? Does the blood of this little lamb mean nothing to you? This wasn't supposed to happen. Sure she was a whore but her soul was innocent. More or less."

She heard the devils' laughter. It sounded like hollow bones dragging on broken pavement at the end of the world.

"Fuck me," she said with bitter resignation. "Fuck me Jesus."

◆　◆　◆

She understood that things had to fall into place. That her place was here in the room that wasn't a room, that the tree that was more than a tree needed blood. The soil barely binding the tree's exposed roots to the earth had already been salted with more blood than a battlefield but it needed *hers*. The demon tree was greedy for her spilled blood, needed it as a bud needs spring rain to blossom. She could feel its dark lust for her. Its sap was up. The air was charged with demonic electricity. The tree had a wicked woody for her.

She saw it clearly now. The former Jeze Bellefleur had earned herself a burial slot here at the foot of the tree. Her blood, flesh and soul were required to replenish what grew here, to bring forth what was yet to come. She had hooked up with the wrong fucking freaks, the Lost City Luciferians, incurred a deep spiritual debt and now the Big Cheese himself was calling in her markers. Lucifer of legend was always up for making a deal, but she didn't have anything to offer that he didn't already possess. She was already in his pocket. Up his ass. Wherever he wanted her. Her plan of becoming a whore for Jesus so that He might save her would by virtue of *no* virtue come to naught.

The devils threw her down so hard her eyeballs clicked like loaded dice. She hit the ground near the bed's brass feet in that *other* room. She caught a distorted glimpse of them in the mirror over the bed. There were three of the ugly fuckers. More hideous than any famed artist had ever imagined or portrayed them, *these* devils.

Hideous enough to blind you, bitch? whispered a scabrous voice.

She turned her head for fear that her eyes would shrivel and die if she looked too long at them. Her eyes came to rest on the tree. Glyphs and strange characters appeared in the trunk's black bark and glowed red with the hellfire dancing a mad caper within the heart of the tree. By some stray sliver of satanic magic she deciphered the flaming symbols:

Eternal death for the damned

Now they were fully visible and she wished she *could* go blind. Homuncular creatures with apelike arms, dragging knuckles and knobby heads, their vulpine faces were fixed with razor-toothed grins and scarlet eyes.

The devils diddled her, teased her terror to new heights, their stunted cockroach wings aflutter and their crooked cocks swelling in proportion to the terror inside her, which is to say, to enormous size. The heads of their phalluses became deadly prongs, and she knew there was no way her body could survive what they obviously had in mind to do to her this time.

Just before they opened her up to an orgy of mortifying torment, one of the horny homunculi mocked her faith with a lisping line from the Gospel: *"Ye cannot drink the cup of the Lord, and the cup of the devils."*

◆   ◆   ◆

She remembers how she came to be buried here, one of countless larva-white corpses.

Human grub worms. Bodies entangled with the denuded roots of the demon tree. Tree roots pulsing in every undead orifice. Corpses impervious to decay, the sleeping dead hopelessly awaiting the call of the archangel's trumpet.

She remembers the unholy trinity of devils' dicks plunging so deep they pulverized her heart and broke her soul.

She remembers Lucifer's beautiful eyes behind shimmering slits, watching her from within the tree. She recalls the way the Devil Himself passed through the tree trunk as Jesus was said to have passed through walls after the resurrection.

She remembers how extraordinarily handsome and angelic Lucifer was as he stood over her and signed the fiery air in malevolent benediction. How he reached down to remove the little golden cross from her neck and the way it softened and rolled into a golden ball between his long hot fingers. Then he parted her cheeks and pushed it up her ass.

She remembers with wrenching clarity what he said: *"You will not need this trinket. The Miracle Man will not come here to the upper reaches of Hell."* His voice was so smooth and sonorously seductive that her undead ears had echoing orgasms. But what he wrote with a fire-dripping finger is a tattoo on the raw skin of her soul.

She has eternity to ponder his fire-writing: *We are all creatures of a cruel Creator.*

THRESHOLD
Fred Venturini

Alexis asked me about my favorite movie, and I told her I didn't confine myself to favorites. She had a sweet-smelling mixed drink with a slice of lime slotted onto the rim of the glass. I noticed her body before her beauty, the way her sweater clung to every curve, the way her jeans underlined her hips. She could be a painting called perfect, her bright hair like a meteor shower, each strand a pure blond vapor trail.

Mason chatted up Christine, Alexis's friend. Christine was almost her equal—almost. I'm sure Mason thought otherwise, and found Christine just as perfect and enchanting as I found Alexis. He was my best friend, brave around women. Humorous but harsh, he reserved his few acts of kindness for his close friends and small family.

"What are your secrets?" Alexis asked me. I told her it was a trick question because the minute you utter one word, they aren't secrets anymore. Secrets have deeper roots and more weight. They offer a feeling of owning something that no one else can ever have. She touched my hand, just grazing it with her own.

They invited us to their place so we could talk in a more casual atmosphere. Mason winked at me on the way out, following his Doberman dick. I didn't resist, and Alexis's hand found mine on the way to the car. Her fingers slinked away as we separated. I would've married her right there and then, but we'll always be connected.

Always.

They took us to the basement at Christine's house out in the country, surrounded by farm fields and woods. The upstairs was dark, and felt small, but the basement was spacious, a garden of glass and steel that grew and twisted everywhere—speakers dangled from shiny metal stands, the plasma TV was flanked by hip-high candle stands. The candles had wax tears and black wicks. They were not decoration.

The coffee table was glass, a single pane perched on top of steel legs directly in front of us. We sat on a black leather couch that curved around the corner of the room. The walls weren't bright enough to be white, not quite dark enough to be gray. They seemed dirty in a way that was pleasing to the eye.

The doors on the east wall, however, weren't pleasing. Unusually high, the doors stopped just before the ceiling. The texture of the paint was different over the doors—the same color, but rough and pocked, like stone. Dysfunctionally wide, as if I were gazing at a reflection of the doors through a funhouse mirror that stretched them to look fat. Fanning those slabs open would be a tough task, even with handles or knobs, which they lacked. No way to open those doors, at least not by hand.

I held Alexis's hand while Mason and Christine flirted further down the couch.

She avoided every question I asked, always turning the lens of conversation on me. I felt interrogated, but it was like peeling off layers of mental clothing, each question more intimate and invasive, each answer making me more barren. In our exotic conversation, I talked about my mother's drug problem, and my failed relationships. I told her I was earning my engineering degree and told her I thought she was the most interesting woman I've ever met—I said this without knowing a thing about her, except for that smile, and knowing that smile was quite enough.

"I think you'd make a nice choice," Alexis whispered. "What do you think Christine?" she said louder. "Do you like what you see, or do we need to go out and get some other guys?"

She said it as a joke, and Mason chuckled it away. But it was her look, a look of hunger that wasn't sexual, but primal, that set me off. My stomach dropped and I felt my erection start to wilt. She rubbed my thigh and then kissed me on the neck, but I eased her away and stood.

"Let's be gentlemen and grab some drinks," I said. Mason looked annoyed, but I curled my finger at him with a "get your ass over here" intensity. "You girls want a beer?" I asked, but they shook their heads.

Alexis was still smiling, her choice made. I imagined her mouth watering.

Upstairs, the only light was from the stove clock and the fridge when I opened it.

"You sense something totally wrong down there?" I asked. "I feel like I was hypnotized or something, and I just snapped out of it. How do you feel?"

He looked tipsy, but I didn't think he'd had that much to drink. "It's called beer and a boner," he said. "And that leads to bangin' and bustin' a nut. Then, the boltin' part. You don't bolt before the bangin' part, for God's sakes."

"Something is wrong," I said. "Did you see those doors? You ever see anything like that in your life?"

"Probably a painted cellar wall or some shit," he said, cracking open a beer. "Don't sweat it."

"We should leave."

He paused at this and sipped his beer. "You really think something's up?"

I nodded.

"You've rarely led me wrong with your brain forecasts." Another sip. "I'll make it quick. I mean, quicker than usual. At least for me—I'll have this chick upstairs riding space mountain before you can have your girl's shoes untied. It doesn't get any easier than this, they're like wounded gazelles down there, and guess who's the lion?"

He guzzled, crumbled the can, belched at me, and smiled.

"Just enjoy your damn self. Let the lion eat the meat and you can be the pussycat that licks the wounds. Hell, that girl of yours down there is hot in all caps and two t's. I'd be licking anything she offered up."

He headed downstairs, not caring if I followed or not.

"What if they're just bait," I said, freezing Mason mid-step. "What if some big game safari-hunters are lookin' for some lion?"

He looked at me from the stairwell. "That's the dumbest thing I've ever heard." He just kept walking and I followed.

We settled back into our conversations. Alexis didn't ease the mood or transition softly into the passion. She cuddled up into my neck, then tossed her leg over my thigh, straddling me.

"Did you miss me?" she asked. "Upstairs is forever away."

Her breath teased my ear, and she caressed my cheek leaving a tattoo of warmth when the hand was gone.

"Do you want to know my secrets?" she whispered.

Her pubic bone pressed against my leg. My erection returned, stripping my gears of conversation bare.

"Be back in a jiffy," Mason said. I looked up and he was standing, holding Christine's hand. "We're going to go exchange some secrets." Another devilish wink.

I glanced at the doors and they were open, but just a crack, creating a sliver of darkness where I could slide my fingers inside and part them, if I insisted on opening them.

I wanted to warn him, but by the time I could break my gaze from the doors, Mason had already left.

"What do you want more than anything?" Alexis asked, grinding into me. She wanted me to ask about her secrets. She wanted me to say that I wanted her.

So I didn't. I yanked her against me and kissed her neck. I put my hands up her shirt and enjoyed her skin, her smooth back. My fingers glided underneath the cups of her bra. I palmed her breasts, kissed her, then stopped.

Kissed her, then stopped, an intravenous drip of passion. The impression was to tease, but we both knew I was stalling.

"Tell me you want me," she said. I ignored her.

"Ask me, I want you to know," she said. "My dirtiest, darkest secrets."

"Shut up," I told her, trying to sound passionate. "Shut up and kiss me."

"I'll do anything you want," she said. "Slide your fingers inside of me, and part me, if you want. Any dirty, filthy thing you want. You tight little boy. You tight, tight little boy. You take it so nice. Don't you?"

A kiss on my lips, cold, with tongue.

"Tight little boy."

And she stopped grinding against me, just letting the words sink in—the words my fourth grade teacher, Mr. Kraemer, whispered to me as he raped me in the boiler room, a secret I didn't spill during her flirty interrogation.

My breath came in bursts, unsteady, black spots dotting my vision, my erection gone, my hands loose, my desire dead. She held me now, anchoring me. Even if I tried, I lacked the strength and focus to buck her. The image of Mr. Kraemer's rape settled in my mind's eye. I tried to shake those leathery hands from my mind, the way they felt against my barren hips, the way a droplet of his sweat fell onto my lower back. The depth and pleasure in his grunts, his announcement that yes, I was indeed tight. A tight, tight little boy—but only her whispers could rescue me.

"Ask me about God," she said, the smile gone. "Ask me about the truth of this place. About the pale faces with small mouths that eat worlds."

Then Mason came down the stairs, his entire face rouge with sorrow. His brow was tight like the lower part of his jaw—almost cramped, distorting his face into that of a crying toddler, his eyes narrowed into slits, the corners of his mouth jutting down.

Christine followed him, smiling, wearing a black robe. The door was open further still.

"Secrets," he said between sobs. "Terrible ones. What touches us now? We are poisoned by secrets."

He fell to his knees by the coffee table. He raised his hands overhead, fists clenched, and brought them down on the glass table, shattering the tempered pane into thick, jagged slices.

"Secrets!"

He screamed this time, a throat-shredding yelp of anguish. I wanted to save him, but Alexis bore the weight of secrets, and I couldn't move.

Mason chose a piece of glass the shape of an equilateral triangle, almost perfect against the chaos. One jutting tooth of glass prevented the perfection. He took it in two hands and drove a pointed edge into the soft center of his throat.

I heard a muted *pop,* and the blood followed.

He brought the shard of glass into his throat again. He didn't just puncture, he jammed in from different angles, then pulled the glass against his naked throat, saw-like, with the last of his breath and power. His long sobs crackled and popped, like a straw sucking air at the bottom of a milkshake. Naked flesh flapped against his neck, like a loose tarp in the back of a pickup. The jets of blood soaked the carpet, spots like rotted raspberries growing more plump as he thrashed and bled. Droplets spackled the door, and it opened further.

Alexis grabbed me by the hair and forced my gaze to the door.

"Now they tell the secrets," she said. The doors eased open, the darkness now beginning to gape—an expanding, black faultline straining to slip and swallow.

Mason should have been dead by now, but he continued to thrash and stab, waiting at the doorway for enough room to enter. He stepped into the darkness, and it appeared as if he should fall, and fall forever, but he found footing and stood, dropping the glass soundlessly into the nothing, his blood-soaked shirt looking like a crimson bib, his destroyed neck hanging in threads.

Then, the men with white faces came. Wearing cloaks of nothing that concealed any further features, I could only see their faces and hands. Their white hands grabbed and pulled at Mason, hungry for his ears and hair and blood. The faces had no expressions, no noses, only small, circular mouths, the twitching mouth of a fish needing air. No eyes, just dents with bruised skin where eyes should be, as if no eyes could bear the terrible void that could've swallowed darkness itself.

Three of the white men wrapped around Mason. One of the white hands grasped for loose pieces of flesh on his neck, found one, then pulled, peeling it away, ripping his polo shirt along with his skin. They unzipped him, skinning him alive, and his only expression was pure relief, pure joy. He stared at me, smiling with his almost skinless face, and winked.

I could feel my pulse in the capillaries of my nose, my whole body throbbing. I found myself standing and then running, only realizing the girls were gone as I bounded up the stairs, then out the front door and through the smacking gravel of the driveway. I ran through the fields, the soft earth sucking at my shoes. I ran until I sensed that I was alone, then stopped. Spent, I almost fell to my knees. Instead, I just bent over, catching breath in whooping sucks, the fall night translating each exhalation into a wave of mist, the moonlight muted by clouds. I looked back. Against all my will, I looked behind me.

The house was gone—there was no home, no driveway. Mason's Firebird was gone as well. All I saw was an empty lot.

Then, she whispered to me.

"Secrets," Alexis said, and I was not surprised. She'd chosen me.

"Brave them." I whirled about, dizzying myself, and there she was, each feature of her perfect face highlighted by light of its own. She wore a black robe and I did not fight her when she took my hand. I gave her my neck to kiss. She did, and eased her lips to my ear—listening couldn't hurt, right? The house was gone. The doors were gone.

Answers. Secrets. Most minds work in mechanical ways, groping for handles, logical things to latch onto, easy ways to open, to solve, to—

"I have secrets to tell you," she whispered.

"Yes," I say to her. She spoke in ancient tongues as clear to me as every contour of her face, and sealed her secrets with a kiss on my cheek.

The doors with no handles hold the secret-tellers with pale faces. Those small mouths held white tongues that whispered all the ways things are. She was more gentle than they would ever be, sparing enough of me to make a decision.

I am imbued the truth of God and gods, of her eternal mission to save blank souls. I keep asking and I look around me, and she's gone.

Cradling madness, I cry. Then I look to the sky out of habit and ask again.

THIS IS MY BODY
Lawrence Conquest

Though they had never before met face to face, Michael had somehow known that the canteen chef was going to be fat. Peter Oakhill's stunted body seemed almost as wide as it was tall, with vast acreages of blubber ill-concealed behind food-spattered white cotton overalls. His bushy beard and heavy brow combined to make him seem like some biological throwback to an earlier age. God save us from the curse of the Cro-Magnon cook, thought Michael, idly wishing for the umpteenth time that he was back in the familiar confines of his office. Or better yet, home, drowsing deep in the comforting fug of herbally induced dreams. Christ, but he could do with a toke right now.

"Do you know what my Mum always said to me when I was a boy?" Michael asked, effortlessly adopting the patronising tone carefully instilled in him from three years of rigorous middle management training, "She said: 'Think of all the starving children in Africa.'"

Peter Oakhill raised his eyebrows in a semaphore of soundless befuddlement.

"Oh, I guess it's a politically incorrect thing to say, these days, but the meaning was clear enough to me then. Finish your food. Appreciate what you've got. Don't waste it. Well, Mr. Oakhill," Michael spread his arms wide, encompassing their surroundings, "*this* is waste."

The pair of them were standing behind the canteen serving counter, a waist-high gleaming metal surface studded with sunken pits of gently steaming food. From each compartment arose the metal handles of either ladle or tongs, the serried ranks of silver stems standing to lazy attention like rows of inebriated soldiers. Michael reached out a hand to the nearest and withdrew a ladleful of baked beans, the semi-congealed goo protesting with an audible squelch that reminded him of the sound of a boot being withdrawn from muddy ground.

"The time is now 7:50 PM," he continued, "and the canteen closes in ten minutes time, and yet here we still have masses of unsold food. What exactly are you planning to do with it all Mr. Oakhill—eat it yourself?"

Oakhill sighed theatrically, making no attempt to hide his contempt for his supposed superior. "Your predecessor was quite happy with how I run my canteen Mr. Roach. There's no need for you to start sticking your oar in now, just because you're new here."

"It's my job to ensure that this company continues to make a profit Mr. Oakhill, and I can't very well do that with your canteen wasting all this food. My predecessor may have overlooked your shortcomings, but I can assure you that I will not." Michael dropped the ladle of beans back into its compartment with barely veiled disgust, spatters of tomato sauce peppering the counter like a soft rain of blood. "And another thing, do you *have* to use the most expensive brands? Most of the people who eat here wouldn't be able to tell the difference between this stuff and economy brand anyway."

"Economy?" Oakhill bristled, visibly offended. "This may only be a works canteen to you Mr. Roach, but I do have my pride."

"Well I'm afraid this company can't afford your pride, Mr. Oakhill. So either you start saving some money, or I start looking for a new Head Cook. The choice is yours. Good day."

Michael Roach picked up his battered suitcase and left the Buckland Studios canteen, eyes wide for the next corner to cut.

• ◆ ◆

"That's a stroke of stone cold genius Steve. I'm absolutely sure he'll love it. Yeah, that's a date, mate—I'll meet you at 10. Ciao."

Michael hit the disconnect button and leaned back in his padded office chair. He stared idly at the crack that meandered across the ceiling and wondered if it was such a good idea after all. Personally he thought it all sounded rather tacky, but then he supposed an element of smut was to be expected at these events. Pity it had to be Japanese though, he'd have preferred a decent curry. Indian or Thai, he didn't mind.

Thoughts of food now utmost in his mind, Michael called up the latest profit and loss spreadsheets on his PC and sighed. Once again, the staff canteen was deep in the red, ordering way more produce than they could possibly sell. What the hell was Oakhill playing at?

Michael checked his watch, reached for his phone, and dialled the canteen extension. After several rings the connection was picked up, and a voice Michael could only presume was human answered with a barely intelligible grunt.

"Oakhill, is that you? This is Michael Roach from Accounts. Listen, I've just seen the latest costs from the canteen and I am not happy about them. At all. I need you to come up to my office to discuss this before you leave work tonight."

A grunt that could have passed for either affirmation or denial echoed back down the line.

"Oakhill, did you hear what I just said?"

A sudden click and the disconnected phone buzzed in Michael's ear like a wasp trapped in a killing jar.

♦ ♦ ♦

For some reason Michael's friends—if he could dignify the gaggle of fellow business school graduates and underachieving hangers-on who got blazingly drunk with him every week in such glowing terms—seemed to think that working in television must be a terribly glamorous business. Whilst it suited his ego to play along with this charade at times, the truth was far more prosaic. Buckland Studios, in common with many similar independent companies, was facing a decidedly hostile marketplace, and it was for precisely that reason that he had found employment there. His friends thought that he rubbed shoulders with glamorous actresses and creative geniuses on a daily basis, but high cost drama was out and cheap phone-in shows were in. Quiz shows, cookery guides, shopping channel auctions, mildly erotic chatlines—in each case the costs were minimal, but the returns could be considerable, especially if the presenters could successfully convince those couch potatoes who bathed in the late-night cathode rays to pick up their phones and dial the premium numbers displayed on the screen.

Or at least they *would* be profitable if idiots like Oakhill didn't continue to spend money like it grew on trees. Hadn't he even heard of the 'credit crunch'? That glorified cook had been deliberately trying to undermine him, thinking that just because he'd been working here for years that he was untouchable. Well, more fool him.

Michael checked his watch again. The canteen would normally be closed to paying customers by now, but the staff took a little longer to finish clearing up for the night. If he was quick he could confront Oakhill with the evidence of his own overspends.

That would wipe the smile off of his greasy fat face.

♦ ♦ ♦

By the time Michael had left his office the studios were practically deserted, with only the occasional dead-eyed technician and slack-jawed presenter crossing his path like spirits of the restless dead. The main doors to the canteen were already locked, but Michael had taken the precaution of signing out the relevant keys from Security, and let himself in without bothering to knock. Oakhill may have hung up on him earlier, but he was damned if he was going to give him the opportunity to slip away without explaining himself.

"Oakhill?" His voice, intended to be issued in a strident tone of authority, suddenly became timid in the prevailing air of silence.

The main canteen lights were out, but the soft blue glow that emanated from the wall-mounted bug-killing electric rings washed about the deserted space like a faint cerulean mist. Michael picked his way slowly through the dining area, his progress hampered by clusters of tables and chairs that huddled together like nervous animals. The drab lifelessness of the eating area was only highlighted by the identical plastic blooms that lent each Formica table top its splash of unseasonable colour. Glossy photos of fading has-beens and rising nobodys lined the walls like trophy heads in a hunter's den, the desperation behind their showbiz smiles impervious to glamour.

A sudden burst of giddy high-pitched laughter cut through the stillness, the unlikely sound causing Michael to start in surprise.

"Oakhill, is that you? Where the hell are you?"

The accountant moved deeper into the gloom, allowing himself to be reeled in by the mocking lure of the laughter. The sound led him over to the far wall, where a currently idle conveyer belt was partially covered with the discarded dishes of absent diners. When in motion this rubbery tongue would bear its burden through a corresponding mouth in the wall, beyond which the canteen staff would clean away any leftover scraps and stack the plates for later washing. It was through this narrow aperture that Michael now peered, sure that the flickering motions of movement within attested to a human presence, but unable to make out any readily identifiable form.

"Oakhill?"

Gaining no response, Michael tried the handle of the door that led to the kitchen area, only to find it firmly locked.

Damn the man, he *must* know I'm out here, Michael thought, and checked his watch to see how long he could spare before his evening arrangements. He didn't have all night to hang around waiting, but he'd be damned if he was going to let Oakhill get away with this. He could imagine him now, skulking somewhere out of sight, laughing at him, thinking his new manager didn't posses the nerve to beard the mighty chef in his den. Well, he was about to get one hell of a shock.

"Alright, Oakhill, if you won't come to me, I'll come to you!"

Michael hopped up onto the conveyer belt, and proceeded to crawl on all fours along the tarry surface, doing his best to avoid the discarded mounds of crockery that lay beneath him. The mouth of the aperture was small, but by hunching himself down and pushing the plates aside he was able to squeeze himself through, and with an ungainly lurch he dropped into the kitchen area beyond.

The light was even dimmer back here, but the awful stench that swept over him gave an early clue to the sight which would await him once his eyes had fully adjusted to the gloom. Piles of abandoned crockery lay scattered about the place, plates and bowls stacked up in teetering mounds like giant ceramic anthills. The stench was indicative of their unwashed nature, as uneaten leftovers clung with grim determination to the assembled horde. Judging by the stench of decay this state of affairs had evidently been going on for some time, but why? What was wrong with Oakhill and his cronies? What did the staff spend all their time doing back here?

"A-huh."

A darker shape moved against the gloom, a crouching figure that scuttled through the mounds of dirty crockery like some gigantic spider. Startled, Michael groped along the wall behind him for a light switch, feeling a giddy sense of relief as his fingers came into contact with the object of their quest. Instantly the room was blasted into burning white nothingness, and Michael held up his hands to shield his eyes from the glare.

As his vision slowly returned Michael groped his way towards the far end of the kitchen, but the scuttling figure was now nowhere to be seen. What was left beyond the drifts of abandoned crockery was something far stranger though, and it took Michael several seconds to fully comprehend what he was looking at.

Laid out prone along the base of the far wall was an immense human-shaped body, stretching fully twelve feet in length from head to toe. It was evident that this giant had never truly lived however, for on closer inspection it was clearly not a man, but merely the simulacrum of one. The inanimate model was a jigsaw composed from countless lumps of edible matter, the scrapings from hundreds of unfinished meals pressed together in a mockery of the human form.

Michael peered at the ensemble with a morbid fascination, trying to trace the remnants of identifiable foodstuffs buried amongst more anonymous semi-masticated muck. Fish fingers depended from gristly burger-meat palms, whilst half-chewed sausages stood in for the creature's toes. Cauliflower ears poked out shyly from behind curls of rotted mashed potato hair. A bread basket chest revealed the tooth marks of the manikin's maker, the indented radiuses peppering the trunk like frenzied bite wounds on a murder victim. Worst of all was the face: two bisected poached egg eyes stared blindly up above a bloated banana nose, the gone-off brownish tube now crawling with a fresh maggoty life; hemispheres of half-buried beans studded the thing's face like a rash of teenage acne, whilst red raw bacon rind lips pursed a slackly yawning mouth shaped from the body cavity of an oven ready turkey. Draped in slack folds across both face and trunk lay stringy strips of melted cheese skin, the semi-transparent substance making the creature seem like some unfortunate third-degree burns victim in the early stages of reconstructive surgery.

The whole obscene mass glistened softly in the overhead lights: gravy, chip fat and drools of human saliva collecting like sweat in the creature's pores. The mingled aroma of fresh and rotting food lent the air a putrid sickly-sweet scent, like the unconvincing disguise of a perfumed corpse at an open casket funeral.

So engrossed was he in examining the bizarre form before him that Michael wasn't even aware of Peter Oakhill's presence until he felt the chef's fingers closing tight about his throat.

◆   ◆   ◆

He's naked.

Out of everything else that had happened this afternoon; the half-rotted uneaten leavings, the giant food sculpture, being strangled unconscious by Oakhill and bound tight to the leg of the kitchen table, Michael somehow found this fact the most shocking of all. He tried in vain to avert his eyes from the sight of the chef's lumpish genitals as they nestled shyly behind a clump of coarse black hair.

"I know what you're thinking," the naked man said, the thick tufts of hair that covered his stunted form making him seem like some overgrown porcupine. "You think that just because I work in a place like this, I don't love my food?"

Michael felt a wave of revulsion pass through him as he saw the bobbing head of the man's penis begin to rise through the matted undergrowth of his pubic hair like a restless snake.

"Well, you're wrong." Oakhill turned his back on the accountant and strode over to where the giant sculpture lay. A series of violent motions attested to his indecent actions, and Michael looked away in disgust. As the chef worked upon himself, Michael struggled in vain against his bonds, but all too soon he saw that Oakhill had finished in his obscene task.

Sweat dripping from his brow, the chef turned back towards Michael and fixed him with a knowing stare. "Now you'll know my love too."

Oakhill moved behind him, and as he slid out of view Michael felt a deeper terror, unsure as to what the madman's next actions might be. No sooner had he disappeared however, than Michael promptly put all thoughts of the cook from his mind, his attention now focused entirely on the nightmarish activity unfolding before him.

A faint wheezing rasp was emanating from the pile of refuse that lay heaped against the far wall, and as Michael looked closer he fancied he could make out the almost imperceptible ebb and fall of the giant sculpture's chest. With an agonising slowness the thing's limbs began to stir, its misshapen fingers clutching and grasping at the air as though it were a newborn child. A sudden lurch and the whole thing rolled itself onto its side, the torso connecting with the tiled floor with a resoundingly wet smack. The creature lay still for a while, seemingly gathering its strength, its body curled up in embryonic fashion while its poached egg eyes stared blindly at Michael across the intervening space.

Michael became dimly aware of the sound of Oakhill chuckling behind him, his mirth increasing as the creature began to drag its way towards where he was bound. The thing grunted in effort as it closed the gap, pulling itself hand over hand across the ground like a slow motion swimmer, a glistening snail trail of fluid and shucked off body parts marking its torturous progress. Stunned at what he was seeing, Michael found himself frozen in inaction. It was only when the thing came to within a few feet of him that he began to struggle anew, but the plastic cord that Oakhill had bound him with held painfully tight.

Having reached his place of imprisonment, the creature paused, bringing itself up onto its haunches in a series of awkward motions. The creature seemed to sense his presence as it angled its face towards him, thick loops of gravy-like tears spilling down the cracks of its half-eaten face. Its meaty mouth suddenly yawned wide, revealing a twitching bacon slice tongue and bone-shard teeth embedded in turkey flesh gums. The impossible creature gulped down a mouthful of air like a drowning man, the resulting exhalation forming words that rode upon the crest of a stinking wave. The thing's voice was barely a whisper, and it struggled to articulate the words clearly through its bacon rind lips, but their meaning was all too discernable to Michael: *"Take. Eat. This is my body."*

The creature placed its stinking paws upon Michael's shoulders and forced itself into a standing position, the weight of its abnormality pressing down upon him with awful reality. Despite his desperate hopes, this could be no drug induced dream, no feverish hallucination. As the creature stood upright Michael saw with mounting horror that Oakhill had fashioned the mannequin with some degree of anatomical accuracy, as a gross penis fashioned from offcuts of scrag and bone depended from the animal's abdomen like some monstrous tail. As he watched, the member stirred with an inner life of its own, twitching with epileptic fits and starts as it fought against the pull of gravity. Michael opened his mouth to scream, only to feel Oakhill's hands inside him, the food lover's stubby fingers digging deep into his mouth as he prised it apart for his inhuman partner.

The golem began to moan as it forced its length into Michael's mouth, the putrid stench of gone-off food making him gag and splutter as he fought for breath. In desperation he tried biting down upon the loathsome appendage, but Oakhill's fingers continued to pull at his jaws, and where his teeth did make contact they merely slid through layers of rotting food. Impossibly the creature's length increased, and Michael struggled not to vomit as he felt the restless member slide past his tonsils and further down his throat. Deeper and deeper the appendage descended, Michael struggling to breathe, snot and tears trailing around his face in a glistening sheen, gagging and choking all the while.

This isn't happening, he thought, trying to will himself away from the scene. It's just one of Steve's tricks, one of his dodgy tablets making me see things. None of this is real.

The golem threw its head back and screamed as it ejaculated its seed into Michael's stomach, and for a time he knew no more.

◆   ◆   ◆

The shrill tones of his mobile phone shrieked in his ear, waking him from an uneasy slumber. With automatic moves, Michael groped for the phone and hit the receive button.

"Yeah? Steve? Hi. Look, sorry mate, I'm on my way. I'll be there as soon as I can, okay?"

Michael pocketed the phone and groggily pulled himself to his feet, unsure of his location. From the looks of things, he seemed to be somewhere in the canteen kitchen area, but what he was doing there he couldn't remember. And what was it with the state of this place? Dirty crockery and scrapings of food littered the area, while the portion of floor in front of him looked as though someone had recently vomited on it. Whatever was going on here, Oakhill was obviously to blame, and as soon as he'd sorted himself out he intended to have some strong words with the man. Just, not tonight.

He bent over and gripped his stomach as a sudden pain passed through him.

Christ, but my guts hurt, he thought. What in God's name *have* I been eating?

◆   ◆   ◆

The cramps continued as he staggered through the early evening streets, but the rolling motions inside him had the feel of a stomach complaining more of a lack of food rather than a surfeit of it. By the time he arrived at the flat, Michael realised he was starving hungry.

"Bloody hell—you finally made it!" leered Steve in his face, his breath a toxic combination of fags and wine. "We nearly started without you!"

Steve ushered him inside, where three other young men sat slumped groggily upon a faux-leather three-piece suite. Rising before them to the height of their knees was a collection of wine bottles and beer cans, the semi-empty containers forming a miniature glass and tin Stonehenge. Gary—the birthday boy himself—already looked half paralytic, a booze inflicted rictus grin plastered greasily across his chops.

"Alright, Mikey boy? Got me a present have you?" he drawled.

"But this *is* your present isn't it?" replied Michael, with barely restrained distaste. "I mean, we all chipped in for it, didn't we?"

"True, true," agreed Steve, "but don't worry about missing the booze, you'll just have more room inside you for the main course."

"Come on Steve, I'm hungry *now*," wailed Gary from the depths of the sofa. "Where is the girl? I wanna eat."

"This way, boys," said Steve, ushering the inebriated celebrants to their feet. "Now Mike's here, I think it's high past time we *all* got stuck in. We wouldn't want the meal to go cold after all, would we?"

A grinning Steve opened the door to the dining room, and led the party-goers through. With a mixture of embarrassed coughs and lecherous sneers, the five diners sat down before their meal. The girl's nudity was covered by artfully placed mounds of sushi, colourful selections of fish, rice and vegetables partially obscuring her golden oriental skin. The young woman stared at the ceiling with a studied indifference, seemingly ignorant of the giggling youths who now surrounded her on all sides.

"Friends, countrymen—let us eat!" yelled Gary, picking up a spoon and digging into a mound of flesh-warmed food.

Where did they find this girl, thought Michael, as he watched his fellow diners begin to eat. How can she stand it? How can she just lie there and let them eat off of her? He'd heard of the practice of *Nyotaimori*, but when he'd looked it up online it had seemed as much urban myth as reality, and he didn't imagine such services were readily available in this country. Or at least, not from any of the regular catering services.

Perhaps that explained it, he thought. Maybe for this sort of girl this was the equivalent of an 'easy gig', a relatively painless way of earning a little spending money compared to her more usual intimate engagements. So maybe he shouldn't feel ever so slightly repulsed at this merging of the pleasures of food and sex, so uneasy at the notion of how unhygienic this must all be. Was she clean?

There was something else about the human platter before him that didn't feel quite right, and he felt a strange kind of deja vu at the sight of the prone dish before him, almost as though he'd encountered something very similar quite recently. Still, it couldn't hurt to take a little bite, he supposed.

Gingerly Michael picked up a fork and scooped up a little of the rice from the girl's thigh. Trying to ignore the jibes of his compatriots, Michael swallowed the food down and was immediately surprised at the reaction from inside him. His stomach positively growled, its hunger threatening to overwhelm him as it pounced upon the morsel like a starving dog.

"This is—okay!" beamed Michael, shovelling down more mouthfuls of food, one after another. He grinned in imbecilic pleasure at his friends. "I love it! I love it!"

The other diners laughed at his enthusiasm, but curiously no matter how much food Michael scooped off of the girl and into his mouth, his stomach still felt empty. His guts roiled in torment, demanding ever more sustenance to sate the growing hunger inside. As he chomped machine-like through his meal, Michael became aware of a certain motion within his belly, almost as though he was somehow pregnant. He tried to dismiss the notion and concentrate on his chewing, but a disturbing image had become fixed in his mind: the dark wet cavern of his guts, now a nest for a mass of squirming white grubs, their blind faces turned expectantly upwards as they awaited the next morsel of food to drop down towards them. Like newborn chicks these parasites waited within, their lusty cries of hunger reverberating through his abdomen in a series of seismic rumbles. The more he ate, the fatter they got. The more he ate, the hungrier he became. With the shrinking of his stomach steadily matched by their increasing size, how long could he last? How much hungrier could he get?

"Easy there, fella!"

"Yeah, leave some for us!"

The other diners watched in amusement as Michael steadily cleared the girl of food, revealing her naked flesh in a gourmet's striptease. Having bared her of provisions, Michael paused only to let out a shuddering burp before continuing on with the next course. Half asleep on a combination of pills and boredom, the girl barely registered the initial thrust, but when Michael turned the embedded fork around in a savage circle and pulled free a chunk of bloody human flesh from her thigh, she soon found the voice to scream. In the noise of the girl's cries the other diners were momentarily frozen in shock, but as Michael hastily swallowed down the meat and aimed the fork at her face the room erupted into chaos.

In the eye of a storm of thrashing limbs and desperate cries, Michael knew only the terrible pain of his unstoppable hunger. As the blows rained about him he felt only the encompassing arms of another beside him, and he moved to step into their warm embrace. He no longer recognised the face of the screaming man who rained repeated blows upon him, but felt touched at the sympathy he saw in his wide-eyed gaze. He reached up for the man's head and drew it towards him, ignorant of the violence being inflicted upon him, determined only to kiss away the tears that now coursed down his face. Oddly, the violence increased as he moved his grazing mouth over the man's cheeks and on up to the eyes, but true to his loving nature Michael dutifully ignored such bashful reproaches, and sucked ever harder at the sweet sadness that now dropped into his mouth like a succulent soft-boiled egg.

The bloody red thing cradled in Michael's hands continued to scream, even as he covered its mouth with his own, gripped its rubbery lips in his teeth, and began to chew.

HUNGER PANGS
Matt Kurtz

"Does *this* scare you?" she asked.

Jack, naked and handcuffed to the steel headboard, stared down at the wide-eyed woman that knelt between his spread-eagled legs. She had a stun gun in her hand, pushing its button as it unleashed blue sparks of electricity that crackled inches from his testicles. The couple's flickering shadows wildly danced over the walls of the dark bedroom like a scene from the mad scientist's laboratory in an old *Frankenstein* film.

The attractive, nineteen-year old woman demanded a response.

"Stop it! That shit ain't funny!"

Sybil immediately released the button on the stun gun and the lighting in the room fell back to warm candlelight.

"Where the hell did you get that thing?" he asked.

"My mom gave it to me. For the nights I couldn't get a ride after work and had to walk home in the dark."

"Well, put it away because if you're trying to turn me on, you're failing miserably."

Sybil slid off the bed and tossed the stun gun into the open dresser drawer. "I'm sorry. I thought you liked freaky things."

"Freaky. Not fucked up."

On her way back to the bed, she stopped to give Chico, her tiny Chihuahua sleeping on a mound of dirty clothes in the corner, a good scratch behind the ears. Chico's eyes opened briefly to verify who was giving the love.

Sybil climbed back on top of Jack and started kissing his chest, swirling her tongue around one of his erect nipples. Jack grunted and struggled a little in the handcuffs.

"SYBILLLLLL!" a screech echoed in the distance.

Both exhaled in defeat and sat motionless in silence.

"HEY, SYBIL! CAN YOU C'MERE?! PLEASSSSEEEE!!!!" the screech got louder.

Jack shook his head. Sybil looked away, afraid to make eye contact; she didn't want to fight. He thrust his body upward, pushing her off of him.

"Uncuff me so I can have a smoke," he told her.

• • •

The morbidly obese woman sat in her bed, spilling over the pillows that propped her up. A cloud of smoke, tinted blue by the glow of the television in the corner, floated in the air. With cigarette in mouth, the woman shifted in the creaking bed, patting the covers in a panic as she stared toward the television screen.

"SYBIL!!!!" she shrieked again.

Sybil barged into her mother's bedroom. "WHAT?! What do you want?!!"

Mother shot her a childish look of utter helplessness. "My favorite program is about to start. I can't find the remote," she whimpered.

• • •

Sybil returned to her room to find Jack sitting on the edge of the bed, slipping on his shoes. She knelt down in front of him.

"Hey. Where are you going, babe?"

"Gotta get up early."

She ran her hands over his thighs and up to his crotch. "But weren't we in the middle of something?"

Jack shrugged. "Yeah, we were. But now I'm tired. I should go."

Sybil exhaled in disappointment. She knew what had to be done; what would, at the very least, bring him back another night.

"Well, let me give you a little something to remember me by." She unlaced his belt and unbuttoned his jeans. By the time he fell back on the bed, his hips were up in the air and she was sliding his pants down. The act was as smooth as a mother changing a baby's diaper. As her head bobbed up and down, Jack pulled a joint from his jacket pocket and lit it up. After a long drag and an exhale, he looked more like a man savoring a smoke after a four-course meal than a guy enjoying a blowjob from his girlfriend.

"Ya know, I really don't know why you just don't give her the pill."

Sybil popped up from between his legs. "I'm not doing it."

"My guy said it would do the trick. With minimal—but temporary—side effects."

"Your guy . . . in Mexico? Oh, you mean the drug dealer?" she remarked snidely.

Jack took another drag and passed it down to Sybil so she could (temporarily) put something else in her mouth.

"That'd be the one," he said, either not picking up—or more likely—not caring about her sarcasm. "He's sold me nothing but quality shit so far. Am I right?"

"Yeah, but we don't even know what the pill really does."

"My guy said he knows a guy that gives it to his girls to make them stay thin. They can continue to eat like pigs and not gain a pound. Which is good for business."

Sybil took a drag and pondered the words, trying to figure out what all this talk of guys, girls, and business equaled. Then it hit her. "A guy and his girls? Like a pimp? And his prostitutes?"

Jack shrugged, taking the joint back from her.

"I am not gonna give my mother a pill like that. Especially if it has some side effects that we don't know about. It could kill her."

"That fatty is a walking time bomb as it is. Her ticker could explode any day. If not from the food, then the smokes. There's always something going in her mouth."

Jack looked down at Sybil who stared up at him with glassy eyes from his insensitivity. Jack didn't notice—or more likely—didn't care.

"Speaking of. How about you finish up down there so I can leave?"

◆ ◆ ◆

After Jack came, he went. When Sybil closed the front door behind him, she heard the screech of the harpy.

"Hey, SYBIL?!!"

Sybil barged through the door and into her mother's bedroom wide-eyed and flustered. "What?! What do you want?!!"

Mother jumped, yanking her hand out of the cookie bag nestled in her lap, sending crumbs everywhere. A lit cigarette, strategically placed at the side of her mouth so she could multitask between her nicotine intake and cookie consumption, fell limp. Again, her look was innocent bordering on ignorant.

"Did Jack leave?" she asked delicately.

Sybil wasn't in the mood. "What do you want?" she hissed.

"Did you two get into a fight again?" Sybil just shot her a look. She really wasn't in the mood for *this*. Mother didn't pick up on it. "Syb, baby. I don't know why you put up with him. You can do so much better than—"

"I put up with him," Sybil exploded, "because he's the only one that will put up with *this* bullshit! This disgusting life we live!"

"Oh, Syb. Please don't say such things."

"It's sick. And it's not fair."

"Not fair?"

"Have you ever wondered why you haven't met Jack? Why he hasn't seen you?" Mother shrugged, scared of what might be coming next. Sybil didn't hold back. "Maybe you've heard of the old saying about how before you marry a girl, look at her mother to see what you're in store for?"

Mother looked down. She relaxed her claw-like grasp around the cookie bag and the cigarette drooped a little lower. She slowly wiped her hand back and forth over the soiled towel beside her to remove the remaining cookie crumbs from her clammy palms.

Sybil knew she crossed the line on that one, but it was a long time coming. And what was said was said; the truth was out. Mother sucked in a deep breath and wheezed it out.

"I know, Syb. I know. I've let myself go. But you know how hard it's been ever since your father left."

"He left over eleven years ago! I mean, Jesus Christ! Get over it! Is that what you're trying to teach me? To roll over and die when things get tough?"

"No. You've always been stronger than me. And I thank God that strength was one of the many good things your father passed on to you."

"Whatever," Sybil said, shaking her head in disgust as she left the room. Mother exhaled and wiped her hand on the towel even harder, like she was trying to remove a scarlet letter.

Sybil collapsed on her bed and hugged Chico, who was curled up in the messy nest he made from her bedspread. Her watering eyes smeared dark mascara on the dog's tan fur. Chico attempted comfort with quick licks to his mamma's nose.

Sybil wondered why her life had to be so hard. What she had done to be born into this. And what she had to do to get herself out of it.

◆   ◆   ◆

The following night, Sybil tried to make it up to Jack by treating him to a dinner at Marcello's, the nicest restaurant on the block within her measly budget. He picked her up at seven and by seven-twenty they were digging into plates of tortellini and chicken parmesan.

Sybil's cell phone chirped before her first sip of soda. Jack eyed her suspiciously as she checked the caller ID.

It was Mother, all right.

Sybil glanced up at Jack for his approval. He shook his head, giving a slight eye roll. "Answer it. Or she's gonna call all night." Sybil knew he was right. Not answering it was only going to completely ruin the evening.

"Hello," she said between clenched teeth. Sybil listened for a bit, noticing that Jack had gone back to his meal. She whimpered and shook her head. "Hold on."

Jack shot her a confused look, thinking maybe for some reason Mother wanted to speak to him. Instead, Sybil reached for the laminated menu between the red pepper flakes and parmesan shaker. Avoiding Jack's glare, she scanned over the menu. "Yeah. They have it," she whispered. "I'll get an order to go. No, Mother. One order is plenty." She lowered her head in her hands, completely defeated. "We'll be home when we're home. You can wait."

Jack dropped his fork in disgust and pushed his plate away. Sybil shut her phone gently and sat there, afraid to utter a word.

The polished black and chrome SUV whipped over to the curb. The bass was thumping so hard it was competing with the beats in Sybil's chest. Jack tapped the steering wheel with his thumb to the rhythm, alternating his glances between rearview mirrors. In his mind he was already meeting up with friends later and leaving this pathetic lump in the passenger seat far behind.

Sybil, a mess of nerves, sat beside him, staring, trying to read just how mad Jack was. She felt like throwing up the knots that were sliding tighter in her belly. She clutched the bag of take-out close to her chest like a child with a teddy bear. Her trembling hand reached over, lowering the volume on his radio. "I know you said you don't want to hear it, but please just listen for a second." She waited until he turned to her, seemingly more out of impatience than understanding. She took what she could get. "I only got her something because she told me she ate all the food in the refrigerator. Which is my fault because I should've gone to the grocery store earlier."

Slightly nodding, he grunted and wished that she'd just get the fuck out.

"If I didn't get her some take-out, I'd have to go grocery shopping right now." She motioned to the bag in her lap. "But now I don't. Which is good, because I don't consider tonight over. Am I right?"

No grunts this time. In fact, not even an acknowledgement. She was losing him and had to act fast. She reached over and slid her hand in between his legs. "Am I right?" she whispered, beginning to kiss his neck. She felt him getting hard. "Why don't you come in for a bit?"

He grabbed her wrist, backing away slightly to look her in the eyes. "What about *her*?" he said, nodding to the house.

"She'll be distracted for at least . . . fifteen minutes . . . by the food. That's more than enough time for a quickie. Right?"

"Babe," he exhaled, "this shit's getting real old."

Sybil nodded, knowing he was right. "Okay, then how about this? How about I run in, drop off the food, then we can go to your place for the full-on experience?" Besides keeping Jack's sexual appetite fulfilled, she was really hoping to see his place for the first time.

Jack shook his head. "Not a good idea. My roommates will be home."

"We could be quiet. They wouldn't even know that we're there. I mean, I'd love to finally meet them but if you think that—"

"I said it's not a good time," he snapped.

She immediately lowered her head. "Please, babe. Please don't be mad at me. I'll do anything to still make tonight good. Anything."

They sat for a long moment in silence, hearing only the hum of the vehicle's engine. "Look, Syb. I don't know what I'm feeling right now. I care about you and all. But it kinda sucks that there's a package deal that I'm stuck with. You're not gonna get rid of her. She depends on you too much. And I think tonight is just a taste of things to come." He shrugged and chuckled, "I mean, I feel like I'm dating a chick that has a retarded kid or something."

Sybil's eyes started to tear up. Then her cell phone rang. It was Mother, calling to see where they were and when Sybil would be home with the food.

Within the span of a minute, Jack was driving away, Mother was slurping up her pile of spaghetti and sausage, and Sybil was on her bed, crying all over Chico.

Within the span of twenty minutes, Jack was taking bong hits with friends on the other side of town, Mother was moaning that her stomach ached from eating too fast, and Sybil was staring at the mysterious red pill that Jack got in Mexico.

A lit cigarette hung out of Mother's lips as she called out for her daughter. Sybil strolled into the room, glaring at her mother, whose forehead was covered in a thin sheen of sweat.

"Syb, baby. My stomach is killing me. Can you get me some antacids?"

"Already have," Sybil said, walking over to the bed. "This is a new type. Maximum strength. Where you just need one." She dropped the red pill into her mother's padded palm. "And you have to swallow this. Don't chew."

Mother looked at the single pill and shook her head. "Just one is probably for skinny-binnies like you. I should probably have two. Maybe three."

"No. You just need one," Sybil replied calmly. "Now take it, so you can feel better."

Mother nodded and popped the pill in her mouth. She frantically pointed to a two-liter soda bottle that sat on the night stand. Sybil got it for her and watched as she gulped the pill down with a swig of cola. She gasped for air, then immediately plugged her mouth with the lit cigarette, taking a deep drag.

After Sybil took Chico out in the backyard for his pre-bedtime pee-pee, she went back to check on her mother. She found her passed out on the bed. The cigarette was wedged between two of her sausage fingers, slowly burning to the filter. One of these days the woman was going to incinerate herself and take the house with her. Sybil paused before removing the cigarette, thinking just a little bit more about that scenario. Maybe next time, she thought and removed the smoking butt, stamping it out in the ashtray beside the bed.

As she turned to leave, a wet, rumbling sound came from her mother's stomach. It was loud and disgusting enough to make Sybil stop dead in her tracks. When it was over, Sybil shook her head and left the room to get some sleep.

◆   ◆   ◆

Sybil woke up to the smell of freshly-cooked bacon. Her first thought was that her mother finally did it this time by falling asleep again with a lit cigarette. But instead of self-immolation, Mother stood in the kitchen whipping up some breakfast on the stove. Sybil couldn't have been more shocked at the sight. When she asked what the hell brought this on her mother told her that she really didn't know. Though she felt absolutely dreadful before passing out, having horrible dreams all night, she woke up with the strong urge to get off her ass and fix some bacon and eggs for her daughter. To show her appreciation. And how much she loved her.

◆   ◆   ◆

As the days passed, Mother became a whirlwind around the house. Straightening up, cooking, vacuuming, doing the laundry, and even the occasional dusting, Mother finally took pride in herself with the knowledge that she was being an asset rather than a liability.

With all this activity, she did find herself eating more, but the strange thing was that she wasn't gaining a pound. Though she didn't have the concrete evidence to prove this (because she knew her massive weight would demolish the cheap drugstore scale that Sybil used), she sure as heck knew the elastic bands around her stretch pants weren't cutting off her circulation anymore—even when fresh out of the dryer! With her energy level skyrocketing (at least when compared to the lethargic lump she was before), she and Sybil just chalked up the lack of weight gain to her metabolism finally kicking into high-gear from all the moving she was doing.

◆   ◆   ◆

With Mother helping out around the house, Sybil found herself with more than enough time on her hands. When not working part-time at the corner convenience store or running errands (such as getting the ever-growing amount of groceries, since Mother seemed to be eating so much more), she tried to spend as much time with Jack—time that was still dictated around his schedule. With her mother managing by herself, Sybil felt boredom for the first time in four months as she waited for Jack's call, either over the phone or on her doorstep. They didn't seem to go out any more than usual but he still stopped by at all hours of the night so Sybil could occasionally feed his sexual appetite. As these rendezvous happened well after Mother's bedtime, Jack and Mother still never had a proper introduction.

Though Sybil loved her newfound freedom, she secretly wished that things hadn't changed to such an extreme. Having a bedridden mother allowed Sybil free reign of the house, especially giving her the much needed privacy in her bedroom when Jack would come over unexpectedly.

One night when Jack and Sybil were engaged in some carnal shenani-gans behind her closed bedroom door, a knock from the other side caused the bedsprings to stop in mid-squeak. When Sybil called out "Yes?" in a flustered voice, she heard the muffled voice of her mother outside the door asking if she could see her for a moment. Sybil came out with her skin all flushed and a bedhead from hell, making it impossible to deny what monkey business she and Jack had been participating in. Mother was polite yet forceful, telling her daughter that as long as she lived under her roof, she would follow her rules. And the first rule to be implemented was the door to her daughter's bedroom was to remain wide open at all times when she had visitors, whether male or female.

Jack was lying under the covers when Sybil came back into the room. He noticed that she left the door open a crack. "What're ya doing? Close the door."

Sybil ignored him, sitting gingerly on the edge of the bed. "You need to get dressed. She wants the door to stay completely open."

"You're fuckin' jokin', right?"

Sybil shook her head then let out a pathetic shrug. "We could go to your place instead?"

"Nope," he replied in a tone that told her there would be no more dis-cussion about it.

Sybil lowered her head. She had been dating Jack for over four months and she still hadn't seen his place. She knew it meant one of two things: either she wasn't special to him, or he already had someone special waiting at home. She didn't want to believe either.

Jack stared at her for a long moment. Sybil sheepishly shrugged again. "She'll probably be asleep in a bit and then we can pick up where we left off. As long as we're quiet."

Jack gave her a smug smile, bolted up and got dressed without a word. Grabbing his car keys, he pushed past her and left the house without a kiss or saying goodbye.

That was the last time he was at the house while Sybil was still alive.

◆ ◆ ◆

A week later, Sybil was returning from a quick trip to the mall as she talked to Jack on her cell. She was trying to set something up so they could get together. He kept telling her that he was busy with work and that it would have to wait. She decided not to push the matter any more because that was the way she drove guys away in the past. Besides, absence makes the heart grow fonder, right? Well, the heart can grow fonder, but his dick is definitely gonna grow harder when he gets a glimpse of the matching bra and thong panties I just bought, she thought, cracking a devilish smile.

When Sybil walked up to the house, she heard Chico barking inside. Upon entering the front door, the smell of feces instantly assaulted her nose, causing her stomach to hiccup and eyes to water. Then she saw the foot-wide brown, slimy trail running across the wood floor. Her first instinct was to swat Chico for being such a bad boy, until it sunk in that there was no way a Chihuahua could provide that much fecal output.

As she followed the trail, Chico yapped away around her feet. The brown slimy mess came out of the bedroom hallway and led around to the kitchen. Only the light from the open refrigerator illuminated the immediate area. When Sybil made it to the switch on the kitchen wall and flipped on the overhead light, she stared around with mouth agape. The kitchen was a war zone.

Boxes of cookies, crackers, and bags of chips were torn open and thrown all over the floor. The canned goods were dented. Jars of spaghetti sauce were shattered, their crimson contents dripping out of the cabinets. The items of the refrigerator were turned on their sides, open or smashed, and dripping onto the floor. A gallon of milk was chugging out the last of its ivory fluid, having obviously just been overturned.

Someone must've broken in. Ransacked the house.

The hairs stood on the back of Sybil's neck as an icy chill trickled down her spine.

What if they're still here? Oh, God. Mother . . . !

Sybil snatched up Chico, pinning him tightly against her chest to quiet his barking. When the dog could only let out muffled whimpers, Sybil crept back into the living room.

The front door was still open, which was good in case she needed to make a quick escape. She bent forward, peering around the corner into the hall. Thankfully finding it empty, she took a cautious step closer—partly out of fear and partly trying to avoid the gooey mess streaked across the floor.

The hall light was off. Mother's door was open about a foot wide. The light from her room spilled into the hall; its reflection bounced off the slick, sticky substance leading through the doorway. She wanted to call out for her mother but dreaded that it might alert whoever might be hiding—waiting—somewhere within the house.

Sybil looked back to the open front door. Maybe she should run out to the safety of the front lawn and call 911?

But what if it was Mother that made the mess? Bringing the police would only mortify Sybil if they caught sight of the trail of . . . diarrhea. If Mother left such a mess in the house, what could she possibly look like herself?

No! No cops.

Not yet.

"Mother . . . ?" Sybil called out in a trembling voice.

Not getting a reply, she forced her legs to step forward and enter the shadowy hall while Chico squirmed in her constricting grasp. With her heart thundering in her chest, she didn't realize how badly she was squeezing Chico until she heard his muffled whimpers turn to squeals. She loosened her grip on the dog and took a couple more steps down the hall. Attempting each step in silence, she strained to hear any noises coming from the other side of her mother's bedroom door.

She finally made it to the half-open door and stopped, straddling the slimy trail on the ground below. Sybil reached out with a trembling hand and slowly pushed the door open until the knob on the other side tapped against the wall, assuring her that no one was hiding there.

She quickly scanned the room. All seemed normal, except for two things: the large lump under the duvet and the glistening, putrid trail that led across the floor, went up and over the still dripping footboard, where it eventually disappeared under the bedspread.

The enormous lump moved. Sybil froze.

"Mom . . . ?" she whispered.

There was a long moment of intense silence before she received a response. It was a moan. Her mother's moan. Sybil zigzagged back and forth, careful not to step in the slimy trail that was leading to the direct source of the disgusting fecal smell. Another moan sounded from under the blankets. Sybil grabbed a handful of the duvet and pulled it back slowly.

Mother was lying in the fetal position. The woman's weight caused her to sink into the mattress where she was partially submerged in a pool of brown liquid. The overwhelming odor of steamy diarrhea made Sybil's stomach leap to her throat. A rumbling sounded from Mother's gut, then bubbles rose to surface in the liquid behind her and popped, making the nauseous smell in the room all the more toxic. Mother let out another groan of pain.

"Mommy . . . ?" Sybil called out. Her mother's eyes fluttered open and looked pitifully up at Sybil.

◆   ◆   ◆

"That's what I'm saying. She doesn't remember anything."

Sybil stood in the laundry room by the tumbling dryer, talking to Jack on her cell phone. "She remembers her stomach starting to cramp, going to lie down and then me waking her up when she was covered in her own . . . shit." Sybil guffawed then looked around to make sure she couldn't be overheard. "I think it might have something to do with that pill from Mexico. I gave it to her last week. What exactly was it again?" Sybil whispered.

"I don't know. My guy told me but it was somethin' in Spanish. He just said it was somethin' that ate away all that gunk down there. Like some sort of colon cleanser."

"Well, Christ! That's an understatement." Sybil rubbed her aching brow.

"I shouldn't have given it to her. What if it kills her?" The pitch grew higher in Sybil's voice with each word of the question.

Jack heard it and just wanted it to stop. "Oh, c'mon. She took it over a week ago. If it was so dangerous, don't you think something would've happened earlier? Like the day she swallowed it?"

"Maybe it's taking time. A slow poison. Incubating or something, I don't know. But obviously something's wrong. Maybe I should call a doctor and—"

"And what? Tell him that you gave her *some* pill but you didn't know what was in it? That's smart, real smart."

"*You* gave it me. I trusted that—"

"Hey! If you bring her to a doctor, that's your choice. But you better leave me out of your little fuckin' tale, ya hear?" he snapped. "I don't need the cops showing up at my door if something happens to your old lady."

Even though she was on the phone, Sybil held up her hand in defense. "Babe, I'm not . . . I'm not gonna call anybody. Just relax. I wouldn't bring you into anything, anyway. I'm sure she's going to be all right. The—*cleansing*—probably took a little longer than usual because she's so big and had a lot of . . . build up." Sybil shuddered at what exactly she was referring to. "Please. Everything's cool. Okay, babe?"

For the first time in four months Sybil was relieved when Jack cut the conversation short since she had a lot of work to do. After cleaning up the mess in the kitchen, scrubbing the now-gelatinous trail off the wooden floor, checking on her mother, and letting Chico out to go to the bathroom, she now had to go grocery shopping (and it couldn't wait until morning because the kitchen was completely barren of food).

While at the 24-hour supermarket, Sybil struggled to push around the two full carts of groceries needed to restock the kitchen and her mother's insatiable appetite. Such a tiny girl buying so much food incited some strange stares, even from the store's variety of late-night weirdoes (where at this time of the night, while the sane and responsible slept, the crazy, drunk, insomnia-plagued, and homeless roamed the aisles like zombies in a Romero film).

When Sybil shuffled up the front walkway with her arms full of the first batch of groceries from the car, she found the front door to the house ajar. She pushed it open with her foot, stepping inside. Again, she was hit with the stomach-churning odor of fresh feces. In the exact same spot where she had cleaned only hours earlier, there was another path of the brown, gushy mess that reeked of crap—as if it somehow grew back!

"Jesus Christ . . ." Sybil whimpered as she found all the cabinets and refrigerator door open again.

No, nothing *grew* back. Rather, something appeared to have *come* back.

Clumps of tan fur blew over the wooden floor caused by the breeze through the open front door. Sybil looked closer, trying to figure out what it could have possibly belonged to. The hair was the same color as—

Sybil spun around, scanning the floor for her dog. Noticing the dead silence of the house, her heart leapt to her throat. *Oh, my God . . .*

She haphazardly placed the grocery bags on the couch then bolted to her mother's room, sidestepping the all too familiar trail across the floor. Barging through her mother's door, she found the woman on her belly laying spread eagle on the bed, the trail disappearing between the "V" where her massive dimpled thighs met. The nightgown around her rear was stained with an enormous splash of brown liquid—with matted bits of Chico's fur stuck in it!

"What the fuck did you do?!!" Sybil screamed hysterically.

Mother moaned, struggling to turn over on her side. ". . . baby . . . ?" she mumbled.

Sybil stepped closer. "Chico?! Where the fuck is my dog?!"

Looking up at her daughter, Mother's eyes rattled back and forth. "I . . . don't . . . know . . ." she muttered, completely dumbfounded.

Sybil searched the house for her dog. There was the distinct possibility that Chico had wandered out the open front door before Sybil made it home from the store. Sybil prayed that was the case; that at any moment, the dog would come running in, hungry for both love and food and exhausted from an adventure in the outside world. But what made that theory difficult to swallow was the fact that there were bits and pieces of her dog's fur scattered all over the house and in her mother's sheets. Even more disturbing was the fact that when Sybil helped her mother get out of her soiled nightgown, bits of the dog's fur were stuck to her large shit-stained ass cheeks. It was almost like the obese woman sat on the tiny dog, and with legs flailing wildly, scooted around the house on her ass, crapping everywhere, while the tiny pooch was pinned underneath her! With hope bleak, she more than welcomed delusion, telling herself that Chico might have still gotten away, more than a little worse for the wear.

As before, Mother had no recollection of what happened. How the gooey trail reappeared. How she soiled the nightgown again. How the front door got open. She didn't even know that Sybil had left to go shopping.

Sybil flew into a rage when her mother hinted that maybe *she* was the one responsible for leaving the door open on her way to the store. Mother immediately apologized for the insinuation, knowing how her daughter was going above and beyond the call of duty for her—especially when it came time for the sponge bath to wipe clean those hard-to-reach places.

In what seemed like a night that would never end, Sybil finally put her sick mother back to bed, unpacked and put away all the groceries, and cleaned up the mess that was stained all over the floor. She left the front door open, still holding out that Chico would return (and for the house to air out). Though she constantly checked the front step for him in between her cleaning duties, Chico had yet to appear. He will, he will, she lied to herself. He's fine. He's probably having a ball somewhere out there. He'll get tired and come home to tell me all about it.

The sun was rising when Sybil finally collapsed on the living room couch. Her back was aching, her head throbbing, and no matter how much she washed her hands, she just couldn't seem to stop smelling crap on them. Thinking maybe the smell was burned in her nostrils, she blew her nose until bloody mucus covered the tissue. It still didn't get out the smell.

Utterly exhausted, she called Jack for comfort. She needed him now more than ever. Jack answered his phone more irritated than exhausted. Sybil rambled on and on about Chico missing, shit-stained nightgowns, open doors, sponge baths, ass cheeks with dog hair, blacking out, slimy trails, more laundry, gagging, grocery shopping, exhaustion, aching back, him picking her up so they could drive around and look for Chico—

Jack stopped her there with not the best choice of words. "Listen. This shit is too much."

"Please, Jack. I need to see you. I need you. *Please.*"

There was a long silence on the phone until, "It sounds like you're do-ing fine without me there. I gotta go, Syb. Good luck." Then, a click on the other end.

The cell phone snapped shut and dropped to her side. That was it. She was done. She could take no more. She just wanted to sleep for a long, long time. Partly to forget, mostly to escape.

She welcomed her drooping lids because in moments she wouldn't have to think. Wouldn't have to feel. Wouldn't have to care. Or care *for*.

As she drifted away, she found herself standing in a beautiful golden field of grass. She was in awe of her surroundings until she saw something dark moving over the horizon of the landscape. She felt like she should turn and run. Far away. Before she could act, a cool breeze blew against her body. It felt incredible, erasing all fears of malevolence. She closed her eyes and inhaled the floral scent it brought. Her body became numb by a darkness enveloping first her body, then her mind. It was peaceful; rolling in like storm clouds, not across the sky, but the ground she stood on like a fog bank. It rose ever so slightly, wrapping around her like cool tendrils of ectoplasm. Sybil let off a moan that bordered on orgasmic. It tightened its embrace, crisscrossing her body, encasing her in what felt like a cocoon of safety. It was protecting her, forcing her nerves to relax for the first time in days. Nothing mattered anymore as long as it stayed snug around her. It worked its way up toward her face; first to her neck, then across her cheeks, gently pressing against her closed lids. As it approached her ears she heard a faint cry in the distance.

"Sybillllllll . . ."

The tendrils of serenity backed away from her ears.

No! her own voice echoed in her mind.

"Sybillll . . . !" The call was closer, more immediate.

She felt the cocoon around her body loosening its grip, starting to drop away. *No, please . . . stay . . .*

"Sybillll!!!"

She flinched from the grating scream that seemed to come from just over her shoulder. The soothing wrap around her pulled back, completely breaking contact with her skin.

Please . . . please, don't go. Come back . . .

Sybil's eyes snapped open. She saw the wall of clouds retreating away from her. It wanted nothing more to do with her. It couldn't help her anymore.

She stepped forward to run into it but it completely dissipated in front of her. Then as if an explosion had gone off, a blinding white light burned her eyes. She winced, shielding her face with her hands. When she eventually lowered them and looked around, the peaceful golden field that was once there was no more.

She stood alone in a muddy field of filth. The air was thick. Hot. Burning her lungs. Pools of brown liquid bubbled around her. When the bubbles popped, the overwhelming smell of diarrhea floated over to her, attacked her nostrils, worked its way down her throat leaving a sickening taste, before finally settling in her lungs.

No! Godammit! NO!!!

She opened her mouth, screaming in agony, only what blasted out wasn't her voice . . . but her mother's. "SYBILLLLLLLL!!!!"

Sybil snapped awake with her heart drumming in her chest and her skin slick with sweat. She kicked her feet up and over where they planted on the ground, the movement forcing her body in a seated position on the edge of the couch.

"Sybillll! I . . . don't . . . feel . . . good . . ."

Sybil's head bounced from shoulders to chest as if her spine had melted away. Only the muscles in her neck pulled taut in all directions as she fought to raise her head. Then, as if a power cord were ripped from her back, Sybil's chin dropped to her chest and remained motionless.

"I'M . . . SOOOO . . . HUNGRRRRYYYYY . . ."

Upon hearing those gut-wrenching words, a backup generator in Sybil's head clicked on. Her head snapped back up.

Sybil rose from the couch, her eyes watery and bloodshot. A strand of drool escaped her parted lips and stretched down to her chest. The young woman's sweet demeanor turned demonic.

Mother lay on her side, her back to the door. She moaned, calling again for her daughter.

The floor creaked behind her.

Fighting to roll over, Mother flinched in fright when she found Sybil already beside her. She was clutching something above her head with both hands. Mother looked from her daughter's bloodshot eyes to the item she was holding. Before she could utter a word, the phone book came crashing down toward her face. There was a blinding pain and a sickening crack that echoed somewhere in Mother's ears. Then another. And another. Then all went black.

◆　◆　◆

When Mother eventually came to with an inferno ripping through her brain she kicked her legs around, trying to pull herself off the bed. She was trapped like a turtle on its back. Her eyes snapped open to find Sybil sitting in a chair beside the bed, looking down at her.

"Stay still," Sybil told her. Her eyes were red and surrounded by dark circles.

Mother was bound to the metal bed frame by her wrists. One was handcuffed, the other zip-tied. She looked around and saw that all traces of food and soda bottles had been removed from the room. It was the cleanest she'd seen the place in a very long time. She shifted her eyes to her daughter, afraid of her little girl for the very first time.

"Please, Syb," she begged.

"Shut up," her daughter coldly snapped back, leaning closer. "When it's time, I'll uncuff you so you can sit up. I don't want you getting bedsores."

"What're ya doing, baby?" her mother asked delicately. Her stomach grumbled causing her to let out a moan. Christ, was she hungry.

Sybil sneered. "I'm doing what should've been done a long time ago. And if you try to scream, I'll gag you. And if you continue screaming, I'll use this." She held up the stun gun and pushed the button. Mother's eyes widened as she saw the blue zigzag of electricity dance between the two prongs. What she had personally bought for her daughter's protection at one time was now being used to keep her captive.

Mother shook her head in utter confusion, not amused at the irony. "Baby? What? . . . Why are you doing this . . . ?"

Sybil released the button and lowered the device. She took a long, deep breath and waited until *she* was ready to answer. "What I'm doing is helping you. For the next three days, you're gonna be fed small meals throughout the day. Small, healthy meals. Things you should've been eating years ago, so you didn't become . . . *this!*" The last few words grew from disapproval into disgust. "You're going to learn self-control. It's going to be like quitting cold turkey . . . which, by the way . . ." Sybil paused to take the pack of smokes off the nightstand. She squeezed her hand around them, crushing them flat. "You're giving these up, too." She opened up her hand, allowing the crumpled cigarette pack to drop to the floor.

She continued on regarding the plan to help her mother lose the weight.

Sybil would feed her the small meals, slowly, one forkful at a time. The days of inhaling her food were gone. She would take the time to taste the food. Savor it. If she screamed for help, she would get shocked. If she screamed for food, she would get shocked. If she annoyed Sybil in any way, she would get shocked.

When her mother asked how she would go to the bathroom, Sybil held up a plastic Tupperware dish. She would be uncuffed, although her other wrist would stay zip-tied to the bed frame (after all, Mother was three times the size of Sybil and could easily overpower her, even more so in a rage of hunger), and she could urinate in the dish. As for the defecation question? She would be fed anti-diarrhea medication that should plug the woman up, making her not have to go for at least a couple days. Her bowels had already been emptied TWICE in the last few hours. With the massive amount of feces that Sybil had already scrubbed off the floor, sheets, and nightgown (again, TWICE!), there couldn't possibly be anything left in her. The well-balanced, small-portioned meals that she would be fed should take a while to filter through her system.

It was a clean slate, so to speak.

In Sybil's sleep-deprived delirium, the plan seemed like it just might work. She had to show her mother that the woman *could* deal with the hunger pangs, move past them and practice some self-discipline. It was an extreme case of tough love, but sometimes desperate measures are called for when the ones you love act so self-destructively.

It was a noble effort on Sybil's part. At least that's how she justified her actions.

When her mother started to silently sob at her daughter's torturous plan, Sybil went to the other side of the room and removed the large mirror that hung on the wall. She returned to the bed, shoving it in her mother's face. She wanted the woman to take a good look at the sobbing mess of blubber that shook on the bed—at the weak, spineless woman that gave up on life years ago. At first Mother refused to look until Sybil threatened her with some shock therapy. Sybil ordered her to stare at her reflection for five whole minutes. After three, her mother calmed down and silently nodded. Either she got the point loud and clear or was afraid of the next tactic her daughter might take to prove it. With snot, spittle, and tears streaming down her plump face, Mother told her daughter that she understood what she was doing; what she *had* to do. Mother also knew that three days might seem like an eternity, but if she didn't do what Sybil said, three days could easily stretch into three weeks . . . or three months . . . or three . . .

There was no other option but to go along with her daughter's demented goal.

Sybil made her imprisoned mother sip bottled water from a straw. "I know you don't believe it right now, but I do love you," Sybil told her before she left.

Mother nodded, not knowing what to believe—besides the fact that somehow she was responsible for making her daughter go off the deep end.

◆ ◆ ◆

As Mother sat alone, strapped to the bed, she couldn't help but think that this is what her life had come to; that her own daughter had to go to such an extreme to prove how pathetic her life had become.

She had always wished that she could redo so much; be a better mother, a better wife, a better person. Oh, to be able to just start over from the very moment she felt Sybil's first kick while she was growing in her belly.

If I could somehow be granted that second chance, I'd change my life forever, she thought, before her lids slowly drooped and sealed shut.

◆ ◆ ◆

Three hours later, Sybil awoke from the beeping of her alarm clock.

Feeding time.

The first (small) meal consisted of a low-calorie and low-fat frozen dinner (Sybil was too exhausted to cook, after all). When she was done spoon-feeding her mother, she heard the first grumble from the woman's large belly. Sybil ignored it, making her mother take a few more sips of water before leaving the room so they could both get more sleep.

What Sybil couldn't ignore was the fact that only forty-five minutes later she was awakened by her mother's howls complaining of stomach pain. Or—goddamn it!—was it hunger pangs?

She entered her mother's room with the stun gun hidden behind her back. "What's the matter?"

Mother shook her head and whimpered. "My stomach . . . doesn't feel right . . . I think . . ."

Sybil waited for it.

"I . . . think I need . . ." her mother continued, "Antacids. Remember those strong ones you gave me . . . where I needed only one . . ."

Sybil nodded, looking away.

"Can I please have one?"

Sybil quickly shook her head. "They're gone. There aren't any more."

"But . . . I thought you said—"

"It wasn't an antacid!" Sybil blurted out, just wanting to shut her up.

"Then . . . what was it?"

Sybil had to come clean. "It was some pill that Jack got in Mexico." Mother shook her head in confusion. "And I shouldn't have given it to you," Sybil whispered.

"I don't . . . I don't understand . . ."

Sybil exhaled. "It was supposed to help make you thinner. I only gave it to you because I thought it would help curb your appetite. Obviously, I was wrong."

"Oh, Syb. How could you?"

"Because I thought it would help."

"Don't you realize that all this started after you gave me that pill?"

They both sat there in silence. Mother shook her head. Upset as she was, she needed comfort, and there was only one thing that could provide it. "Please. Please, get me something to eat."

"You've already eaten. You don't need anything else."

"Sybil! This bullcrap is gonna stop right now! Untie me and get me some food!" her mother screeched.

And there it was.

"It's the least you can do. I mean for Pete's sake! Look at what you've done to me!" Mother jerked her bound arms up as far as the restraints allowed, punctuating her statement. "I'm hungry! Go and get me some food!!" she screamed, with eyes bulging.

Sybil's eyes began to tear up at the thought of what she had to do. "I'm sorry. But I warned you."

Sybil lunged at her mother, shoving the stun gun deep into a fat fold of her stomach. She depressed the button and held it there for a good second or two. It was long enough to cause her Mother to convulse and grit her teeth. She gasped in agony, and with the air rushing into her lungs, she puffed up even larger.

Sybil pulled the stun gun away and started to cry. Her mother's body slammed back to the mattress, and between the spit bubbles that percolated out of her mouth, she let out a harrowing groan. She turned to her daughter with a newfound reason for terror.

"Please! Don't make me do that again!" Sybil sobbed. "You know the rules!"

Before mother could speak, her stomach grossly rumbled. A long, wet fart puttered out from under the sheets. The obscene noise seemed to last an eternity.

Both Sybil and her mother looked down at her belly in shock.

When the bubbling flatulence finally subsided, her stomach loudly grumbled again.

Sybil's shock turned to disgust. Her mother looked up in horrified embarrassment.

"Oh, my God! What's wrong with—" Before Sybil could finish, her mother unleashed a torturous scream and began flailing around on the bed, her legs kicking wildly in all directions. Even in Sybil's twisted state, she knew this wasn't right.

Something was definitely wrong.

Her mother needed medical attention. And needed it now.

But before she could call for help, the restraints had to be removed. They'd probably question the raw lacerations already starting to bruise around the woman's wrist. Maybe Sybil would be charged with abuse or neglect. But at the rate her mother was flailing about, the sooner she removed the restraints, the less damage her mother would cause herself. Maybe . . . just maybe . . . the wounds would go unnoticed.

Sybil fumbled in her pockets for the handcuff key as her mother began to wail in excruciating pain. She pulled out the key, attempting to stick it in the tiny key hole. As her mother frantically yanked on the cuff, Sybil missed the hole. Once. Twice. On the third attempt she stuck the key in and turned it, unlocking the cuff. Her mother's hand shot out of the metal restraint and clutched at her rumbling gut. Sybil ran to the other side of the bed, ripped back the covers and looked at the wrist bound by the zip-tie. She knew she'd have to cut it off before it tore, even more so than it already had, through her mother's soft pudgy flesh. Sybil ran out of the room to get the scissors.

When she returned her mother was bouncing back and forth on the bed, clawing at her stomach with her free hand. The grumbling was louder and in unison with the wet farts that were escaping again. Sybil screamed when she saw that her mother's pupils were missing; just the whites were visible as her eyes had rolled back into her head.

"Mommy! I'm sorry! I'm so sorry!" Sybil sobbed, frantically attempting to cut at the zip-tie. Using her knee, Sybil pinned her mother's forearm down against the mattress. In her trembling panic, the metal point of the scissor slid under the tie and slashed across her mother's flesh, causing a stream of crimson to flow over both mother and daughter's hands. Sybil tried again, finally snipping at the tie. She was half way through it when Mother ripped her hand free, breaking through the remainder of the uncut plastic bond.

Mother bellowed an unholy howl and clutched at her stomach. She frantically clawed at her nightgown, pulling it up, to see if what she was feeling down there could possibly be happening.

Mother and daughter screamed in unison at the sight of the bloated, bulging belly.

Sybil scuttled off the bed, stepping over Mother's arms and legs, and causing the bed to bounce wildly. She landed clumsily on the floor then scrambled to her feet, whirling back around to her mother on the bed.

The pink smooth flesh of her mother's stomach was squirming like a bag of snakes. Something large wiggled and flopped around just below the skin, pushing and stretching as if at any moment it was about to tear free. The rumbling now took on the sound of muffled growls buried under a mound of flesh, fat, and muscle.

Mother flipped over onto her stomach and raised her large, padded rear into the air. There was an ungodly explosion from under the woman's nightgown that let loose a torrent of brown liquid, shooting out like a geyser across the room. It was as if the woman had been a crimped garden hose (her spigot all the way open for minutes) which had finally been straightened out. The goopy spray *splattered* against the opposite wall.

Sybil jumped back to avoid getting hit by the warm, liquid projectile, her back slamming against the opposite wall as she let off a bloodcurdling scream—not from pain but from the obscene sight she was witnessing. Between the wet, gushy sounds of the liquid hitting the wall, something solid shot out, bounced off the wall with a metal clang, and landed on the floor at Sybil's feet.

Sybil's jaw went slack as she stared at the object on the floor. Chico's dog collar lay there, covered in a brown gelatinous mess. Sybil opened her mouth to howl in horror but her mother stole her thunder.

Mother unleashed another scream but buried the climax of it into the padding of the mattress. She jerked her body up and clawed at the sheets, tearing through them as if she had razorblades for nails. Her frenzied movements caused the duvet to flip over and cover the lower half of her body, as if an enormous invisible hand was somehow trying to restore the woman's dignity as best it could.

Then there was another explosion. Only this time it wasn't a liquid projectile but deafening flatulence with enough force to ripple the duvet—followed by what sounded like something very large and wet squeezing its way out of a hole that was too small for its girth. As the disgusting noise continued, Mother's body seemed to deflate to half her size, sinking deeper into the soiled mattress.

Sybil wanted to rip off her ears, tear off her nose, gouge out her eyes—anything to put a stop to this insanity that she was seeing, hearing, and smelling!

Before Sybil could self-mutilate, Mother went limp, passing out cold. Though the woman fell completely still, the bed hadn't.

Something large coiled under the bedspread causing the mattress to shift upon its box spring from its massive movement.

Sybil stood frozen, bound by dread.

A growl bellowed from under the rumpled covers.

Sybil shifted her eyes over to the door. If she could make it, she could slam the door behind her and lock in whatever had just *slid* out of her mother.

The movement on the bed stopped. The growl silenced.

Sybil shifted her gaze back to the bed.

All was still. This was her chance. She had no other.

Sybil leapt on rubbery legs.

She made it to the doorway, grasping at the brass handle, ready to slam the door behind her.

Before Sybil could escape, a tapeworm the size of an anaconda sprung out from under the covers, flew through the air, and clamped its glistening mouth completely over her head.

With a mighty tug from its other end, the worm yanked Sybil off her feet where she landed on the wood floor with a hard *thud*! As she was dragged back across the ground toward the bed, Sybil dug her heels into the wooden floor while beating and clawing at the slick, fleshy behemoth that encased her head.

The thing's shit-covered, slimy, segmented body convulsed as it began to chomp down, stretching its mouth forward—inch by inch—over Sybil's flailing arms, until it quickly enveloped her down to her hips.

The other half of the worm, still attached somewhere within Mother's rectum, started reeling itself back inside where it was warm and safe. With Sybil attached to one side and Mother to other, the tapeworm looked like a gigantic, glistening Chinese finger-cuff locked in a demented tug of war with itself.

As the air was crushed out of her lungs, Sybil finally went still. She slid across the floor, leaving a trail of brown slime and one dislodged shoe. She was pulled up onto the bed. She inched her way across the sheets, a death nerve causing one of her legs to twitch its final resistance, as she headed toward the center of her mother's spread-eagled legs.

◆　◆　◆

Mother awoke two days later. Though she prayed it was all just some horrible nightmare, this time she remembered key events from two days ago. The reality of it all was confirmed when she repeatedly called out for Sybil and got no response.

Except for the rumble in her belly.

With her enormous protruding stomach, Mother wobbled around the house, clutching at the walls for support. As she continued to plead for her daughter, her stomach rumbled even more.

She eventually collapsed on the living room couch and started to weep.

Then she felt the kick.

Mother wiped her eyes dry, fought back the final sniffle and wondered why she was crying. She was finally given a second chance. Somebody up there had listened to her prayers and was willing to give her another shot at life with Sybil. And this time she wasn't going to take it for granted.

◆ ◆ ◆

Mother rested for the next few hours to build up her strength. She spent the down time rubbing her belly, feeling the movement within, and singing nursery rhymes. When she felt strong enough, Mother rose from the couch to clean up the house.

Then she searched for Sybil's cell phone.

Because there was unfinished business to take care of.

◆ ◆ ◆

Jack got the call from Sybil's mother later that day. She told him that she had to see him. When he informed her that he was too busy, she informed him that she knew about his little pill from Mexico. How it made her . . .

. . . sick.

Almost poisoned her. And if he didn't get over there right away, she'd put in a call to the police.

Jack quickly replied that he could be at the house within the hour.

As Mother waited on the couch for him, she rubbed her bloated, squirming belly. She smiled as it growled up to her. She patted it very delicately.

"I know, Syb. I know, baby. Don't ya worry. Food will be here shortly," she told it.

◆ ◆ ◆

POST SCRIPT:

There seemed to be a rash of disappearances just south of the border. All the missing had various things in common: young men that just got paid on a Friday that wandered to the seedier parts of town looking for professional companionship only to never be heard from again.

One young man, found wandering the streets completely naked and bloody below the waist, kept mumbling the same phase over and over: "gusano de mierda". He was hospitalized with a large unknown bite mark on his inner thigh and died quickly from sepsis. Mexican authorities believed the man to be insane and that the bite came from a wild dog that he might have provoked.

Because of the latest massacre between warring drug cartels just shy of the Texas border, the story was pushed to the back of the paper where few of the local citizens noticed it.

Besides, who really wanted to read an insane man's tale—of being attacked at a whorehouse by a gigantic "shit worm"—while consuming their bacon and scrambled eggs?

FLY ON THE WALL
Stephanie Bedwell-Grime

Joe knew he was going to have to kill his boss that first day because of the flies.

They littered the floor beside his dust-covered desk. He even found a fat fly corpse in his top drawer. A few buzzed sluggishly around the fluorescent lights. The sound of flies hitting the Plexiglas window punctuated the slow morning hours. By lunchtime he couldn't think of anything else.

Finally, out of desperation, Joe used a piece of letterhead to sweep some of the flies into the trashcan. But by the time he finished, a new layer of fly bodies covered the floor. Big fat furry flies, long skinny flies, all lying on their backs with their hairy legs curled inward.

Mid afternoon, the boss came to check on how Joe's first day had gone. As she stood in the doorway to Joe's office, he noticed that a halo of listless flies buzzed around the boss' head.

It didn't matter if the boss was half his age, drop-dead gorgeous and stacked. Because of the flies, the boss would have to go.

"Can we do something about these flies?" Joe asked irritably. Better that than admit to the boss that he'd done nothing except swat at them and step on them by accident all day.

The boss looked at Joe as if reconsidering her choice of an employee. Blonde curls tumbled over her shoulders. She wore a navy blue suit, with a skirt that barely covered her crotch for all its austerity. She had great legs. Legs that went on forever, disappearing under that tiny skirt. A couple of fat flies buzzed lazily after her as her heels tapped a rhythm against the tile floor. "What flies?"

"Never mind," Joe said sharply. How could the woman not notice the flies? She looked well put together, the kind of woman who never missed a detail.

Like his ex-wife, who'd certainly taken note of the nights he insisted he'd worked late. Joe frowned.

"Everything okay?" the boss asked, those blonde brows creasing in concern. A real blonde, he thought. Unless she dyed them.

"Fine," Joe said, trying not to sound like a lunatic. He needed this job. Especially after he'd been fired from his last job for sexually harassing a female co-worker. Who would have thought smacking a woman on the butt would classify as sexual harassment, he thought bitterly. What was the world coming to?

"I could use your input on a new project," his new boss said with a smile. "Well, unless you have to get home to your wife."

"Oh no," Joe blurted out. "I'm divorced." Divorced and until today, unemployed. He winced. Why on earth had he told her that? If she hadn't noticed the flies, she probably wouldn't want to hear the sordid details of his private life.

"In that case," the boss said with another of those megawatt smiles, "Why don't we share a late lunch? I just hate to eat alone."

Joe had already eaten lunch, but he neglected to mention that to the boss. Flies or no, Joe mused, life was definitely looking up.

The boss' name, it turned out, was Denise. Joe being one of those people who promptly forgot a person's name as soon as they were introduced, had already forgotten it twice. Once after his interview. And again after she'd reintroduced herself this morning. But as they sat there enjoying margaritas at a local Mexican restaurant, he vowed never to forget it again. Denise looked like the kind of gal who wouldn't mind getting her butt slapped. Joe hoped he would get a chance to find out.

The boss, Denise, he forced himself to remember her name, leaned across the table and clasped his hand. "I'm so glad you came to work for us, Joe."

"Why thank you," replied Joe's tequila-soaked tongue. He poured himself another margarita from the pitcher. Those tacos were taking an inordinately long time, he thought distantly. The tequila was going to his head. He really should eat something. That's when he noticed the fat fly sitting on his salt-rimmed glass. Another circled above like a furry vulture looking for a place to land.

"I've been needing someone like you for some time," Denise added.

The comment hung between them. What had she meant by that? That the company needed him? Quite honestly, he had no skills that couldn't be supplied by someone smarter and cheaper. Or did she mean that she liked him?

Joe tried to twist his mind around it, but the amount of alcohol in his blood made thinking difficult.

"Hmm, it's getting hot in here," the boss mused. She shrugged out of her navy jacket, revealing a very low cut blouse.

Joe took one look at her cleavage and decided higher-level intelligence wasn't required at the moment.

Denise ordered another pitcher of margaritas. By the time the tacos arrived, Joe's stomach rebelled at the thought of food. But the boss ate voraciously, consuming Joe's portion as well as her own. It didn't seem to bother her that a huge black fly swam in the salsa beside her plate. One look at it was almost enough to send Joe lurching down the hall to the washroom, but then Denise looked up at him and smiled. Joe took one glance at that inviting smile nicely framed over that cleavage and promptly forgot about the flies.

"Well, I guess I should talk about the Smith account," the boss said. "We've got that meeting first thing in the morning." She dipped one long-nailed finger into the salsa and licked it clean.

Joe took one last gulp of his margarita. "Right, the meeting," he slurred, the details of which they were supposed to be discussing.

"We can have coffee at my place," Denise suggested. "That'll give me a chance to bring you up to speed."

He definitely needed that coffee, Joe thought. The boss seemed to have attracted a crown of flies that buzzed erratically around her head. The movement was making him dizzy. Yeah, coffee was a great idea. Coffee and sobering up so he could at least think somewhat coherently about the upcoming meeting. Not that Joe put much effort into anything he did at work. But the lovely Denise made him want to hang on to this new job. Even if it was just for her company.

The sun was still high in the sky as he staggered to the boss' Jaguar and tried to brave the drive without spewing all over its leather interior.

Joe expected Denise (he was certain that was her name), to live in some swank downtown condo, something to go with her silver Jag. But she drove for what seemed like hours into the country. Overhanging trees cast a pattern of light and shadow that swirled about the interior of the Jag making him all the more likely to puke. But he found the soft purr of a well-tuned motor comforting.

He must have dozed off because suddenly Denise said, "Here we are," in that got-it-all-together, I'm-a-hot-woman voice.

Joe stared into the green jungle of the country lane. The Jaguar was parked at the end of a long gravel drive. A stone garage stood beside the car. But Denise got out of the Jag in those navy spike pumps and walked around to open the door for him.

Finding his machismo, Joe tumbled out of the Jag and stood up before Denise rounded the back of the car. He blinked, wishing for all the world he'd passed on this afternoon rendezvous and just gone to bed. His stomach was starting to violently protest the over abundant influx of tequila coupled with a lack of food. To add to the torment, a fly buzzed persistently by his left ear. That tiny sound jumpstarted his hangover headache.

He opened his mouth to plea the headache, but just then Denise said, "It's just down there." She pointed to a very quaint renovated schoolhouse at the end of the drive.

Maybe they could play schoolteacher, Joe thought, his libido overriding his hangover.

"I'll put on some coffee. Then we can talk."

What Joe had in mind involved speech of the nonverbal kind. But he knew from past experience that to say such a thing would only earn him a slap in the face. So he followed Denise down the gravel drive. One of the flies floated after them, buzzing on the still air.

The inside of Denise's cabin was warm and dark. So warm that a trio of flies had made a pool out of a coffee cup abandoned from her breakfast. Oh well, Joe thought, his brain finally working again. This was the country. You had to interact with the wildlife once in a while.

Denise rinsed the coffee cup, drowning the flies, and put on a fresh pot. Joe sat on the couch. The inside of the schoolhouse had been gutted. A loft bedroom perched above them among the rafters. His libido leapt into high gear as he imagined hammering into her up there on that platform bed, her long legs wrapped around his waist. He nearly spilled the coffee Denise handed to him.

"Thanks." He pulled his thoughts back to the present and drank a mouthful of coffee. Hot liquid trickled down his throat, followed by the sensation of something furry moving against his tongue. Joe gagged. Denise looked at him in alarm.

"You okay?" She bent over him, hiking that short skirt higher.

"Fine." Joe took another quaff of coffee and swallowed. Whatever it was, it was gone now, swirling in his stomach with all that tequila.

"Let's go out on the patio," Denise suggested. "It's stuffy in here."

She led him through a dark hallway out into the green light of overhanging trees. A wrought iron sofa with a soft cushion, two chairs and a small table furnished the patio. Silence reigned, except for the persistent buzz of insects. Denise sat beside him on the couch, all long legs and cleavage and looking fresh in spite of a day at the office and an afternoon spent drinking. Joe wished his mouth didn't taste like garbage and his shirt wasn't wrinkled beyond hope, but the boss didn't seem to notice.

"So," Denise began. "About the Smith account. I know this is your first day, but I could really use your input."

"Uh-huh," Joe said, trying to look intelligent and less bleary-eyed than he felt. He hadn't so much as glanced at the Smith account all day. Having nothing halfway intelligent to say, he leaned over and kissed her.

Now came the moment of truth. He never knew until the moment came which way it would go. This could be his first and last day of the new job. Or the start of something way more exciting. Admittedly, his track record wasn't good.

To his surprise Denise kissed him back.

Her tongue snaked into his mouth, hot and . . . furry.

The sensation shocked him at first. But he realized they'd both been out drinking all afternoon. No wonder her tongue was furry.

That was Joe's last coherent thought for some time.

He'd made the first move, but Denise was the boss and she took charge.

Her tongue probed deeper into his mouth, plundering his tonsils. He twined his hands into her silky blonde hair. Her ample breasts pressed against his chest as she leaned even closer, seeking to devour him.

His hand slid inside her blouse and cupped one of those breasts. Her nipple hardened against his palm. Denise moaned, a low sound that buzzed in his fuzzy mind. Her skirt hiked even higher as she straddled his leg and pressed her heat against him.

Desire spiked through him, hot and demanding in spite of the liquor. The caffeine high hit, dragging his libido with it. His hands skimmed her ribcage, realizing suddenly that for all the office-appropriate camouflage of the navy suit, Denise wasn't wearing a bra. The boss' tongue left his mouth and diligently went to work on his right ear. His lips felt sticky. But then Denise had been wearing a ton of red lipstick. His fingers toyed with the tiny pearl buttons of her blouse, but he'd lost dexterity on that second pitcher of margaritas. Still, he fumbled through the task. Her breasts spilled into his hands.

Oh for bigger hands, Joe thought.

But Denise busied herself coating his neck with the same sticky stuff that ringed his lips. She hummed, a deep contented rumble.

Odd. Joe's brain formed the dim and seemingly unimportant thought, but then Denise's probing fingers found his belt buckle. Joe hoped that weird buzzing would soon turn to screams of delight. No neighbors out here in the country. They could make all the noise they wanted.

The rasp of his zipper interrupted Denise's humming. Her fingers twined around his erection. Joe pressed himself into the soft fuzziness of her palm. Strange, but who cared? He glanced up at the sun setting through the trees and briefly imagined how much more comfortable a bed would be.

Then again, the braided wool rug in front of the fireplace inside had definite possibilities. Ones that didn't involve standing up. By the way Denise moved her hand, he doubted he'd last that long.

He groped for the zipper of her skirt, getting it undone without too much damage. Perfect long legs stole his breath, as Denise stood up and divested herself of her thigh-high stockings and the whisper of a lace thong.

Joe skinned out of his hopelessly wrinkled pants and not-so-clean boxers and hauled Denise back down on top of him.

She fit around him like a hot, sticky glove, and he groaned aloud as he entered her. His eyes drifted closed as he savored the sensation of her soft skin surrounding him. Skin so soft it felt like . . . fur.

Joe's eyes shot open. Denise's mouth covered his. Her tongue thrust into his mouth, mimicking his movements. He caught a blurry up-close glimpse of her eyes. Far too close for proper perspective, he suddenly thought he saw four sets of eyes looking back at him.

Must be the tequila. Joe's body stole the rest of his thoughts as it rushed toward orgasm.

Gripping Denise's hips, Joe spun her over on the loveseat. Her long legs wrapped around his hips, the way he'd so hoped they would. He hammered into her. The wrought iron creaked with their exertions. Joe hoped the welding would hold. Denise was making that high-pitched sound again. But for once he had no nosy neighbors downstairs to complain about the noise, or to tip off his now ex-wife to his afternoon's entertainment.

The buzzing rose to a shrieking crescendo. Joe slammed into her. His pelvis met the resistance of her pubic bone. Then Denise seemed to go soft around him. Joe gripped her shoulders.

Only to find his fingers sinking into something soft and furry, something that whirred contentedly. He opened his eyes to find himself shoulder-deep in fat, furry fly bodies.

Slowly the flies undulated, just as Denise had done beneath him, pulling him deeper into their mass. He screamed.

Orgasm hit, blinding him with its intensity. He didn't remember anything else for a long time.

He awoke groggy and disoriented in his own bed and with no recollection of how he'd gotten there. His hung over brain surrendered memories unwillingly. He'd gone out for drinks with Denise, like that had been a good idea after what had happened at his last job. He'd drunk far too much. Didn't take a rocket scientist to figure that out. His head hurt like holy hell and his mouth tasted like something vile slept in it. And his stomach lurched at the vague memory of food. Oh yeah, he'd drunk far too much and eaten far too little. And God knew what he'd said and done.

A fleeting memory of undressing Denise on her own patio flitted through his mind. And then they'd . . .

That's when those fleeting half-memories got weird.

His stomach picked that moment to rebel. Joe fled for the bathroom.

He spent the next half-hour hunched over his grimy toilet, the alarming suspicion he should be somewhere else ringing in his aching head.

Finally, after what seemed like an eternity, he stopped spilling his guts. Joe lay down on his bathroom floor and rested his head against the cold tile.

Oh no! The meeting. The one Denise had supposedly lured him back to her place to discuss. Linking his fingers over the porcelain sink, Joe heaved himself upright.

He caught a glimpse of himself in his bathroom mirror and screamed.

A horrifically disfigured Joe screamed back at him.

Raised red welts covered his face. He looked like a victim of measles or smallpox. The trail disappeared past his shoulders where the mirror ended. Sucking in an apprehensive breath, Joe looked down.

And screamed some more. Red welts covered his entire body. Every single inch. He looked like he'd been chewed up and spit out. Clear blisters covered most of the lesions. Whatever he'd done with Denise last night, he'd caught something . . . terrible.

And still the blistered welts reminded him of something from his childhood, something not chickenpox or measles. Something that bit and then itched and left scars.

He peered into the mirror, trying to not look at his blistered body, trying not to think about how long it would take for those blotches to fade and whether they'd leave scars. He scrutinized one of those liquid-filled blisters, forcing his brain to remember . . .

A camping trip up north in the summer. A tent with a ripped screen. A hot muggy afternoon when the black flies had made a meal of him while leaving his companion practically unscathed. Joe gave the welt another skeptical glance.

He wasn't imagining things. Those marks did look like black fly bites. Hundreds of them.

Well . . . Denise did live in the country. He had a dim memory of driving for what seemed like hours down deserted roads.

And then his mind offered him a more sinister memory.

A strange image of hammering into Denise, her body soft and giving under him. Wet and sticky and soft. That strange contented humming she'd been making.

And then her body seemed to dissolve . . .

One moment he'd been staring down at Denise, his face inches from hers, looking into those luminous eyes, her lithe body wrapped around his. And in the next, things had gone kind of blurry and strange.

Like staring too closely at a newspaper photograph, Denise seemed to dissolve into little black dots. Black dots that buzzed and bit!

He'd come then, hard and fast. Horror and desire warped into one. And if he'd seen what he thought he'd felt and seen, all he remembered after that was pouring into Denise and the blank lassitude that followed.

Somehow he'd ended up in his own bed. Something had chowed down on him before he got there. Joe intended to find out what.

His medicine cabinet turned up an ancient bottle of calamine lotion.

He'd tossed the box of tampons his ex-wife had left there, but other than that, he hadn't bothered to clean it out. Well, the old ball and chain had been good for something. The Ex had also left a bottle of insect repellent there. He checked the label. Sure enough it contained an impressive assortment of chemicals that promised to kill mosquitoes of all kinds. That ought to do the job, Joe thought.

Joe stepped into a steaming shower, but the hot water stung his bites and he added a fair measure of cold just to make it bearable. His towel felt like sandpaper. Wincing, he dried himself off and slathered on what was left in the bottle of calamine. The pink lotion made him look even more like leftover hamburger. He rubbed as much as he could stand into the skin on his face and covered the rest with a shirt and pants. He shoved the bottle of insect repellent into his pocket as a last minute backup plan.

The meeting about the Smith account was just wrapping up when he arrived. Denise sat at the head of the conference table in a navy suit and very low-cut blouse, looking powerful and undeniably hot.

Caught between the blinds and the window, a fly buzzed at the plate glass. Everyone else ignored the high-pitched percussive sounds of its efforts.

The meeting dispersed. People checked their watches, entered a few last notes in their PDAs. Chairs scraped against the floor. A few of the departing staff gave Joe an odd look. Joe slipped into the room and took the seat nearest Denise.

"Joe!" She seemed surprised to see him. "I told them you wouldn't be in today. You seemed under the weather when we parted yesterday."

"What time was that?" Joe asked.

"I don't know," Denise hedged. "Late."

Joe resisted the urge to seize Denise's leather portfolio and deal with the fly that didn't seem to bother anyone else. The thought of its fat body squashed against the glass excited him. But there was Denise to deal with instead. Another fly circled lazily above her head.

He swatted at it.

Denise jumped. "What are you doing?"

"Trying to get rid of that fly." He pointed indignantly to the space above her head.

Denise raised her eyes and studied the space over her head. "What fly?"

"What fly?" Joe repeated stupidly. He yanked up his sleeve, exposing the bites that covered his arm like freckles. "Why don't you tell me about this!"

"Oh dear," Denise said. "This is all my fault. You seemed unwell yesterday evening, so I drove you home with the window open. The bugs are murder this time of year."

She looked completely sincere, but the word "murder" rang in his ears.

He'd have to kill her, he thought with cold certainty. All because of the flies.

The ghost of a plan drifted through his mind. Joe turned his most engaging smile on the boss, the one he'd used to mollify his wife. Like that had worked. "Sorry I missed the meeting. Why don't we have lunch and you can bring me up to date?"

Denise glanced at her watch. A slow smile spread across her face. Whatever they'd done together last night, the boss had enjoyed it. "Good idea."

She gathered up a sheaf of papers and stuffed them into her portfolio. "Why don't we have lunch at my place? That way we can work through the afternoon without interruptions."

"Sure," Joe readily agreed. He patted his pocket.

This time Joe paid more attention to the route as they left the congestion of the city. But after many twists and turns down unfamiliar roads, he grew confused. He thought they were still heading north, but they could have veered east. Didn't matter, he reassured himself. He could always hitch a ride if he had to, maybe even with another Jaguar-driving blonde.

"I admire your dedication," Denise said, as she led Joe through the damp stuffy interior of the house and out onto the secluded patio. "Especially on a day when you're feeling under the weather."

"I'm fine, really," Joe insisted. Truth be told, he felt like death warmed over and he looked the remnants of someone's lunch. But he had to unravel the mystery of what happened between them last night, besides the obvious. And whether it was all as freaky as his memory insisted.

"Coffee?" Denise asked standing in the doorway. She looked immaculate in another of her seemingly endless supply of navy suits, except for the fly crawling out of her cleavage. If she noticed the tickle of its furry black legs, she gave no sign. "Or perhaps you'd prefer something a little stronger."

Joe glanced at the fly and nodded. "Stronger is good."

The boss reappeared with a silver tray containing a chilled bottle of wine and two wineglasses. She'd shed her jacket. The fly that had made such an intimate inspection trailed behind her.

Denise sat on the loveseat and patted the space beside her. The fly crawled along the decorative wrought iron back of the sofa. Joe reluctantly joined her. The boss poured wine. The bottle disappeared quickly and she ventured inside for another one.

Joe seized that opportunity to coat himself with insect repellent. He glanced at the shadowed windows. No sign of the lovely Denise. He undid the buttons of his shirt and slathered it on his chest. He even coated a healthy handful on his crotch. A little extra lubricant couldn't hurt, he thought. The chemical smell of it hadn't chased off the fly, Joe observed with a frown.

Another bottle of wine and neither he nor Denise had spoken a word about the Smith account. It could be that Denise's attraction to him overrode her work ethic, but Joe just didn't have that kind of luck. Since when had a gorgeous successful woman been interested in him? Joe squelched his conscience and decided to put his savvy to the test. Leaning over, he placed his empty wineglass back on the tray. Straightening, he found his vision eye-level with Denise's cleavage. He buried his face there.

He waited for Denise to push him away, but instead she uttered that high-pitched humming sound and pulled him closer. Joe raised his head and plundered her mouth. A fly circled his head like a furry voyeur.

He reached inside his pocket and patted the bottle of insect repellent.

Denise moved, taking the offensive and positioning herself on top. Joe's body responded to her aggression. She rubbed herself against him, all the time uttering that keening sound. Joe let her push him back against the cramped confines of the loveseat. The metal armrest cut into his back, but he ignored the discomfort.

Against his best intentions he became aroused. He pulled Denise against him. One hand reached beneath that scandalously short skirt, finding to his amazement that she wore no underwear. The thought of her sitting through the staff meeting in that condition made him rock hard.

She seized his belt buckle and flung open the clasp with her thumb. The sound of his zipper was nearly drowned out by the chorus of flies buzzing around her head. Her fingers closed on the neck of his shirt. Buttons popped as she tore them from their fastenings. Buttons leaped into the shafts of sunlight coming through the trees, then fell with tiny pings to the flagstone patio. Denise nuzzled his chest hairs, now flattened against his chest by a liberal coating of bug repellent.

"Hmm," she murmured, "you smell good."

Good? Joe's brain tried to process the information, but all the blood that should have been in his head raced south toward the spot Denise's mouth was heading.

He bucked against her, his body soaring toward fulfillment, even as he tried to coax it back. His head spun as the wine he'd consumed hit his bloodstream. A cloud covered the sun. Shadows drifted over the patio. The sun began its descent across the sky.

He reached for Denise, deciding he had time for her to finish what she'd started before he did something they'd both regret.

But instead of Denise, his fingers closed on a furry mass that buzzed and undulated above him.

Teeth pierced him. His hands groped toward his groin. But Denise dissolved into a multitude of fly bodies, which all decided to take a synchronized bite out of him.

They latched onto his face, biting his lips, stinging his eyes and even investigating his nose. His chest had grown another layer of hair that buzzed and bit. Dozens of them clustered around his nipples, finding the blood supply better there. Following the lines of his veins they formed an arrow heading toward his groin.

And still his traitorous body responded, dragging him against his will toward completion.

Joe fumbled for the bottle of lotion in his pocket. The flies seized this new target and latched on. He managed to maneuver it out into the open and pop the catch.

The flies stilled. Silence settled into the secluded patio. The sun dropped below the horizon. Crimson spears blazed above the trees.

Joe squeezed a handful of bug repellent into his palm. He smeared it over his groin, heedless of the flies he coated in the process.

As one the flies sprung into action. Their buzzing and humming increased in pitch and tempo until it filled his ears. They left his face and chest in a dark cloud.

He raised the bottle and glanced at it in the dimming light. "Does not protect against black flies," it said.

Like a storm cloud breaking, the flies dived for his crotch. Joe screamed as thousands of flies simultaneously found their target.

He climaxed. Darkness claimed him.

◆　◆　◆

Denise sat across the boardroom table from her newest employee. Joe had been special, she thought with a sad smile. Yet, this new recruit showed definite potential.

"Welcome aboard," Denise said. And held out her hand. A fly buzzed above the newest hire's head, investigating.

He swatted at it. "What's with the flies?"

LEGACY OF THE LAST INVADER
M. Shaw

The invader-themed S&M clubs were still around, if you knew where to look. Of course, the last invader had died a little over two years ago, but they were a legend among the underground and a bogeyman for everyone else. You heard the odd conspiracy theory, all of them along the same lines: the invaders were still around and the government was covering it up to study them blah blah blah and one day they were coming back to kill our men and fuck our women. Having been part of Operation Flypaper, I knew that it was all BS. If there were any invaders left, I would still have a job.

Not that I completely resented being able to sit around and goof off with my government pension. But I was always fascinated with the wet machines that we are—if I wasn't then I never would have had my medical license revoked, sat around in federal prison for six years, and finally been pulled by the Flypaper group to do some dirty work. Now that all that was over, I could no longer practice, which was why in a messed-up way I missed the invaders. I guess that's why I decided to track down one of the clubs. For old times' sake.

I found one on the North Side, past Belmont and into some alley that ran off Halsted. It took a while to get there from McKinley Park and waiting for the El was like standing in the middle of the Yukon (as usual), but I had time to kill and nothing better to do. When I finally found the address I wasn't surprised to see that the place was unmarked by any sign, other than the muffled remnants of drum-and-bass sounding from inside.

The bouncer gave me a dirty look as he let me in, but he seemed content that I wasn't up to anything. The first thing I noticed inside was the lack of women, which was something I hadn't picked up on when I'd looked the place up. I wasn't there to hook up anyway. Just to reminisce, and maybe even collect some interesting observations.

This was what I did know: these people got off on pain in a big way, or else they wouldn't be here. Specifically, the kind of pain that came from being penetrated by something twenty inches long and about as thick as a human leg, that would eventually inject you with an acidic substance liable to produce ulcers, and that was connected to an animal three times your weight with claws that would rip your spine in half if you moved wrong. If you can think of it, it's somebody's fetish. I'd heard that some even made costumes, although I imagined that the problems of not having four legs or being radially symmetrical would get in the way of their realism.

It became clear to me that these were not exaggerations. I didn't have enough fingers and toes to count the kinds of freaky shit going on here, and I decided to ignore the black doors on the back wall with their windows painted over. There were murals too, acrylic paintings of aliens proudly displaying tremendous members. The things didn't look much like invaders, but then not everyone had had as many close encounters as I. There weren't many actual photos of them, so most people just had to let their imaginations do the work, which clearly hadn't been a problem for this artist. The crowning achievement was the wall behind the bar, showing what was clearly intended to be an invader having intercourse with a leather-clad man on his hands and knees, though the business zone was cleverly blocked by a liquor cabinet full of bottles that seemed especially phallic in this context.

I'd been contemplating the bar for a while before I noticed the person sitting there. What stuck out first was that she was the only woman in the place and from behind she looked like she'd come to Chicago in the back of a garbage truck. I semi-consciously wandered toward her for a better look, putting my fingertips together in a spear-point to part the crowds of men engaged in something that made freak dancing look graceful. The closer I got, the more it confirmed that this woman looked like absolute shit. Her hair hadn't been washed in weeks, maybe months, and had dirt clinging to patches of it. I couldn't be sure through the musky sweat-booze odors fogging up the place, but I had an impression that she smelled like she'd spent the last twenty-four hours rolling in garbage and piss. Her sweatshirt and wrong-fitting jeans were standard shelter issue, and severely worse for their wear.

All of which begged the question: why would someone in this kind of shape come here, of all places?

But the biggest shockers didn't hit until I was within a few feet of her, staring right into what would have been her eyes if she'd bothered to acknowledge me. One: she was pregnant. Two: I knew her.

I knew her from Operation Flypaper. And after our final mission, I'd watched our C/O shoot her. In the head. In the middle of the Alaskan tundra.

"Bessie?" I said tentatively, invoking her codename. It was her only name that I or anyone else directly involved with her knew. None of the executioners kept their names and there was a double-blind system that made sure of that.

I was fully aware that this was insane. A woman who I'd seen die, in a bar dedicated to the sexual worship of the extinct aliens she and I had helped exterminate, on the one night when I happened to wander in on a whim. The second following my speaking of her codename was the only one in my entire life when I believed that there was a Hell, some sort of supernatural realm centered around the ironic torment of its inhabitants, because where else could I possibly be?

I also knew that if this was real then I was talking to a woman who might kill me at any moment for no reason at all. Given these bizarre circumstances, though, I was feeling slightly detached from mortal concerns.

I waited a moment, but she didn't turn. The fact came back to me that I was in a place where I could barely have heard a gunshot over the music-noise, and so I shouted, "Bessie!"

This time she did turn. She said something I couldn't hear, got up and headed to the door, pushing through the crowds as if they weren't there, which in her mind they probably weren't. I followed as best I could, which left me trailing a good distance behind, lacking whatever quality it was that led her through the maze of bodies unhindered. The bouncer didn't pay me any regard on the way out other than a slight smirk. I guessed I wasn't the first person to leave minutes after arriving.

My ears were ringing, if only slightly, a sensation that served to preserve the air of unreality to the situation outside the club. I couldn't help but be thankful.

Bessie kept walking. I called after her again. When she stopped and faced me, I saw that I'd underestimated her when I thought she was pregnant. She was carrying a womb that looked like it could fall out if a fly landed on her belly. I noticed her appearance again, and thought I remembered seeing a drink in front of her at the bar. I was horrified to consider what condition her small resident might be in—and yet was fascinated to do so at the same time.

"That's not my name," she said. Her voice was a dispassionate waver, almost lost in the chalky hum of traffic noise that rose from the city in the background.

"What?"

"I don't know who Bessie is." She advanced a few quick steps. "I'm Jess."

Her pre-Flypaper name. I couldn't have known the contractual obligations of executioners, but I was fairly sure that her telling me would revoke the freedom she'd bargained when she joined the program. Like all the executioners, Bessie had been pulled from death row. Her service had gained her a pardon, with the caveat that her probability of surviving to make use of it was extremely low. She was the only one who did—apparently, since my impression until now had been that none of them had.

More importantly, I was struggling to remember the terms of my bargain and what would be brought on me as a result of having made contact. Legalese, unfortunately, was never my forte.

"Jess," I said. "Of course."

"You know me?" Her face was blank; no incredulity, no sadness or happiness, no suspicion or straining to remember. Blank. The only expression she gave was a slight shrug. "I'm missing about six years. I was in solitary, what seemed like a few weeks ago, and now here I am. I always keep track of time. I don't know how I lost them, but there it is. So do you know me?"

I nodded.

"How?"

Six years. That was before Flypaper, even before the invaders. If she couldn't remember any of that, then nothing I could tell her would make any sense. It would sound like complete fantasy to her. Again I pondered the question of what she was doing in the club, if she'd had any idea what was going on around her.

In the end I decided to break it down to the most basic level. I knew nothing, and apparently neither did she, so we'd have to go from there. "I'm your doctor," I said.

◆   ◆   ◆

The invaders came down with a winter meteor shower, packed inside the rocks in hard-shelled, spore-like ova that burned away on entry. They scattered around the border of the Arctic Circle, mostly around northern Canada, a few in Greenland and Siberia, where the ocean currents carried them. Days later they started terrorizing human settlements, and reports of deaths and massacres started trickling in: monsters the size of a VW bus, with the legs of a spider and the torso of a man, that would mate with anything female they could mount and kill whatever might try to stop them, including the female if she got uncooperative. There was video footage of polar bears trying and failing to take down an invader, of an invader absorbing a point-blank shotgun blast to the torso and sweeping the assailant away like a rag doll.

Within a week of their arrival, two things became clear to the government. Firstly, the invaders were a parasite of galactic proportions, an all-male species that hijacked the reproductive machinery of any world they could land spores on. There were an undisclosed number of successful couplings, and the invader promptly expired after each. None resulted in fertilization. Their semen was mildly corrosive to us and would never cause anything but devastating uterine ulcers. Which didn't seem to discourage them.

Secondly, the only reliable way to wipe them out would be with heavy bombing that would destroy settlements, oil pipelines, and forests, and cause a significant rise in the sea level. That, or let them die the way they were apparently meant to. That was where Operation Flypaper came from.

They pulled from death row first, then on to anyone else who didn't have a choice. People who were serving multiple life sentences, or who clearly had no hope of parole—both of which described me. I'd been in federal four years by then. I'd been ass-raped a few dozen times and beaten a hell of a lot without a word from the guards, who all knew why I was there. The prospect of governmentally-sanctioned free rein on what promised to be groundbreaking autopsies, with the implied possibility of actual vivisections if opportunity presented, was my version of finding the golden ticket. I signed everything without reading it and was thanking the invaders for my freedom the next day.

They recruited two types of people for Flypaper. I fell into the first category, researchers and advisors, the stoop-shouldered, bespectacled guys who came in looking as pale and brow-beaten as I must have, and spent the project accumulating the kind of excited momentum that builds empires. Flypaper wasn't the best days of my life; the samples I studied were extremely interesting, but I never got the spectrum of material that I did from my free-range work in the ICU. Still, I wouldn't trade the experience for anything. That was a glorious time to be an against-ethics surgeon.

The second type—Bessie's—were the executioners, for whom life was anything but glorious. Only people with the most hopeless sentences would agree to the work they did. But given the harshness of the penal system on women who perpetrated violent crime, there were plenty of candidates. The Pentagon's recruiters told them their chances of survival were low (in fact, there was no basis to think those chances existed at all), but they sprang for it anyway. Having glimpsed what I guessed was a shred of the prison life some of them had known, I could understand why.

Their job, simply put, was to mate with the invaders, destroying them one by one. It didn't sound easy, and was much harder than it sounded. Invaders weren't exactly tolerant of unruly subjects. If an executioner so much as flinched wrong, or screamed too loud, she'd quickly be reduced to fleshy ribbons. If she survived, she'd have to contend with the chemicals she'd been injected with, which tended to cause permanent damage and stayed very painful for very long. Few of them made it past their first "mission"—either they were killed, or they died of internal injuries afterwards, or they developed acute psychoses that made it impossible for them to redeploy. In the event of the last, they were killed. Their contracts forbade them to discuss their work with anyone, an agreement which no psychotic could be counted on to honor, regardless of whether anyone might believe her. In addition to being a covert operation, Flypaper (as I understood it) was one of the biggest human rights violations since World War II. The policy on rumors was strictly better-safe-than-sorry.

There was one exception: Bessie. She saw my exam table six times, and came under my knife five times, once after every mission. Surviving a full five missions gave her the record by a wide margin. Each one had required some creative reconstructive surgery, but she didn't die and she didn't go crazy.

By my observations she must have owed both of those to the fact that she was already as crazy as they come. I didn't know how Bessie had ended up on death row, but she was a true sociopath. Pain meant nothing to her, hers or anyone else's. No matter what happened around her, or to her, she was cold as ice and scary as judgment day.

It was during her sixth mission that she ran into problems. I was there, as I had been her previous five, under a codename like every operative. Our chopper held seven in all: the two of us, a pilot, a medic, a sniper (the purpose of whom had always confused me), another executioner, and the commander, a frog-faced guy who spoke broken English and swore in German to remind us that Flypaper was an international cooperative. We didn't know it at the time, but this mission was to exterminate the last invader; all our briefing told us was that this would be a routine execution and that was all we needed to know.

This was the Yukon, an area with nothing resembling civilization within at least a twenty-five-mile radius. The weather wasn't quite a blizzard, but the snow and wind were strong enough, and both those things always have a way of blocking out everything—sound, sight, and touch when it gets cold enough. That had always been a positive aspect of our missions: after a point it didn't feel like you were really there at all.

We found the invader after a few hours, and right away I noticed it was acting funny. Its movements were random, more like pacing than traveling pointedly the way they usually did, and it kind of hobbled. I couldn't put my finger on whatever was really unusual about it. Understand, invaders looked fucking horrible to begin with, so any unusual quality one might have was an afterthought. They were between seven and ten feet tall and covered with three inches of darkish hair. Their heads were human-like, except the underdeveloped forebrain and deeply cavernous brows. They had a couple two-segmented arms with three six-inch-long fingers and one opposable thumb. Their legs were placed radially, two before the torso and two behind, with four-toed, hawk-like feet. Their genitalia was disturbing. Internally, they had both endoskeletal structures, such as a sophisticated spinal column and rib cage, and armor reminiscent of an exoskeleton covering the vitals, feet, and legs. In essence, a giant gorilla-mantis centaur with a cock that put baseball bats to shame. When one sees something like that, whether it's walking strangely isn't the first thing on one's mind.

Even though we were half a klik away when we landed the invader spotted the copter and charged, though it still looked like it was fumbling a bit through the binoculars. Every time a copter touched down, the first thing on the squad's mind was *please, please don't let it charge*. That was how we lost entire squads and got their copters thrashed for good measure. We had to send our first executioner out *post haste* to intercept.

She bought it within forty-five seconds. By the time she started screaming we'd already sent out Bessie behind her, hoping she could reach the target under slightly more stationary circumstances.

"Anybody else notice some unusual coloration of the exoskeleton?" It was the medic, who I think we were supposed to call Sheldon. "Unusually thin layer of hair too."

I looked. "Now that you mention it," I said. "It seemed like its movement was hindered, too. Sort of limping. Could be signs of invader aging." I thought for a moment. "Or illness. Is it possible that we could spread diseases to them?"

"Or that they could spread diseases to us," Sheldon added gravely.

We'd all been over that before, enough to make us dizzy. Exotic microbes were a nervous point. Every returning squad had a thirty-day examination period, but so far the Space Flu had never surfaced. Looking at an invader that actually appeared diseased was something different.

"Could it be that invaders metamorphose?" I said, trying to crane my head toward Sheldon from within my fortress of insular clothing. "That it's entering some stage of its life-cycle we haven't observed?"

"Maybe," he said, the implication being *but maybe not, and that's what's important.*

Bessie performed as flawlessly as on her previous missions. The Invader's eyes slowly pushed shut inside its trembling head, as if every fuse in its brain was slowly being blown. It backed off from her and crumpled to the ground with hind-limbs still spasming. Bessie stood and began walking back toward the helicopter.

"Target eliminated," said the commander. "Execute."

I didn't understand that last part until I realized that he was talking to the sniper. Through the snow and wind and the massive garments I was wrapped in, and probably also through the filter of my memory, I never heard the shot, nor did I hear Bessie hit the ground. I never heard the commander say "return to base", but that happened too.

That was how we dealt with the threat of invader-transmitted illness. We dealt similarly with just about everything during Operation Flypaper, and from the standpoint of twentieth-century ethics there were a million things wrong with all of it. When there's enough collective stress, though, there's little that the brass, suits, and white-coats alike won't suddenly approve of. Psychologists call it nine-eleven syndrome, a variant of post-traumatic stress that affects entire populations. I call it doing what you should, which is why they need to bring in guys like me down the road, when their sensibilities start to return. Guys who aren't afraid to bend the rules in favor of scientific progress or, in this case, survival. When it came to survival, what difference did a few shady moves and lost records make? We survived as a species. I had no regrets about that.

♦   ♦   ♦

Bessie was sleeping on my couch. She still looked worse than I'd ever seen her (and I'd seen her naked with lacerations all down her back, pale-orange acid dripping down her thighs), but any doubts I had that it was her were dispelled by the scar on her forehead, slightly left-of-center where the bullet had gone through. I was willing to temporarily put aside the fact that there should be a charred grey matter donut where her left temporal lobe used to be. How she'd gotten back from the Yukon—well, I wasn't even going to touch that one.

The first of my suspicions had crept in on the street outside the club. That, of course, was that she was carrying the invader's baby, that the sick-looking thing she'd killed out on the tundra hadn't been old or diseased, but somehow adapting. Could the invader, an interstellar parasite built to mate generalistically, have some mechanism of retrofitting itself to the nuances of its host species' bodies, evolving at geological warp speed to suit? It seemed unlikely that their bodies would somehow just *know* how to adapt, but if the invaders taught us anything it's that unlikely is not impossible. After mating, their bodies would break down so quickly that we still knew little about their physiology.

The way to know for sure—*maybe*—would have been to take Bessie for an ultrasound, but that would be a big no-no. Members of officially nonexistent government programs who were supposed to have double-blind ignorance of each other's identities didn't just walk into hospitals where their names and faces would be cataloged. And while I could rig up a makeshift surgery in my apartment if need be, maternity wasn't my area. Bessie (or Jess, rather) would have to wait for the big day, and so would I.

My second suspicion had hit somewhere between the club and my place, probably on the El where thoughts had the opportunity to ferment. This whole meeting-up seemed *monstrously* orchestrated. An amnesiac dead woman who just happens to need off-the-books medical attention for something invader-related just happens to show up in an invader S&M club on the one night of my entire life when I just happened to be there? Sure. Right. I was well-acquainted with the Pentagon's spooks, having been one myself, and this bore all but their gilded seal of approval. They wouldn't have been the ones who dropped me the tip for the club online, but they certainly had every telecom function in my apartment monitored around the clock. They would see the opportunity for a drop-off at the club and use it to put Jess in my hands.

The spooks wanted something—this I was sure of. They thought that handing Jess over to me like a lamb to the surgical slaughter would tickle my fancy, that I'd do everything I could to make sure whatever was inside her made its way out and keep it all under wraps. Which it did, and I would. What can I say, the spooks knew me like an old friend.

I leaned on the side of the kitchen counter that faced the living room, watched her sleep. "Screw 'em," I said aloud, refusing to think of myself as a pawn. I'd see this through because I had to know—for myself.

None of it was especially shocking to me. Jess's survival, probably aided by some protein or microorganism transmitted with the invader's sperm, and the way she made her way to me, were not by any means beyond belief. Flypaper had desensitized me to anything so over-the-top. What I had a hard time believing was that I'd told Jess all of this the morning after we met: about the invaders, the operation, even her death. All she'd done was nod and accept it. *Oh, well that explains the years I'm missing, thanks for filling me in.* She never said as much. She never said anything directly related to what I'd told her, beyond hushed, wordless acknowledgment. After I'd finished, she asked me when, in my professional opinion, she was going to have her baby. I had no idea, of course.

She began to move around on the couch. She propped herself up on her elbow and sighed the way people do when they're waking up, so that a few small movements sound like they must be physically draining.

"Hungry?"

Even in her grogginess, she didn't look at all upset by the notion that I'd been watching her sleep. "I'm never really hungry," she said, "but if you've got something good then sure." Apathetic as hell. It was how Bessie had survived to turn back into Jess, I figured.

I chucked a couple breakfast burritos in the microwave and hoped that would qualify as good. If not, I'd eat them myself.

"You said you're my doctor," she called while I waited for the microwave to chime. "So do you know when I'm going to have the baby now?"

There were a few seconds left, but I popped the microwave door and took out the plate. "Jess," I said on my way into the living room, "who is the baby's father?"

She shrugged.

I pulled up a chair across the coffee table from her and set the burritos between us. As harmless as she'd been so far, I knew Jess well enough not to get much closer than I needed to. "You don't know? Not even any possibilities, men you slept with, one-night stands?"

"Nope." She looked disdainfully at the burritos, but deigned to pick one up and scarfed it with all the ceremony of a car crash. I watched her start on the second one, pondering her *never really hungry* remark.

I didn't know Jess's story specifically, but I wasn't blind. The woman was untouchably cold, and not just emotionally; the mental disconnect she showed in everything she did was scientifically astounding. The way she moved, the way she ate and looked at things, was like she wasn't even there. No cares, no personality, no pleasure principle, superego, empathy—a psychological vacuum.

That was how I knew what she'd been doing on death row. Jess had to be a killer. The fact that she was barely conscious of what she did eliminated the possibility of self-hindrance, much less morality. I'd seen that in action. Not that Jess was a particularly immoral person, there were just certain concepts that she could never grasp. Two of those were rules and other people. I'd seen her do things, and heard about her doing others: random acts of small destruction like smashing up furniture in her room or breaking bowls in the executioners' mess hall, unprovoked violence—stabbing people's hands with forks and such—and fiddling with equipment in the copters. She did things when and because she thought them, and didn't do things because she didn't.

At some point, she must have got it in her head that she could kill some folks. Why? There would have been no 'why'. It would come just like that.

"I still don't know when the baby will come," I told her. "Jess, there is the possibility that the invader was the father."

"Okay," she said. "Why?"

I explained my theories about invader adaptation, which she absorbed easily enough. I asked about abdominal pain, odd feelings from the fetus, anything else unusual.

"Yeah," she said, "cause I'm pregnant. Those things come with the territory, right?"

I reiterated that I wasn't a midwife.

Jess gave me a penetrating look. "I thought you were my doctor. If you don't know this stuff, shouldn't I just go to a hospital?"

Not happening. The spooks sent her to *me*, dammit, this was my patient. If Jess was carrying an invader, I was the one for the job and that was that. I toyed with how to convince her, then remembered who I was dealing with. "Because Flypaper people sent you to me and they know best."

"Okay," she said.

◆   ◆   ◆

What's it like to live with a mass murderer? You could probably ask a particular family of mostly orthodontists and orthodontists' kids in Oregon who still think I'm dead. They'd probably tell you it seems normal enough until the SWAT team shows up, but they'd be wrong. People oblige themselves to ignore things, and my family was no exception. At my trial they said I'd been a normal kid, but normal people don't start their careers at age nine by taking a bunny rabbit apart, then putting it back together and trying to figure out why it doesn't live anymore even though everything is where it should be.

Besides, I'm not a mass murderer. Mass murderers murder people, whether it's for revenge or politics or God or the rainbow-colored chinchilla in the corner who tells them to. I'm a scientist. I did research, and any death that resulted was incidental—party to the plot, but never the plot itself.

Jess was a mass murderer, and living with her was anything but normal. She spent the remainder of day one working on a crossword puzzle book I bought to keep her busy, looking up the answers online. She did that most of day two until she set the computer on fire, triggering the building's alarms and sprinklers.

I used a fire extinguisher to get the blaze out fairly quickly, but there was still the matter of what to do next. The correct thing would be to evacuate, but I didn't want Jess seen if I could avoid it. If we stayed inside, though, the fire fighters would find us and that would lead to a whole series of questions.

In the end I had Jess hide under the bed and evacuated myself, out to join the legion of chest-hugging residents. Some spoke to each other in rapid Spanish, but the building's few white folks were, as usual, uncommunicative, their stony expressions suggesting *Nobody had better say he's more eager than I am to get back inside.* A strong wind was funneling onto us from between a couple five-story buildings on a nearby corner, so I couldn't blame them. There was an old man out there who looked like he'd shatter like an icicle if he fell.

All I could do was hope the firefighters wouldn't find Jess. Their truck showed up within a couple minutes.

It was the truck that caught my eye. Was it just me, or did it look not completely like the standard Chicago firetruck? Was the paint job a little fresh? Was the station number right? If I was more of a community kind of guy, maybe I would have recognized the firemen themselves. All I could tell was that they looked professional enough.

To my relief, they emerged from the building a few minutes later and told us it was okay to go back inside. I breathed out, probably for the first time in five minutes, and returned to my room.

"Can I come out?" said Jess.

"Better not," I said.

She was still under there when I passed her a cup of Easy Mac for dinner. I finally let her out around 8:00. "No more fire," I said.

Later, I noticed the firefighters had never asked any questions at all, even the normal ones, or mentioned whether they'd found the cause of the fire. Nothing about it appeared in the *Tribune* either—I even bought the *Sun Times* to make sure I wasn't hallucinating. I didn't know how the spooks had done it, but there it was: the fire never happened.

They didn't have to cover it up. The threat to whatever they expected me to do was mild at worst. This was just how the spooks communicated. They knew I wasn't stupid, that I'd pick up the cues they'd dropped. It was their way of saying both *Nobody's going to interfere* and *We're watching you, motherfucker.*

◆　　◆　　◆

Preparations started with supplies. Assuming at least a semi-pseudo-natural birthing, I thought in a pinch I could do a cold read without equipment, but it never hurts to get in the mood. Anyway, I wouldn't need much.

First the grocery store, where I bought latex gloves and rubbing alcohol, posing as germophobic by adding every stripe of household cleaner available, plus brushes, mops, plenty of tissues and a surgical mask—since I was still forbidden to practice medicine. I left out pain relievers. I'd summarily decided that Jess didn't want to be doped up during childbirth. Physical thresholds were always an interest of mine, and if the baby was human then I didn't want to go through this completely without new data.

Next, the hardware store. All I needed there was an X-Acto knife, which I stuck down my pants before buying a few how-to books about bathrooms so it couldn't be traced to me. The buzzer went off on my way out, but the clerk let me go after making sure everything in my bag was on my receipt. An X-Acto knife wouldn't do one tenth the job of a scalpel, but the feel of it was similar, and a successful surgery is as much about mentality as equipment. If things got serious there would be other, more effective instruments handy.

When I got back to my apartment I smelled gas. I mumbled, "Shit," plus a selection of other curses, and pushed open the door.

It was all over. My head immediately revolted with pain that threatened to make my brain not okay if it went on too long. I knew what happened just by looking at the kitchenette: Jess had turned on the stove without lighting it and been inhaling the fumes. Presently she was lying on the floor, pupils dilated, staring through the ceiling at whatever new reality she'd introduced—or, probably, reintroduced herself to.

I shut off the gas with the hand that wasn't covering my nose and mouth. "Stupid. Hey!" I yelled at the human blob on the floor. "What if you blew yourself up? What if you killed the fetus?"

I opened the living room windows, then went to the bedroom and bathroom and did the same. I didn't dare leave the door open. Prying eyes and all. I got a box fan out of the closet, but stopped short of plugging it in.

I couldn't risk a spark. I hung my head out one of the windows. It didn't stop my headache, but I felt my skull depressurize a little bit. It would quit hurting—in a few days.

I didn't go back in until my ears felt close to frostbite. I dragged Jess over to the same window, 200 or so pounds of dead weight. Her belly made it impossible to drape her over the windowsill, so I grabbed a chair and propped her up on it, arranging her so that her head lolled in the general direction of the window.

It was getting cold, so I grabbed the blanket off my bed and wrapped up in it, sat close to the window to help clear my head. I thought of going to a hotel. How would I check us in? It would raise a few eyebrows if I walked into the lobby carrying an unwashed, unconscious pregnant woman (Jess hadn't asked for a shower and I didn't want to press any issue too hard). I imagined she'd become even more troublesome once awake.

Staying here could be disastrous, though. We could die, or explode, or one of the neighbors could smell the gas and call somebody. I had to decide, quick, which choice yielded stronger odds.

I let out a deep breath, coming down from my adrenaline high just enough to reflect on the fact that this was some terrible shit. This was the second time Jess had put my life, or at least my freedom in danger this week, and I was beginning to wonder if taking her in could be worth the insights I might gain from her childbirth. *Too late to worry about that*, I thought. I wasn't about to try and evict an impulsive psychopath. I wondered how anyone could live with her, then remembered that they probably hadn't—for long, anyway. She clearly lived with herself just fine, and would until she pulled some stunt just like this and pushed herself a little too far in the process.

I'd never been, and never would be more completely sure of my hatred for any one person than at that moment. The thought entered my head of revenging myself upon her sexually, but I dismissed it, knowing it was only a marker of the degree of my scorn. As the court ruled, I am not criminally insane; I'm perfectly aware of what I do, aware of the ramifications and legality of my actions. I may be governed by different moral codes than most, but I'm not *immoral* and I'm not a rapist.

I did give her a swift kick in the hip though. She stirred, muttered something incomprehensible, and drooped back over.

"Stupid," I repeated.

◆   ◆   ◆

In the end I took her to a $35-per-night motel I knew on the southeast side. I threw my makeshift instruments in a backpack with a box of Honey Nut Cheerios to keep myself fed over the next day or two. We took a taxi, which was unfortunate because I didn't have enough cash and had to use my debit card, but it was still better than the El or a bus. The driver didn't ask any questions. I knew how bad off most cab drivers were, and in that business you can't afford qualms about taking a guy to a motel with an unconscious woman under his arm.

When we got there I told the driver to pull around back and wait. I checked in as just myself, under a fake name, and paid cash (I had that much, thankfully). I went back to the taxi and dragged Jess into the motel room. Then I paid the driver, adding a 50% tip for good measure.

Jess came around three hours later with a light comment about how wondrously fucked-up she'd been.

◆   ◆   ◆

Jess would give birth soon. I knew this. Maybe a few days, tonight, the next second. When I fell asleep on the motel bed—by accident, since I had no intention of falling asleep anywhere near that woman—I had nightmares about that birth. In the nightmares the birth happened over and over, but I never saw what came out, was always left staring at an open void, confronted by the horrifying mystery of what might emerge. I supposed that for someone else this might be an expression of fear. Being on the edge of knowing would be yet another terrifying threshold in the sequence of thresholds that most people spend their lives trying not to cross. But what I felt more than anything else was the pain of not knowing, born from the desire to know.

I was growing impatient.

I awoke in the motel, suddenly aware that I couldn't take anymore. This whole affair had me over the edge. I'd survived Flypaper, sure, but in Flypaper we'd all known where we stood. From the start, there had been too much here that I didn't know. I could be making most of it up. Hell, Jess might not even be "Bessie," just a random, pregnant, amnesiac homeless woman with a scar I'd met by coincidence. Was that any *less* credible than what I'd assumed so far? How could I know? Anything?

I sat up and looked at Jess, who was sitting on the bed, drinking water from a plastic cup and watching Letterman on a TV with the color messed up. I thought about her bizarre psychology and the uncanny way she operated. I thought about all the hormonal factors involved in inducing labor, and even emotional responses that had been known to trigger it. And I realized then that there was one thing that I could know.

"Jess," I said, "why don't you go ahead and have the baby?"

And she did.

◆   ◆   ◆

The time and place seemed right. The motel room looked like it had seen several particularly messy births—blotchy, off-colored carpet, odd stains on the bedclothes, marks climbing the wallpaper that must have been water damage or mold or both. A couple surgeries, at least, and no sterilization. Or just the kind of shithole I'd grown to believe suited Jess.

The labor went for 14 hours, which I'd spent applying compresses, monitoring Jess's contractions, looking for cervical dilation, and drinking nasty coffee made from a very old complementary bag of grounds. She was ten centimeters and we were getting nowhere. Whatever was inside was just too big.

Jess never screamed once. Nothing more than an irritated groan the whole time. What surprised me, though, was her almost complete lack of fatigue. Jess hadn't eaten anything since her stunt with the gas. She'd been giving birth to something that was clearly inhuman for more than half a day, yet she hadn't lost consciousness and continued to be fully coherent, almost relaxed. Throughout the night we'd been holding conversations about mundane topics—sports, movies, celebrities—and she'd responded as if we were sitting at a table in a bistro over tea and muffins, punctuated occasionally by a strain or grimace.

What had the invader done to her that let her survive the gunshot to the head? To make her way back—from the Arctic—and stay alive this long? The gas probably should have killed her too. One thing was for sure: we'd underestimated this parasite during Flypaper. The spooks must have been slavering when they saw what I was uncovering.

Speaking of which, where were the spooks? All along I'd assumed that they'd reveal themselves at some point to reclaim their quarry. Here we were now, on the point of it. When would they show up?

"You know how I ended up on death row?" said Jess, in a tone that made it sound like *You know what's just totally weird?* "I killed my friends while they were asleep in my apartment." She chuckled. "We got so wasted that night." As if that explained everything.

"Why?"

"What?"

"If they were your friends, why did you kill them?" I said.

"I dunno."

"You're crazy, Jess."

"Whatever." She drummed her fingers on her knee in a pattern I could have sworn was *Uptown Girl*. "I just was thinking of it. Your mind wanders when you've got nothing to do."

"I bet it does," I said. Then, "Did you ever think of killing me, Jess?"

She shook her head. "Really briefly one time I started thinking about how much I sort of hated you, so I lit your place on fire. You rem—"

When it came, it came all at once. Whatever had sustained her pain-free this long was betraying her, and for once in her life, she was feeling pain. I could see it was beyond anything I might conceive.

Jess bled, not just from her vagina but every other available point of exit as her body snapped under its own pressure. Her fingers clutched madly at nothing, then stiffened. She banged her head against the wall, rolled onto the floor and started banging it there too.

"It's eating me! Oh for fuck's sake cut it out cut it out cut it out—" she screamed right before going into shock.

It was all I needed. I grabbed the butcher's knife from my backpack and made my best attempt at a C-section. I had no ideas of saving her—she'd passed the point of no return already—but I wanted to see this.

The incision revealed a massive dome of something that wasn't exactly flesh and wasn't exactly carapace. Something that still wasn't coming out.

Time to get sloppy. I slipped the knife under Jess's skin above the central cut of the C-section and extended it all the way to the base of her sternum. Her body peeled open like a banana. And there it was.

I counted at least fourteen stubby, amorphous legs along a bloated body that ended with a sphincter two inches wide. At the front was a head, but nothing like an invader's head. More conical, like an ant's head only with a toothed mouth that stretched around half its circumference. No eyes. Two extensions that might be nostrils or antennae. The color was a uniform brown.

"Multiple life phases," I breathed. This must have been some kind of larva. *A very hungry invaderpillar.* It was too funny to laugh.

It certainly was hungry too. Jess had been right: it was eating her, indiscriminately. Her reproductive organs and lower digestive tract were gone, except one kidney. It finished her liver, sort of turning its head and snapping parts of it up, like the way a tortoise eats, and moved on.

It took a few minutes to hull out her entire chest cavity, growing steadily more bloated the whole time. It left the rest of the carcass. It stuck out a fat proboscis that it used to suck up some pools of congealing blood, then crawled out of Jess and toward the crack of light coming under the door, its nostril-antennae moving around like little satellite dishes all the way.

I followed it cautiously, taking everything in. I thought I'd have to open the door for it, but it chewed through, so I only had to open it for myself. I closed it behind me when we were both out. Once there it rose up, lifting its front legs off the ground and poking the proturbances on its head toward the evening sky. I saw the sphincter on the back open. Then it started expelling a yellow gas that smelled of sulfur and carrion, which propelled it upward like a rocket. And it was gone.

"God damn," I muttered. After just two years, all the excitement I'd grown out of during Flypaper had come right back. I mean, you just don't *see* shit like that. I didn't have it in me to be amazed or shocked or anything. All I could do was stand there and appreciate it.

I walked to the far end of the parking lot and sat next to a telephone booth, on a bench that carried an ad for pest control service.

"So what?" I yelled to the encroaching night and, assumably, the spooks. "That's it? That's what you wanted me to do?" I waited for a reply. "Are you satisfied?"

I got nothing, of course. These people don't keep their jobs by being transparent.

Within a couple minutes I had four police cruisers in front of me. Two of the cops looked into the motel room while the rest surrounded me. Had a maid come in to clean the room and found the body? Not likely: it was after six o'clock. Someone else had called them in. I could guess who.

The cops were rough, knocked me around a lot. The final butcher's bill was a black eye, six cracked ribs, and a punctured kidney that got fixed up in a solitary room in a hospital I didn't recognize. Not that I'd ever been to any hospital in Chicago, but all the same. They never read me my rights.

◆   ◆   ◆

I've been in federal prison for twelve years—minus a six-year vacation. Fly-paper and all, plus a couple years off for good behavior. I'm serving more life sentences than I have fingers. I get beaten a lot. Raped less often since I got a case of warts from somewhere. The guards don't do anything.

I'll be here a while, but not a long while. I know these people. Sooner or later something will happen, something that makes them lose their petty scruples just long enough for them to need me again.

I think about the invaders every day. Every time I'm alone—or at least, as close to alone as I can be in a cell I share with three guys—I go over my observations about invader reproduction, invader life-cycles, annotating my theories and revising when necessary. I haven't written anything down so that it will be me they need, not just my work. And they'll need me because we were wrong.

We were wrong about the invaders. They don't just haphazardly send spores to any planet they can and hope that there's a compatible species there. What they do is find the most compatible species, and adapt. The adaptation comes at the expense of an entire generation, but it's worth it for a long-term investment; because now that they *have* adapted, they'll be back. That's when they'll call me up again. Up from prison. Up from the bullpen.

All I don't know now is when it will happen. And even on that I have my theories.

ACCEPTABLE LOSSES
Simon Wood

The landing craft bobbed clumsily on the waves. The damned things were so unstable when they didn't have a full accompaniment of men to act as ballast. Captain James Clelland's six-man team was no substitute. The ride back would be better. The boat would be full.

They were half a mile out and Clelland could see the carnage on the beach. He didn't want to look at it or think about it. There would be plenty of time for that when they arrived. There would be sights and sounds that would eat through his soul for a lifetime. He leaned on the side of the boat and stared into the sky, ignoring the flotilla of boats approaching the beach in a fan formation.

Puffy white clouds passed gracefully across the sky. He was astounded by how similar the clouds were to those back in England. Somehow he expected them to be different, at least exotic. Clouds from the North Pacific should have been different. He didn't know how or why, but they should have been. Floating on the wrong side of the sky maybe, he thought. He could have watched the clouds all day but the stink was invading his nose. The beach was close.

"Right, kit-up everyone," Clelland ordered.

"Make way for the Lord Mayor's Bucket Boys," Sergeant Williams announced in a pompous, officious voice.

Clelland hated the term that had attached itself to his men like a limpet mine. It had started in the mess hall after their second or third mission. The problem was the phrase was too apt. The real Lord Mayor's Bucket Boys picked up horseshit after the annual procession. His Bucket Boys picked up something different after the battles were waged. The stench of what they handled was no less disgusting, and most couldn't stomach the work. Turnover was high. His men always had a choice, of sorts. He didn't. He was Oracle's right-hand man. He was the only man perfect for the job.

Clelland tied a handkerchief around his head, over his nose and mouth. Others did likewise. The Lord Mayor's latest Bucket Boy pulled on a gas mask. After a couple of trips, the mask wouldn't be necessary. The stench would offend, but not disgust. A handkerchief, scented maybe, was all that was needed for a Bucket Boy.

Clelland tapped the private with the gas mask on the shoulder. "Take off the mask," he told him.

Confused eyes stared back from behind the mask.

"Take off the mask, soldier. That's an order."

The private did as he was told. "Sir, the stink?"

"Harris, it's in your best interests to keep the mask off. You'll throw up."

"But if I have the mask . . ."

Clelland raised a hand to silence the lad. Hysteria was creeping into the private's voice. "You'll vomit. If the stench doesn't do it, the sight will. So, it's better to vomit with the mask off than on. Then you won't have to breathe in the stench of your own spew. So, keep the mask off."

Williams, not wise-cracking for once, nodded. The Australian knew better than most. He'd been with Clelland since the discovery. "Puke now. Mask later."

Clelland pulled out a scented rag and pressed it into the private's hand. "Use it when you're done."

Harris couldn't speak. Fear, anguish, whatever it was Clelland saw in those innocent eyes strangled the private's vocal chords. In a month's time, those eyes would be hollow and darkness would be the only thing lurking behind them. Nothing would ever disturb the private again. Clelland knew. He stared into those same eyes in the mirror every time he shaved.

The sapphire blue ocean changed to blood red. Pink caps that should have been white rode the tops of the red waves as they crashed onto the decimated bodies of fallen soldiers.

"Brace yourselves boys," the helmsman warned.

Clelland's team grasped handholds and waited for impact. The boat ground to a halt on the beach. The bow door dropped, digging into blood-stained sand and crushing dead bodies. No one rushed off the boat, ready for action. There were no Japs to take on. No one left to kill. Clelland's men took their shovels and trudged onto the beach ignoring what they trod on. As Clelland disembarked, he patted the vomiting Harris on the back.

The place was different but the story was the same. The Japs had won at the expense of the British. They'd been particularly ruthless on this occasion. Besides the bullet-riddled and grenade-ravaged corpses, he recognized the hallmarks of ritual decapitation and disembowelment. The battle over, they'd set about the wounded with their samurai swords.

Blood from hundreds saturated the beach. Clelland hadn't realized until he became a Bucket Boy that blood had an odor. It wasn't unpleasant, just overpowering, suffocating, like being trapped in a room filled with stale air.

The soldiers had been dead some time. Twelve to fourteen hours, by Clelland's estimates. The blazing sun had had a chance to cook the flesh. What should have been pink had blanched and turned beige. Instead of just the usual stench of shit and rotting flesh, a human barbecue was in progress.

Clelland blew his whistle. Soldiers disembarking the four other landing crafts turned to their commanding officer. All of them were close enough to shout to. "Right, gentlemen. The routine is the same as it always is. Take the dog tags, leave the weapons, no souvenirs and . . ." Clelland's voice faltered, losing power. "Let's get these boys back on the boat."

"Poor bastards," Williams said.

"I doubt they envy us, sergeant," Clelland remarked. "They don't have to do this."

The Australian mulled the thought over and nodded. "I reckon we're gonna have to come back for a second go."

"Then we'll come back, sergeant." Clelland was sharp with Williams. He knew he was wrong to snap at the Australian. The man was only making small talk. And God knew they needed something to take their minds off their jobs. He'd make it up to him, a beer in the mess hall tonight. Another to go along with all the others he owed. "Are you finished there, Harris?"

The private ran a hand across his mouth. "Yes, sir."

"Well, let's get stuck in."

Clelland didn't have to get stuck in. He had rank. He could have overseen the operation without getting his feet wet like a good officer. But he was compelled to be involved. No man should have to do this and setting himself apart from his men didn't sit well in his stomach. Better he got in the thick of it. His complicitus actions had caused this. If he'd been half the man he should have been, then maybe they wouldn't be here.

They snagged dog tags, placing the ID plates in the satchels over their shoulders. They shoveled up chunks of men and dropped the pieces into wheelbarrows, then emptied the barrows into the landing crafts.

They were about half an hour in when Williams let loose with the jokes— right on time. He had a never-ending stream of them. Mainly bawdy stuff Clelland had heard in the not-so-classy music halls. He couldn't remember how many ops they'd been on together but he knew he'd never heard a joke repeated. His gags weren't just blue. He launched into scathing attacks on the crew and the British in general. It was all taken in good jest. The men forgot they were shoveling human slops as they attacked Williams and Australia. After the bullets, personal attacks strafed the battlefield.

"Alright there, Harris?" Williams called out.

The masked private nodded, his filter hose flapping.

"Harris, you look like a fucking monkey with that thing on," Williams said.

"Yeah, one wiv an elephant's trunk," another soldier chipped in.

"You're right, mate. A fucking monkey with an elephant's trunk." Williams started a chorus of laughter. "You want to lose that thing, Harris."

Clelland knew it was the wrong time to pick on the private. Williams' ribbing would have consequences. But some situations were best resolved between the men and not their senior officer.

Harris blew. He tore off his gas mask and threw it. It struck the side of a landing craft and splashed in the surf. A wave carried it back to shore. The private stared daggers at Williams.

The Australian and the men froze, waiting for Harris' next move. He breathed heavily, as if he was building enough oxygen in his lungs to give Williams the tongue lashing of his life.

But he didn't.

He sang.

Harris possessed an astounding choral voice. He sang a hymn. Clelland didn't know which one, not being much of a church man. But it was beautiful.

The men remained silent. Williams nodded his approval to the private and got back to work. The other men followed his lead.

Harris' voice soared and could be heard across the beach. The men joined in with the private when he came to a hymn they all knew, adding to the heartwarming sound.

Clelland was amazed at man's ability to cope. He couldn't believe that beauty could exist in such a place. Why was it when man was at his absolute worst, it inspired others to create their absolute best? Clelland didn't know the answer to his question. He wasn't one of those men whose enlightenment raised them above the situation.

As soon as Harris sang, Clelland knew the private would survive his time on the HMS Vulture. Some hadn't, but he would. He had his singing, like Williams had his corrosive humor. All his men had their outlet, something to put between them and the horror.

Except him. He had an officer's burden that came with command. He could never distance himself from the job. Oracle made sure of that. He was just a cog in the machine; integral to the monstrous acts committed in the name of war. If he was granted an outlet, it would be to take Oracle's life.

Williams was right. They had needed more boats. The landing crafts made two runs each to clear the beach. By the time his men returned to the landing crafts not a scrap of soldier remained. But they couldn't do anything with the tainted sand. Clelland didn't like to think how long it would be before the crimson tide washed the crimson beach clean.

His men looked like savages, ancient warriors returning from a successful raid. Their khaki uniforms were as red as the gore that doused the inside of the boat. It was as if they'd bathed in blood. Clelland knew his soul had. It was drenched with the stuff.

Reaching the HMS Vulture, Clelland's men stripped off, tossing their clothes overboard. No one wanted to bring their part of the mission back to the ship with them. Hoisted aboard, they turned hoses on themselves and let the day's toil run into the bilge.

HMS Vulture was a converted salvage ship, kitted out with armor plating and 50mm cannons. The last of the landing crafts filled with Britain's fallen was raised into the air. It swayed above the open cargo hatch that was large enough to hold what fifty landing crafts had to offer. The bow was tilted and the landing craft's contents spilled into the hold. The suspended boat was rocked to make sure nothing remained.

Lieutenant Rodgers threw Clelland a towel. The young officer was Navy and ran the ship with a small detachment of sailors. But the Army had authority. It was their operation.

"Is that the last one?" Clelland asked, nodding at the dangling boat.

"Yes, sir. The other boats are moored on the starboard side."

Damned mariner-speak, Clelland thought. He had to remind himself which side was starboard. No more port left was the mnemonic. So, port was left, which made starboard right.

"We'll slop out the boats in the morning," Rodgers continued.

Clelland shook his head. "I want those boats slopped out tonight. I don't want their stench to contend with in the morning."

"Very well, sir. I'll make arrangements." Rodgers turned to leave, then stopped. "Will you be talking to Oracle tonight?"

Williams, Harris and several others waited for Clelland's answer.

"Yes. Is Oracle eating?"

Rodgers nodded.

Clelland didn't need to ask. He knew Oracle was eating, because the son of a bitch wasn't screaming his name. The bastard didn't complain as long as it was fed. Some aide to Allied forces.

"I'll speak to our guest after I've had a drink. I think these men deserve one."

"At least one," Williams chipped in. "Today's been a bastard."

◆   ◆   ◆

The Vulture's chugging engine reverberated off the hull, sounding like a beating heart. The ship was on a new course with another rendezvous with synchronized slaughter the day after tomorrow. Would Oracle have anything for him that might save some lives?

Entering the cargo hold, it was as dark as the night sky on deck. Feeble lighting came from a daisy chain of bulbs suspended by their own wiring.

Oracle preferred the dark and Clelland was more than happy not to see his guest.

British forces had pulled off a few coups during the war. One had been the capture of the German's cipher generator, Enigma. The other had been Clelland's battalion discovering Oracle in Papua New Guinea. No one knew about Oracle, not even the Yanks. Oracle's information was shared with the Allies but the source was unknown. Oracle was too significant to share.

Clelland had been a corporal when they found Oracle a year ago, but because he was the only one who understood what Oracle said, he was elevated to captain and given the unholy task of working with it.

The hold stank. Oracle stank. Even though they slopped out the hold on a regular basis. The creature's filth clung to the ship and its natural odor didn't help either. Its perfume was rancid at best. It wasn't the best way to make friends and influence people, but luckily for Oracle, its talents lay elsewhere. People were willing forgive a lot of things if you had something to offer.

Oracle sensed Clelland's presence before he opened the cargo hold door. Clelland felt it traipsing through his mind in spiked boots. After tonight's encounter, he would have a headache that would last their journey to the next island.

"Clelland, are you there? Have you come to see me?"

Oracle's unspoken words sloshed through Clelland's skull. He winced, closing his eyes, and massaged his sinuses. It was always like this, at first. But the jarring pain would pass. The first time the creature had tried to communicate, he thought his brain had been cleaved in two. But he had learned how to tune Oracle to the right volume and frequency so its thoughts would come through at a steady throb.

"You know I have," Clelland answered.

"A lot of casualties today, Captain."

"Yes. Let's hope you can help minimize the chances of more."

"I'll do my utmost. As long as our arrangement continues."

"You have my word. As always." Clelland's words tasted metallic on his tongue. He kept his bargain, at the cost of others. "I need to know the locations of the Japanese fuel dumps for it's Pacific fleet. And . . ."

"Don't hang back Clelland, come closer."

Clelland edged forward and his foot brushed against pulsating flab. He blocked out his disgust. He had learnt to suppress his feelings in front of Oracle. He couldn't show his revulsion. It would hear his thoughts and be offended. Clelland retracted his foot.

Oracle was getting bigger, a side effect of living off others. Clelland glanced up at the hold's bay door. Oracle could only have been ten feet from the top. Soon they would have to find a bigger ship. The creature wasn't the twenty-five ton mass they had found in a dormant volcano crater.

Christ knew what it was. Oracle had tried to explain, but either it couldn't articulate itself or Clelland couldn't comprehend it. Not that it mattered. It was of use to the Allied cause. Beyond that, Britain had no further interest.

It was a creature though. The professor who examined Oracle at the discovery site had said that it was alive and pronounced it as such.

"A creature is defined as an organism that possesses a mouth and an anus."

Physically, that was all Oracle was—a gelatinous hillock of shit-brown flab with the ability to process food. It possessed no eyes to see, or ears to hear and was incapable of movement. But that wasn't important. What raised Oracle from biological curiosity was that it had intelligence. It could communicate.

The downside was that Clelland was the only one who could understand. The creature was to be shipped off to the British Museum, until Clelland realized that Oracle possessed the power to read men's minds. Distance wasn't a problem. Oracle could tune in anyone on the planet like a radio and listen to their thoughts. Its gift made up for all its physical shortcomings and the creature became a military deity and Clelland, its interpreter.

"You were saying, Captain?" Oracle prompted with its sickly sweet voice.

"I need to know the location of the fuel dumps and the movements of the Japanese fleet in the Philippine Sea."

Clelland didn't know why he did it. He always spoke to the spout at Oracle's peak, the opening that consumed food. Oracle didn't have a face. Clelland was astounded at his reliance on convention. He relied on the visual, the creature on the mental. He needed a face to talk to, but there wasn't one, so he spoke to the next best thing, its mouth. He wondered if Oracle could sense his presence. The hairs as thick as straw and just as rasping that covered Oracle's mass might have been able to detect rudimentary shapes. His theory was further reinforced by the heavy concentration around its mouth.

"Let me see what I can find out," Oracle said.

Oracle scanned. The creature breathed in and out, much more deeply than when it communicated with Clelland. It inflated, pushing Clelland back, then deflated. The creature expanded by at least ten percent when in deep thought. Its mouth opened and closed in time with its swelling and contracting bulk.

After several minutes, Oracle responded. "I have the information you need."

"Good." Clelland wasn't overjoyed. He didn't much care for the information. The price was too high.

Oracle relayed the information and Clelland made shorthand notes for his superiors.

"Will London be pleased?" Oracle asked.

"Yes."

"I'm their best agent, aren't I?"

"Yes. Yes, you are, Oracle."

"My information has the best mission success rate in the Allied forces, doesn't it?"

"Yes. Eighty percent."

"Always eighty percent." Oracle exhaled and its spout opened then closed. "I wish it could be more."

Clelland was shaking. Oracle was tearing him apart. It was hard to hold back the tears. He insisted on showing Oracle a brave front every time it teased him. It was a futile gesture. Oracle knew exactly how Clelland felt. How much it all hurt. How much he hated himself for being the one who had to deal with the informant. Clelland covered his nose and mouth with his hand, holding in a cry.

"When do we arrive at Wotje Atoll?"

"Thirty-six hours." Clelland wiped away a tear and sniffed.

"Wasn't Wotje Atoll one of my bad predictions?"

Clelland nodded to a creature that couldn't see.

"Have they fought yet?"

"No. Oh-five-hundred hours."

"Do you think many will be killed?"

"You know it will be slaughter." Clelland's words crawled out on barbed wire. He fought the urge to scream.

"Do you blame me?"

"Does it matter?"

"Because London is happy with my successes and not too bothered by my failures? Because nobody's perfect? Because no one can be right all of the time?"

Clelland was already walking away. He had what he came for. He didn't have to listen to Oracle. He wasn't the creature's friend or nursemaid. He was just the message boy.

"I'll relay your information to London."

"I've given you five missions there. One has to fail, to maintain my eighty percent success rate. I'll let you choose which one."

"Bastard," Clelland hissed under his breath. He didn't care that Oracle heard his thought before the word was out.

"Remember, Clelland. We have a bargain."

Clelland slammed the cargo hatch. The resulting clang rebounded off the hull and bulkheads.

How could he forget? The bargain came after a string of successes at the expense of Oracle's health. In the Vulture's hold, the creature had been dying.

London told him to keep Oracle alive at any cost . . . any cost. The problem was its diet. The food they fed it, the cows, pigs and sheep, were killing it. It needed what it had always needed, what it had survived on in the volcano's crater and what it needed to thrive to read the enemy's minds—people.

London wasn't about to sacrifice people to the creature, but they did have plenty of dead. Clelland fed Oracle the carcasses of soldiers that fell in battle. The families of the dead didn't need to know the final sacrifice their loved ones had to make for King and country.

Nobody was perfect, except Oracle. But the creature had to be wrong, or it would never eat. The flow of dead was drying up. London had told Clelland to do whatever it took to keep the information coming. Oracle and Clelland made a deal. Every fifth mission, Clelland sent London the wrong time, location or position. Thousands of soldiers died unnecessarily, just so Oracle could eat.

He never shared their secret. Who could he tell? The Lord Mayor's Bucket Boys would have hacked him and Oracle to pieces. London would have turned a blind eye, uninterested. The cost was small compared to the tens of thousands that lived. Acceptable losses, as they liked to say.

"Our bargain, captain," Oracle reminded Clelland, as the officer headed for the radio room.

Not that its reminder mattered. Oracle was finished. The Pacific theater was at an end. The Yanks had the bomb and intended using it. And Clelland had his transfer papers. He was an artilleryman again. His destination was number three on Oracle's list. He circled it as the mission to fail.

AN UNFORTUNATE INCIDENT AT THE SLAUGHTERHOUSE

Harper Hull

Being in England we wrongly assumed we just had another mad cow on our hands.

It was Jack who spotted it first; he was putting out the feed in the main dairy pasture when we heard him shouting out *'B.S.E! B.S.E!'* at the top of his voice. Myself and Will, who were on a smoke break in the yard by the slaughterhouse, sighed and heeled out our Rothmans, ambled around to the pasture fence and got ready to give Jack some ribbing. He saw us coming and gestured wildly towards a large black-and-white Friesian that was snorting and grunting towards the back of the herd. I immediately nudged Will in the side, knowing this did not look like your classic mad cow. The rest of the herd, obviously quite upset, had moved away from the crazed cow as far as they could, pressing up against the fences and mooing in agitated, high-pitched tones. The sick Friesian, making noises I had never heard come from a cow before, began stamping and tripping its way towards the main part of the herd. It looked as if it was about to fall over with every step it took but somehow it kept its footing each time. I noticed that its eyes looked like they were green around the pupils. Dark green like seaweed on the beach. Jack took off running, saying he was going for help. Will and myself just watched, quite bewildered at what we were seeing. This wasn't supposed to happen here.

The farm we worked on was the first organic beef and dairy farm in the great County of Cheshire. What had once been an old-fashioned *pack, rack and stack* blood-and-guts killing compound was now a state-of-the-art exercise in modern farming. There were nutritionists and geneticists employed here these days, as well as regular workers like me who took a pride in their job. No more cider-soaked village idiots who would blast a bolt between a cow's ears and cheer while they did it; all the simple, inbred bumpkin bully-boys who had actually enjoyed bleeding out cows and often made sick games out of it were long gone. This was a highly monitored operation of organic perfection. Everything was carried out with complete professionalism and to the letter, as written out by the new owners. The idea that something could have diseased one of our pristine cows was unthinkable. We had the finest herd of Friesian milkers in the country, and our beef Herefords were top of their class. With no chemicals, nutrients or altered genetics our beef was pure, which is what made Will and myself wonder how what we were watching could possibly be happening.

The sick black-and-white milker got into the cornered herd and started attacking the other cows. They frenzied and started trying to launch themselves over and through the fences. We ran back, away from the sudden chaos, and watched in static shock as the sick 'un took bites out of its herd mates, causing them to react and nip out at those around them. Some cows fell at the fences and were trampled; the sounds they made were awful, the type of sounds you never want to hear from a living creature. As we watched, helpless to intervene, Jack returned with a gang of the other workers, a couple of them lugging rifles with them. After an initial moment of complete disbelief where the entire group of men seemed to run into an invisible wall and just gape, the two blokes with the rifles carefully approached the fence and, finding an angle, took out the sick cow with several shots to the skull. It went down with a thud, but now several more of the Friesians were acting in the same sick manner. Someone cursed, and more shots were fired, a tattoo of cracks that sent crows scattering from the distant tree-line, until all the infected cows were down on the grass, still and bloody. The main herd, the ones that lived, scared by the guns and sensing safety behind them now, stomped back away from the fences leaving the dead sick 'uns and the injured, stampeded animals behind. A quick check and the wounded cows were dispatched swiftly. Everyone looked around at everyone else.

Someone said we needed the bosses out here, and we all looked at the ground.

◆ ◆ ◆

Clean-up was quick and efficient. Doctor Bloom, known to us as Doctor Doom, the company boffin, arrived with his small science team and took away the dead cattle. They also took blood samples from the rest of the dairy herd, promising results by the end of the week. In the mean-time we were to halt commercial milk distribution until further notice and just dispose of the liquid we pumped. They didn't bother with the beef herd; none of the dairy cows mixed with the red skinned, white faced Herefords in any way so contamination seemed an impossibility. As quickly as that everything seemed back to normal. The company had lost twelve head of cattle and at least half a week's milk income. Not great, but not the end of the world either. By the next day everybody seemed to have forgotten about the crazed cow, but I couldn't help but wonder on those tests; unless they found out why the cow had gone batty, I assumed it could happen again.

◆   ◆   ◆

Friday rolled around without further incident; sweet, glorious Friday with the promise of a late night winding down at the town pub chatting up the local totty and maybe swinging a shag once the days toil was done. I was disposing of the days milk haul with Jack and Will when we heard a ruckus from the slaughterhouse. It was noisy in there at the best of times, but this was something different and unusual. We stopped our swilling, put down the pails and ran towards the building.

"What the buggery now?" said Will, throwing a worried look my way.

As we approached the slaughterhouse workers came running out, almost colliding with us. We asked the manager, Bonehead, what was going on. The horrible sounds were still emanating from inside the metal building. He told us to take a peek, but be careful. He told us it was the most fucked up thing we would ever see. He told us he was off to fetch the rifles. We paused at this and then Will clapped his hands together and said he was going in. Everyone else but Jack and me took off towards the old farmhouse that now acted as the general office for the facility, Bonehead in the lead cursing and spitting.

When I was a kid I used to play that game *Doom* on my computer. It scared the shit out of me and actually gave me nightmares. Things behind doors, around corners, making noises that turned my bones to liquid in the dark of my bedroom. The sounds coming from the slaughterhouse took me back to *Doom* in a second; it was as if all my life since playing I'd been moving forward attached to an enormous rubber band and it had finally stretched too far and snapped me back. I was completely terrified and looked at my own hands which were shaking like pink blancmange. Will opened the door, slowly, and peeked inside. He swore once, under his breath, and disappeared inside. I looked at Jack and wondered if my eyes were as plate-like as his were. We breathed deep and followed Will into the building; I fully expected to be face to face with an army of axe-wielding Minotaurs based on the grunting, snorting reverberations that were assaulting our ears.

There was deep red blood splattered across the walkways. In the holding pens a group of Hereford cows were acting just like the milker from earlier in the week—evil looking things they were, with their red skin and white faces. All of them had those same green eyes as well; lips pulled permanently back exposing bloody, yellow teeth, ears completely flat against their heads. A number of Herefords were down on the floor of the pen, unmoving. They all had bites, gouges and wounds showing; a few were missing meat from their bodies, one seemed to have had its entire face ripped off leaving a single eye still in its socket. The infected cows made a gurgling sound when they saw us three lads and threw themselves against the iron rails of the pen, clumsy yet very powerful. I was about to ask Will if he thought it would hold when he pointed down the walkway towards the killing zone, mouth agape. I looked and about fell to my knees.

"Bloody Hell!" said Jack as he saw it too. "That's plain wrong, that is!"

Three cows were up in the air, suspended upside-down on hooks. Their throats had been slit and they had bled out significantly judging by the amount of claret running down them. Normally, these animals would have been dead. These three though, these three were flipping and shaking around as if they were performing seals. The hooks were pulling on the ceiling moorings and I had a horrifying vision of them getting loose and charging us, blood splattering from their smiling throats as their loose heads flopped up and down. Will must have had a similar thought, as he suddenly ran the length of the walkway, almost slipping over in the blood outside the holding pen as the crazed cattle in there all lunged at him. He made it to the stunning area before the killing zone and grabbed a captive bolt pistol, weighed it in his hands and made his way towards the jerking, hanging cows. I immediately realized what he was planning and shouted his name, began to run towards him. As someone who had actually worked in the slaughterhouse, unlike Will who was pure dairy boy, I knew that we used stun guns, not penetrative, and all he was about to do was piss off the angry beef even more. He gave me a quick look as I ran towards him, nodded, then reached over and placed the gun hard against the nearest Hereford, right between the eyes. There was a whoosh and a pop, and the cow made a roaring sound. Will went in again but this time the cow clamped its jaws around his hand. He screamed, tried to use his free hand to beat off the animal as it crunched down on his wrist but it had no effect. The cow made a frantic jerk and pulled Will down onto the ground beneath it, his right hand severed and in its mouth. Blood and spew poured from the cow's mouth all over Will's upturned face leaving him with a sticky crimson mask, screaming and choking at the same time as his damaged arm leaked life. By the time I got there he was (mostly) silent, almost thankfully in my mind. The three hung cows were moving more than before and sensing that the hooks wouldn't hold I turned tail and ran back towards a white-faced Jack, telling him we needed to get the fuck out of Dodge. I still feel bad for leaving Will, but now I know he was beyond saving. Not that it helps.

We burst out into the sunlight and looked around for Bonehead and his crew. They should have been back by now with the rifles but there was no sign of them. Behind us the sound of crazed cattle and hard skulls hitting metal was getting louder and louder. Jack groaned and gestured towards the farmhouse.

"The bastards . . ."

I looked and it took a second, then I realized that Bonehead's battered old Land Rover was gone. The filthy cowards had left us.

An engine sound came along the glorified dirt path leading to the main road and for a second we thought the slaughterhouse lads had returned, but it was a small, red car that came into view. We ran towards the farmhouse as it pulled up, trying to get as much distance between ourselves and the killing cows as we could, and Dr. Doom stepped out of the vehicle, a terrible look on his face. He heard the awful noise and looked towards the slaughterhouse, dropped his head and muttered something about being too late.

I grabbed him by the arm and demanded answers, spat out something about Will and zombie cows as I did so.

"I have answers, I do, but let's get inside the office first," he said, then turned to Jack.

"Jack isn't it? Would you take a jog over to the dairy pasture and check on the Friesians for me? Good man, we'll be in here"

With that the Doctor led me inside the farmhouse.

Neither of us sat down, and as we stood in the farmhouse kitchen he explained to me what had happened. His team had integrated a new feed supplement nicknamed *Agent J* into the diet of our cows; it was from Japan and was supposed to significantly increase resistance to common disease. I rolled my eyes at that and laughed bitterly. He explained that a bad shipment had gone out from the lab in Japan, something had contaminated it pre-shipping and they hadn't realized until too late. His tests this week had confirmed that this *Agent J* was indeed responsible for the reactions in the cattle. There had been other reports of infected cows across Europe but absolutely nothing as severe as what we were experiencing.

Jack came bounding into the farmhouse at this point, breathing heavily. He got his breath back and told us the dairy cows were breaking through their enclosure. All of them were turned. I cheerfully suggested we jump in the good Doctor's car and bomb off towards town, as quickly as possible, but the Herefords busting out of the slaughterhouse put the scupper on my plan. I spotted them first; their distinctive white faces which I once thought quite delightful were now snarling, sunken-eyed death masks splattered with blood. The one we'd seen dead on the floor with its face ripped off was now amongst the Hell herd, moving towards the farmhouse with them, its exposed skull and one remaining green eye showing above bared teeth. They seemed to know we were in here, and I pushed the Doctor out of the way and asked Jack to help me barricade the door with a small desk. As we carried it across the room we both spotted the mass of dairy cows across the yard; like their beef cousins they were coming towards us with that disturbing ungainly trot that made them look half drunk, half brain damaged. We moved faster, planted the desk and started looking around for what else we could use.

Whilst we were trying to turn plastic filing cases and empty milk crates into a reasonable barricade the good Doctor was entranced by the oncoming hordes that his magic ingredient had created. He made his way to the window and pressed his palms flat against the glass; he froze there, absolutely still, just watching. We didn't pay him any heed, at least not until the terrible sounds of the demon cattle seemed to be all around us and turning our attention to the window we spotted him there, unmoving. The first of the Herefords were already banging their heads and jaws against the glass right in front of him, spraying it with dark blood. Jack shouted that he should move back, but he stayed exactly where he was, leaning against the glass in this weird trance. I could see the window pane pulsating beneath his hands as the cattle barged into it, and as I moved to physically pull him away the window shattered. Doctor Doom fell forward; I think he snapped out of his weird trance in this final moment because he shouted something about being a vegetarian as the infected red and white cattle gnashed at his arms. They pulled him completely out of the window and my last-gasp diving reach only made contact with a notepad in his back pocket as he disappeared from sight, his kicking feet the last thing we saw. They were on him like huge locust, knocking each other out of the way to get a piece. We couldn't see him being eaten, but we could hear the tearing, cracking and snapping sounds far too clearly. Jack suggested we head for higher ground as the front door started to buckle. I slipped the notebook I had inadvertently grabbed into my waistband and quickly followed Jack down the hall, up the stairs and into the front room overlooking the yard where the cattle masses were gathered.

We could now see poor old Doctor Doom. Or what was left of him, which wasn't very much. He'd barely feed a cat now.

"His name was Bernard," Jack said quietly.

Before I even had a chance to give the old bugger a few final words my eye was drawn back over towards the slaughterhouse. Oh no, please don't let this be happening. I poked Jack and pointed. He looked across and actually started to sob.

Our good friend Will was walking towards the farmhouse. He was missing a hand, was covered in blood and shit and his eyes had the same creepy green color to them as the cattle. His gait was off too, like an over the limit driver trying to walk the line for the traffic cop. We both knew he was dead and really wasn't Will anymore. It didn't help.

He staggered up behind the massed cattle (which now included the black-and-white Friesians) and they actually made way for him! A pathway to the farmhouse door opened up, as if he was the Moses of cattle! This was an unexpected turn of events and no mistake.

• ◆ ◆

"Attic!" I shouted, and ran, Jack on my heels. After some fumbling with the attic ladder it finally unsheathed and came sliding down; we were up it like circus monkeys, the increased banging downstairs pushing us on. There was a huge crash way below us and we panicked. Jack tried to pull the ladder back up but it was jammed. I pushed him aside and attempted it myself but it was well and truly stuck. There were footsteps on the stairs.

Forgetting the ladder I dropped the hatch down on the hole in the attic floor and looked around for a weapon. It was practically barren up there; no farming tools, no table legs, nothing we could club or stab with. I did see a wooden bookcase and a squat black box over in an extra-cobwebby corner and scooted over to it as fast as I could. The box was an old safe, rusty and obviously unused in a long time. Made from cast iron, the thing was too heavy to lift. I had an idea and started pulling and then pushing it across the floorboards until it sat a few feet in front of the hatch. I explained quickly to Jack and we both got behind the safe, our feet behind it and our legs bent at a sharp angle, knees almost touching our chins.

The footsteps were on the landing below us now. We could hear a moaning, gargling sound as well—it was at the ladder. Our ex-friend the Will-thing was at the ladder. Bracing ourselves, we listened hard and watched the hatch across the top of the iron safe, waiting for the Will-thing. It sounded like it was having trouble navigating the vertical steps but by trial or error it was making it up, missing hand or not. Slowly, slowly it got closer and finally with a great groan the hatch lifted up and fell back, a stumpy arm pushing it and smearing blood across the wood. We watched in complete disgust as the red-masked Will-thing's head appeared through the hole, those nasty green eyes dull in the barely lit attic. I think we froze for a moment, but then someone (I forget who) shouted out and we pushed our legs forward with every ounce of muscle we had. The safe slid quickly across the floor and smacked that face dead on with a satisfying crunch. Will-thing was sent tumbling to the floor below with the safe following right behind. I leaned over the hatch and looked down. The initial hit from the safe had smashed the nose and mouth of the zombie; it was barely a face at all anymore. When the safe had fallen it had landed on Will-thing's chest, crushing his ribs and sitting inside the pocket the impact had made. But it was still moving. Its legs and arms jerked around and even through its broken face it was moaning and groaning, snarling up at me and spitting pieces of tooth. I sighed, sat on the edge of the hatch, balanced myself and dropped down feet first, landing on that angry face. It finally went silent and stopped moving.

"Jack mate, it's safe!" I called up into the hatch, and made my way to the top of the stairs to see what carnage awaited us below. The noise was deafening and it was obvious the infected cattle were inside the farmhouse.

At least they couldn't climb stairs, I told myself.

One of the Herefords was climbing the stairs. It had its legs splayed out at what looked like impossible angles, practically pressing itself against the walls, but it was slowly moving up a step at a time, bloody hoof by bloody hoof. Jack arrived at my shoulder, looked and went straight back the way he had come from.

At this moment, as I listened to Jack scrambling back up the ladder and watched a huge undead bull attempt to navigate a staircase, I was struck with a wonderful instance of serenity. I don't know where it came from, but it was welcome on this particular day and I embraced it like a long-lost lover. Seeing the snails pace at which the Hereford was gaining ground, I sat down on the top step, suddenly and ridiculously feeling completely safe and calm. It's snarling, nipping mouth and bloody horns were mere feet from me but I didn't care. I felt something poking into my side and pulled Doctor Bloom's notebook from my pants, started to flick through it casually as though I was on a park bench reading a Sunday newspaper. A lot of it made no sense to me—scientific jargon *a little* above my head. One section caught my attention though. As I read it my calmness dissipated, replaced by shock, then anger. I closed the notepad, put it back into my pants and went back towards the attic, spitting down onto the horned devil below me as I left.

Jack was up there, sitting in the far corner. I went over to the one small window that overlooked the approach to the farm, wiped away the cobwebs and dust with my sleeve. I moved the wooden bookcase from the far corner in front of the window, slipped it onto its side and used it to perch against, watching through the window as I rested my buttocks against the wood of the shelving.

"What are you doing?" asked Jack quietly.

"Those things will leave soon," I replied, no tone in my voice, "they can't get to us and they'll head off towards town before long. Maybe that old bastard Bonehead actually alerted the right people and they'll be ready for them, maybe even on their way here now. More likely he went straight to the pub and is telling scary tales to his drunk mates and any pretty lass who will listen. Either way, it doesn't matter."

Jack had moved over and stood beside me, scratching himself nervously.

"So are we going to make a run when they leave?" he asked me. "Take old Doom's car?"

I gave him a quick glance then returned to staring out the window, over the dirt path to the main road that led into town.

"You can, Jack mate, you can. I'm going to stay right here. I found a notepad on the Doctor before he died. Interesting reading. Oh look, there they go."

I nodded outside where the stumbling Friesians were starting their ragged march away from the farm towards a denser civilization. The red-skinned Herefords were right behind them. Jack ran to the hatch, peered out and disappeared. He came back a few moments later whooping and whistling.

"The big nasty bad 'un is gone, must have given up or fell arse over tit back down again! Stairs are clear, downstairs is clear, we can get out mate! Go get help!"

I pulled the notebook out and flicked to a page near the middle.

"Listen, Jack. The day this *Agent J* stuff started turning the cattle, they'd been consuming it for two days already. Doom and his crew stopped us shipping the milk that very day. They didn't stop shipping beef though. It still went out. And the Herefords had been getting the stuff in their feed as well."

Jack rubbed his chin; he didn't understand what I was telling him.

"Look what happened to poor Will," I said, "the stuff got into him either through being bitten or the cow blood going all over his face, in his mouth and nose and eyes. He went over pretty quick didn't he?"

Jack nodded, and I saw that he suddenly understood what I was getting at. He seemed to deflate in front of me; all the hope and relief drained from his face.

"All that beef," he whispered, "all that beef out there, across Cheshire, being ate, whole families will be turned at once."

I kept my eyes on the undead herd outside as it got to the main road and, by instinct perhaps, turned in the direction of town.

"Yes mate, all across Cheshire. And then all across England, Wales, Scotland . . . then the rest . . . and I bet we're not the only farm to get it this bad despite what your friend Bernard told me."

I sighed.

Jack made for the hatch, shouting at me to go with him, how we could warn somebody.

"Too late Jack. You go, be a hero. See how far you get."

I could see smoke pluming up into the sky way off in the distance towards town and knew that it had already started before the infected cattle could even get there. I didn't tell my friend this.

"I'm bloody out mate—please come, what are you going to do here?" shouted Jack as he slid through the hatch.

"All I can do. Sit and watch the world end."

ROTSWORTH
Kurt Bachard

He heard a snatch of the hymn again as he dragged his trolley down the concrete walkway to the shops. All night he'd been hearing the same hymn, which sounded nothing like the ones he remembered from primary school sixty odd years ago. Most schools nowadays had banned hymns anyway, he remembered, unless they referred to God as Allah. He'd read that in a Sunday paper. Come to think of it, apart from the singing, he'd heard only one other English voice on the housing estate in months.

Reed limped toward the Co-Op, buffeted by a chilly December wind that somehow wormed its way into his prosthetic leg, to numb what was left of his right thigh blasted on a landmine in the bloody-conflict of the Falklands.

He thought the carol singers might be part of the Christian vanguard he'd spotted loitering on the quadrant a few weeks ago in the run up to Christmas. He'd seen the Christians, if that's what they were, singing outside old Maud's door some nights ago, though they'd yet to bother *his* flat. He smirked, thinking that maybe they picked their targets carefully and had deemed this sinning old veteran a lost cause.

Sleet drummed on the awnings of the little parade of rundown shops where graffiti in a foreign tongue covered the walls and windows like threats, and where the usual rabble of teenage sluts and their cretinous boyfriends hung about outside. If their fathers hated them enough to abandon them, why should anybody else care? They plagued the estate night and day, drinking, and smoking pot. Reed squinted at their ugly faces, but this lot were too old to be the Carollers. Sniffing his disgust at the sickly-sweet fetor of marijuana, he pushed open the Co-Op door with his walking stick and entered.

The girl at the cash register needn't snigger with her ninja friend when she saw the wonky wheel on his trolley. *Not everybody has the privilege of rich shop-owning parents*, he thought, and dragged his trolley down the hemmed-in aisle. He poked at the biscuit rack, looking for ones without the indecipherable cuneiform on the packets. "Some of us still speak English around here," he grumbled, and then paused to listen, for there it was again, the hymn.

The stale warm air in the shop drifted down from the humming vents, tearing the hymn before he could hear the chorus. He was beginning to wonder if it was anything he knew, when it faded.

He remembered the police at Maud's flat the day after he'd seen the Carollers there. An old bird he didn't know from a "cooey" on the corner had approached him on the overpass.

"Hear about old Maud?" she said. "Poor Cow. Funny thing is, one of the coppers said it weren't no robbery. Not for money anyway. Whoever did it, cut her up bad and took her new hip joint."

"Some pervert's idea of a joke," he said, and decided not to mention the Carollers.

She leaned toward him, her lips like a roughly used anus, and smelling as rancid. "I'll tell ya," she whispered, "there's not many of us left. We're all for the chop. You mark my words."

He'd frowned, puzzled by her remark. Now in the Co-Op, he shivered as he remembered.

The assistant followed Reed around the shop, as usual, eyeing him up as if he were a common thief. Reed was too agitated to turn on him, so he screwed up the ten-pound note in his fist on purpose and slammed it down on the counter like a dog turd. The girl looked at the canned beef and his money as if he had exposed himself. "That's the government's facetious Christmas bonus for us pensioners," he grumbled. The girl scowled, as if she had no idea what he was saying. Of course, nobody spoke proper English anymore. Her ninja friend was still sniggering behind her scarf. He could see the hate in her eyes, no matter what she wore to mask her hatred.

Reed pulled his trolley back up the walkway, where the tower block leaned forward, as if urging him under. The Wandsworth council housing estate, dubbed Rotsworth by the tenants, had been heralded as a model of mixed tenure living, but potential owner-occupiers hadn't bought the lie, leaving the humongous ugly sprawl of concrete to Disability-Benefit claimers and crack addict scum. No wonder it resembled the wing of a prison or hospital complex for the insane. Fit for purpose, he thought, sneering. From the overpass, he eyed the taped-over front door of Maud's flat, twenty feet below, on the second floor of the adjacent block. The police had sealed off the balcony, but it would need more than yet another murder and the ubiquitous crime tape to rouse the residents from their sociopathic disaffection.

Inside his block, which felt like a cold metal tomb, Reed wavered between the stairs and the elevators. Only one worked; the other they'd destroyed. It was still blackened by fire, a deep pit ten feet to the basement. But the dark stairs looked forbidding, and he refused to wear himself out just for them; coming down was easier than going up. In defiance, he'd rather suffer the piss-stench of the elevator, he thought, as he entered its dimly-lit cage.

Some clever clogs who had never been potty trained had defecated in the corner, big as a cowpat. Another, or the same, had used the shit as ink to scrawl a protest on the elevator wall. Reed couldn't decipher much of it, for the scribe was obviously illiterate, unless they had meant to spell the name that way as "BLIAR". The majority of the message looked like Arabic. Not wanting to touch where their fingers had been, Reed jabbed the third-floor button with the knobbly head of his stick.

None of the numbers lit up, but the doors still shut him in a rattling cage, the bell jangling when he reached his floor. The elevator doors scraped opened only midway, broken deliberately. As usual, he had to push back one of the doors on its roller to escape.

In the corridor, wind moaned through the cracks under the closed doors. Graffiti faces leered at him from stained walls under the only working fly-flecked lighting strip, which stuttered like his pacemaker whenever he woke from a nightmare. Reed dragged his trolley over broken glass, was rounding the corner when the door to one of the flats creaked open.

He paused to look inside. In the living room, a group of figures, five or six of them, sat facing away from him, bending over. It was too gloomy to see what they were doing exactly, except someone on the far right was genuflecting with a candle while another muttered foreign words.

The unpleasant smell reached him; was it their incense, which smelled thicker than the marijuana? If they hated the smell in this country enough to mask it, he thought, then why come here? That stink, dark and mouldy, made his gut turn over.

That was when he saw it.

Evidently, it was the cause of the stink. He thought for a second it was a pinkish hairless dog, but it had too many irregular joints to be anything normal. It shifted like an injured crab, or someone upside down with a broken back who couldn't stand.

Whatever it was, they had wanted him to see it, perversely. *Why else leave the door ajar?* They must have heard him coming, unless they'd spied on him from the balconies again. He refused to be terrorised, which was what they wanted. He'd seen enough in Falklands to steel his nerves.

The freak scuttled away from the genuflecting figures, though not to hide, but to skulk. Reed saw its albino eyes watching him through the door crack. It wasn't afraid of him. It palpitated like a spider, and he could hear it breathing excitedly, a *phlegmy* sound like a soggy lung. When it moved again, he saw it in the candlelight. It *was* a person, after all, a child at that, but only half of one, for it was missing some body parts, half-limbed; and when it crab walked, its limbs faced the wrong way and it couldn't look up with its head on upside down between its legs. No wonder it couldn't wear clothes like a normal person.

The figures in the room turned their heads to look at him, but all their faces looked smudged, as if their features had been rubbed away to blur their original identities. Wind blew through the flat from an open window somewhere and slammed the door shut.

Reed turned and hurried down the corridor, trolley wheel scratching at his ankle, telling himself that in the New Year he would be down that bloody Council to give them hell over the broken lights in this building.

The familiarity of his own door made him feel safer, despite the ugly lie they had sprayed across it. If they hadn't meant to spell the word *racist*, then maybe it was the same illiterate who had shit-scrawled words across the elevator. The rapist on the sex register known to everyone hadn't lived in *his* flat; the rapist had been one of their own, living a few doors down before the police had carted him off for good.

Inside, Reed threw the bolts and dragged his trolley down the hall, hurrying to switch on all the lights and the television to fill the flat's emptiness. His toilet flush sounded too loud, unnerving him with the fear that he might not hear someone creeping up on him. He hurried out of the toilet, his hands still wet, and into the cubbyhole that the architects of Eaton Towers wanted to pretend was a kitchen.

The naked bulb's jaundiced light made the shopping he unpacked look as if it belonged on an operating table. When he put the broccoli on the boil, it bled green goo. No doubt injected with a dye to fancy it up. Fake, like everything else these days. The corned beef looked like diseased strips of flayed skin, and smelled as dead. He folded the meat on his plate beside the anaemic vegetables, intent on getting his Sunday dinner one way or another. Hard times during the seventies hadn't defeated him, neither would Blair and his thieving cronies; or was it Bliar? he thought, carrying his meal into the front room.

Even before he loosened the uncomfortable strap on his prosthetic leg and plonked himself down on the sofa, he had to change the TV channel when he saw it was a repeat of the party political broadcasts. Since the government dismissed his kind in favour of foreigners, he wouldn't listen to any codswallop now. But the next channel was worse; some jumped up *Social* who couldn't even speak English properly was going on about immigrants. ". . . worrying tide of xenophobia among the disaffected in an increasingly marginalised British minority in and around the . . ."

Just because she had gone to Oxford, she thought she could tell people what they were thinking. "Up yours," he muttered, and snapped off the set. As he ate, he watched a shadow of himself in the dark television screen tucking into his grub, and he had to look away, afraid that his movements might not match the ones on the blacked out screen.

Everything tasted over-salted, which was down to these Halal butchers, no doubt. Couldn't even get a decent bit of beef these days without some religious fanatic sticking in his big conk. Reed spat out a wad of processed gristle, which landed on the side of his plate and stuck there, looking like the malformed head of that monstrosity in the other flat.

He looked up when he heard the hymn. The TV was still off. The sound must be coming from somewhere on the estate again, faint and distant.

They might have driven his Carol crazy before she died, but they weren't having him as well. Little scums couldn't even let people have their Sunday dinners in peace. "Silent Night, my arse," he shouted, and banged his plate down on the floor.

◆   ◆   ◆

Night settled over the estate's labyrinthine alleyways, as if glued to the wet brickwork, the light from the old amber lamp standards pooling on the pavement like dried blood. Reed limped along the twisting paths between the blocks in the gusty rain, needled by an icy wind. The discord of a domestic argument drifted down from one of the balconies; it poked at his slumbering memories of a violent upbringing and made his stomach tingle sickly. He deliberately looked up at the sprinkle of lights in irregular columns, seeking the thin comfort of crepe-paper optimism. But in none of the windows was there any evidence of Christmas cheer—only Maud had had glitter and fairy lights in the window. No wonder people were depressed these days, he thought. Between the tower blocks, he could make out a few stars in the blackness of the sky, but no sign of a Holy star in that vast emptiness beyond which Reed could feel nothing. Regardless, he went to midnight mass every Christmas Eve, and put flowers on Carol's grave in the Tooting churchyard, even if his belief in Mercy was rotting as fast as Carol's body.

Going there meant using the old river Wandle as a shortcut, but why should he alter a tradition because of a bunch of heathens who'd decided the Wandle was a place to grunt and groan like sex-starved animals? The Wandle had been one of Carol's favourite spots in the early seventies. With its overhanging trees and the delicious smell of the hops from the Young's Brewery beyond the embankment, it had been almost a country pocket away from their concrete cell. Now it looked like a cesspit, Reed thought, hobbling along by its low embankment, and it smelled like one. Condoms, shopping trolleys and spilt black sacks of rubbish lay tangled in the mire; and unless he was mistaken, even the river's name was wrong, a foreign jumble of letters where some misguided do-gooder at the Council who cared nothing for heritage had campaigned to change it.

It was usually deserted around Christmas, but as he reached the bridge, he saw hooded figures, like a pagan procession, moving above him.

Reed passed underneath them, the tap-tap-tap of his cane echoing back from curved damp walls. As he came out of the tunnel, he heard the little group scrabbling down the strip of overgrown wasteland at his right. They called him mockingly when he reached the pathway, "limpy, limpy!" as if calling their crippled dog.

He swung around, brandishing his walking stick. The faces beneath the hoods were sexless blurry blotches, visions of congenital retardation and nothing like the Carollers. Clammy, fumbling hands reached, grasping for his weapon, but he clung firm to his only means of self-defence. A badly aimed fist clipped his neck. His pacemaker fluttered briefly, filling his head with a boom-boom as they smothered him. He felt the heat of their shitty breath. Grunting, Reed struck out again. The cane connected this time, and his target cried out. Although it wouldn't happen again, for Reed was already falling to his knees, and his attackers were running away, whooping as they fled. Whoop for me you *cowsons*, he thought, feeling elated at his success and lucky they hadn't stabbed him, or worse. But his elation turned sour when his efforts to stand weren't bringing any success. His bad leg wasn't responding and he had to push himself up with the cane. Although he wasn't really standing when he eventually got up, because his right leg was missing. They hadn't cared about money they knew he didn't have. They had wanted his prosthetic leg.

He understood now who had taken Maud's hip joint. But they weren't keeping anything of *his*, he thought, heading back. Before the army had discharged him on medical grounds, he had fought valiantly for his country and he would act no differently now. He used his tower block's lights to guide him home, the way a sailor might use the stars.

The steady, self-regulating beat of his pacemaker encouraged him, though he had to keep stopping to catch his breath. The cold night air had grown barbed hooks that scratched at his lungs.

When he reached his block almost an hour later, the working elevator was lit, as if waiting. He rode it to the third floor, and hopped out warily. They'd smashed the only remaining light in the corridor, leaving it dark. Without the corona of light from the elevator, he would have been practically blind. Blind and legless, that was how they wanted him, the cowards.

A door creaked open ahead and pattering of feet sounded on the tile. A shadow was approaching, slowly at first, creeping, and then rapidly. He saw the shadow like a huge spider crawl across the wall and stretch towards him. Reed used the wall by his side for support so that he could level his stick.

Anger overwhelmed the fear he had expected when he finally saw what it was and what it had done to itself.

"I want my leg back, you freak," Reed screamed, as a warm wetness spread through his pants. "What have you done with my leg?" The question was pointless, for he could see it well enough now.

Its head like a carbuncle still hung between its legs, upside down, and the whites of its albino eyes stared wetly out of the dark from below its damp black mouth. Only half of its body was twisted, with the other half almost upright, held aloft on a deformed limb attached to Reed's prosthetic. The impromptu surgery forced it into a spastic mockery of Reed's shambling, lurching gait as it came at him, claws outstretched, incoherent words bubbling from the dribbling tar mouth.

What was it after now, his pacemaker? "Over my dead body," he yelled, hitting out when it came within striking distance.

It dodged the blow, parried, and reached out to him again, mewling as if trying to speak. Reed's cane snapped across its bony excrescences, leaving him holding a stump, catching him off balance.

But his mistake saved him, forcing the other to over-reach. In the blink of an eye, it tumbled under his body where his leg should have been, and fell over the lip of the empty elevator shaft. It hung there a moment clinging on, before Reed, oblivious to the plea in its damp eyes, made a grab for his prosthetic, which tore away with a juicy sucking sound, releasing the other. It screamed a high-pitched note, pathetic and horrifying, like the squall of a terrified baby, as it fell away and plummeted down the shaft.

Reed dropped to the floor, cradling his leg on the rim of the elevator shaft. His own voice rang in his head against that lunatic shriek. A squelchy thud punctuated the scream, cutting it off in the damp well below.

Reed lay on his side waiting for his pacemaker to stabilise, panting. He couldn't move and he wasn't sure if he felt immobilised with a sick fear or guilt. Confusing thoughts pounded against his skull where his temples already throbbed. After a time, the sound of muttering voices woke him from the shock. Using the prosthetic as a crutch, he pulled himself up and dragged his body away and along the corridor, to his flat, reached up to insert his key, and heard the Carollers again, this time coming from the stairs below.

He recognised the hymn at last. "Come let us convert you," they sang, in corruption of "ye faithful". It wasn't "Christ" the lord they sang about, in any case. It was that foreign muddle of scribbled graffiti he couldn't pronounce. Thinking of Maud, he realised what they did.

Well they were too late this time, he thought, crawling into the safety of his flat. They hadn't won. There would be more crime tape in the morning, but not for this old soldier.

EVIL, BENT, AND CANDY-SWEET
Tim Curran

Here the trees were dead and grotesquely formed, thick with spidery roots coiling from dank soil. And if the trees were thick, the shadows were thicker . . . full and fat-bodied things dripping a black and vile sap. And it was in that skeleton forest of bone-pipes and scratching limbs that brother and sister found themselves.

It was nearly dusk.

The sky had been slit open, oozing tangles of red blood and seams of yellow fat at the horizon. The air was heavy and moist-smelling like the steam from freshly-plucked gizzards. All around were the secret sounds of the darkening wood: creaking and rustling, a wind of whispered voices and something like sharp fingers scraping bark.

"This is the Witch's Wood," said sister, a palpable dread knitting a hemp noose around her throat. "I know it is and we're lost and we'll never get out alive."

Brother laughed and that laughter was thin and dry. "Oh, don't be silly. Even now, people are looking for us. Even now mother and father are shouting our names. We're just not close enough yet to hear them."

But sister did not believe him.

For this was the boy who also said he knew the way back to the cottage by the glen. The boy who told tales taller than himself. He would take fragments and flaps of nonsense and sew them into whole cloth, things about villages of macabre marionettes that lived deep in the forest and of evil dwarves that dwelled in tree stumps and played eerie tunes on flutes of hollowed human bone. So what brother said and what sister believed were often two different things.

"We should . . . we should go back the way we came," said sister.

But brother would not have it. "And which way is that?"

Sister looked behind them, seeing the trail that was narrow and winding, an artery that had diverged into vein, vessel, and capillary a dozen times, reaching back into itself and around and through. A skein of trails leading neither here nor there, but only to this lonesome spot.

She trembled and sighed, choked something down in her throat. But if to go back was to be more lost, then what was ahead? What shadows might creep and shades might crawl in that sepulchral wildwood of skeletonized deadwood? Sister did not know and did not want to know. All those trees and thickets and sunless stands of driftwood were grim ossuary sculptures of bone that had put out roots and twigs and vines of dead sinew and deader tissue, skeletons growing into one another, welded into a latticed weave of thorny bramble and femur and flaking vertebrae.

No, sister did not like what was born in her at the sight of that congested forest. Things skittered in her belly, spinning webs at her spine.

"Just woods," brother said, licking fear from his lips. "That's all."

Yes, just forest. Just dead trees and rotted logs, loam and pine needles boiling to mulch. That was all. But why did she sense horror there? Things hungry and sentient, multi-legged and malignant?

But brother took her hand and said, "Come on."

He pulled her forward and away and together they dissolved into the shadowed depths of the woods. And as they pressed forward, the forest reached out to them. Seized them and tasted them and swallowed them whole, putting them down somewhere light and warmth could never hope to touch.

Sister did not like it, of course.

For here there was a blackness and a chill, the sour smell of rotting pelts and charnel breath, the distant murmur of chattering teeth, the sense of ravening eyes watching and breath held behind gnarled fingers.

"Here," brother said, his wind coming fast. "Quick! Through here!"

Hand in hand, brother and sister ran up the trail and down, ducking under clutching limbs and corkscrewing boughs, feeling twigs scrape their cheeks like fingernails split on coffin lids.

Then the forest fell away like a morbid veil and a misty hollow opened before them. Wisps of gray fog twisted like wraiths from corrupt graves. There was a cottage down there surrounded by a braided wreath of thorny briars. They could see the remains of squirrels and woodchucks impaled in that tangle, leeched and mummified into mats of dirty fur.

Brother led sister down there, through the opening in the briars and they saw an enchanted sweetbread cottage with its frosted cake roof and spun sugar windows, stacked chocolate chimney from which a finger of maple smoke reached into the twilight.

Brother did not move.

Such a thing could not be . . . yet he was smelling it and his stomach was rumbling. For it could not have been his fevered imagination that the cottage smelled of candied raspberries and lemon crème, glazed cherry pies and apple tarts fresh from brick ovens. The odor was real and rich and wonderful, filling his mouth with wetness.

"Do you see it?" he said. "Can you smell it?"

Sister could, but her voice had dried-up. The stench of that place was honeyed and gagging, overpowering. But what stole her voice was that just before the odor of candies and confections blotted out her senses in a luscious storm of nectar, she had smelled something else and seen something else.

It was not there now, but it *had* been there . . . crushing her with its repellent physical weight. She had seen not a delightfully half-timbered candy house set with mints, cookie crumbs, and coconut crumble . . . but a gray and sagging skull-house with pitted walls and empty socket-windows. And what she had smelled was neither delicious nor inviting, but the stench of rancid soil and corpse-slime. But then it was gone. Maybe it never was.

"I don't like this place," she said, still smelling a ghost of the smoke from the chimney which had not been maplewood, but the fumes from a cremation pit. "This is the Witch's Wood, this is the place of the Child-Eater."

"A story," brother said. "Just a story. There is no Child-Eater of the Black Forest . . ."

Yet, he did not seem sure . . . but those good, hungry smells made it hard to think and harder to reason. They pulled him in and owned him, saccharine alchemies and sugar-coated bewitchments. Under that candymaker's spell, that cloving cabalism, he was soon at the cottage, grinning in its sugared shadow, sucking almond frosting from his fingertips and crunching horehound trim, licking honey that dripped from peppermint rainspouts, filling himself and being filled, seduced and suckled and fattened.

"Oh, please," sister said, trying to pull him from that sticky sugar web that ensnared him before the candycane spider showed dripping sucrose from its dire fangs. "We must run! We must get away before, before—"

But her words evaporated, for a syrupy and toothsome voice said: "Nibble, nibble, like a mouse . . . who is nibbling at my house?"

Swallowing down a mouthful of butter cream, brother said, "It is the wind."

"The wind?" said that voice, at once hideous and serene. "Does the wind fill its belly with candy-meat and candy-wine? Is that wind pink-cheeked and fat-bellied?"

Then the door swung open and a bent-over old woman hobbled out, grinning with a mouth of yellow ivory teeth. Brother called to her and she was harmless, was she not? Certainly. How could a woman with eyes of Swiss chocolate and skin of vanilla butterfat, who smelled of baking treats and brown sugar, be anything but kind and joyful?

Yet, like the cottage itself, there was a momentary suggestion of something else, something twisted and hunched and tumescent-fleshed: a dead-eyed nightmare wrapped in mildewed baby-hides with a face that was yellow and white, horribly seamed and puckered like that of a waterlogged corpse.

But then . . . gone. Never was. Never could be.

Just that fine and plump old woman who called herself Mother Honig and smiled with summer sunshine, a thousand stolen August afternoons knitted into a shawl at her sloping old lady shoulders. Leaning there on a cinnamon stick cane, she smiled and her eyes were juicy blueberries, ripening and swelling.

"Lovely, lovely, lovely, are my children," said she. "Sweet and bounteous and delightful. Come in then, your bellies I would fill with a thousand dreams."

Being pulled into that fairytale cottage was like being drawn into a village bakery and drifting on warm rafts of shortbread dough, drowning in the succulent odors of hot pies and sweetcakes, gingerbread houses and buttery pastries. Even sister could not deny the ecstasy of it all.

At a sturdy wooden table, Mother Honig brought food by the platter and bowl and dish. Milk and pancakes, candied apples and caramel nuts, and finally, from a bubbling cauldron atop the blackened stove, plates of spicy meat steaming with hot juices.

"Ah, my children," said Mother Honig, "now we'll have our daily bread, will we not? Come children, your fingers to your mouths, eat of the meat, tear it in your teeth and fill your narrow bellies . . ."

Sister did not want to.

She was too full, too dreamy, lost in some morphic cloud that wanted to lay her out in gossamer feather beds. But brother was eating, chewing slabs of meat and salty fat, hot grease running down his chin. At first taste, there was disgust. Then confusion. And finally a ravening need for those rich-smelling cutlets and shanks dripping sharp-juiced wine. Then sister was eating, wanting to stop for the taste was peculiar and obscene, but she hungered for it, gnawing on steaks until her own face was oily with blood and sweet blubber.

"Now to bed, to bed, my fine plump muttons," said the old woman. "Even now you fatten and grow full."

Then there were two beds and sleep coming fast, darkness unwinding and looms of dream that took them and tucked them away in soft, silken places.

Sister knew good thoughts and good dreams, but when she awoke early the next morning, brother was gone. His bed was there, but his body had gone to vapor, became a mist that slipped out under the shutters.

Sister could hear a voice singing and humming, a voice that was sweet and corrupt and somehow perverse. A voice that was not to be denied, for it took hold of her and webbed her mind, cocooned her thoughts and hung them in high dusty places.

Sister shook herself awake.

She was apprehensive and nauseous and her heart was fluttering, a thousand cabbage moths taking wing. The voice was not singing now, but rhyming. It was Mother Honig's voice, a spinning wheel casting fine yarns and soft virgin's wool gathered into blankets.

But sister would not have it, she blinked sleep away.

She got to her feet, shaking the dust of slumber from her head. At the door, she paused. Mother Honig was still rhyming. Her voice was hollow and haunted, singing sonnets of moon-tide:

> *"I'll skin you, I'll boil you, I'll eat you alive.*
> *I'll salt your flesh and I'll wear your hide.*
> *Your meat is my blood and your blood is my meat,*
> *I'll stew you up tender, I'll serve you up sweet."*

This is the verse the old woman rhymed, cackling and hissing and grinding her rotting teeth. Sister felt dark dimensions open up within her, vortices and sucking holes that pulled her down into nightmare depths. Mother Honig was the witch, the Candy-Witch and Child-Eater, the daughter of ogres and cannibal necromancers.

"Eh?" said the witch and her voice no longer dripped with dandelion wine and honeysuckle, now it was hot and grinding like metal on a wheel, the snapping of leather. "Spying on me, you little tart? Eavesdropping, my fine savvy minx? Aye, so it would be. Bring yourself forth, my little charmer."

Sister, oceans overflowing her eyes and splashing down her cheeks, did as she was told. She stumbled out into the kitchen that was no longer bright and sunny, but a dissection room and a slaughterhouse, a vivisection parlor lit by guttering corpse-fat candles in black carven stems. A place shadowed and cobwebbed, stinking of marrow and bone and meat boiled to broth.

The witch's kitchen.

Not a good place. The reflection of dark myth and darker legend.

The air was heavy, flower-sweet and dog-breath sour. A place of jars and retorts and alembics, fans of bone-saws and cutting knives and cleavers, wormy books on webby shelves. A profusion of the arcane and nameless: dried herbs and powders, runic scrolls and yellowed anatomy charts, jugs of birth fluid and snake innards, mummified hands and strung wreaths of mourning lily. Skeletons and grave-dirt and greasy pelts, briny glass vessels of pickled boy-meat and salted girl-meat drifting in oceans of pale serum. And bones . . . everywhere child bones and gnawed skulls heaped and mounted and scattered.

And like the cottage itself, Mother Honig made no more pretense of who and what she was. A witch and a crone and a child-eater and happily so. A hag that sprinkled mummy dust and powdered rats' gut, a hellcat that slept in the coffin of a suicide and fingered the gizzards of black crows and made a grim mischief in the woods. She sat at her scarred table and grinned with a mouthful of black teeth, her eyes red blood-scarabs.

Pushing aside a pile of worm-holed bones from a chair, she said, "Sit, child. Sit so I may look upon you, my little enchantress. Ah, dry those tears or I'll bottle them! No mother or father has come a-knocking for you and your brother, you are mine and I would do as I please with you!"

"Where . . . where is my brother?"

The old witch cackled. "Where indeed? Dear boy, dear child, so pure and sweet, I give him to the moon, a tender treat."

"Please, he—"

"Sshh!" the witch warned, finger to withered lips. Before her was a blackened pot and she hummed a dirge as she reached into her mildewed cloak and dropped fat brown spiders into the stew she was making. Then she said words over it, words that were barbed and hooked and nonsensical. She added a tin cup of flies, the contents of three green dusty bottles, then an assortment of buzzing and whistling and hopping nature in its juiciest forms: fat grasshoppers, shiny crickets, plump, silky caterpillars.

"Go ahead, child, ask your question," she said, "for naughty children always have a question, don't they?"

Sister felt very small, a toy on a dirty shelf, her eyes drawn into black moist stars. "Will you . . . will you let us go? Can you please let us go?"

"Why in crystal Heaven or frozen Hell would I want to do that?"

"To be good, to be kind . . ."

Mother Honig's eyes were pink scabs now. "I am none of those things, haven't you heard? Has not your nurse and your grandmama told you the sort of thing I am and what it is I feed upon?"

"Yes," sister said. "But . . . but . . . this once. If not me, then my brother. You can have me in your stewpot and let him go."

"But, child! It is the boy-meat I crave! And you? You have tasted of the meat and now you are as me."

"Please, let him go. I . . . I will give you my soul . . ."

The witch stroked the graying straw of her hair. "Child, dear sweet child, I am not a demon! I have no use for souls! What, praytell, would I do with it? Keep it in a jar? Admire its soft radiance? Take it out and pet it like a wet, homeless kitten?"

"Please . . . I'll give you anything."

"Would you?" the witch purred. "Would you indeed? Your child-flesh and child-bones?"

"Yes."

"A lock of hair?"

"Yes."

"A sliver of skin?"

"Yes."

"Sweet things? Candy-blood and candy-meat and candy-gullet? All the luscious candy-yummies in your fat hog's belly?"

"Yes. Anything."

Mother Honig laughed at the idea of it. "But I have all those things for the taking! Can I not nibble on your goodies and nip at your sweet treats? Are the jewels in your gut not mine for the chewing? Can I not roast your candied heart on a stick or braise the butter-meat inside your skull?"

Sister did not say anything. There was nothing to say.

"Enough of your foolishness, child," the witch said, inhaling the vile stench of her stew, feeding off the putrid heat. "Your brother, my little enchantress, is out yonder in a fine, tasty cage. You would go to him, yes? He has had very little to bite or sup this day and you would feed him . . . fatten him for my pot."

"I won't!"

"Won't you, my sly little chavy?"

"No! I'll run! I'll get help!"

"Yes, you may run, girl, you may do that." Mother Honig seemed to think that was possible. But the idea made her grin with sawblade teeth, her breath like cooling tallow and bubbling cane sugar. "Go back to your mommy and daddy, eh? Bring them back to stretch my neck and burn my hide? Aye, you may, you may. But would I not ask vengeance and would I not receive it? Would I not call something up from the cold cellar-ooze of creation? Aye, the One Who is All Teeth and Terror . . . the eater and the grinder! An ogre, a beast of the wood! And he would come if I were to call, slithering along with the smell of sewers and graves and black blood in buckets! His mouth so big it would eat first your mother, then your father, then the very house you live in!"

"No, no, no," sister whimpered, "I won't run!"

"Won't you, child? Mayhap I would call the hungry one up, the Bogart, him that loves fresh meat and quiet mausoleums!" Mother Honig cackled at the very idea. "Juice on his lips or in his belly, in the Bogart's mouth you are warm, red jelly!"

The witch ground those glass-shard teeth together, her graveworm lips coveting an evil smile. She sat there, a hag woven out of cane straw and filthy hay, sheathed in dusty rags and maggoty skins, stuffed with sawdust and dead insects, a sprinkle of crematory ash and graveyard soil. Her crone-eyes in that crackling wicker face were melting rubies and scarlet-flamed blast furnaces. Her bosom rose and fell, her breath strident and scraping like flutes clotted with dirt.

"Off with you, child, before I make a rich gristle-soup from your bones!"

Sister had no choice.

Outside she went, around back and through the litter pile of child bones that were sometimes old and sometimes new, gnawed and licked and sucked clean of marrow. Hundreds of bones and maybe thousands, a playhouse of femurs and tibias, ulnas and vertebrae and jawless skulls. Here, in this bone kingdom, were secret places and dark holes. You could crawl in the osseous litter of stripped and scraped children, hide in the white and towering pockets of their shattered skeletons.

But sister did not hide.

She walked through that morbid bone carnival with her crocks and platters, watching storms of flies rise and fall, blown through those hollows and charnel sculptures.

Once she was through, sister could see the cottage. Ah, no more candy and sweet dreams, just a tall and narrow cottage like something worked from the black iron of cemetery gates. A weird and sepulchral high house like an upended casket, long and tall, thin and rising, creaking and trembling in the breeze, exhaling a pall of child-soot and child-dirt.

Sister crept on fairy-feet out of the tomb-shadow of the witch's house, something waxy and cold lodged in her throat. She found brother in a cage of leg bones and arm bones stitched tight with child-sinew and catgut.

"Run," brother told her. "You must run now."

But sister shook her head. "The witch . . . she'll call the Bogart."

Brother, poor brother, already looking weak and empty-eyed. He did not want the platters of butterscotch cupcakes and rich puddings that sister brought. Nor did he wish to taste that crock of stewed insects and spicy meat. He refused.

"I will get you out," sister told him. "You watch me."

After that? Minutes that bled into hours that wrapped themselves fatly into days. Mornings that stank of morgues and afternoons that were exhumed earthen boxes. And the witch, of course. Mother Honig, the Child-Eater of the Black Forest. A cloven-hoofed hag with outspread silken wings that picked at cadavers beneath a red Cyclops moon. Something vomited from a Medieval burial ground, a writhing mass of excrement, worms, and decay.

And sister was her apprentice.

Each morning the witch donned her cloak of tanned child-skins, gathered up her sacks and flesh-bags, saying, "I would go now to check my traps and make a grim merriment in the wood. You would be here when I return, child."

Sister always was.

Mother Honig would return just before dusk, those sacks bulging with fresh treats, often a curl of blonde hair or a pale, tiny arm dangling free.

When the witch was gone, sister would hatch plots and string together schemes like pearls on a thread. Sometimes she would go into the witch's bedroom, stare in cold, restless terror at that bed made of bones, the kidskin blankets, the skulls on the bed posts, the soft pelts of infants adorning the walls. And this more than anything, would make her hate.

When the witch returned, she would always check brother, poking him through the bars of his cage with a fleshless skeleton key finger. With her crackling voice, she would say, "Ha! You must eat of the sweet goodies and the meat, boy! You must fill your belly, my fat Christmas goose! I'll not feast on bones and scraps, I want fat yummy boys!"

And for sister, there was always the cooking and the preparing, the searing and stewing, the braising and the slitting. At Mother Honig's side, meat was cut from bone, moist loops of goodies were boiled in black pots, gizzards were seasoned and yellow globs of fat made into rich and satisfying gravies. Disemboweled lambs offered up succulent steaks and dripping roasts, fine loaves and salted filets. The kitchen was a wonderland of meat smells and sputtering grease, bubbling juices and joints of marbled beef, thick loins and tasty briskets. Organ meats were stewed to sweet jellies and savory brown sauces, blood-soups were ladled into bowls, and bones were nibbled clean of tasty tidbits.

And fingers were busy, always busy with dressings and tender niblets, with spices and herbs, knifes and needles and mallets.

And Mother Honig was always there, in the oven blasts and abattoir blood-stink, mouth watering and belly growling, nibbling and licking and tasting. Devouring plates of delicate finger food and vacuuming creamy confections from the hollows of white bones. Always singing her vile songs:

> "A basket of bones, a bag of skin . . .
> So much yummy goodness, where shall I begin?
> Sage and pepper, sugar and spice,
> Will you be naughty or will you be nice?"

And then suddenly, it ended.

One gray and lonesome afternoon as the oven grew hot and sweetmeats steamed and smoked there in that slaughterhouse of gutted things and decapitated things. Sister had been eating of the meat so long that she could not remember eating of anything else. Her face was sallow, her teeth sharpened on bones, her eyes sparkling cherry crystals.

"The oven is hot, child," Mother Honig said. "Push in the pot, push in the pot so that we would fill our bellies."

"I don't remember how," said sister.

"Oh! You fool child! You fool, fool child!" The witch pushed her aside with skeleton hands, opening the smoking mouth of the oven wide. "Like this! Like this!"

And as the old woman made to push in the pot, sister's hands came alive, forcing the witch into that yellow flaming hearth. But it was no easy bit. The witch fought and screamed and clawed with blackened fingers. Things rattled off shelves and doors slammed, bogarts shrieked in the forest and haunts howled from shallow graves and tombstones toppled in windy churchyards. And in that kitchen, fire belched and sparks roared as that feral red oven-mouth accepted its screeching sacrifice. But the witch would not be broiled so easily. Her face was baked brown as gingerbread and her iron fingers scratched at the grating. Her hair blazed and her skin blistered, she spit venom and steam, blackening and burning and fleshed by popping embers.

But finally, ultimately, that grating was closed and the witch was roasted.

Sister freed brother from his cage and he was happy to smell good odors rising from the chimney.

"I must eat of the meat," he said. "Fingers to mouth, I must fill myself with the meat."

Then, inside, the hunger scratching at the walls of their bellies, there was a feast. The witch was drawn from the oven, a smoking husk, and there brother and sister opened her with fingers and blades and sharp teeth. The candy witch. Yes, blackened outside, but inside? Vanilla and chocolate, ginger and gooey taffy. Her eyes were hot gumdrops and her fingers salty pralines, a treat of peppermint teeth and candy cane bones. Candy-witch and sugar-witch, orange and lemon and spice, shortbread and oozing molasses. Brother and sister filled themselves, pulling out sweet globs of nougat and dripping bags of goodies, licorice whips and candy ropes, licking sticky toffee from their fingers and quenching their thirst with running rich cherry syrup and sucking marshmallow cream from that glistening sugar skull.

All in all, a fine sup of witch-flesh and witch-meat.

And afterwards? In the days and weeks and years?

Ah yes, there was still the Witch's Wood of spider-roots and serpent-trees and malefic hungry shadows. For once tasting of the meat, brother and sister knew it was good and filling. Brother would lay the traps and collect the bounty. He was the scraper of hides and the de-boner of fat, pink mutton, little girl lost and little boy found. And sister would make merry in that dank, dark kitchen, cleaning and gutting, skinning and scalding and roasting. And together, they did make a grim and loathsome mischief in those dark woods.

HEAT
Daniel I. Russell

Hanlon leaned back against a cedar and held his breath against the stifling night. Cloaked in shadow and leaf, he counted off the seconds and strained to hear the scuff of Tessy Mae's boots on the road. He'd tailed his target for the last half hour, ever since she left the gates. Heading east along Seventh Star road, she'd been oblivious to her silent companion, until she'd stopped and peered through the tree line.

The moon, a lone spotlight in the empty stage above, illuminated the forest with a glow that glinted from the barrel of the shot gun. Hanlon focused on this as he clamped his mouth shut and waited for her to move on.

Come on, y' old hog, he pleaded.

He flinched and snapped the shotgun down hard, hearing a rustling close by. Probably a rabbit or 'coon, but tonight . . .

He gripped the weapon tighter, the arthritis in his knuckles moaning in protest. He ignored the familiar pain and swept the barrel back and forth, covering the dark bushes and shrubs.

A bird called deep in the forest, and silence reigned once more.

His barren gums felt tacky, like the back of a licked stamp. He worked up some saliva, lubricated his mouth and dared a glance around the tree.

Between hanging branches and thick foliage, he spied his chubby folly. She'd placed the basket on the road and stood looking back the way she'd come, probably contemplating a return home. The irritated chicken clucked in the basket.

"Whatcha thinkin', ya tub o' goose fat!" he hissed. "Gettin' yer sorry hide home?"

She stared vacantly down the road like an abandoned dog before sighing, her mountainous chest hitching up. Picking up the basket, she returned on her plodding path through the dark.

Hanlon followed, staying among the trees, constantly aware of the shadowed forest around him.

Dangerous night to be out on Seventh Star road these days, what with the killin', he thought. *Gots to be careful.*

He eased a leg over a fallen tree, feeling all of his sixty-something years in his knees and back.

Tessy Mae paused once again, scanning the darkness either side of the road so fast her jowls shook.

"That you, Bobby?" she slurred. "If that's Bobby James I'll 'bout tan yer hide when I catches ya, hear? I ain't got no time for no silly games, ya hear me, Bobby?"

Hanlon almost chuckled. *Young Bobby James be in his bed in town. Simple lyin' boy ain't got the grits to step outside on nights like these.*

"I gots me a sick chicken," she said, marching on. "Yes, sir. One sick chicken."

Hanlon kept pace.

The killing had begun six months ago, starting with a goat at the McKeetly farm. Since then, every month or so, another farm had its chicken coop torn to shreds or cattle go missing. Teenagers had been blamed by the Sheriff Norton; drug-smokin', fast car drivin', rock 'n' rollin' teenagers. Hanlon knew different. His old man had told him of the changers.

"And they gots a taste," he whispered. "A taste for blood when the moon goes fat as ol' Tessy Mae down there."

He'd followed her right into the heart of the killing fields.

He cracked open the shotgun and squinted to check the round. It glistened like a penny in the soft glow of the full moon. His poppy said only silver'd kill these things, but Hanlon dared the fiend to walk with half its skull blown off.

He snapped the gun shut and listened to the trudge of Tessy Mae's boots on the asphalt.

"Come and git it," he said.

Tessy Mae froze, and for a moment that creaked his ancient heart, Hanlon thought the game was up. He cursed, but then stopped dead himself.

The growl resonated from the trees, buzzsaw jagged and deep as thunder.

Hanlon's gaze darted from Tessy Mae to the surrounding trees.

The changer . . .

Tessy Mae slowly lowered the basket to the ground. The chicken trapped inside clucked and bustled, causing the straw box to shake from side to side.

"Bobby James?" she called, placing one podgy leg before the other and easing towards the far side of the road. "That you, Bobby James?"

Hanlon readied the shotgun and loitered behind a tree.

"Shit for brains," he mouthed. "Why'd I marry such a—"

It burst from Hanlon's side of the road, darting out of the forest straight towards the back of Tessy Mae.

"Holy Mother," cried Hanlon, his tensed, stringy muscles almost sparking with the need to move. He sucked his rubbery lips into his toothless mouth and fought to stay still.

The beast moved with dazzling speed, reaching the abandoned basket in seconds. With a single slash of its head, it tore through the flimsy straw. The chicken managed a single panicked squawk before exploding in a geyser of blood and feathers.

Tessy Mae slowly turned. Seeing the powerful animal crouched over the remains of the basket, she swallowed and trembled. Hanlon watched the fat of her bare arms wobble.

That's it, he thought, creeping closer. He broke his cover. *That's it.*

The creature held the doomed chicken between its jaws and shook its muzzle back and forth; a bad tempered dog with a chew toy. Poised and taut, its body was packed with tight muscle, coated in a thick, fine hair. Hanlon noticed the bumps of its spine were visible through the fur, like a greyhound.

"N-N-Nice doggy." Tessy Mae struggled to speak through quaking lips. "Nice! N-Nice doggy . . ."

It growled.

The few hairs on Hanlon's sunburned scalp stood to attention. Another step forwards and he coiled his finger around the trigger.

The mangled corpse of the chicken flopped onto the road.

Tessy Mae quit her babbling and ran.

The beast seemed to watch her go for a moment, enjoying her waddling trot up the road, before it pounced. It cleared the short distance between them and crashed into her back. Tessy Mae cried out and hurtled forwards, striking the road hard on her front. The snarling changer thrashed on her and whipped its snout down to her neck. She screamed.

Hanlon ran into the road past the destroyed basket and leveled the shotgun.

The ears of the beast pricked, and it glared back over its shoulder.

Through a dark fringe of matted hair, golden eyes shimmered with a sickly, halogen glow. It smiled a happy, canine grin, revealing teeth stained with the pink froth of blood and drool.

"Ain't you a gorgeous lil' thing," said Hanlon, aiming.

The changer's smile dropped, replaced with an intense stare. Its growl seemed to make the very air shake. It leapt.

Hanlon thrust the barrel high and squeezed the trigger.

The slug caught the beast in the upper-right of the chest by its packed shoulder muscle. The animal turned in the air, knocked by the force of the blast. Blown back, it struck the road on its side and skidded to a halt.

Hanlon ran to his wife and, lifting a heavy arm, rolled her over, onto her back.

"Tess?" he said, looking into her pale face. "Tessy Mae? Sugar?"

He kneeled and checked her pulse. Slow, but steady.

"Burt?" she sighed. "Burt . . . thank the Lord . . . a dawg . . ." She gulped. "A dawg . . ."

"I know, pumpkin. I gone taken care o' that dawg."

He peered up.

The changer had gone, leaving a dark patch like oil on the road.

"The chicken . . ." she forced. "It . . . got the chicken."

He stroked her face.

"What's one chicken? I shouldn' have gone sending you to Rooney's farm over one sick chicken. Damn truck breakin' down . . . This be ma fault. Frickin' dawg . . ."

She shook her head and winced. "Neck . . ."

"Okay, Tessy Mae. I'll getchya back home." He hooked an arm around the back of her head, ignoring her screams of pain. Her skin was slick. "You be right as rain in no time . . ."

He looked up at the moon as a howl echoed from the forest, pained and lonesome.

• ◆ •

"Gurd mornin', sunshine!" said Hanlon, briskly opening the curtains. Sunlight beamed in.

Tessy Mae covered her eyes. "Darn it, Burt. Why you gotta be such an asshole all the time?"

She lay in bed, taking up most of the mattress, which had been stained yellow over the hot, sweaty nights. The thin blanket was wrapped around her lower half in a shroud. Bandage had been wrapped around her neck, pushing up her double chin. She gazed up from the pillow like an angry bulldog.

"Asshole, huh?" he said and tugged on his braces. They held up his baggy, decrepit brown pants. The morning had been too hot for a t-shirt. "I'm just bein' a lovin' husband, pumpkin. Looks what I gots fer ya."

He left the room and entered the kitchen. From between piles of newspapers, sacks of chicken feed and soiled plates, he picked up a tray containing her breakfast. He walked the length of the farmhouse back to the bedroom. Tessy Mae watched him with piggy blue eyes, her face ruddy and sagged.

"Whatchya got there?"

"Breakfast," he said, triumphant. He placed the tray on her chest and, though the weather was hot and he'd neglected the shower for the past two weeks, he still smelled *her*; piss, vinegar and a weird burning odor.

She licked her lips, the corners already glistening, and picked up the knife and fork from the plate. She dug into the pile of sausages and bacon.

"I wants to go out today," she said with her mouth full, spraying half chewed flecks of meat on the bed. "It's been a while and I feels much better."

Hanlon shook his head.

"You been through somethin' nasty wit' that ol' dawg, Tessy Mae. You gots to rest. I'm lookin' after you, ain't I?"

She nodded and shoveled in another half a sausage. After swallowing she said, "I just worry. I means, you're ain't no spring chicken, and what with the farm and such—"

"I cans look after the farm, no mistakin'," said Hanlon and returned to the window. His one horse, Prince, stood by the fence to its paddock, watching the road. The magnificent creature held its head high, almost noble. A steed fit for a knight. Its thigh muscles were round and compact, and it shook its tail playfully.

Hanlon watched it, a dreamy smile on his wrinkled face.

"Burt!"

"God pound it, woman!" he cried, turning away. "What?"

"Be a dear and change m' bandage while I eat?"

He forced a sigh and rubbing his aching back, headed for the squalid bathroom. He found fresh gauze and bandage in a pile he'd dumped by the sink. Returning, he kneeled by the bed and held his breath.

"Lean forwards, you ol' sow . . ."

"Burt Hanlon! If I weren't so poorly I'd break yer boney ass, ya hear?"

"Yeah yeah."

Still, she did as ordered and leaned forwards. Hanlon unwound the bandage from around her neck and peeled off the gauze. Only her sweat held it in place.

"How's it look this mornin'?" she asked through another mouthful of meat.

Hanlon examined the skin. Apart from a hairy mole the size of a dime, the hot pink skin was flawless.

"Time be the best healer," he said. "Looks like you gots a lovebite from a grizzly bear."

He threw the used gauze aside and replaced it with the fresh one.

A knock at the door boomed through the house.

"Darn it!" Burt cried, stomping out the room. "Cants they leave us be?"

He left his wife behind, hearing her click on the television with the remote. She'd be happy for the day, providing he brought her lunch and dinner and plenty of snacks in between.

Maybe I goes down the sheep paddock later and—

He opened the front door.

"What?" he demanded.

The man standing on his porch dipped his Stetson. Pinned to a grey uniform, a badge shone in the morning sun.

"Oh. Mornin' Sheriff. How it suitin' yer?"

Norton smiled. "Suitin' me just fine, Mr Hanlon. One helluva morning we got going on. Shame I gotta come with some bad news."

Hanlon raised a bushy eyebrow. "News?"

The Sheriff jerked a thumb over his shoulder, pointing back towards the long, dusty driveway. His cruiser was parked at the head.

"They're back," he said. "They brought posters and signs this time. I managed to keep 'em off your land, but they're blocking your gates. Not expecting guests today, are you?"

Hanlon bared his gums and cackled.

"An ol' coot like me don't gets many guests." He spat and wiped his chin. "Damned hippies saying I mistreat m' animals. Ain't no beast treated better this side the ol' bridge."

The Sheriff wiped his brow. The morning heat bore down, and the sheep in the distant field shimmered like a mirage. With no breeze for eviction, the suffocating stench of manure hung heavy. Yet the Sheriff breathed deep though his nose unperturbed.

"You know what they're sayin', Mr. Hanlon. They don't think you're starving them or nothing. Just that day young Bobby James saw you with that lamb—"

"Was a misunderstandin'!" Hanlon cried, hoping his voice reached the meddlers at the gate. "That boy got nothin' 'tween the ears but chicken shit. Lies. Lies!"

The Sheriff held up his hand.

"Easy there. No need to go all rowdy . . . 'specially in this heat."

"You tell 'em," said Hanlon, waving a finger, "that I ain't standin' for this kinda treatment! I gots a sick wife that needs tendin' and I ain't gots the time fo' this. I gots a gun. Mighty fine one. You tell 'em that, Mr. Sheriff."

"Tessy Mae? She okay?" The Sheriff leaned to his side, trying to look through the doorway. "You okay in there, Tessy Mae?" he called.

Hanlon stood firm.

"Dog bite s'all," he said. "She be restin'."

Norton sucked in a long lungful. "There's an odd smell 'round here, Mr. Hanlon. Any idea what that could be?"

Hanlon stared at him. "Shit, Sheriff. Whole piles o' shit." He spat again and shooed a fly from his face. "Anythin' else I can do for ya?"

The Sheriff dipped his hat. "No need for more of your precious time, Mr. Hanlon. Pass on my regards to the good wife. I better keep an eye on those young 'uns. Look a rough bunch. One of 'ems the hairiest boy I ever damn saw . . ."

•   •   •

In the dream, a young Hanlon ran through tranquil green pastures, the pain in his joints a distant memory. The animals of his farm frolicked about him: Prince the horse, the sheep, chickens and the goats. He reached for one of the kids, grabbing it by the short horns.

"Such a purty thing," he said, stroking its neck with his other hand.

A deep-throated growl rumbled across the heavenly glen.

Hanlon's eyes flicked open. He lay on the sofa in worn, crusty underwear, a torn blanket draped over his scrawny legs. Staring up at the cracked ceiling, he shook his head to shift the dream-induced fog.

"Purty thing?" he asked, and sat up, sluggish, wondering where the fresh-scented field had gone.

The front door rattled.

Reality snapped back.

Hanlon gazed at the wooden door, which lead from the lounge out to the porch. The heat of the day had refused to budge, and the room had seemed to bake him through the night. He licked his gums, desperate for a glass of water.

The door rattled again.

"Darn it," he hissed and slid his legs from the sofa. "Who got loose, eh?"

Scratch scratch

Hanlon paused. The occasional escaped goat or sheep had banged its head on the door in the past . . . but a scratching?

"You just go on outta here," he said, sounding firm despite the sudden trembling of his fragile, rotting heart. "I gots me a gun!"

The shotgun lay in the kitchen.

Hanlon stood and crept across the room to the door. He laid a gnarled hand on the wood.

The scratching increased, sounding like a carpenter sawing on the porch. The door vibrated with each quick score.

"Sweet Jesus and the saints," Hanlon whispered and backed away. A rapid sniffing accompanied the scratching. "Sound like a dog wantin' its supper."

He turned and hobbled into the kitchen on sleep-stiffened legs. His knees, rusty hinges of bone, seemed to grate with each step. He spied the shotgun leaning against the back door frame.

"I gots yer number, fella," he said, arriving at the weapon and checking the fresh cartridge in the chamber. He clacked it shut and grinned. "Last time yer come ta *my* farm!"

He limped back through the dark house and back to the front door. He propped up the barrel with his left forearm, and gripped the trigger with his right hand. Pressing his ear against the wood, he strained to hear any scratching or sniffing.

"I knows yer out there," he growled. "Ain't no slinkin' away this time!"

He swept the door open and leapt out, weapon raised.

The porch was empty.

Out in the darkness, Prince neighed.

"Sum' bitch!" he cried and lurched down the few steps onto the driveway. He squinted, identifying a few familiar shapes: a water barrel, the truck, an old, decayed plow.

An engine fired, and Hanlon spun around, shotgun aimed. The taillights of a car glowed in the night like the eyes of a dragon.

"Damn you, changer!" Hanlon roared and fired.

The vehicle engine revved, and tires crunched on the sandy dirt track. It sped off, kicking up a cloud that floated up through the sparse treetops like a pale spectre.

Hanlon cracked open the chamber, and the spent casing pinged out. The rest of the ammo lay in the kitchen drawer. Powerless, he shook his fist at the lights of the departing car.

"Damn you!" he cried again.

"Burt! What in God's name you doin' out there?"

Narrow chest billowing, he shouted back into the house, "Nothin' Tessy Mae! Just scarin' a fox from those there chickens. Go back ta sleep, pumpkin."

"But . . . but I'm *hungry* . . ."

Hanlon sighed, cast the empty driveway a final glance and stomped back into the house, closing the now deeply grooved door behind him.

◆　　◆　　◆

Hanlon dragged one of the kitchen chairs into the bedroom and, placing it at the foot of the bed, dropped his flat rear into the seat. He watched his wife in her restless sleep, leaving the bedroom dark.

"Burt . . ." she moaned.

Hanlon sat straighter. *How long she been 'wake?*

"Burt . . ." she said, louder.

"Yeah, pumpkin?"

"I wanna go out some," she said and yawned.

Hanlon leaned forward, trying to inspect her teeth.

"I been in here some weeks now. I wanna go outside."

"Can't go out," he said, settling back. "Need yer rest."

She opened her golden eyes and tried to move her arms. Chains, linking her arms to the bed posts, rattled.

"Burt? Why'm I all tied up?"

He smiled. "Why, for safety, Tessy Mae."

She frowned, her unibrow creasing. It looked like a hairy boomerang.

"What's goin' on?" She sniffed three times in quick succession. Deep. "Why's you wearin' aftershave?"

"My my," said Hanlon. "What a good nose yer have."

"All the better to smell yer with," she said without humour. "Now what in God's name you doin'?" She writhed on the bed, like she had an itch she couldn't quite reach. Her breathing quickened. "I means it, Burt. You gots to let me out!"

He silently watched her movements ascend to a violent thrashing.

"Burt!' she cried. "Please! There's . . . there's . . ." She threw her head back and wailed.

"That's it, Tessy Mae," he said, finally rising. He approached the window and pulled back the curtains. Silver light filtered through the clouds from the moon. The changers' moon.

The moonlight fell across the bed, and seemed to burn Tessy Mae like acid. She increased her kicking, but the chains held firm.

"We been married close ta thirty year come summer," said Hanlon. "I was a thinkin' . . . we ain't lain like husband an' wife fer some time . . ."

Tessy Mae's scream warbled into a deep coughing din, and another noise joined the cacophony. She wailed in several deafening voices.

Thick matted hair sprang up along her arms, weaved by invisible looms, and the strands of dark brown wavered in the air like spider legs. Her jaw stretched, drawn out easily as hot toffee, and the teeth within sprang up, elongating.

Hanlon, still holding the curtain open, slid his other hand into his baggy pants and massaged his swelling rod. Feeling almost sentimental, it had been years since Tessy Mae had got him hard.

She howled over the rattling of the chains. Her nose had caught up with her chin, and now a full snout poked proudly from her face. Whiskers blossomed into existence either side. She snarled, drooling over long canine teeth. Her golden eyes glistened with pain and panic.

"Not much to go now, Tessy Mae," said Hanlon, cautiously approaching the bed. "My poppy, he saw a changer once. Said it took minutes before sumabitch were a full on dawg . . ."

Her bed clothes seemed to grow on her, but Hanlon realised his wife was shrinking. Folds of fat tightened, becoming lean and packed. Her legs buckled, the bones within realigning with a wet crunch.

He stroked his growing member, and crept further still.

The creation lying on the bed had lost all resemblance to his wife. It glowered at him, and its lips curled back, baring its teeth. Wicked, hooked claws were still locked within the chains. She'd managed to kick her voluminous flannel pants off her now slender legs, and Hanlon picked them off the mattress and flung them aside. His groin throbbed with animal need, stirred by the strong heat that radiated from between the creature's legs. He slid his braces from each shoulder.

The dim room suddenly fell darker.

Hanlon stopped, his thumbs hooked into the waistband of his pants, ready to tug them down. He glanced towards the window. The gentle lunar rays barely penetrated the hanging curtain.

"Damn it!" he moaned and climbed off the bed. "Don' want yer changing back. Not tills we consummate our weddin' vows o' course."

He walked over to the window, hunched from his engorged shaft.

The creature continued to growl and fight the restraints. Its hind paws kicked circles in the air.

"Let's get yer top up, pumpkin," said Hanlon. He grinned and spread the curtains wide apart.

Golden eyes peered back at him through the glass.

"What in God's name—"

The window exploded in a cascade of glittering shards as the claws burst through. They grabbed Hanlon by the shoulders, parting the flesh with ease and gripping the bone.

Hanlon screamed and strained to pull backwards. Blood jetted from the wounds and poured down his chest.

The hulking changer leaned inside the vacant window frame, snot and thick saliva dripping from its muzzle. It opened its mouth, blowing a fetid breath of decaying meat into Hanlon's face.

"God pound yer!" he screeched. "She's mine, yer hear? She's ma *wife*!"

The beast opened its maw wider and pulled Hanlon forwards. His face slipped into its mouth like the old-time lion tamers he'd seen as a boy.

He stared into the teeth-lined cavern, focusing on a cavity on a rear molar. He gagged from the warm, dank stench.

"God pound ya," he whimpered, feeling points press under his chin. "I love ya, Tessy Mae! This was fo' our marriage, damn it!"

The jaws slammed shut, ripping through Hanlon's weathered, screaming face.

◆ ◆ ◆

Tessy Mae blinked in the early morning light and sniffed. Eggs and bacon. Her head throbbed.

"Burt? Ya ol' dawg! Get me all liquored up, ya snake?"

Sitting up, she found herself lying on her belly on the floor of the lounge. Groaning, she pushed her heavy body up and winced. Her sex burned like a hot coal had been shoved inside. She grinned.

"Burt, ya ol' dawg . . ." she said to herself. "Make a nice change from all those sheep y' been porkin'. Bet Prince be mighty relieved too."

She yawned and stretched. Rubbing her wrists, she staggered into the kitchen, following her nose. Seemed Burt was cookin' up one helluva feed.

She stopped in the kitchen doorway, her mouth hanging open.

Sheriff Norton stood by the stove, completely naked and holding a spatula. Despite the shock of finding the lawman butt naked in her house, Tessy Mae couldn't help but stare at the scar on his chest near his shoulder. Bullet wound? Warmth spread through her already hot loins. She loved a dangerous man.

"Mornin', Tessy Mae."

She blinked, glanced down at his hanging manhood and then back up to his face.

"Did we . . . ?" she asked, aware she too wore nothing.

He smiled and nodded. "Yes ma'am. All night long."

She inhaled the succulent meaty smells he'd cooked up.

"Where's . . . Burt?"

The Sheriff ignored the question, instead raising his nose and sniffing, watching her all the time. He tilted his head. "You smell so sweet, Tessy Mae. There's somethin' 'bout you . . . I just can't keep away."

She blushed. "Gee, Sheriff. I ain't never been told that 'fore. You makin' me breakfast?"

He nodded. "Last night's leftovers. Nothin' too pretty. Certainly not as pretty as you."

She felt heat rush to her cheeks and somewhere else. Somewhere lower, past her belly button. Hot waves seemed to emit from her lips. She spread her legs, worried her thighs might burn.

"There's something 'bout you," he said again and pounced forwards, hands exploring her slick skin. "I just can't keep away."

Her heat bloomed.

"Why Sheriff," she giggled, looking into his eyes. "You be actin' like a dawg in heat."

He sniffed, lower and lower. "Not me, Tessy Mae. No ma'am, not me at all."

THE NEGLECTED
Sean Logan

The house looked the same as it had when he was a child, only smaller—and very, very old. The same could be said for Dom's father. There were older houses, and older men, in this neighborhood, but none of them *looked* older. They had all been cared for.

The two of them sagged, of course—one leaning to the south, the other curling forward. They both had dark, rotten patches on their facades and seemed asymmetrical in various indefinable, but unpleasant ways.

Dandelions and starthistle were now squatting in the two square patches of dirt in front of the house that had once been inhabited by grass. Was there an equivalent to this in Dom's father? Probably. Maybe the old man's jock itch.

As they started to climb the stairs to the front porch, the father curled his hand around the crook of Dom's arm. He *needed* to; he had to steady himself—Dom knew this—but it still seemed strange to him that he *would*.

The father aimed a key at the door knob, his hand shaky and wandering, quivering toward the keyhole like a drunken man stumbling for the bathroom in the dark. Dom wanted to grab his hand and jam the key into the hole, but he had more patience than that. He could wait. He could wait all day if he had to.

The father unlocked the door and Dom stepped into the dark living room. It had a distinctly familiar smell, nothing he could name, just the house's particular combination of building materials and humidity and ventilation and the lifestyles of those who lived there. It was an odor he never knew he smelled throughout his childhood, but probably the first thing every visitor noticed. And Dom noticed it now. Sixteen years had turned him into a visitor.

"Do you want to take a nap, Dad?" Dom said. "Are you tired?" Dom said this like he was talking to a child. If that gave Dom a perverse sense of power—if there was a delicious justice in the fact that he could make his father feel the same helpless dependence that he'd felt for the first half of his life—Dom didn't recognize it. He felt like a dutiful son.

"Yeah, I think I could use a rest."

Damn, the old man really was sick. The doctor told Dom that, said he'd been sick for a good long time, implied with his tone that Dom should have been involved before now. The doctor showed him X-rays; they looked like any other X-ray he'd ever seen, but the doctor pointed with his pen and said that the little shadow he was looking at was "quite serious". He *believed* the doctor, of course—he didn't think the guy was making it all up for a laugh—but he didn't start thinking of his dad as sick until he'd asked him if he was tired and the old man didn't tell him to piss off and go watch TV.

Dom put his old man to bed and went to his own room, the room he'd slept in for twenty-three years. It hadn't changed. It had just gotten dusty and a lot less awesome. His Iron Maiden and Heather Locklear posters where still there. The Star Wars blanket was still on the bed. He wasn't still into Star Wars in his twenties, but he never made an effort to get a new one. And damn that bed was small! How the hell did he ever fit in that thing? He lay down to test the size and decided he could probably use a nap himself.

As he stared up at the acoustic popcorn ceiling, waiting for that warm pool of sleep to rise up and engulf him, he heard the steady sound of clinking metal. The pipes under the house. A problem with the plumbing. He could fix that tomorrow, make himself useful. His only job was making sure his dad took his medicine three times a day. Other than that he just had to hang out and wait for him to . . . get better. So he could take care of a few things, fix the plumbing. Get under the house and check the pipes. He remembered that the hatch to the crawlspace beneath the house was in his closet.

And then another memory came back to him. It was something he'd made a great effort to forget, because it was the worst thing he'd ever done.

◆ ◆ ◆

The kitties were so cute that he couldn't choose. The boy kitty had the cutest black nose and the girl kitty looked like a tiger. He wanted them both. He'd please-oh-pleased and promised and it *wouldn't* stink because he'd clean the litter box *all the time* and *he'd* be the one to feed them, yes, twice a day, every day, and no, of course he won't forget.

And to his great surprise, they agreed. He had been shocked once when his parents agreed to get him a kitty, and he was shocked beyond measure when his pleading and promises actually worked and they agreed to get him *two* kitties.

He kept up his end of the bargain and did everything he'd promised. For most of a week. But sometimes he'd forget because he was tired when he got up in the morning, and he had homework when he got home, and by nine his mom told him to go straight to bed. She said "straight" to bed. If he fed the kitties, that wouldn't be "straight" to bed, would it?

His parents didn't check up on him. The kitties were his responsibility.

His, not theirs. If they had to remind him, that made it their responsibility. That was part of the deal. They didn't nag him. But the kitties did. Constantly. Long, whiny meows while he was trying to sleep. Crawling on him. Rubbing their cheeks against his forehead. Jumping off his nightstand onto his back early in the morning, way before his mom was supposed to wake him up for school. They were totally being deliberately annoying on purpose.

One morning it was too much. He'd forgotten to write the last two pages of "Who is your favorite historical figure and why?" and it was due tomorrow and it was going to count for ten percent of their grade. So he stayed up until almost midnight and finished the paper (but didn't type it, which would take off one whole letter grade).

Meowing, rubbing, crawling, jumping. It was barely even light out. There was a fuzzy, dizzy weight in his head like he'd only just fallen asleep. He swung his legs out of bed and stomped his feet to the floor. He scooped a kitty into each hand and stomped to his closet. He'd tried shutting them in there once before, but they scratched at the door and meowed all morning, which was nearly as bad as them crawling on him. So this time he stuck his big toe into the small gap in the carpet at the edge of the roughly cut rectangle that surrounded the hatch to the crawlspace. His dad didn't use it anymore, but it's where he used to throw out anything that wasn't supposed to go in the regular garbage—used motor oil, gasoline, household cleaners. If they couldn't go in the garbage, he'd throw them down there, until Dom's mom figured out what he was doing and made him stop.

Dom lifted the hatch enough to toss the kitties to the grey plastic three feet below, then closed the closet door behind him as he went back to bed.

He fell asleep and slept all morning until his mom woke him. He was still tired when he woke. That was one thing. He slid out of bed and slouched to his dresser to get dressed. His clothes were in his dresser, not his closet. The closet was for blankets and linens and extra pillows. He didn't have his clothes in there, so he never used it. That was the other thing.

Dressed. Breakfast. Off to school. It was stupid as usual. He'd be lucky if he got a C on his history paper. Chad and those guys were being jerks at lunch. In PE, he missed a super easy pop fly in kickball. The ball bounced right off his chest. So when he got home, he was exhausted. He flopped onto the couch and watched TV. He did his homework while his dad hogged the TV for Magnum P.I. and the news, then he went to bed.

The next day wasn't so bad, but he had extra homework and soccer practice after school.

The day after, he went over to his friend RJ's house to play cars and he stayed for dinner, so he got home late.

The next day . . . it was just a regular day, pretty much. He didn't have an excuse. He just forgot, because he'd already forgotten for three days.

On Friday, as Dom was sitting down in front of the TV with a plate of meatloaf, his mom said, "Hey, I haven't seen your cats around."

Dom felt like he'd been punched in the gut. A sick twisting guilt washed over him. How could he forget? Jesus, had he not fed them in almost a week? They'd be dead by now.

"They ran away," Dom said. He was starting to sweat.

"Oh, good God, we spent forty dollars on those cats," she said. "You should have taken better care of them." But a minute later she was talking about how the dryer was making a funny noise.

After dinner Dom went to his room and stared at the rectangle in the carpet of his closet. He should open it. Go in there and see if they were all right. They could have been eating rats. Maybe they were just fine? Maybe he'd open the hatch and see them playing with each other, rolling around on that grey plastic having fun.

He imagined opening the hatch and seeing them lying there emaciated and still, worms crawling on them. Or even worse—almost dead, squinting at the light coming down on them from the open hatch, barely enough life in them to turn their heads in his direction. He'd carry them out of that cold, dark space and take them to his mom, tell her what he'd done, admit he'd lied. They'd get in the car and drive to the emergency vet, but they'd die on the way and he'd have to walk into the vet's office holding two dead kittens. He'd have to say he killed them because he'd just forgotten about them. He killed them because he was selfish and bad.

He decided not to look. They were probably dead. Definitely. There was nothing he could do now.

That night he had dreamed about them. He was in class, in his seat at the back. Mrs. Dunning was asking for their homework, but he'd forgotten to do his. He had plenty of time, but he'd forgotten until now. He decided to look in his backpack anyway, maybe there was something he could turn in. He put the backpack on his lap and zipped it open. Inside were his cats, almost dead.

In his dream, Dom remembered putting those kittens in his backpack days earlier and forgetting about them. Now they were trying to crawl out of his bag, barely able to move, eyes closed, straining to raise their paws up toward him. They were practically dead. Dom couldn't let them go on like that, they were suffering.

He was at the back of the class and everyone was facing forward. He took the boy kitty with the black nose out of the bag and put him on the speckled yellow linoleum floor. The kitty was limp, breathing heavy, reaching out with his paw like he was dreaming about chasing a mouse. Dom wanted to end his suffering quickly, so he put his foot over the kitty's little head and pressed down.

There was a sickeningly loud squishy crunch and the cat came suddenly to life under his foot, jerking and twitching like it was being electrocuted. Dom raised his foot and stomped down again, trying to make it stop, but the kitty wouldn't die, there was more life in him than Dom realized and the kitty just twisted and squirmed as Dom brought his foot stomping down over and over.

"Dominic!"

Dom turned around to see Mrs. Dunning and all of his classmates staring at him in horror. He looked back at the kitty, who was dragging himself across the floor by just his front paws, trailing blood. He picked up the kitty and held him close as his classmates sneered at him, disgusted. The kitty wasn't going to die, but he'd probably be crippled and have brain damage. But Dom was going to take care of him now. Forever.

When Dom woke up the next morning, he dragged his steamer trunk into his closet. The trunk was filled with all the old toys he used to play with when he was younger. It was heavy. He slid it over the door to the crawlspace, shut the door to the closet and never went in there again.

◆　◆　◆

"Dom, I think I was supposed to take my medicine."

Dom woke to see his father hanging like wet laundry in his bedroom doorway. The green LED numbers on his alarm clock said it was 3:15 PM. He was supposed to give the old man his pills three hours ago.

"Sorry, Dad. Let's get you taken care of."

Dom spilled the bag of pill cases onto the kitchen table. There were six of them, two labeled Morning, two Noon, and two Night, and each had compartments marked with a day of the week—M, T, W, Th, F, S, Su.

The doctor had gone on for ten minutes giving Dom instructions on when and how to get all of those pills into his father, shuffling through bottles and tapping on labels with a fingernail that was surprisingly dirty. Were doctors allowed to have dirty nails? Weren't they supposed to wash their hands all the time? And how did it get so dirty? Was it from something he was doing to a patient, sticking his fingers in something?

"So does all that make sense?" the doctor said, and Dom realized he hadn't been listening.

Dom stared at the bottles for a minute, with his mouth hanging slightly open. "Uh, what was that one thing you said about the one with the 'oxy' in its name?"

The doctor stared at him for a moment. "Why don't we make this easy for you," he said and separated the many, many pills into all the little compartments. Now all Dom had to do is remember what day it was and know whether it was morning, noon or night.

Dom opened the M compartment of a Noon case and poured four pills into his father's hand—a small red pill, two big white capsules and an amber gelcap. "There you go, Dad. Those are suppositories, so shove them up your ass."

The old man looked like Dom had thrown a drink in his face.

"I'm just kidding. I'll get you some water." As Dom filled a glass in the sink, he heard the pipes clinking again. "Hey, Dad, you got plumbing problems?"

"I don't think so."

"I think you do," he said, handing the old man his glass. "I'm gonna take a look under the house."

"I don't think you should."

"What, you think I'm gonna bust something? Don't worry so much, you're gonna get yourself all worked up."

Dom went to the closet in his room and opened the door for the first time in nearly thirty years. His trunk was where he had left it. He slid it aside and uncovered the rectangle cut in the carpet. He felt sick to his stomach and tried not to think about how long it had taken his kittens to die. Would he see their bones?

He lifted the hatch, and cold, dank air poured out at him. A patch of light fell on the grey plastic below, surrounded by blackness. Even though the sun was shining outside, none of the light made it down there.

He went to the kitchen, grabbed a flashlight from the junk drawer and returned to his closet. He aimed the flashlight around the crawlspace, and didn't see any rats (or bones), just uneven dirt, sheets of torn plastic and a mound of bottles and tubes and cans, some filled with used sludge, others with nothing more than toxic fumes. The dirt around the mound was streaked chalky yellow and green from the chemical runoff, like watercolored riverbeds, a pastel alluvial fan.

Dom lowered himself through the spiderwebs into the small, cold space, acutely aware of all the darkness that surrounded the weak beam of his flashlight. The area was long and narrow to the north, with a small alcove about six feet wide to the east, and another passageway to the west about thirty feet ahead of him, in a configuration that seemed to have no relationship to the floorplan of the house. He didn't see any pipes in this section, so he crawled forward, listening for clinking metal.

As he approached the alcove on his right, he heard a wet sound, but it didn't sound like a leak, more like squishing. It sounded like movement. Dom felt a chill tingle down his back. He couldn't run out of here if he needed to, the ceiling was too low. And the thought of crawling back as a herd of rats came chasing after him made him feel like the floorboards above him were pressing down on his back.

Rats. That's what it sounded like, didn't it? Like rats playing in mud.

You're overreacting, Dipshit, he told himself, applying his dad's favorite nickname for him. *You see a rat, you get to leave. Until then, keep crawling.*

Dom aimed the flashlight at the alcove ahead of him, the light creeping along the far wall, deeper into the narrow space as he got closer. The squishing sound grew louder, and with it, another noise, squeaking. Like rats? No, it wasn't squeaking.

Mewling. Like cats.

Dom felt a cold hard shock to his chest, as his heart forgot to beat for a moment. But he kept crawling forward, even though he was beginning to feel detached and light-headed. He came around the corner and shined the flashlight all the way into the alcove, the faint yellow beam hitting the back wall ten feet away. And something else. Something shock white and moving on the ground. It looked like something spilled, a puddle, a vomited milkshake, but chunky—and moving. Dom's light reflected back at him, two small objects glimmering red. And two more, and another two. Little rat eyes. Rats playing in wet dough.

Dom wanted to scramble out of there, but in the moment it took to rally his limbs into action, he saw that these rats, or whatever they were, weren't chasing after him. They seemed to be feeble and straining, rolling over one another.

Like a basket full of newborn kittens.

Dom's panic turned to acid in his gut. He crawled forward, and the closer he came to the writhing mound in front of him, the less clear it became. There were a dozen or more little creatures, but Dom couldn't tell where one began and the next ended. They were hairless and stretched, pale twisted flesh, knotted and tied.

As Dom came closer he could see distinct shapes, animal shapes, like little . . . creatures. But between those fully defined bodies were less distinct forms. There were legs the size of Dom's thumb, little jaws with bone-sliver teeth, and small red sightless eyes; but the proportions and relationships between them weren't correct. A stubby tail near a muzzle. A paw bulging out above a blind eye. A small twisted leg near one much larger.

Dom stared at the writhing mound of burn-scar flesh in dizzy horror. He couldn't tell what these creatures were, or had once been (though he suspected), but he knew they weren't rats. In fact, two of them—connected to each other by the hip, and to the others by warped and stretched hind legs—were gnawing at the half-eaten carcass of a rat.

Another sound, scraping through the dirt, snapping Dom out of his daze. It came from the far end of the crawlspace, and it sounded too big. That sound didn't come from one these little monsters.

"Hey, Dad? Is that you?"

The silence that followed squeezed at Dom's chest. He heard someone shuffling. Some*one*, not some*thing*. It came from around the far dark corner to the west, opposite the hatch through which he'd entered.

And that hatch seemed like a good destination right now. He thought he might like to head toward that hatch.

Dom turned away from his surreal litter of damaged animal parts and bolted for the exit, crawling with the knuckles of his right hand punching at the dirt, the flashlight curled in his fist, throwing shaky circles on the wall beside him. He didn't turn around, didn't know who might be scurrying up behind him, what might be nipping at his heals. He didn't want to know.

The glow from Dom's closet shone down through the hatch like a heavenly light breaking through the clouds. Dom scrambled for the light, and though he didn't want to know what he was crawling away from, what was shuffling in the dark, he aimed his flashlight behind him. He didn't want to—he didn't want to know what was back there—but his instinct was to make sure he was clear to climb up out of the crawlspace and into the safety of his closet without something snapping at his dangling legs.

There was nothing directly behind him, so he lunged for the hatch. But the beam of his flashlight had fallen on something that hadn't been there before. As he raised himself out of that sarcophagus of a basement, he registered the blue-veined flesh and bony form that had been hunched against the far wall. Because his mind acknowledged the image only after he had turned away from it, he was immediately able to dismiss it as a trick of the light, a conjuration of an overstimulated imagination. And this dismissal needed to happen, because the idea that the pale figure crouching in his brain might be real was beyond madness.

Dom pulled himself into the cleansing light of his room, slammed the hatch door back into the open rectangle and shoved his trunk back into place over it. The trunk was heavy—he had to lean in and shove hard—but was it heavy enough?

Dom lifted the TV from his nightstand and placed it on top of the trunk. Then he went back for the nightstand. He shut the closet door. He wanted to lock it, but the door didn't have a lock. There was his dresser. Should he move that in front of the door? No, that was a little too real. That was like an acknowledgement. That was an admission. There was no reason to block the door. He just wouldn't go in there again. He didn't need to. And for that matter, did he *really* need to be going into his room? No. No, he didn't. He should really be sleeping in the living room to be closer to his dad, right?

Dom gathered his Star Wars blanket and his pillows and joined his father in the living room. The old man was staring at the TV, which wasn't on.

"So what you watching there, Dad?" Dom said, focusing on the TV and trying his best not to think, ready to force any negative thoughts out of his short term memory at gunpoint if he had to.

"I'm just resting."

"What, you just get back from a jog?"

"No, I'm just a little tired."

"Well, sure, you've been up for, what, two, three hours now? You must be about ready for a nap."

"I think I'd just like to sit a little while if you don't mind."

He didn't say this sarcastically. He really seemed to be asking Dom's permission. It was sad. And a bit pathetic. And it made Dom a little angry, but he didn't know why. "No, I don't mind. You mind if I fix myself a drink? You got anything?"

"There's a bottle of whiskey in the hall closet, on the left next to the jar of batteries. Did you find something under the house?"

Dom froze for a second, trying to figure out what the old man meant by "something"—a leak, or something else? He quickly realized he didn't want to know and found that bottle. "Nope," he said. "I think we're just going to have to live with that clanking noise."

"Yeah, I know."

"So what about you? Do you want a drink?"

"Am I allowed to have one? With my medication and all that?"

"I don't know."

"Okay, pour me a drink."

◆　◆　◆

Dom was watching a paid program for a meat dehydrator. The program was like a talk show with two happy hosts, one male and one female, great hair both of them, and an audience full of applauding people who had a lot of questions about dehydrated meat. They broke for a commercial. The commercial was for the same meat dehydrator they were talking about on the fake talk show—a commercial within a commercial. Dom turned off the TV, and remembered why he'd turned the volume up so loud. His dad was moaning in the bedroom, a low monotonous wail. He sounded horrible. Didn't those pills do anything?

Dom's stomach knotted. Had he given the old man his pills tonight? Or this afternoon? Dom went to the bathroom and found the pill case labeled Night. He opened W. The pills were in there. He poured them into his palm. He found the case labeled Noon, opened W, and poured the pills into his palm. Morning. It was full. He didn't want to look in T. This was bad enough.

Dom brought the handful of pills to his father with a glass of water. The old man was twisted up in sweaty sheets, his fuzzy green blanket piled next to his bed like debris from a landslide. Dom shook his bony shoulder. It was wiry, clammy and spotted, and it seemed to belong to an older man. Even older than his father. Mid-moan, he looked up with confused, watery eyes.

"Hey, Dad. You've got to take your pills. You forgot to take them earlier." Dom might have felt bad about transferring his guilt to his father, but he didn't realize he was doing it.

The old man sat up with barely enough energy to wince. He took the pills one at a time. By the time he reached the twelfth pill, it looked like he was trying to lift bowling balls to his lips. The water dribbled down the sides of his mouth and soaked the worn gossamer fabric of his boxers.

"All right, that's good," Dom said, taking the water glass. "You just relax now. You'll be feeling good as new in a minute."

The old man flopped back into his damp pillow. He lay on his back breathing through his mouth—with his eyes open, which was a bit creepy. There was a faint nasal moan behind the huffing of air. Dom sat in the hard-backed chair next to the bed to wait for the pills to kick in. Some of those had to be for pain, something fun so he got a little buzz for his troubles.

Dom sat for several minutes doing nothing, just watching his dad breath like some sort of creep. It was a bit ridiculous just sitting there. He picked up a pen from the nightstand and drummed it on his knee, clicked the point out and back, out and back, click, click, click, click, drum, drum, dubba dubba, drum drum. His father looked over at him. Didn't turn his head, just his eyeballs, which added to the creep-factor. He didn't say anything, just breathed and stared. Dom put down the pen and picked up a National Geographic. Buffalo, native kid drinking a Coke, big grey giraffe tongue snatching an apple wedge, skinny men swimming in a river, saggy dancing native boobs. So was that why this was the only magazine on the nightstand? Was his dad beating off to swinging African knobs?

Dom dropped the magazine like it had gotten sticky. He stood and strolled around the room. It felt pretty good, walking around his dad's room with impunity. He took the old man's Timex from the dresser, pulled on the stretchy band. He opened the drawers, looked at the balled socks, folded T-shirts, white striped boxers. It all looked dusty and stagnant, like the old man hadn't been in his own sock drawer in decades. Dom slid open the flimsy fake-wood door to the closet, saw the old short-sleeve shirts, a half dozen scratchy wool coats, shiny uncomfortable shoes, a Super-8 projector, shoe boxes filled with bills from back when his mother was alive. There was a photo album among the shoe boxes. He flipped it open to a middle page and saw pictures he didn't recognize, shots of his dad's second wife, who Dom had barely met, maybe a half-dozen times, a thin-lipped, raspy-voiced woman with frizzy blonde hair who's ass had probably made a permanent imprint in a bar-stool somewhere.

"Hey, you put that away," the old man said, his voice slurring, the pills starting to work.

Dom felt like he'd been waiting for that. He brought the album over to the chair next to the bed and turned to the first page. Wedding photos, his dad and the barfly. The pictures picked up right after Dom's mom died and he moved out.

"Come on, you," he said, mumbling like his lips were numb. "Just put it away, why don't ya?"

Vegas, his dad standing next to a slot machine with three blue sevens in a row. Disneyland, the two of them standing in front of the Matterhorn. Some beach, the skank drinking a red frozen beverage. The living room couch, his dad's ex-wife pregnant.

Pregnant? What the fuck?!

"Hey, Dad? Your ex-wife? Did you knock her up? Did she have a kid?"

His dad rolled away from him and mumbled into his pillow.

Dom turned the page. The ex-wife, in a hospital bed, her belly like an overfilled laundry basket in front of her. His father kneeling next to her smiling half-heartedly, her in an oxygen mask.

"What the hell, Dad? Does this mean I have a little brother or some-thing?"

Mumbling, spitting unintelligible protests.

Dom turned the page. His former step-mother, looking exhausted, holding a stubby, miserable infant. His dad sitting on the brown leather recliner in the living room, looking at the infant's face like a math problem he couldn't solve.

"So you have another kid out there somewhere?"

The baby, a few weeks older, red and puffy-faced, sitting in his former step-mother's lap. She looked like she didn't want to be photographed. And she looked like she didn't want that kid on her lap, holding it away from her on the end of her knee.

"Jesus, Dad. Where's this kid now?"

Dom turned the page, but there were no more pictures. He stood over his father and rolled him onto his back. "Where'd she take the kid?"

His father grumbled belligerently, sputtering and stumbling over the words, half of them unintelligible. ". . . didn't take him nowhere . . . god-damn woman left me alone . . . what the hell do I know about . . . what was I supposed . . . ." He rolled onto his stomach and pressed his face into the pillow, pushing the sides up around his ears.

Dom went back to the living room couch, pulled the cover over himself and got into a similar position.

◆　◆　◆

Dom had the TV up so loud it was almost painful, but it didn't entirely block out the sounds of . . . the other noises. He was trying to concentrate. He was really, really trying to focus on the questions Oprah was asking her guest. But then a commercial came on for a pill. It didn't say what the pill did—it just showed an old couple holding hands, and a young couple riding horses on the beach. But it showed the pill, and Dom couldn't stop the thought he'd been pushing back. All of those pills, all the pills he hadn't given his father over the last few days. Those did things. They stopped pain and cured things—or made them not get worse, he didn't know. His father needed those pills. Dom didn't want to hurt him, didn't want him to go without his pills. He just didn't want to see the old man. He didn't want to talk to him and think about him having another son. He just didn't want to think about it. So he didn't go in there. Then days had passed. How could he face the old man now? His father had hobbled out of the room on his own a few times for water or to use the toilet, hunched and grimacing, calling his name, his wispy grey hair disheveled and his ratty brown robe hanging from his bony frame like it was melting off him. How could Dom face him now? And how could he face another day of this, hearing that old man wailing and not being able to do anything about it? Why couldn't it just go away? Just go away. Just go away. Just go away!

Dom darted into his father's bedroom and scooped him out of bed. He barely weighed anything. He marched him into Dom's old bedroom and dropped him on the bed. The old man was talking, confused, but Dom tried not to hear. Or think. Or feel anything. He opened the closet door, moved the TV, nightstand, slid the trunk aside, opened the hatch. Dom grabbed the delirious old man, knelt next to the hole and lowered him into the cold and dark. He focused on the task at hand and tried not to think. If he was screaming somewhere inside himself, he didn't acknowledge it.

As he lowered the old man, a hand clasped his wrist, bone white and cold, pulling, shifting him off balance. He fell forward into the hole after his father, landing hard, half on the grey plastic and half on the old man, who grunted under his weight. Dom rolled to see the wiry, long-limbed body scrambling out of the hole and into the light, its pale skin almost grey. It looked down at them with crazed, clouded eyes and a gaunt face that looked like his father's. The haunted figure slid the hatch into place above them, the rectangle of light disappearing into blackness.

Dom heard the sound of the toy chest sliding over the hatch. He got to his feet, put his back to the hatch and tried to lift. He knew it would be hopeless, and it was. He lay back down next to his father and listened to the old man's ragged breathing. Between breaths, he began to hear another sound.

Dom got to his hands and knees and crawled blindly along the dirt. He followed the sound, felt the corner when he reached the alcove. He crawled to the end, until he felt something like skin. He lay down, got comfortable there in the dirt. He was staring into darkness, but the sounds of mewling and writhing were so distinct he felt like he could see the life in front of him.

"It's okay, I'm not going anywhere," he said, reaching out and feeling slick skin rubbing against his fingers. "You have my full attention."

BETTY AND THE CAMBION
Ralph Greco, Jr.

Between the muted mauve tableaus of stucco walls, the sound of Betty's bare foot fell. Dressed as lightly as she was, a ruby red paper-thin sheath hanging from her wide collar, sides split from her neck to her ankles, the chalky October breeze undulating through the deserted house blushed a cold shiver cross the young woman's rising sheen of sweat . . . though not an altogether uncomfortable sensation. Hesitating on the Italian marble floor, the freckled-nosed girl bit her lip and stared down the empty hallway to the solid wooden door that faced her. Betty's plan, such as it was, was to open that door, cross beyond the threshold and become a woman of legend among her peers, to break the pattern and actually *remember* this night as those who had come before her had not. But the pretty college sophomore secretly feared she'd come to love what happened to her in that room beyond the door—as much or more as her sisters before her had—and she'd be sent from this house unable to recall what had transpired, while a longing urge and a sinister comeuppance haunted her for the rest of her days as it did the young women who had dared try this walk through this house and the horror it held.

◆　◆　◆

Julia's tape made the rounds through school; from freshman to seniors (though the older girls acted as if the secret of Delino House could never entertain their 'mature' sensibilities), some teachers were even rumored to have heard it. Played nightly for rapt live audiences, even downloaded into e-mail, Julia Bents' secret recording of her 'time in the room' kept every girl who heard it in a perpetual 'state'.

A junior at the private college, lanky Julia had secreted a mini-tape recorder under the flouncy flower-patterned skirt she had worn her night in Delino House. Her plan had been to close her thighs hard—as she actually *had* done—engaging the record button to hopefully capture what would engage her after she closed the wooden door and faced whatever it was all the girls before her had but had not been able to remember. After being picked up in the woods behind the Pizza Hut, as every one of the girls before her had, Julia produced her 'secret' tape.

Of course Julie didn't remember ever producing the scream and low taped 'mewing' let alone recall activities that could have caused her to do so. As *every one of the girls before her had*, Julia's only proof of her ordeal was the requisite nickel-sized scar dead center of her right buttock, a similar shape just over her right nipple and the deep sensation (and low ache) of having been 'filled' with something, the size of which she could never have imagined. As with the other eight girls who had ventured beyond that door in Delino House, Julie only remembered crossing into the small room at the end of the hallway, closing the door behind herself then waking up in the parking lot silently nursing an ache she could not remember the cause of.

Julia became addicted to her oratory submission though. Returning again and again to her tape she was quickly driven mad by the things she heard that reminded her of the things she could not remember.

Betty arrived the very day the ambulance came to 11 Norton Way to 'escort' Julia from the dorm.

◆　◆　◆

Man or beast, Betty Fect—for that was who she was—was going to know this cool leaf-blown night just what it was that was bequeathed in this house of her uncle, the wily exiled Antony Fect Delino.

She stood at the door then, wiping the palms of her hands on the material of the smock tickling over her knee. Despite her fear, Betty still felt a dollop of wetness between her legs, saw and felt her little nipples poking far out from under her sheath. There was a pull in her belly, like the gestating coil of a snake that will neither strike nor sleep. Familiar only with clumsy rumblings in backseats and family-room groping (and only with one boy, as a matter of fact) the Virginia native was rattled with how hot she was just standing here. In fact, Betty suddenly stepped right up on tiptoe and pushed her wet pelvis into the fat doorknob

Spreading herself so her bare sex below the material could flatten hard against the knob Betty was amazed at her sudden brazen masturbation; in fact she couldn't really be sure she wasn't dreaming. She had not heard of any of the girls before doing this (not that anyone would admit it), but Betty pushed and shucked until the sheath was sticking heavy to her front. Like the proverbial wave crashing against a rocky shore, the young woman climaxed in seconds.

Writhing, Betty came off the doorknob shaking with as much fear as she was with lust.

◆　◆　◆

The Delino family had lived four generations in the red brick house until Antony Delino Fect, a distant cousin to the original owner and supposedly the only Delino living in the country now, donated the house to the college in the summer of 1995. The Delino family had amassed a sizable fortune, their money gaining the family both recognition and reputation on the east coast.

But the house quickly fell to a strange state of stasis. Not actually disrepair—with college maintenance keeping-up appearances, the school simply didn't seem to *want* the place. It was rumored that the money the Delinos had made, especially of late, had come from rather nefarious dealings (it was reported that Antony Delino Fect *had* to leave the country) and the college administration grew skittish of such a 'questionable' donation.

So the house stood quiet and uninhabited that year . . . and the next.

Stories began to be hung on the quiet Tudor like the dark shuttered windows it wore. Every new girl who passed through the tree-tunneled streets of the suburban Massachusetts college campus heard the tall tales as much as they did gossip about freshmen and teachers. In the fall of 1996 Delta-Ti-Delta, the premier sorority on campus, held their hazing ritual on the lawn of Delino House. Daring new members to take a celebratory walk through the 'haunted' house at the very end of pledge week, but by the fall of that next year, after four school seasons of this specific sorority hazing, Delta-Ti-Delta 'tired' of this new ritual. It was rumored that for the girls who had entered the house, both the pledges and older sorority sisters alike, the Delino place really 'spooked them'. All the girls reported feeling an unmistakable 'presence' in the house, even in the middle of the muted sexual mayhem and mind-numbing drinking of pledging

That October the quick cold breeze carried leaves and courage away as Delino House was more or less left to its own devices.

◆   ◆   ◆

"Shit," Betty sighed.

Settling her breathing, letting the after-shock of the quick orgasm wash through her, Betty stood back and placed her hand on the warm doorknob.

"Get a hold of yourself!" she scolded silently, managing the single step, turning the knob and pushing the door in. It made no sound as the darkness bade Betty forward.

The room was devoid of smell, the only light pouring in from the doorway Betty was framed in; the room had no windows, very much like a large walk-in closet. It was just an empty room in an old house with four high walls, a deep stained wood floor and the thick wood-beam ceiling that she had spied throughout the house.

It really was *just a room.*

Betty's breasts ached though, a heavy fullness to them as if she was getting her period. She didn't feel as frightened as she had when she had walked down the hall—certainly not as loosed in abandon as she had been with that damn doorknob!—but she was ill at ease. This dread both excited and scared her . . . because it excited her so much. As she took another step into the room she reached for and lifted the two thin parts of her sheath-dress up and off her voluptuous pale body. Having taken her cue from what she had heard of the girls before her doing, she really did regard this all as a most pagan ritual.

She only hoped she had not gotten all dressed-up—then undressed—for nothing!

◆   ◆   ◆

It wasn't until the spring of 1998 that Patty Ebberts and her twin sister Rachel ventured into the house to find what really was, if anything, living there. Their vowed 'duty' (both girls were physics majors) was to dispel rumor and reputation. Armed with video recorders and foodstuffs, the Ebberts girls planned the entire weekend; silent sexy sentinels supporting their scientific sit-in.

Patty was first into that room beyond the door at the end of the hall-way.

Rachel had turned away for the briefest of moments when Patty called to her but by the time Rachel turned her sister was slamming the door at the end of the hallway. Rachel reported (and Rachel's would be the only true accounting) hearing Patty's guttural moans beyond when she ran to and found a suddenly locked door. Forgetting her video recorder (and some would later scold, her *good common sense*), Rachel was torn whether to run for help or stay. The thinner sister stood pulling and pounding for fifteen minutes, reluctantly recognizing in Patty's pleas—though Rachel would only ever admit this to Patty!—a sexual abandon so visceral Rachel grew aroused enough herself she thought she was pissing herself in fear. Thankfully, Patty's moaning subsided as quickly as it began and the single wooden door swung open a smidgen for Rachel to dash to her sister's aid.

Rachel had stumbled into the darkness of what she could only describe as a small wooden-floored room, and like her sister—and every other girl since—she had turned to close the door behind herself for no reason she'd later understand. The next thing Rachel knew she found herself in the Pizza Hut parking lot with no further memory of her time in that room. A weeping Patty was waiting on the gravel roadway to regale her brave sister with the same experience.

It wasn't until the next night when the twins noticed the scars on their right buttock and over their left nipple that either girl would admit to the soreness in their vaginas. In the cruelest of sexual temptation, the girls were left with the knowledge that they had experienced a moment they'd never fully recall nor relive. Like a fluttering memory hovering on the peripheral of their mind's eye, the twins would agonize together and separately on what they couldn't remember.

A legend was born that night. When Betty Fect saw the Internet posting and connected the house to her relative, she knew that when she could manage the grades and was old enough, her fate lie in Massachusetts.

◆   ◆   ◆

The rush came on her so suddenly.

As her dress fell to the floor Betty felt a pushing deep in her belly, a yearning to turn and close the door. It was a palpable sense of wanting to be alone, wanting to accept, wanting to be open and ready. She felt eyes watching her, inspecting her body, like electric tendrils tap-tap-tapping her skin; her inner thighs were wet with flood, her eyes were tearing; she felt a blood madness taking her, as if she was a thing of liquid, to be thirsted upon, drunk . . . drowned in; she was frightened to her marrow for how much she wanted to release.

There was a bulbous, pulsating crotch just out of her reach . . . God, Betty could taste it! A live thing from the body that surrounded it; Betty actually brought her hands to her inner thighs and pried them apart as she stood there, willing that thick phallus to find her, Like a fleshy worm periscope the picture she conjured in her mind was nearly comical if not so dangerously seductive. How can there be such power in the world, Betty ached to understand. One second she had been standing here naked, a little cold, but breathing steady, now she was a girl unhinged.

Could she keep that door behind her open much longer?

Arching her back, Betty threw her head back and grabbed each big breast in hand, smushing her diamond point nipples through her wide fingers, kneading her flesh.

"Feast" she said in her mind, knowing fully well this thing could hear her loud and true. "Feast."

◆   ◆   ◆

The house was guarded by a small, yet efficient college security contingent and it was only on those busiest of school nights, when extracurricular activities abounded, that a girl would even try to pass onto the Delino lawn. Julia had been the last, armed as she thought best with her recorder, but it had literally cost her her sanity.

What Betty was hoping was that her lineage, her family history, would allow her a 'leg up' on her sisters before her.

Grandmomma couldn't be more specific but *those* northeast Fect's had always courted a smuggler's past; it was rumored Antony Fect's business dealings became more shady as they became more lucrative. The man had been described as odd to say the least, handsome to a fault, bearing some of the same strong facial beauty as Betty, with a thin nose, high cheekbones and dark deep-set almond-shaped eyes. But although women were attracted to the man he never took a wife and held no mistress for long enough for them to report much about his sexual proclivities.

No, Antony Fect Delino, it was said, was a man concerned only with money. It was even whispered among the family that the curly-haired man had made a pact with the devil to gain more of it.

Of course Betty's grandmomma didn't support such idle talk.

◆   ◆   ◆

"Pretty little one, close the door," the low liquid voice taunted from the dark center of the room.

At first Betty thought she was going to faint, but clutching her big breasts harder, she eased her breathing, quelled her fear and held onto the idea that here she was naked before this thing—which she had yet to accept truly as *a thing*—yet she was holding her ground. The young girl had what the wielder of this voice wanted, here deep between her wet legs, here in her heavy breasts. Sooner more than later Betty feared she'd give herself to that thick pulsing cock she could just about smell, the hot breath she could just about feel, the skill this thing possessed she was aching to know, but as of yet Betty had not closed that door behind her wide quivering ass.

Yes, Betty reasoned, her lineage might be allowing her these few extra moments a girl like Julia hadn't been privy to.

"Who are you?" Betty groaned through her thin-parted grimace.

She felt her vagina parting as she stood there, her clitoris engorging; the thing was not touching her but her body was reacting beyond her reason. She held herself tighter, the weight of her chest scaring her so much she feared that maybe they were even growing for this thing!

"I have no name," the thing teased and this time Betty swore she felt a cool breath tickle her belly.

She leaned to the source in the center of the room.

"Close it," the male voice boomed and Betty even slightly turned to the door but stopped herself in time, stood straight up, re-grabbing each breast so the pain pulled her back to what she was about.

"You cannot resist me forever," the thing said. "You need me."

"I don't need you," Betty tried, but even then she felt her will easing out of her, like a good steam heat. God, she wanted to lie down on the floor, feel the unforgiving hard wood on her full ass as she spread her legs and just let this fiend do what it would.

"Tell me what you are . . . please," Betty said.

Her eyes were adjusting to the light and she discerned a shape. It was about her height, wider if she could see right, but to her surprise, definitely human in form. The fear in her head subsided a bit; some solid ran back to her squishy body.

"In your tongue I am called a *Cambion*," the thing said and the very utterance of this word slightly cooled Betty's roiling body. She stopped kneading her breasts . . . but kept her hands on them.

"I don't understand?" she said.

Good, feeding her curiosity was keeping Betty from feeling as light-headed as she had been. She was still flooding, her nipples achingly hard, but she was focusing her mind now, feeling the cold air of the hallway behind her ass as a reminder to what was real outside of this room.

"You need to see," the Cambion said and from out of that center of darkness the thing stood tall.

For all intents and purposes he was mostly a man. Standing as tall as Betty's five foot nine height, maybe a smidgen taller, his human face was unlined and featureless, quite an unremarkable looking man in his early thirties, Betty'd guess if she didn't know better. There was no luster in what should have been tantalizing green eyes, no true purpose in his strong square chin.

Not wanting to, but loosing the battle to curiosity, Betty's gaze drifted downward.

She feared what she would see.

The creature's long neck was mottled red flesh, not scaly really, but certainly a leathery surface. Across its broad chest was a coarse plot of matte black hair, the same color as that on its head, but deep in color and texture, much like the bristles on a horse's mane. In the center of this puke of tuft hung a sight Betty could simply not get her mind around, but knew all the same what it had to be.

"In the end it was a good trade, I'd say," the naked Cambion added, noticing Betty's gaze to his ancient makeshift necklace.

Around its neck the creature wore two tiny petrified testes on a thin yellowing cord. Betty knew whose they were. What kind of a deal had her great uncle made to grant this thing residency here in this room, to rend daring young women? Were his business dealings that important that he would trade his manhood? And what dastardly machinations had this thing, this Cambion, granted her fated evil uncle?

"Jesus Christ!" Betty sighed.

"He was a man more given to money then sex," the demon continued.

"I came when he called. I am always available."

"But you don't want to know of my history, pretty little thing, you want ..." the demon continued and stood back as Betty's eyes fell involuntarily to the erection jutting out from between the Cambion's thin hairless legs.

She had yet to see a cock that beautiful, even in the few *Playgirls* she had secreted from her sister. True, Betty had never been with any men beyond Brody and that time with Jon when they had been playing a sixteen year-old version of 'show and tell' but she assumed this perfect thick erection to be a good eight and half long. Strangely enough Betty thought, for the briefest of seconds, that it wasn't as big as she had thought it might be from all the tales told about the sensation the girls felt afterward ... but God it was a great looking cock.

But then a clutching fear hit her even deeper than any had before. The Cambion's skill, its evil brute power was what rent girls not only sore and wanting but forgetful. This was a thing not of the clean 'play-by-the-rules' world outside. This was a creature sporting a supremely aesthetic member but more dangerously, a demon's lust and skill.

"It will not hurt, but you will ache," the Cambion assured and it was then that Betty saw both the thing's middle fingers. They were flattened, wide, and sizzling for Christ's sake! The Cambion noticed her gaze lifting and smiled his thin red lips.

"One for your tit, one for your ass, to leave my mark," the thing explained. "Your memory will not allow much else, even one as strong as you."

"Why?" Betty asked but even then knew she was loosing control.

She feared the thing's hands more then its cock. They were so alien to her and therefore so unclean, like freed reptilian things, slithering and repulsive to her very sensibilities as woman and human. It unnerved her to look at them, but she couldn't turn her gaze away even with that fantastic cock wagging below her.

"I need to know," Betty pleaded, but even then felt her knees quivering. She was trying to stop herself but she could feel her body twisting even then so she could reach behind her for the door.

She could just shut the door and not see those wet fingers.

"You will not remember anyway," the Cambion said and took another step to her.

Betty looked down at the clipping sound and saw the thing's three-toed blunted feet. The Cambion's large erection was just touching her bare thighs now!

"Please, tell me more of what you are," she pleaded as she turned. "Please."

This close Betty could feel the heat off the thing; she dared not look down at that jumping cock below her. She eased herself to face fully forward, steeling all of her nerve to face the thing head on and know it . . . if it would tell her. She had now been in here longer looking at this thing, standing before her, then any girl had been before; would that help her remember?

She needed to remember?

"Sweet Betty *Fect*, it will just make you miss me all the more," the Cambion snickered and Betty fell to the floor.

The thing could read her mind.

"Yes, I know who you are, little pretty one," the thing seethed over her.

Betty was terrified. The trump in her stunted juvenile deck was in keeping her identity, her lineage secret . . . and her thoughts to herself.

"Yes, your blood has allowed you to get this far," the thing over her sneered and Betty looked up, though she feared doing so. Damning her senses for it, she began to salivate for the thick erection bouncing just above her bent head.

Betty could not get up from her supplicant spot under that swaying cock as much as she didn't want to. Reaching up for it she grabbed the alive warm thing in both hands as the Cambion groaned.

"Yes," the thing cooed from above her. Betty leaned back her head and opened her mouth as wide as her lips could stretch.

"Anyway you like, little pretty one," the thing cooed and Betty pulled at the warm thick shaft, stretching the sweet warm flesh to a fraction away from her lips. Scooting her behind down hard, she opened her legs, rolling her pelvis forward, attempting to smush her fat squishy clit to the wooden floor, planting herself in that impossible dark of the room and her mind.

"This will be a first for you young girls," the thing jested and Betty began to cry with the realization that she was so lost now and needed so deeply. She stuck out her tongue to lap at the head of this creature's hardness.

"History is a demanding teacher," the demon continued, standing as still as stone, willing the girl below him to begin her complete submission.

Poised with the big round head in her two fists, feeling the hot tears streaming down her face, the hot juices out her vagina, Betty looked up and smelled smoke and opened her lips even wider to accommodate.

It was then that she noticed the door to the room was still open . . .

"A small matter," the Cambion said. "Close . . .

"No," Betty moaned, sitting back away from that fleshy trunk in her fists.

The slanted bit of light, the cold air from the hallway, her knowledge of what this thing had revealed it was; Betty *knew* that there was a world outside that door and this thing, this Cambion (whatever the hell that was) could not venture into it. She knew. She knew. She kn . . .

In the Cambion's priapismic pride, in its tease for this 'unique' oral copulation, in equating Betty with all the girls before, it just assumed Betty would simply shut the door just before she took him in her sweet soft mouth. The demon could not perform until she did, until he truly had secreted the girl in this room and Betty, like all her contemporaries, had to be the one to close the door.

Betty had no way of knowing what the ritual was that this demon had secured with her uncle all those many years ago. In exchange for acute business acumen and unprecedented wealth Fect had assured the Cambion this one single room in his house. He had allowed the demon to castrate him to show his loyalty and sexual disregard but the Cambion, being a great wanderer of the earth, the half-human half-animal offspring of a succubus and male was bound by the deals he struck. Fect had assured the creature he would have plenty of human females for his picking (the private girls' college was just down the road, for Christsakes!) but he made the Cambion promise not to leave this room. Only the creature's supernatural sexual animus (aided by Fect's very manhood around his neck) could send out a scent.

The Cambion was a patient creature and had waited; his picking, while few, had been wonderfully nubile and spry with those who had come so far.

But, the demon could not perform until that door was shut, until he truly had secreted the girl in this room completely and *she* had to be the one to close the door.

Betty sensed all this, if not the particulars. The thing's massive penis released from her hands, it brushed her legs as she stood.

"I will remember," she said, keeping her distance from the thing. If she had been strong enough she would have reached down for her dress; as it was let the bastard get his last look at what is denied him, she thought.

"It will be worse Betty Fect," the creature said. He was still raging, hard, glistening, and dangerous if she got too close, but Betty could sense some of his seductive strength dissipating. "Your longing will be worse, little pretty one."

"Read my mind all you want, you fuck," she thought hard, looking at the creature, "you will not have me."

"Do you think you will be able to live the rest of your days not knowing?" the thing said. "Even the others sense me in their dreams. Their memories won't allow what you have seen and will now want for the rest of your days. Do you think your puny males will ever be able to satisfy you now that you have seen, touched, me?"

The Cambion stood back then, into the darkness of the room, deliberately obscuring its face and body until all Betty could see were the tops of its knees and its perfect huge cock bouncing there in the light; it retreated into a darkness of its own making she knew, not the darkness this room held. Betty stared at that erection for a very long time, wanting it, aching deep in her belly for the sensation of having it in her, but she didn't move.

"The rest of your days, pretty little one," the Cambion whispered. "The rest of your days, you will wonder."

•   ◆   •

Tammy's cell rang as she sat with Jill in the Pizza Hut parking lot. Smiling in her shock the tall red head steered her lime green Echo out of the gravel lot giggling with Jill all the way back to their dorm.

•   ◆   •

"You just have to believe what I say," Betty regaled her two best friends as they sat huddled in her attic room.

Nobody but Jill and Tammy knew about Betty's outing, the prevailing thought being that the fewer people who knew if you were planning a trip into Delino House the better. And though Betty still wasn't sure how many she would tell about her experience, she'd share what she could with her two best friends now.

"It's the half-human offspring of either a succubus or incubus mating," Tammy said from the computer screen. She had logged on the minute Betty began telling her tale of what the thing called itself.

"Or it's a real guy with a huge cock that hides out to fuck girls' brains out."

"Could be that too," Tammy agreed and they all laughed.

"Whatever the hell it was, it was kinda sad," Betty agreed and Tammy turned from the computer screen to look over at the girl with the wide eyes, as did Jill.

"I mean, just standing there waiting, the anticipation must be almost too much to bear."

"And you didn't even give him a piece," Jill coughed and the trio laughed again.

But Betty Fect knew she had given the Cambion her curiosity and in a way that was worse then giving up her loins. As sure as she knew she was sitting there with her two best friends, her Pearl Jam T-shirt and thick blue sweats covering her body, Betty knew that there was a supernatural thing living there in Delino House. And she knew that she would be venturing back to again meet that thing in that room. The creature had been right: "the rest of your days you will wonder."

There were so many questions one could ask of a creature like a Cambion. Betty wanted answers to who Antony Fect Delino was and how he had come by this creature that now occupied his house. And she wanted another chance to stand in the light from that open doorway, face a darkness not of this world and ache for what she knew sooner or later she had to break down and give herself to.

JIMMY STICKS AND THE OUTLAW CRITTER OF DOOM
Michael Boatman

Jimmy "Sticks" Bohannon broke the surface of Lake Michigan just after 9:00 PM. He staggered the last few steps toward shore, dragged himself up onto the pebble-strewn sandscape of Oak Street Beach, along Chicago's "Little *Riviera*," fell to his knees, and puked his guts out.

Beneath the fat Midwestern moon, Jimmy hawked up three gallons of lake water, a half-pound of sediment, six teeth, one shredded condom: X-tra large and ribbed for maximum enjoyment, and two feet of his own intestines.

"Jee . . . sssus," Jimmy breathed. It was the first utterance of his dark new life. It was also remarkably similar to the last utterance of what he would soon come to think of as his "old life." "What's . . . happening . . . to . . . me?"

As if in answer to his query, a bright flare of—

PAIN

—*something* erupted in his head. It wasn't a physical pain so much as *psychic* distress, a remembrance of agonies too vast to fit into the decayed hard drive that was rebooting itself behind his eyes: See, Jimmy Sticks was beyond pain in the traditional sense, at least any kind of pain he'd ever understood.

Still—

HURTS

—*something* was gnawing at the insides of his skull like a rabid badger on crystal meth.

Jimmy reached up with one extremely long fingernail and poked at a spot between his eyes, the area from whence the ghost pain signal seemed to emanate the strongest.

His fingertip punched through skin-crust, plunged through the ugly hole in the center of his skull and into the soft meat of his brain. To say that Jimmy was confused was like saying Naomi Campbell had anger issues: both insufficient and unsavory.

Jimmy's forefinger hooked something hard, unyielding in that perforated jellybowl of fish-gnawed graymeat goodness, hooked it and *pulled*. As the hard knot moved through his cracked brain-box, a flood of memories came with it.

I love you, Jimmy!

Miyoko!

Somebody shoot this bitch before I puke.

A shock-surge of memory punched Jimmy in the lower 'taint. He tugged harder at the thing in his brain.

And . . . *Chink Bitch hits the water with a huge splash!*

Haw. Haw. Haw.

Ouch! That's a Two from the French judge!

The hard knot fell out of Jimmy's head and hit the sand with a soft 'plink.' Jimmy looked down: A bullet lay between his splayed finger bones like a smashed miniature beer can. The slug had pancaked after blasting through the failed bulwark of Jimmy's skull. Now it glittered like a nugget of tainted starlight upon the oblong shelf of stone atop which he knelt.

And Jimmy remembered it all.

He and Miyoko had gone out to dinner to celebrate their wedding anniversary: Twelve years of happiness that a two-bit jazz drummer and a struggling graphic artist had little right to expect. They'd just exited *Nolane's*, Miyoko's favorite French-Asian-Cuban fusion place, and decided to take a moonlit stroll along the Miracle Mile.

As they'd wandered down Michigan Avenue, a black BMW loaded with glowing skull-masked teenagers approached, the occupants' howls accompanying electric piano and heavy bass guitar: a 'techno' remix of the Doors' *Riders on the Storm* droned from the luxury sound system.

"Trick or treeeeeaat!" one of the luminous skulls shrieked, his laughter scaling up into a maniac wail as the BMW thundered past. Jimmy and Miyoko had laughed at the daffy bastards and made their way toward Millennium Park, arms entwined against the crisp autumn deadwind blowing off the Lake, as deeply in love as they would ever be in their short, happy life together. They'd barely crossed into the park when three men stepped out of the darkness, grabbed Miyoko and put a hunting knife to Jimmy's throat.

"Well look at this," one of the men, a stocky blond, snarled. A large strawberry birthmark in the shape of an arrowhead covered the right side of his face. "Blackboy and his trusty chink sidekick out for an evening sabbatical."

The other two men were a study in contrasts. One, a hulking, heavily-tattooed brute, sported a head like a mutated pink bowling ball. The smaller one affected a long brown ponytail, bad teeth and shitty mustache.

They laughed like the good beta males they undoubtedly were and took turns kicking the shit out of Jimmy. Then Arrowhead and Signor Mustache dragged Miyoko off into the darkness while Bowling Ball sat on Jimmy's chest and pounded his head against the pavement.

After a century in Hell, Arrowhead and Signor Mustache returned, dragging Miyoko, her clothing ripped and bloodied, by her hair.

"Gotta compliment you on your taste, my *brothuh*," Arrowhead sneered. "Crouchin' Tiger here's got a great rack."

"Yeah," Signor Mustache giggled, zipping up his fly. "Nice shitcutter, for a cum dumpster."

This comment elicited gales of laughter from the three thugs. Meanwhile, Jimmy tried to stand up. Unfortunately, his right leg was broken in three places.

"Hey, I *like* that jacket," Bowling Ball rumbled. "Looks like my size."

He'd stripped the black leather coat, a birthday present from Miyoko, from Jimmy's back. It slid, with a hard, tearing sound over his massive shoulders. He turned toward Signor Mustache. "Well?"

"Looks good," Signor Mustache said.

"You really think so?"

"Yeah. 'Specially in the shoulders."

"Thanks."

"Hey, *faggots*," Arrowhead snarled. "If you're finished with the fashion show, let's do 'em and dump 'em. There's a Whopper with my name on it waitin' at Mickey Dee's."

Signor Mustache snickered, "They got the Whopper at Burger King, Lonnie."

"You wanna shut your shit-dribbler, Leon," Arrowhead snapped. "Or I'll shut it *for* ya."

They'd driven to the Michigan Avenue Bridge. At nearly three o'clock in the morning the Miracle Mile was free of potential rescuers. Bowling Ball and Signor Mustache propped the Bohannons against the railing. Then Arrowhead pulled a silver Smith & Wesson nine-millimeter automatic.

"Hold 'em still, douchebags!"

Jimmy fought then. Bucking and rearing like a bull with its nuts in a bear trap, he'd managed to smash Bowling Ball's nose with the back of his head. Bowling Ball squealed like a girl scout who has discovered her favorite hamster floating facedown in the toilet.

"Oooeeee! Fuck!"

Signor Mustache kicked Jimmy in the balls. Arrowhead did something . . . *wet* to Miyoko, and *that* was when she gasped, and cried out in a surprised, *hurt* kind of way, "I love you, Jimmy!"

"Miyoko!"

"Somebody shoot this bitch before I puke," Signor Mustache griped.

Arrowhead complied. The shot echoed out over the river, hiccupping between the Wrigley Building and her younger, uglier stepsister, the Chicago Tribune Building. Then they threw Miyoko's body off the bridge.

"And . . . Chink Bitch hits the water with a *huge* splash!" Arrowhead crowed.

"Haw. Haw. *Haw*," Bowling Ball laughed, the sound somehow strangled and honking through his busted schnozz.

"That's a Two from the French judge!" This from Signor Mustache; he of the ponytail and punch-fucked facial grill.

"Kill you!" Jimmy snarled. "SweartoGodIllkillyouuu!"

Arrowhead laid the barrel of his nine-millimeter against Jimmy's forehead. "Look out, Leslie," he said to Bowling Ball. "I don't want to get Blackboy's brains on that fine leather car coat."

Jimmy Bohannon had a moment to think, *Jesus, this is it.*

Then a bright red flash.

Then darkness.

Now, Jimmy Sticks looked up from the bullet that lay between his rotting knuckles, a howl of fury boiling up from his rotted guts.

That was when he saw the possum.

The minute he laid eye on it (He only had one. The other one had been eaten by a trout) he knew it was no *ordinary* Possum. For starters, it was black. Jimmy had lived his entire life in the Midwest and never seen a pitch-black opossum of the variety that regarded him from the branch of a nearby maple: gray, brown, and on one sad but memorable occasion *hairless*, but never black.

The black possum was bigger than your run of the mill tree-rat too; its rippling musculature suggesting a capacity for branch-clinging and telephone line-scampering that would have sent Satan's Own Monkey Brigade whimpering to their dens. The three-inch long claws on the ends of its paws, however, made it plain that line-scampering was the last thing the black possum was about.

Its eyes were even weirder; lucid black pools, obsidian orbs that fairly throbbed with force. Dark gravity. *Power.*

"*Vengeance,*" that force whispered. "*Blood for blood.*"

"What . . . do . . . you . . . want?" Jimmy croaked, his voice a ragged rasp. "Where's . . . Mi . . . yo . . . ko?"

"*I can give you peace,*" the force inside the possum whispered. "*Would you have justice?*"

"Miiyokooo . . ."

But Miyoko was dead. And, as far as Jimmy Bohannon knew, so was he. The men who had murdered them, however, were free to stalk the night, pouring ruin down upon the innocent like venereal thunderheads pregnant with gonorrhea rain. Jimmy could *feel* them out there. He could *taste* their laughter, like acid smoke carried on a burning wind.

"Jus . . . tice . . ." Jimmy Sticks rasped. "For . . . Miyoo . . . ko."

The black possum spread its arms, and Jimmy saw the final difference: Gray sheets of skin unfurled from beneath its limbs; red-veined membranes stretched from the undersides of the possum's wrists to the sides of its tiny rear paws.

Wings, Jimmy Sticks thought. *It's got wings.*

The Black Possum reared up from its perch, its eyes blazing with that terrible force. Then it leaped into the air and flew into the night, gliding toward the dark sprawl of the South Side.

Jimmy Sticks lurched after it.

◆   ◆   ◆

He'd seen the movie a dozen times.

He and Miyoko had rented it only a few weeks before their anniversary. It was one of his favorites: the one where mobsters killed Bruce Lee's kid and rape-murdered his innocent but hot young wife.

But Bruce Lee's kid had returned from the grave as an ass-kicking in-vulnerable super-wraith; a knife-wielding, shotgun-jacking, pistol-packin' kung-fu boogie bastard with a hard-on for Justice: all of this cinematic *uber*-bluster brought to you by a supernaturally sentient blackbird. Jimmy had memorized every line.

But the movie got it wrong.

The creature that soared above him, carried aloft on leathern wings was no crow, raven or giant golden eagle, but it was a scary little motherfucker nonetheless. And powerful: Jimmy Sticks was dead, but he was *alive* too. His bones showed through his mottled, rotten flesh; he would never star in any movie that didn't have ". . . *of the Living Dead*" featured prominently in its title.

But he was getting stronger.

As the Possum banked over the rooftops of the sleeping city, Jimmy fol-lowed, long dreadlocks flying as he leaped across chasms that would have claimed the boldest crackheads. His waterlogged leather boots made barely a sound as they hit, darted forward and sprang into space.

Barely an hour after his resurrection, the Possum touched down in an alley behind a bar just off Cicero.

The back door of the bar was emblazoned with a huge shamrock. Perched above the shamrock was a rosy-cheeked leprechaun with a pot of gold under its ass. The name above the lintel read, *Dougal's Irish Pot.* Despite the artist's best intentions, the leprechaun appeared to be taking the most expensive dump in the history of Irish alcoholism; the fabled "Pot" a receptacle for a shower of shimmering golden fecal flakes.

The air here tasted like one of Jimmy Bohannon's murderers: cheap tobacco and second-hand motor oil. It rang with the sound of the killer's laughter.

Sheer homicidal rage rose up from what was left of Jimmy's balls. He growled, reached for the doorknob . . . and wrenched it out of its socket.

The dead man lifted the mangled brass doorknob up to his good eye and rasped appreciatively. Inhuman strength ran like electrical current through his bones. The ropes of decayed muscle that hung from his frame vibrated with black power that had nothing to do with his daddy's membership in the NAACP.

Jimmy Sticks drew back his right foot to batter down the door. Then the Black Possum hissed. Jimmy Sticks froze, mid-kick. The Possum hung by its tail from the arm of a nearby lamppost, its obsidian eyes radiating that weird force.

Patience

And in a crackling burst of rodent telepathy Jimmy Sticks understood. In his present state he'd cause a riot the moment he burst through the door. Even twenty drunken Irishmen were bound to notice the revivified corpse of a dead black jazz drummer backflipping across the bar. Miyoko's murderer might escape in the confusion.

Jimmy Sticks slithered beneath a parked SUV and fixed one dead white eye upon the front door of *Dougal's Irish Pot*, dreaming dead dreams of love and vengeance.

Miyoko.

Sometime before midnight, the front door of the bar swung open and eight partiers tumbled out, laughing, screaming with mock terror. One of the two women in the group wore a white wedding dress stained with red. A fake butcher's knife protruded from her ironing board-flat chest.

The other woman resembled a 1970's Midnight Shock Cinema queen; black Tina Turner fright wig, purple eyeshadow, rouge and lipstick, a skimpy black dress contrasting a peaches & cream complexion and tits that jiggled like the ass-cheeks of a panicked white rhino.

One of the men wore a Chicago Cubs uniform with the name *M.C. Gravy* stenciled across the shoulders. M.C. Gravy carried a baseball bat casually over his right shoulder.

Every once in a while, he would swing the bat in big, wavy circles around his head as if he were stepping up to the plate at Comiskey Park, not standing in front of a white trash Irish juke joint in the middle of the night.

The biggest of the men stood nearly six-foot-seven, his identity hidden beneath a life-like George W. Bush mask. He was also wearing Jimmy Bohannon's black leather coat.

Miyoko's coat.

Jimmy Sticks wondered at the mask the big man wore. The women's clothing seemed *unnatural,* somehow out of synch with what he remembered from his pre-mortem existence. He struggled with that wrongness, frozen beneath the SUV, while his busted synapses sizzled like Puppy Chow on an old man's hot plate.

The Possum chattered into that meaty confusion.

Jimmy Sticks spasmed as the streetlamp in front of *Dougal's* flickered; a Morse code flutter of illumination. The fog of fatality that enshrouded his thoughts began to lift. Mental faculties that had gone slushy in the meat-locker of Death's Diner of Damnation unlocked the doors, flipped on the lights and fired up the big gas grills.

It's Halloween.

Halloween. Exactly one year since he and Miyoko were murdered; 365 days since he'd been dumped like a hot stool sample into the Chicago River. *Hal-o'-friggin'-ween.*

"Gooood," he snarled.

Jimmy Sticks shot out from under the SUV like black tar squirted from the depths of Lucifer's bowels. He didn't leap up onto the sidewalk beneath the flickering streetlamp so much as *congeal* there.

"Look at *this* asshole," M.C. Gravy sneered.

'George W. Bush' turned toward Jimmy Sticks.

"Nice costume," he grunted.

Hey, I like that jacket. Looks like my size.

Jimmy Sticks whirled, and punched 'George W. Bush' in the side of the head. 'George W. Bush' flew face-first though the plate glass window of the bakery that sat next door to *Dougal's.* The sounds of shattering glass and a tripped burglar alarm pierced the night.

Shock Cinema Slut screamed. M.C. Gravy and the third man, a big biker type with a long red beard, moved on Jimmy Sticks. The biker pulled a bowie knife from the leather sheath strapped to his right thigh.

"I'm gonna cut you bad, asshole," he said.

At the same time, M.C. Gravy feinted to the left and swung his bat at Jimmy Sticks's head, or at least where Jimmy Sticks's head *should* have been: Jimmy Sticks had collapsed into a pile of bones and rotting flesh.

Shock Cinema Slut screamed again.

"Shut up, Britney!" M.C. Gravy snapped.

The biker and M.C. Gravy leaned curiously over the bubbling sack of cadaver *con carne.*

"Is that *teeth* in there?" Biker said. "What *is* that shit?"

"Damned if I know," M.C. Gravy shrugged.

The two men leaned in closer, and the flesh, the rancid, liquefying necroplasm that was all that remained of Jimmy Bohannon's body, spewed up like the ejaculate from a masturbating cyclops, smashed through the biker's front teeth and shoved itself down his throat.

"Donnie!" M.C. Gravy yelled.

Shock Cinema Slut stopped screaming and bolted, her high heels clicking away into the night. M.C. Gravy dropped the baseball bat and fled, the sight he would carry to his grave seared into the meat of his eyeballs: Donnie, choking and kicking as the six foot long flesh worm forced its way down his throat. His long red hair was braiding itself into dreadlocks, his skin turning first brown then grayish black.

Donnie the Biker's boots thrummed against the concrete for nearly half a minute. Then he lay still.

The bloody bride shimmied up to where Donnie lay, the handle of the fake butcher knife bouncing against her chest like a wayward hard-on.

"Donnie, honey?" the bride whispered. "You okay?"

Donnie opened his eyes and sat up.

The bloody bride, whose real name was Sheila Dumbrowski, hawked mystery meat 'nuggets' at the cafeteria of the Richard J. Daley Forensic Hospital For The Homicidally Incensed. Sheila knew what madness looked like; as a longtime food-service provider to Chicago's ambulatory fruit basket community, she'd seen it in the eyes of many a fucked-up customer as they slobbered over their Thorazine fish-sticks.

But Donnie's eyes were the worst.

Because they weren't Donnie's eyes anymore.

The thing that had once been her boyfriend Donnie but was now a horrible amalgam of Donnie and a dead percussionist, stood up. Donnie was six-foot-four on a *short* day. Now he *towered* over her, his face a black rictus of rage, cheekbones protruding from his ripped flesh like twin white tongue guards, his shattered chest heaving from the exertion of his transfiguration.

Sheila remained absolutely still beneath the burning eye of insanity. Her time spent in that luscious realm had inured her to the panic that might have crippled a weaker woman: panic would only draw the madness to her. It would laugh as she fell, screaming, beneath Death's iron heel. It would pee its pants while she bled real blood. Instead, Sheila watched as Death bent over and scooped up M.C. Gravy's baseball bat.

'George W. Bush' came barreling out of the window of the bakery, his berserker's scream muffled by the rubber mask that still hid his real face, the studded brass knuckles on his massive right fist promising to take Jimmy Sticks on a one-way ride to Torture Town. He ripped the mask off as he came.

Bowling Ball.

Jimmy Sticks turned and took a hard shot to the jaw. Bones snapped, flesh ripped, and his newly acquired lower lip flew across the street and hit the windshield of an '87 Volkswagen Beetle. The lip hung there for a moment, clinging to the glass like a pink/black slug. Then it slid down the windshield on a tiny river of blood and spit.

Bowling Ball swung a brass-bound haymaker toward Jimmy Sticks's right cheek. There was a wet 'splat' of metal-on-flesh-on-bone, and Jimmy Sticks's right eye bounced out of its socket. It dangled on his cheek, rolling and glaring at Bowling Ball like a witch's curse.

"You ain't so tough," Bowling Ball said, raising his hands. "In fact, you ain't nothin' at . . ."

And that was *all* he said, because Jimmy Sticks's right eye shot forward on its stalk and wrapped itself around his throat. Jimmy Sticks braced himself, took one step backward . . . and his elongated eyestalk swung Bowling Ball around in a wide, staggering circle and slammed him head-first into a nearby fire hydrant—

Bam. Bam. *Bam.*

—until his skull gave way with a rotten-melon *smush.*

After that, Bowling Ball simmered right down.

Sheila Dumbrowski took to her heels while Jimmy Sticks removed his leather jacket from Bowling Ball's shuddering shoulders and shrugged it on. Then he beat on Bowling Ball with the baseball bat until what was left looked like a smashed watermelon in a cheap Brooks Brothers knock off.

Above them, the Black Possum chattered its dark litany of death and revenge.

◆   ◆   ◆

Signor Mustache had just shot his ex-wife's dog when the smell of Death crept over the back fence.

"What the hell is that stink?" he said to the canine corpse at his feet. "You fart, you useless piece of crap?"

He kicked the Rottweiler in his disgust and shot it again for good measure. He'd climbed Tiffany's back fence a few minutes earlier, violating a restraining order, hoping to throw a good scare into the bitch, maybe grab a shotgun handjob in the bargain.

She'd recently remarried: some schmo from *Des Moines*, fer Christ's sake. But the schmo had money and lots of it from what Signor Mustache (whose real name was Leon Van Sweringen) could gather. The house into which he was about to break had to run a cool mil. Maybe two.

Leon stepped over the dead Rottweiler. Any man who trusted the security of his property to a dog like that had to be a first rate *numero uno* Assholio Supremo. Leon preferred Akitas: Japanese hunting/guarding dogs. They weren't as solid as the Rotties, but they were mean little shits if you abused 'em right. Rottweilers were passé.

He moved toward the darkened mansion that sat at the front of the yard. It was an ancient colonial, recently remodeled, with four, maybe five bedrooms. He could smell fresh paint even from where he stood.

"Lah dee friggin' *dah*," he sneered.

Leon pulled on his ski mask and crept toward the back door. He'd brought along his favorite tools: files, knife, rope, rape kit, (with condoms and plenty of handi-wipes) and Vera, his favorite automatic. He could just see his ex-wife's face as he forced her to watch him kick the crap out of the schmo. Hell, maybe he'd kill 'em both: Leon was feeling generous tonight.

The gleam of silver and chrome caught his eye. Leon looked over at the driveway and froze.

"Holy . . . *shit*."

It was a Silver Shadow.

A Rolls Royce Silver Shadow. The car sat, perched in the moonlight like a big-tittied blonde who has just won the Illinois Super Jackpot.

"The King of Kings," Leon whispered. "You gotta be greasin' me."

He approached the Silver Shadow like a man in a dream, heedless of the shadow that dropped from the trees behind him, how it watched him from the darkness. Leon had dreamed of this car since he was old enough to realize he'd never be able to afford one.

He touched the front fender gently, almost fearfully, a high priest stroking the nipples of a menstruating war goddess. He brushed the skin of the hood, ran his hands over its shining contours with something like lust in his eyes. He bent down, laid his cheek on the hood of the car: he might have raped it if he'd known how to get the gas cap off.

"Ooohh, you little junkyard *whore*," Leon whispered.

It took him less than twenty seconds to jimmy the door, another thirty to get his clothes off and slide, naked and shivering, into the driver's seat. The feel of the cool leather seat on his nude buttocks ranked among the finest experiences of his life. The sensation of the leather-wrapped steering wheel in his fists made him shiver, and the pink invader between his skinny thighs slithered into wakefulness.

"You hot little twat," Leon hissed, fingering the leather knobs on the steering wheel while grinding himself against the seat. "You like that? Huh, bitch? Tell . . . daddy you . . . like . . . ."

He was three strokes away from a Red Letter Day when the asshole in the stupid Halloween rig stepped into the moonlight.

"Hey, shithead," Leon said, Vera in his free hand with a speed that was almost supernatural. "What the hell are you lookin' at?"

The big intruder didn't answer. He just stood there, half-illuminated by the autumn moon. Leon had to admit, the getup was good, even a little scary. He wondered how the intruder managed to make the phony eye hanging down from the mask's eye socket roll and glare at him.

"Nice costume, dickbreath," Leon said. "Very realistic. Now why don't you bugger off and leave a guy to enjoy the fruits of his labor?"

No answer.

Leon was starting to get scared. And when Leon got scared, Leon got mad: the way the guy was just standing there, head tilted, as if he was listening to a distant voice only he could hear. And that goddamn dangling eyeball tracking his every movement . . .

That's just goddamn creepy is what that is.

"Hey, shithead," Leon said. He got out of the car and pointed Vera at the shadowy figure. "What are you, deaf as well as queer? I said clear off."

Then the big intruder stepped forward and Leon started to laugh.

"Les? Is that you?"

The guy in the mask cocked his head sideways, as if listening to that distant voice again.

"Jesus," Leon breathed. He stooped and grabbed his underpants off the driveway and shrugged them on. "I almost popped a cap in your stupid Irish ass," Leon chuckled. "If I hadn't recognized that jacket you lifted off that porch monkey last year I would'a drilled ya good, ya stupid son-of-a-bitch. What the hell're you doin' out here?"

The big intruder moved forward, lurching like a cheap 1950's movie robot. Leon had a moment to think, *That smell. It's coming from Leslie.*

Then: *That ain't Leslie.*

Instinct kicked in a moment later. Leon lifted Vera and pulled the trigger an instant before the barrel punched through Jimmy Sticks's chest. The first shot bounced off Jimmy's ribcage and blasted part of his spine out through his upper back: chunks of spinal column smacked the white backboard of the basketball hoop in the neighbor's driveway.

The second and third shots went high and wild; Leon's gun hand was stuck in the hole his first shot had made. One bullet struck a passing goose on the wing. The lonely goose, mortally wounded, fell out of the sky with a despondent squawk.

On the ground, Jimmy Sticks grabbed Leon's balls and ripped them off. Leon screamed. He took two staggering steps toward the Silver Shadow, clutching the gushing crater where his nuts had been, his eyes wide with horror.

"Why?" he whispered.

The dark figure lifted his manhood, dripping, into the moonlight, and rasped, "That's . . . Two . . . from . . . the . . . French judge."

Leon's eyes grew even wider.

"You!" he whispered. "But . . . we *killed* you. You and . . . and . . ."

"Mi . . . yo . . . koooo," Jimmy Sticks moaned.

Then something flew out of the night and attacked Leon, a black furry animal of some kind. It moved like a whirlwind, burrowed under his chin, ripping at his throat and his face with long sharp claws, tearing at his eyes. Leon opened his mouth to scream and the Possum tore his tongue out.

He fell, spewing red across the windshield of the Silver Shadow, and the Possum ravaged him like a streak of black lightning, clawing at his flesh, gnawing his bones with such savagery that his face was reduced to a smoking ruin.

Jimmy Sticks shut the door. He watched as the Silver Shadow jumped and rocked back and forth on its wheels. He watched as the interior of the Rolls Royce turned red and various organs smacked against the windows. Then he opened the door and let the vicious little bastard out.

Jimmy Sticks reached into the mess on the front seat. Two minutes later, he'd replaced the parts he'd lost to Leon's bullet. Meanwhile the Black Possum licked its paws.

One more, the Possum said, its muzzle dripping red.

Then the final darkness.

◆   ◆   ◆

Lonnie LaFleur was just about to skull-pop the rich bitch from Birney when the screaming started. Birney was a skidmark suburb an hour west of Chicago, home to Big Eagle Country: the crown turd in the Seven Stars Amusement Parks crap-chain.

The rich bitch and some of her rich-bitch girlfriends had staggered up to the Big Eagle Nosh Nest, dressed (respectively), as a Sexy Witch, a Sexy Nurse, a Sexy Librarian and Pope Benedict the 16th. They'd demanded candied apples and popcorn. Lonnie obliged them, filling their buckets while eying them over the counter.

None of the girls was a day over sixteen, and in their tight costumes, 'belly shirts' and 'hot pants,' every one of the little whores was asking for it and Lonnie told them so.

"You're *disgusting,*" the Sexy Witch (the blond one with the nose job, of course) snapped. "My father is Charles Devereaux, *freak,*" she hissed, whipping out her cell phone. "I'm calling him right . . . frickin' . . . *now.*"

"He's not even *cute,*" the Sexy Nurse lisped through her braces. "What's with that goofy birthmark?"

"Yeah," Pope Benedict chirped. "Nice leprosy, shit-for-brains."

The rich girls laughed. Lonnie reached under the counter for his gun.

Charles Devereaux was the billionaire CEO of Seven Stars USA, the corporation that fronted Big Eagle Country. He was also a notorious ball-buster, and the star of the hit reality TV sex show, *'Hey, America: Go F--k Yourself!'*

It was just Lonnie's luck that Devereaux was hosting his bitch daughter's sixteenth birthday/Halloween bash at the Park tonight: two hundred of

Jennifer's closest sycophants, each and every one of them the demonspawn of some corporate asshole or assholette.

Lonnie drew a bead on the Sexy Librarian. The girls had all turned their backs on him, gawking as Jennifer poured out her horror to Lonnie's boss. It was well after midnight and this part of the Park was empty: he could off the three losers, abduct Jen at gunpoint, do her in his pickup, dump her body along I95 and be at Burger King before they opened at sunrise.

"Oh, girrllls," he sang, his finger on the trigger.

That's when everyone started screaming.

◆ ◆ ◆

After the forty-mile forced lunge up from Chicago, Jimmy Sticks looked like Hell. The energies that powered him were as puissant as ever; his eyes fairly burned with the fever of the animated damned.

His remaining human parts, however, had been beaten to a gristly frazzle during his quest for vengeance. What shambled through the employee entrance to Big Eagle Country looked like motivated road-kill on a hot summer day.

But the Possum had summoned reinforcements.

Seven bitter *mariachi* players from the 'How America *Really* Won The West' show grumbled past Jimmy Sticks on their way to the employee parking lot. Most of them ignored the obviously fake zombie with the glowing red eyeball on his chest, but a few of them fell to their knees and vomited: as bad as Jimmy Sticks looked, he *smelled* like a garlic-infused bowel movement on moldy onion loaf.

Only the bass player, Oscar Corvado, recognized the danger for what it was. Corvado saw the Possum perched on the dead man's shoulder, and the roiling carpet of gray forms writhing in his wake.

Let the *gringos* in their stinking white funhole deal with *el muerto caminando,* the walking dead man, Corvado shrugged. Then they'd understand how the West was *really* won.

Jimmy Sticks cut a wide swath through dozens of stoned and/or drunken teenagers. The Black Possum chittered into what was left of his right ear, drowning out the screams of upper middle-class teen horror. The heaving ocean of squealing gray bodies that surged behind him was growing hungrier by the moment: many of the party-goers would be carted away with multiple bites that night.

Jimmy Sticks took a hard left past the Heartland-America Chinese Railroad Workers Exhibit, staggered across Native-American Memorial Parade Way, and stopped just in time to see 'Arrowhead' aiming his gun at the Pope.

Jennifer Devereaux and her friends took one look at Jimmy Sticks and shrieked. His body was crawling with rats, some as big as their mothers' Shar

Peis. They dropped their candied apples and bolted into the night, followed by nearly four-hundred angry vermin. For her birthday present, Jenni-Lynne Devereaux would receive seven different strains of rabies and one bitch of a yeast infection.

Lonnie LaFleur and Jimmy Sticks squared off. There were no dramatic speeches, no declarations from man or monster. In many ways, Lonnie was as much a predator as Jimmy Sticks: he instinctively recognized the monster that had come to kill him.

"Mother . . . *fucker*," he whispered. Then he shot Jimmy Sticks in the face. His first shot shattered the creature's lower jaw and right cheek. His second shot tore a chunk out of Jimmy Sticks's throat. His third and fourth shots took out the nose and blew off the top of Jimmy Sticks's head.

Jimmy Sticks kept coming.

"*Motherfucker*," Lonnie chanted, squeezing off a shot with each breath. "Mother . . . *fucker*."

To his credit, he didn't stop shooting until his gun was empty. Then Jimmy Sticks grabbed him, shoved his finger bones up Lonnie's nostrils and *pulled*. Lonnie shrieked as the top half of his face came off like a wet meat mask. His lidless eyes rolled wildly in their bloody sockets.

"You . . ." he squealed. "Yoooooouuuuuuuu!"

Jimmy Sticks leaned down and spoke clearly into Arrowhead's exposed ear hole, "Her name . . . was Miyoko."

Then he lifted Lonnie up by the lapels of his Big Eagle Nosh Nest uniform and punched him in the nuts. His fist hammered those dangling pleasure-berries, exploding them like overripe cherry tomatoes before shattering his pelvis and sinking elbow-deep into Lonnie's intestines.

"Gah . . . gah . . . gaaaaahhhhh," Lonnie replied.

Jimmy Sticks yanked his arm out of Lonnie's guts and let gravity do the rest. There came a sound, like a punching bag stuffed with manatee blubber suddenly giving way. Lonnie took three steps backwards, snagged his foot in the loop of gut dangling between his knees, stumbled and sat in a steaming pile of himself. The last thing Lonnie LeFleur saw was Jimmy Sticks feeding his face to the Black Possum sitting on his shoulder.

Then the rats took him.

They chewed his liver and lights; chewed their way up his ass and ate like rude relatives. They devoured his unruly penis. Fortunately, Lonnie stayed conscious for the whole thing.

Until they got to his brain.

◆   ◆   ◆

Dawn found Jimmy Sticks standing on the shelf of rock that looked out over Lake Michigan. He could feel her out there, waiting for him.

Come home, my love.

Miyoko's voice was in the waves. It whispered across the wind that tugged at Jimmy's melting flesh.

Jimmy Sticks looked up at the Black Possum, unsure if what he'd heard was possible.

"Miyoko?" he whispered.

The Black Possum's obsidian eyes sparkled with a malicious glee. Then it spread its wings and took off over the Lake, soaring toward the distant mysteries of western Michigan.

It's time, my sweet.

Jimmy Sticks took seven steps toward the water and fell flat on his face. His skull struck a large outcropping of rock and ruptured, spilling his brains across the sand. It didn't matter. By the time his cerebellum was gull chow he was in the spectral arms of his beloved, nestled in the eternal darkness.

He was home. With her.

And that didn't suck.

RANCHING THE SLEORE
Aaron Polson

Harold Talbot's world was splitting apart even before he demolished the moldy sheetrock in his basement. His wife, Molly, insisted on maintaining the nursery, even after their baby was born dead. The second fissure in Harold's world was ten years his junior, had the body of a swimsuit model, and carried his bastard child. Of course, Harold didn't know. Not yet. He spent his nights with a broken woman and his days wishing her father was dead. Daddy had deep pockets, and they stood to inherit most of his wealth. Maybe he could sew his life back together with a little of Daddy's money. A pry bar and hammer channeled his frustration, and Harold joined the destruction of his world on a Sunday afternoon.

On the stereo, Johnny Cash sang "Cocaine Blues" live to a group of inmates, and Harold imagined working on a chain gang as he struck and smashed through the walls. Gypsum dust and sweat mixed together, coating him in a pale cast like cheap ghost make-up from the community theater production of *A Christmas Carol*. He had met Molly during rehearsals.

Jacob Marley and the Ghost of Christmas Past . . . but those days *were* past. The Molly of the present was sleepless, wild-eyed, and numbed with medication.

Harold's work slowed, the sheetrock crumbled in small bits, and he cursed under his breath. When he found the thing in the wall, he was just thrilled to remove a piece bigger than his hand. He pried loose a large section, and the thing tumbled to the floor with a dull thump, coming to rest on a dirty pile of gypsum dust and old nails. Harold straightened, rubbed sweat from his forehead with a dirty sleeve, and stared at it.

He'd heard about folks making money selling hidden treasures they'd found while remodeling, but the *thing* didn't look like treasure. It was small-ish, just longer than a football but about the same width, and looked to be wrapped in yellow-brown paper the color of his still-born child. The shape was thick and round at one end with a point of sorts at the other. *An egg?* He stooped, reaching out to touch the thing, but hesitated. A shadow moved across his back.

Hide it.

He tapped the thing with the toe of his old running shoe.

Hide it now.

Harold shook at the thought. The thing, the egg, was alien. Wrong. Johnny Cash coughed and asked for a glass of water. Harold set down the pry bar and picked up the thing. It was heavy. Solid.

Hide it from Molly.

* * *

The next morning, Harold Talbot left the house before Molly stirred. He drank his coffee quickly and choked down a piece of dry toast as he steered his Honda through neighborhood streets toward the highway. It was cooler that morning, but still warm enough to leave his window down and taste the damp air. He merged into highway traffic and sped toward the head-quarters of Blatek and Dvorske, surprised that he felt so clean after hiding the thing under a trash bag in the dumpster beside the house, unaware that Naomi waited with a surprise of her own. She had started as an intern and had found her way into Harold's pants almost three months ago, shortly after the stillbirth of his child.

He was southbound on I-55, caught in stop-and-go traffic. His eyes drifted to the rearview mirror. Clear. Harold accelerated and cranked his wheel, sliding into the open lane to his left.

So did the car in front of him.

Harold's foot pressed against the brake pedal, jamming it to the floor. "Motherfucker," he muttered. His face burned and beads of sweat popped out on his forehead. With a deep breath, he checked the mirrors again, and accelerated after the car—a blue Buick. *An old man's car.*

They sped past the log jam caused by a tractor-trailer with a blown out tire and continued on the highway. Harold's silver Accord trailed the blue Buick. Both of Harold's hands held the steering wheel like the hilt of a sword in battle. Grooves in the rubber bit into his palms. He boiled with the desire to drag the Buick's driver from his car by the neck.

When the blue car pulled from the road, Harold hesitated, fuming on the inside. But his exit was only three miles away, and such an act of brazen anger wouldn't do. The sky was clear. Monday morning marked a whole week of work—time away from the damaged creature that used to be his wife. A whole week of sneaking into an empty conference room with Naomi for carnal negotiations.

Harold glanced at the Buick as it disappeared down the exit ramp. The driver was an old man—*of course*—and he turned to look at Harold. For a moment, their eyes met. Harold's blood went cold. The old man grinned, showing a mouth of jagged, broken teeth. From a distance, Harold imagined the man had no eyes, just empty pits of black.

◆   ◆   ◆

"I'm pregnant. I'm going to have a baby," Naomi said as she slid her hands down the back of Harold's pants, squeezing his buttocks lightly. "I'm two months in."

"Shit." The blood dropped from Harold's face.

Naomi pushed back. Her large, brown eyes burned. "What do you mean, shit? *Shit* you knocked up the intern at work, or *shit*, I'm going to have a kid with this fine sister?"

Harold closed his eyes. The thing from the wall crawled toward him, still wrapped in its yellow skin. It morphed from an egg of brittle paper into a crawling, mewling baby. He shook his eyes open. "Sorry. Really. *Shit* . . . I'm happy. But . . ."

"But you're married." Naomi puffed out her full lips in a pout. "I got it."

His mouth was dry. Too dry. The room started to rock. Naomi said the word baby, and he heard Molly's voice. He saw Molly's father signing his will and the thing's brown, wrinkled skin showed under the yellow wrappings.

"That's not it," he said. "This is good." With effort, Harold Talbot forced a smile.

"Good, good? As in, getting that divorce you've been talking about good?"

He looked at Naomi. She was a thin woman—not skinny, but athletic. Her firm, round breasts pushed her blouse out just enough, her sloping hips fit her pants just right. *She could be a model. Or a stripper.* Naomi was his affair at work . . . not someone he would marry. She was ten years younger than him, anyway. Ten years and a thousand worlds away.

"Yeah . . . yeah. Divorce," he lied. He lied again with his smile.

"That's what I want to hear," she said. Her hands worked his fly, pushed inside his pants and pulled out his manhood. "A little celebration, then." Naomi knelt and slipped him inside her mouth.

Harold leaned back, letting the blood disappear from his brain as it left in a warm rush to his genitals. He needed a vacation from thinking.

◆   ◆   ◆

Late afternoon shadows brushed across Harold's car as he guided it through the quiet streets toward home. At a stop sign, he watched an older couple shuffle across the street, hand in hand.

How romantic. Harold sneered. *What bullshit.*

The old man turned and stared at him, his eyes empty and black. It was the man from the Buick that morning. Harold's throat tightened. He couldn't breathe. Inside the car, the air grew thick, humid, too hot. The old man smiled, opening his mouth enough to show the broken line of teeth—near teeth. *Those jagged things couldn't be teeth. Not human teeth, anyway.*

A blaring horn snapped Harold to the present. In the car behind him, the driver shook a fist. Harold accelerated from the corner, his heart rattling in his chest.

When he entered the house, Molly was at the kitchen sink. She washed her hands in slow, deliberate movements. Harold staggered to the table, still shaken. Almost hypnotized by the sound of running water, he shook his head as she turned off the tap.

"Harold?"

He turned his hands over, examining his palms.

"Harold?" she repeated.

"What? Sorry." He looked up, and Molly was picking at something under her fingernails.

"Are you okay, Harold?" Molly crossed the room and laid a hand on his shoulder. Harold bristled—the muscles in his shoulders and neck tightened. "You seem tense," she said.

"Fine. I'm Fine."

There was a smell in the kitchen that didn't belong. A heavy, cloying odor like blood—but not quite. Blood and dirt, mixed together . . . muddy and pungent. He hadn't noticed it at first. Turning his head slightly, he glanced at Molly's hand. Something dark was caked under her nails.

Dirty.

Harold pulled away and stood. "I'm . . . going to shower before dinner." As he made for their bedroom, he paused outside the closed nursery door. Was it the smell again? Harold shrugged, and continued down the hall.

◆   ◆   ◆

Around midnight, Harold reckoned from the blue silence of the house. *Around midnight, and too damn hot.* Molly slept next to him crumpled under a section of blanket with her dark hair splayed on the pillow. Her skin shimmered like liquid silver in the moonlight, and he touched her bare shoulder. She pulled away. Glancing at her hand, he saw she'd cleaned under her nails. The smell was gone, too. He rolled on his other side and glanced at the alarm clock resting on his nightstand. 1:37 AM. *Damn.* His feet slipped from under the covers, touching lightly on the hardwood floor. He peeled his t-shirt from his chest padded into the hallway.

Too hot in here.

He stopped at the door to the nursery. A sound, a small, whispered noise, crept from inside. Scratching, clawing at wood. His hand touched the doorknob, but he pulled his fingers back. The noise stopped; the house fell silent and still again. Harold moved down the hall and flipped open the thermostat.

"Damn thing's probably on the fritz," he muttered, poking the "Run Program" button.

On the way back to bed, he shivered as he walked past the nursery, despite the humid air.

◆ ◆ ◆

Molly sat at their small kitchen table with her hands around a hot mug of coffee. Her hair was up, pulled back again in her standard ponytail with a few rogue strands dangling by each ear. She sipped slowly, bringing the mug to her mouth, blowing across the dark liquid, and then touching it to her lips. Harold rinsed his breakfast dishes at the sink. His memory toyed with the dark matter under her fingernails when he came home from work last night.

None of this shit is healthy, he thought.

"Babe," he said, turning to face her, "I think we need to talk about clearing out the nursery. For the time being at least." He remembered the sticky warmth in the hallway during the night. He could almost hear the scrabbling noises behind the door.

She glanced down as if searching for something in the coffee. "I'm not ready yet . . . not ready to quit . . ."

Harold moved to the table and sat down. "I'm not either. Really." He took her hands and squeezed. "I think it might be best, right now at least. I don't want you thinking about the baby—"

"I'm not." She pulled away.

Harold glanced at her hands, noting her nails were dirty again. His stomach lurched. He turned back to the kitchen window, saying, "I'm only trying to do what's best . . . really."

"You don't know what it's like, Harold. Having something alive inside you."

She's lost it Harold. Cut your losses. He started counting to himself, working to maintain the suggestion of empathy. *Daddy can't live forever.*

He carried out the trash that morning on the way to his car and paused before dumping in the new bag. A chill braided up his spine. He dropped the bag to the ground, lifted the dumpster lid, and checked inside. The shell of the thing was still under the other bag. The shell. Empty and split open, like *it* had hatched, and black sludge, thick like dried blood covered the inside.

Harold stumbled on the way to his car.

◆ ◆ ◆

Traffic backed up on I-55 again. Harold tapped out a tune with his forefingers and thumbs as he waited for the blockage to clear. No lane hopping today, just patience. As the cars crept forward, he thought of Naomi, their baby. He focused on *anything* to avoid the specter of the thing in his trash. Did she really expect a divorce? That he would throw away his inheritance and marry the office hottie?

Harold's gaze drifted out of his passenger window as he passed the flashing lights of the emergency vehicles. A body lay on a gurney, strapped tight and covered with a blanket. The ruins of a car—a dark blue Buick—lay in a disordered twist on the shoulder, still smoldering.

A dark blue Buick.

He looked ahead, tightening his hold on the steering wheel as if that would prevent him from going to a darker place in his mind. The gurney. The body. The old man had been in his neighborhood last night. He had looked into his empty eye-holes just twelve hours ago.

Couldn't be the same guy.

No way.

Harold rubbed the back of his neck. His chronic headache had returned, tapping at the base of his skull. Naomi. The old geezer. Molly and the thing from the wall. His world upside down.

Traffic loosened once he drove past the wreck, and Harold Talbot pushed the accelerator to the floor. The speed made him drunk. He could just drive his Honda into one of the bridge supports ahead. Crash-boom. Dead.

Harold laughed.

Maybe life would be simpler, dead.

◆   ◆   ◆

"Where the hell were you this morning?" Naomi whispered, but her face was shouting.

Harold looked up from his desk, catching the brunt of her angry eyes over the top of his cubicle wall. He rubbed his chin with the back of a hand.

"Accident on I-55." Harold's fingers pulled at the corner of some papers on his desk.

"Oh." Naomi's fierce gaze melted. "You okay? I heard about that wreck. Weird."

Harold pulled at his collar. "What do you mean, weird?"

"The old guy driving . . . well, my girlfriend Taira, she's a dispatcher. She told me he was dead before he wrecked."

Harold's stomach tightened at the word *dead*. "What . . . heart attack? That kind of shit happens all the time."

"No. She said the EMTs were freaked out. He'd been dead for about a week."

As she spoke, Harold's eyes went blind, running through his memory of the old man on the street last night. Black eyes. *Dead* eyes. He swallowed—tried to swallow, but his mouth was dry. "You sure Taira's not—"

"Back off my friends, man. I'm still pissed at you. Glad you're okay, but pissed you didn't come find me this morning for our usual . . . meeting. We've got shit to talk about tomorrow." Naomi's face disappeared from his cubicle wall.

Bitch. Harold tapped the papers on his desk into a pile. He sorted a few into separate stacks and clipped them together. *At least it looks like I'm working.*

"Damn, she's hot."

Ed, the mail boy, poked his head around the corner of Harold's cubicle. In a former life, Ed must have been either a skateboarding champion or meth addict. Maybe both. His necktie, required Blatek and Dvorske attire, always hung loose about his neck. His shirts were never ironed, and seldom matched the rest of his wardrobe. The kid—Harold always thought of him as a kid, even though he was at least twenty-four—never really learned how to use a comb.

"Hi Ed." Harold shook his mouse to coax his computer screen out of hibernation.

"Dude." Ed stepped into the grey office-box, reeking of something too sweet for tobacco smoke. "You hitting that?"

Harold's shoulders tensed. "What?"

"The intern. What's-her-name. She's fine, dude." Ed made a lewd gesture with his hands in front of his groin. "I'd be all over that shit."

"Goodbye, Ed."

"Later, man."

That evening, on his way home, Harold Talbot took a different route. He avoided the highway completely, still spooked by the old man's accident. He circled his neighborhood, approaching down a street on the opposite end of the subdivision.

No old men with black eyes found him.

◆   ◆   ◆

Harold dreamed that night, or what he believed must have been a dream. He lay in bed, realizing that Molly was not next to him. A low, whispering scratch sounded from the wall behind the head of the bed. He saw tiny fingers, like swollen, drowned worms, padding across the sheetrock, searching for a way out of the wall. Harold tried to move, but his body was locked in a block of ice, frozen, immobile. The sound stopped abruptly.

Molly came into the room then, cradling something in her arms. Her face—pale as it was—still shone like silver in the darkness, but the thing in her arms was yellowish-white, the color of raw chicken fat. She was naked from the waist up. The thing squirmed, and little fat tentacles—maybe fingers—worked open and shut against the edge of Molly's naked arms. She bent her head forward and nuzzled the thing with her nose. Its mouth—if you could call the groping, ovular sucker a mouth—reached out to Molly's nipple and latched on. She let out a low moan, a peaceful, slow sound.

Harold closed his eyes.

When he opened them, Molly was climbing into bed. He was coated in a thin layer of sweat. The house was too hot again. Too humid. The fecund, muddy odor hung in his nostrils.

"What's going on?" he mumbled, disoriented.

She pulled the comforter to her chin. "Nothing, nothing. I just had to go to the bathroom." Her hand brushed his forehead, and Harold could smell the rich odor of blood. He lay awake the rest of the night, staring at the wall away from Molly.

In the morning, after his shower, Harold stepped into the nursery, flipped on the light, and scanned the half-painted walls. His eyes rested on the crib. A sheet covered the mattress, and, for a moment, he imagined a dark smudge on the sheet. Pulling the door shut, he returned to the bedroom and undressed as something cold began to writhe in the pit of his stomach.

When he looked in the mirror, he noticed marks on his chest.

Five little red rings—raised and bumpy like the sting of a bee.

◆　◆　◆

Harold downed three cups of coffee: two at home and one in the car. Ed found him in the break room after he arrived. Steam rose from his fourth cup of the day, and Harold's hand trembled from the caffeine zinging through his veins.

"Man, you looked like shit. Wild night?" Ed poured the remainder of the coffee pot into a cup and proceeded to dump in sugar packets, one after the other, until the mixture was at least half sweetener. In went the cream until the coffee mellowed to a tone closer to Naomi's skin.

Harold closed his eyes, pinching the bridge of his nose between forefinger and thumb. "I'm fine."

"You don't look fine, man. I've seen dudes like you before. What is it? Coke? Heroin? Tell me it ain't heroin, man. That shit will mess you up."

One . . . two . . . three . . . Harold to himself, trying to outlast Ed's presence. The smell of super sweetened coffee filled the room and crawled inside Harold's nostrils. He felt sick to his stomach, but continued counting.

"Whatever dude. Later."

Harold let out a long, slow sigh. He sipped the black coffee in his own cup, but the sweet odor of Ed's concoction lingered. Turning to the break room sink, he poured the black liquid down the drain.

Someone entered behind him.

"You all right?" Naomi asked, closing the door to the break room with a soft click. "Ed told me you were in here. He said you look like shit. You do. Like that funny white shit that comes out of birds." Naomi smiled at her joke.

"Funny," he muttered. "Couldn't sleep last night."

She crossed her arms. "I'd like to think this means you've had a hard time deciding how to tell that crazy bitch you're through." Her head wagged from side to side. "Too bad that wasn't it."

Harold crushed the paper cup. He frowned. "It's not that . . . well . . . things have been happening."

"I'm pregnant Harold. Things have been happening, like you sticking your dick in me for the last few months."

Harold's eyes flashed to the break room windows, scanning for anyone that may have heard. "Quiet, okay?" He waved his hands. "Molly's just . . ."

Naomi squinted at him, tilting her head slightly. "This going to be good, Harold? Molly's just what, suspicious? I'll give her some shit to be suspicious about." She jerked a finger over her shoulder. "Cush gig, right? Fast track for one of those corner offices with the windows and 'vice-president' chalked up next to your name?" Naomi's lips spread wide and curled at both ends. "I'll make sure that shit doesn't happen."

Beads of sweat snaked down Harold's forehead. He brushed his face with the back of one sleeve. His mouth opened, started to move. "Look—"

"Look what? Do you love me, or not? You said plenty of shit with your pants down in the conference room downstairs." Naomi turned and grabbed the door handle. With a last look over her shoulder, she added, "I'm not going to be played like this . . . not by some uptight, white asshole like you. Let me know what you've got to offer by tomorrow, or I'm going to your wife and the boss."

The break room door slammed home with a rattling crash, but Harold didn't hear it. He still leaned against the counter, heat radiating from under his arms and the back of his neck. Harold glanced into the drain and imagined black eyes in the drops of dark liquid. His inheritance washed down the drain with the coffee.

Later, when he fell asleep at his desk, he dreamed of fleshy, pale things with tails like giant sperm. They climbed his legs with scuttling claws and whispered dirty things in his ears. The office melted away, and he was home again. Harold stepped from his bedroom, crossed the hall, and pushed open the nursery door. In the rocking chair, the dark maple heirloom in which his mother had rocked him, Molly sat with a white, writhing thing in her lap. She bared a breast, and held the overgrown grub to her nipple. The worm-thing undulated, and Harold's ears filled with an awful wet, sucking sound. Its pincers opened and shut in a broken rhythm. Molly looked up, smiled at

Harold, and mouthed, "They need me."

◆ ◆ ◆

"The door to the spare bedroom was open when I came home." Harold drummed his fingers against the Formica counter in the kitchen. He'd left before Molly roused in the morning, sure that all the doors were shut.

Molly prodded two chicken breasts with a spatula as they sizzled in a skillet. "The *nursery* you mean?"

"For God's sake, Molly." Harold rolled his eyes. "Call it whatever you like. Did you go in there today?"

She continued shoving the chicken around in the pan. "Why would I, Harold?"

He stepped closer, his face reddening. *Easy, easy.* He unclenched his fists. "I don't know Molly. I had a dream, okay? I thought I saw mud . . . blood in the crib." He shook his head and massaged the back of his neck

"What are you saying?" Molly's voice was curt.

He grabbed her arm. "Why won't you look at me?"

Molly pulled away. "Don't you care about me? You're trying to make me hurry through something—my grief—*you* didn't carry our child for five months before, before . . . I'm not ready to move on, Harold." She turned to him, facing him for the first time in their conversation. "Can't you understand *that*?"

He backed away, confused and startled and tired. "All right. Whatever. Call me for dinner." Harold turned to leave the kitchen. "I'll be in the garage." He slammed the door behind him. The red bumps on his chest itched like poison ivy he'd had as a child.

◆ ◆ ◆

Harold's thoughts oscillated between Naomi, the dead old man, and the fire on his chest. He and his wife didn't speak during dinner. Molly called her father after washing the dishes, and the rest of the evening passed in cold silence.

She called to remind Harold what was at stake. He was sure of it.

After two hours, Harold slid out of bed, checked the door to the nursery, and sprawled on the couch in their living room. He'd stared at the ceiling in the bedroom without drifting off; he wanted his full awareness that night.

Outside the house, the breeze toyed with the trees, forcing odd shadows to dance and play on the living room walls. Harold waited for them to take shape, to do something, but it wasn't until he heard a noise in the kitchen—a light, scraping sound against the tile—that he knew his wait wasn't in vain. He sat up on the couch, his nostrils sucking in the pungent, earthy smell. It was the same blend of blood and dirt that Molly's fingers stank of earlier in the week. The scraping came closer, and then muted against the hallway rug. Harold looked toward the hall, but saw nothing. *Where's Molly?*

He rose from the couch like a ghost and floated into the hall. Shadows laced across the floor, crossing against both walls. The nursery door was still shut, and Harold took a few quiet steps into the shadows toward the door. "Molly," he whispered. The walls swallowed his words without answer. He stood inches away from the door and reached out with one trembling hand, but withdrew it. *What am I afraid of?*

Small noises sounded from the other side of the door, wet, sucking sounds. *I'm dreaming, right? If I open the door . . .* Harold backed away, his mind bending toward something awful, and the thing in his stomach turning flips. He made a few more awkward steps away from the nursery before spotting Molly at the end of the hallway.

"Hey." Harold rubbed his sweaty hands against his pajama pants.

"I've been watching you. You tried to hide it from me."

"What are you—"

"In the trash. But it found someplace *warm* and safe. Not a cold womb in the earth, but a place it can grow, a place it will be nurtured." Molly pulled open her robe, revealing her belly, silver-blue like the rest of her pale skin. One hand came to rest just above her belly-button. Below the hand, her uterine wall bulged and shifted, like a great worm pressed from the inside. She stepped forward, taking Harold's hand.

"Touch it, sweetie. It waited for so long behind that wall, waited for me. It's home now." She pressed his palm to her lower belly. "They can all come home now. The one you found . . . it wasn't alone."

Harold yanked his hand away. His stomach flopped. "God . . . Molly . . . I'm dreaming . . ."

"No, babe. You helped it find me. It called the others."

"You're nuts. You've been fucking nuts since . . . since . . ."

"No." Molly stepped closer, a black shape moving through the night. "No. We lost the baby so I'd be ready for them. Like fate."

It was too much. Too much on top of all the other crazy shit since Sunday.

Harold pushed his wife aside, still clinging to a vestigial hope that the night, the thing inside her—that it was all part of a lucid dream. He tore through the house, grabbed his keys and a wad of cash from their emergency stash in the bottom of the cookie jar, and was in his car before Molly could catch him. Before she even tried.

◆ ◆ ◆

"Fuck, fuck, fuck," Harold muttered into the windshield. The dashboard clock indicated 1:49 AM, but he wasn't going home.

I imagined it, Harold thought, remembering the strange, moving bulge in Molly's skin. *That's it. Imagination. Not enough sleep. The drama with Naomi. The weird old dude, dead in his Buick.*

"Bullshit, all of it."

Harold drove to a Motel Six on southbound I-55. "Vacancy" was broadcast in neon outside the building. The clerk, a scrawny nineteen-year-old hunched over an open College Algebra text, looked up with half-closed eyes when Harold stumbled into the lobby.

"Yeah?"

Harold glanced around the dim room with quick, sudden turns of his head. "I need a room."

"Right." The clerk craned his head to see over the counter. Harold's pants were filthy and his feet bare.

"All I have is cash. You take cash, right?"

"Whatever, sure." The scrawny clerk looked at Harold, studying him like an algebra equation, and then turned to his computer.

◆ ◆ ◆

Harold never imagined he would own a gun. His father never took him hunting and his mother abhorred the things. But the next morning, after lying awake all night on an uncomfortable motel mattress and a trip to the Goodwill store for a change of clothing, he drove to Larry's Pawn and Loan. He didn't plan on going to work that day. He never planned on buying a pistol under the table at a seedy pawn shop, either, but reality had started to come undone, and Harold Talbot was not going to face the day unarmed.

Not after last night and the writhing shape in Molly's gut.

"We got a waiting period in this state, mister." The man behind the pawn shop counter—maybe Larry himself—was thin and dark, his skin wrinkled too much around his eyes and his voice hoarse.

Too many cigarettes, Harold thought. *Smoking will kill you.*

"I said we got a waiting period, buddy."

Harold rubbed his neck at the base of his skull. Another headache. "Waiting period?" He knew bags hung around his eyes. *Does that make me look more suspicious? Would that be a problem?*

"If it's money," Harold said, pulling a stack of large bills from his pocket—money he'd taken from the bank that morning to back up the emergency fund. "I can pay double . . . triple."

The thin man leaned back on his stool. His eyes, razor-sharp blue, flicked to the pawn shop door. They cut across Harold's face.

"You a cop?"

Blood rushed to Harold's face. "No."

"Why you need the gun so bad?"

Harold shifted his weight between both legs. He felt his stomach twist again. "I'm afraid something—someone is trying to kill me." His hand rubbed across his shirt over the raised red bumps on his chest.

"Why not go to the cops then?"

"They won't believe me."

◆   ◆   ◆

Later that day, after driving aimlessly down I-55 past the remnants of south suburbs and back again, Harold bought lunch at McDonald's and drove to Suson Park to eat near the duck pond. He remembered the ducks from his childhood, how his mother used to bring stale bread to feed them on a Saturday morning. The ducks would waddle around, muttering in duck-speak, odd honks which sounded nothing like quack. Only now, Harold was not little, he had no stale bread, and there was a loaded .38 revolver in a brown paper sack sitting on the picnic table next to him.

His head was on a swivel, rotating around the park, watching for someone he might know. Someone who would wonder why he was eating McDonald's with a loaded gun in the park on a Thursday afternoon. Old people milled about. Kids should be in school.

One old man walked in his direction.

Harold took a bite of his cheeseburger.

The old man continued, quickening his pace as if Harold was an old friend.

Harold's hand inched toward the brown paper sack.

As he came closer, the man had no eyes—just empty, black pits in his face. He smiled, showing a mouth of broken, jagged teeth. It wasn't the old man from the Buick, but something was similar. Wrong.

"Don't bother," the man said as Harold's hand slipped inside the brown paper sack and touched the handle of the gun. The man's voice was low, broken and indistinct.

"Leave me alone."

The man coughed. "Damn flesh bags."

"What?"

"These bodies. So easily broken."

Harold swallowed his bite and set the cheeseburger on its wrapper. Slowly, he pulled the other hand from the gun bag. Clouds obscured the sun, casting a shadow across the park. Harold's eyes made a quick circuit; other old people approached, staggering toward the shelter.

"What the hell are you talking about?"

The old man sat opposite Harold. His eyes were black—not a shiny, living black like the eyes of a dog, but empty. Absent. Hollow. Each time he spoke, Harold could see the flash of jagged teeth inside his mouth.

"These flesh bags." The old man pinched a bit of his arm. "One member was killed trying to guide his flesh bag in one of those metal boxes. He didn't jump in time."

"The Buick. The accident on the highway." Harold pushed his McDonald's sack away.

"We've been looking for the open gate, Mr. Talbot." The old man leaned forward. "You have the stink on you."

Harold scowled. "The stink?"

"You opened the gate. We've been trying to find you. Ask you how you opened the gate. Thank you for the new discovery. Our Sleore are happy in their new ranches."

Sleore . . . those things. Like the thing in Molly's stomach. Harold felt the crowd closing in on him, the group of eyeless old people smothering him. He was too tired. Too worn out. His hand crept toward the paper sack holding the gun. Dozens of empty eyes focused on him.

"Your wife. She showed us a new way. Our yields will increase."

"Yields . . . what?"

"You opened the gate, but she called them. She gave them ranches, a warm, safe place where our stock could hide and grow. She increased our yield. The Sleore meat will fill our S'clar pit again."

Harold rubbed his face with his left hand as the right worked into the gun sack—an old stage magician's trick. *Yield. Sanctuary. Warm, safe place.* In Harold's mind's eye, he saw the wormy-thing move under Molly's skin.

"Have you been to the lower level of your dwelling lately, Mr. Talbot?"

"The basement . . ." Harold's hand wrapped the pistol grip. His forefinger found the trigger. The crowd pressed closer. He could smell them. Their breath was hot and rotten—the breath of corpses on his back. "Not since Sunday."

The old man didn't move for a moment. If he had eyes, he would have looked thoughtful.

"It is harvest time, Mr. Talbot. Thank you for the ranches."

Harold squeezed the trigger. The shelter amplified the gunshot, and Harold's ears began to ring. The bullet struck the old man in the throat, but there was no blood. His head tilted to one side where the bullet sliced through his waxen skin. The mouth opened. An unearthly howl rose from the gaping maw.

Spinning around, Harold fired at two more of the old people, hitting one woman in the chest and a man with glasses in the forehead. Harold pushed free of the group and ran for his car. Other people in the park began to shout. Harold scrambled for his keys, and climbed into the Honda. With a quick glance behind him, he sped from the park. The group of old people had barely moved, but all were facing him. All with their black stares.

Jesus, Molly . . . what have I done. What have we done?

•   ◆   ◆

Harold's neighborhood was deserted in the early afternoon, and he tore through several stop signs without slowing. His back was tense as he expected the howl of sirens and flash of lights to find him at any moment. Careening around the corner of his block, Harold noticed a strange car in the drive. No—not strange. He'd seen that rust-bucket before.

Ed's at my house?

He slowed into his driveway, scooped up the pistol, shook a box of cartridges out on the seat, and reloaded. The house was quiet. Molly hadn't come out. No sign of Ed. Gulping a lungful of air, Harold counted to ten one more time as he let the breath slowly escape. Then, Harold Talbot climbed out of his car and headed into the house.

The front door was open—not a bad sign as they lived in a good, clean neighborhood. When Molly was home, she usually left it open. Harold pushed the door closed with his back and locked it. He pulled back the living room curtains and glanced outside.

Nobody out there. Yet.

"Molly!"

No answer. Harold's heart started to pound against his ribs. He wiped his face with his shirt tail and walked through the hall to their bedroom. With the barrel of the pistol, he pushed the door open. Nobody.

"Molly!"

The nursery. Harold pushed open the door and nearly retched at the stench—a smell of dirt and blood. The humid, hot air caught him in the chest, almost pushing him back into the hallway. He scanned the room, starting with the wall next to the door and working his way to the crib.

They were in the crib . . . five of them. They were from his dream: the pale, writhing lumps that looked like overgrown sperm. Albino tadpoles with fragile, crab-like pincers snapped at him. The things wriggled toward him, their sucker mouths pinching open and shut. Harold touched his chest, feeling the raised red bumps.

Fuck.

He heard the car door slam and stumbled into the hallway. Leaning against the wall, Harold doubled-over and vomited. More car doors. He staggered into the living room and glanced into the yard.

The old people had arrived, and now they shambled toward the house, led by their black eyes. Through the window, Harold could hear them talking to each other in strange, low tones that weren't human.

"Molly!"

The basement. The old man said . . .

Harold ran through the kitchen as the old people began to try the front door. He heard glass break in the living room. He yanked open the basement door, and nearly tumbled down the steps. He caught himself at the bottom, wholly unprepared for who—what waited for him.

He thought the floor was moving. His eyes adjusted to the low light, and realized those *things* nearly covered everything. The wall he'd started to demolish a week ago was almost gone. The air was hot and sticky, just like the nursery upstairs. He'd found Molly, though. She was naked, her skin grey in the dim basement. Naomi was with her, also naked, and they stood on either side of Harold's old recliner.

Bent over the chair on his belly, pants around his ankles, lay Ed.

"Oh, Harold." Molly smiled in his direction. "Good."

"M-Molly? Naomi?" Harold felt his world spin. "W-we need to go." He waved the gun to the stairs. "These, people have come for us. I don't think it's safe."

"We're not going anywhere, Harold." Molly stooped and picked up one of the things. It twisted and undulated in her hands. "This is where we are needed."

"Yeah, Harold. Molly showed me." Naomi bent over and scooped one into her arms like an infant. "They need a warm, safe place to grow." She nuzzled the thing to her chest. "They're better than your bastard child, any day."

Harold glanced at Ed and noticed that his hands were bound behind his back. Ed's eyes were shut. Naomi rested the thing on the chair and pulled Ed's pants off completely. She spread his legs, propping them up on the arm rests of the chair. Meanwhile, Molly pushed her fingers in his mouth, and pulled it open.

"Stop," Harold said. He raised the shaking gun in his hands.

Footsteps sounded from the kitchen upstairs.

Naomi looked at Harold and smiled. "Ed was nice enough to give me a ride over here, Harold. Then Molly showed me. I was scared at first, just like you." She picked up the thing and held it between Ed's buttocks. It wriggled and crawled into his anus. Ed's body shook once and fell still.

"Stop!" Harold sobbed. He fired the gun, hitting one of the fleshy things at Naomi's feet. Her ankles sprayed with black fluid. Strong hands clamped around his arms from behind, forcing the gun from his grip.

"Now, Mr. Talbot. Look at your wife." The voice was next to his ear, hot and foul and dead.

Molly smiled at him. She beamed, looking the picture of matronly health—just like people say about pregnant women. As Harold watched, she fed a smaller thing into Ed's mouth. Harold pulled and struggled, but the hands held him fast.

"You fucking killed Ed," he muttered.

"No Harold." Molly started toward him. "Ed's fine. He'll be even better when he wakes up."

The eyeless people milled into the room. An old man stooped and picked up a thing, holding it like a squirming fish. His black eyes seemed to flicker, and then he sank his crooked mouth into the pale flesh. Black juice streamed out around his teeth, down his chin, and across the front of his shirt. Others began to pick choice morsels from the ground. They began to hum with delight.

Harold was being herded for the chair. Naomi, with the help of an elderly woman with white hair, pulled Ed away.

"It's a win-win, Harold." Molly was talking to him in the soft, sweet voice he fell in love with back on the set of *A Christmas Carol*. "The Greeton'thull, well—they're ranchers, sort of. They need the Sleore to survive. Like food, Harold. The Sleore grow better inside us . . . it was an accident with the first one, the one from our wall. And it feels so good to have them inside you, babe. Really good." Her warm breath was in his ear.

"No . . . no . . . no . . . they *bit* me . . ." Harold was crying. He didn't want to cry, but he had nothing left. The old people brought him to the chair. Naomi knelt between his legs and started to undo his pants. Any other time, he'd want to fondle her nubile breasts. Any other time, he'd have an erection.

"Sometimes they nip when they try to suckle . . . but this doesn't hurt, Harold," she said.

Molly fondled his hair. "No. The Greeton'thull aren't bad at all. In fact, they only take bodies that died of natural causes. Isn't that nice? They could inhabit anything, and they only take dead people."

Harold's thoughts spun. He was vaguely aware that Naomi tugged off his pants and underwear.

"That first one we found, the one from the wall. It wasn't dead, Harold. Just molting. I nursed it back to health. More of them started to come through." She patted his head. "With your temper, I wasn't sure how you'd react. I tried to keep it a secret."

Naomi's slender fingers walked up Harold's legs. "Not excited to see me anymore, Harold? Don't worry. I promise . . . you'll feel so good."

He closed his eyes, hoping to somehow squeeze the world away. A half-dozen pairs of hands latched his arms and legs and flipped him over, face down across the reclined chair. As they spread his legs, Harold held his breath. Harold Talbot hadn't been to church in at least ten years, but he uttered a silent prayer, the best one he could muster:

Let me die now, please.

The tubular thing was rather warm as it slid in. It emitted a slime with narcotic properties, and his bowels tingled, radiating to the rest of his body.

No, it didn't hurt.

In fact, it was rather pleasant.

PAPER ANGELS ON FIRE
John Shirley

"Mr. Cordell, I know how you must feel." Bret Sage gazed into Cordell's eyes as he said it, projecting sympathy with a carefully honed skill. "Yes, you've lost Muriel—for awhile. But you'll see your daughter again. I promise you." Sage realized he had his hands in his jacket pockets. It was chilly on the front porch but hands in pockets didn't look right, at a time like this. He took his hands out and clasped them in front of him. He'd seen funeral directors use that pose. "What happened was part of Muriel's journey. Death is just a freeway interchange, Mr. Cordell."

Cordell smiled coldly, and nodded to himself. "Yeah, it's almost funny to watch—the way your mouth moves and those words come out, like puffs of smoke." Cordell was a balding middle-aged man in a black sweater flecked with what looked like dog hair; the sweater's sleeves were drawn back show-ing beefy forearms. Sage could see the big dog waiting in Cordell's SUV—a German Shepherd. Cordell was wearing opaque dark glasses hiding his eyes, and maybe his intentions. "Just means nothing at all," Cordell went on. "You are one empty son of a bitch, Sage." And Sage saw that Cordell's right hand was hidden behind his back.

Sage licked his lips, took a step back, edging towards his front door. Maybe he'd been hasty, coming out on the porch alone. He'd met Cordell on the porch of the Sage Foundation's New Mexico ranch house to try to work something out, maybe some kind of settlement, get the guy into the right state of mind . . . after all, Cordell had come here without his lawyer. That was a sign he might negotiate. Starting to sound like this wasn't about a settlement . . .

Little Bear was out back somewhere, fixing the hot tub. The sunset bite was in the northern New Mexico air. The shadowy pine woods around the house rang and chattered with birdsong. The ranch house was isolated—no neighbors around to call out to, if he needed them.

Something moved clickingly through the patch of prickly pear under the front window. Funny how vivid everything seemed, in this instant.

Cordell took a step toward him, and the birdsong, all at once, suddenly quieted.

"My daughter trusted you," Cordell said, between clenched teeth. "And that is just goddamn amazing to me. Just look at you! Shabby middle aged long haired unlicensed therapist in beaded moccasins. A slick line of bullshit. Lots of worn out clichés. And your slogan. 'Give me your trust and I'll give you life'!" Cordell shook his head sadly. "She was always a bit lost, that girl. We sure as Hell tried to help her—and she was getting on track! And then *you* got hold of her."

That's when Sage noticed the tattoo on Cordell's left forearm. Faded blue ink, but you could make out an anchor slanted through the Earth, topped by an eagle and *Semper Fi.*

Sage swallowed. "Mr. Cordell—we've had hundreds of people in that sweat lodge with no problem and . . . she probably had some . . . some pre-existing condition . . . a bad heart valve or . . ."

"No. She didn't. You gave her drugs. You wouldn't give her water. You wouldn't let her leave. She died in that hole in the ground you call a sweat lodge. And those others too . . ."

"We never, uh . . ." They had, actually, given the Experiencers a rather large dose of Ecstasy. People expected a powerful experience for their three thousand dollars seminar fee and that was the only way to guarantee it. He told them the pills were made of Sacred Herbs. They were supposed to take the pills *after* the sweat lodge ordeal. But the timing got mixed up, maybe because Sage himself had been stoned that morning. "She may have taken something on her own . . ."

"Uh huh. That's what your lawyer says. Says you didn't give her the stuff. But you did, Sage. *Ecstasy.* Now, that wouldn't have killed her—but that stuff makes a body overheat . . . and then you put her in a sweat lodge! Wouldn't let her leave. She begged to be let out . . ."

"We've . . . we've been in touch with her, we've channeled her, since then, and I know it's hard to believe but . . . she's actually, um, happy where she is . . ."

"Shut the Hell up, Sage. You're gonna choke on your own lies. Starting with your name. What's your real last name, again—Mazoosky?"

"Um—" It was Mezinsky. Didn't have the right ring to it. He'd stopped thinking of himself as Mezinsky long ago. "I am—Sage."

"You're *a hustler* who doesn't care who he hurts, is who you are. A hit and run charlatan. Doesn't care who he runs down. But your pals in the local DA's office, looks like they're gonna let you get away with it! No prosecution! Sure I could win a lawsuit. But that doesn't make it, 'Sage'. That's not restitution for my daughter. Not in my book."

Sage licked his lips. Mouth seemed so dry. "I can see this attempt to communicate was a mistake. I understand your feelings in this time of bereavement. But you'd better talk to my lawyer. Good day to you and may the Spirits bless you, Mr. Cordell."

He turned away and fumbled at the door. *Get through it—fast. Damned rusty knob. Open the damned door.*

He felt Cordell punch him hard in the right kidney. That's what it felt like, at first. But there was a funny *sound* with the punch. A snake-hiss sound . . .

Then his legs wouldn't hold him up and he was slipping down the closed front door, still clutching at the knob. Waves of blazing sensations rolled in furious rhythm from his lower back—he'd never before felt anything like it. So far beyond any pain he'd ever felt. It was like being hit by lightning over and over in the same spot.

Cordell's voice came to him as if from a telephone held at arm's length. "That's a bayonet, you feel there, 'Sage'. I angled it up, gave it a little twist. But you won't die too quickly. My daughter didn't die too quickly. You're going to . . ."

Sage couldn't hear anymore. He leaned forward against the door, on his knees, hands skittering at the doorknob, convulsing, all his feelings, all his senses, sucked through the spike of ice in his lower back—and the process went on forever.

And then forever ended, somehow, and he fell through his own door.

The wooden front door had become gelatinous, and then foggy. And he fell through it and lay on the floor, face down, half in the house, and half outside. He thought he might sink through the floor, but somehow it held him up.

Then he realized the pain was gone. He felt almost nothing at all. Not even fear. Just a faint, sickened wonder.

He drew his legs up under him, and somehow, very awkwardly, managed to stand.

Sage turned and looked at the front door. It was closed. He stepped over to the window onto the wide porch and saw Cordell walking away from the house, toward the SUV and the German Shepherd. Muriel Cordell's father was running a hand over his bald head as he went, looking limp, drained, barely able to trudge along, his sunglasses now dangling from his other hand.

Another man, a middle aged man with a graying pony tail, remained on the porch, slumped against the front door, on his knees. There was a bayonet grip sticking out of his lower back. His left arm was faintly twitching. Blood was running down his hip, pooling around him.

The sick feeling entirely replaced the wonder.

Sage turned away, went to the kitchen, and called out, "Little Bear! George, get in here!"

Little Bear's name was actually George Valdez. He'd never had a traditional Native American name. He was a quarter Comanche, three-quarters

Mexican, really. But he played the wise Native American medicine man exactly as Sage needed. He was also the Foundation's handyman.

"George, goddamn it!" he called.

The back door opened, and George came in, wearing overalls. Long gray-streaked black hair, features right out of an Aztec temple painting. Chewing gum, wiping grease from his hands on a red rag. "Hey Sage!" George yelled, looking around. From ten feet away. "I got the hot tub fixed!"

Not seeing Sage—walking right by him. Sage tried to stop him with an outstretched hand, and it was like Sage's hand was boneless, all made of rubber—it turned away from George's arm, couldn't get a grip on it.

George kept on, into the front room. Sage numbly followed. "I'm right here dammit, George, look at me!"

"What the fuck!" George yelled from the front door, seeing blood oozing under the door. George opened the door and Sage's body sagged forward like a sack of fertilizer.

"Madre Dios!" George muttered. He pushed at the body with his booted foot. Stepped back from it. Shook his head once. "Not gonna blame this on me . . . No fucking way, man."

George turned and bolted, charging through the house, banging out the back door.

Sage shouted after him in a sort of blurred fury. "Why you son of a bitch! You could call nine-one-one! I might still be alive, for Christ's sake!" He heard George's old Ford pickup starting. Revving. Screeching off down the gravel road.

"No, you couldn't still be alive," said the figure in white, matter of factly. The man in the glimmering white suit was perched casually on the window-sill to Sage's left, legs stretched out to the floor, like he was a comfortable old friend making himself at ease in Sage's house. But Sage had never seen that bland, pale, blue-eyed face before. "Actually, you kind of lost track of time when you were stabbed, Bret. It took some minutes for you to die. That young woman's father was watching the whole time till he was sure you were dead."

"This whole thing an acid flashback?" Sage asked, approaching the figure sitting casually on the windowsill. "Or . . . am I on Ayahuasca again?"

"You were *never* on Ayuahuasca. They just told you it was Ayahuasca. It was a stew of handy, random drugs they sell to the white people from the north."

"Why those crooked bastards!" Sage looked more closely at the translucent figure leaning against the sill. "So I'm definitely dead?"

"You definitely are." The figure in white chuckled with angelic conde-scension.

So that meant life after death was real. Sage had talked about it thousands of times, at lectures and seminars, but he'd never believed a word of it. Well, what do you know . . .

He looked more closely at the angelic visitor—he seemed vaguely reminiscent of a vice principal at Sage's old Junior High school, in Santa Fe. Mr. Wallace, wasn't that his name? "Are you Mr. Wallace?"

The figure in white bobbed his eyebrows. "Who's Mr. Wallace? I am the angel Abnegas, Bret. I work for the Cleansing Authority."

Sage didn't like the sound of that. "I don't actually need Cleansing," Sage said, thinking aloud. "I don't know you. You could be lying about my being dead." He put his hand to his chest, felt for a heartbeat—then he felt for his chest itself. It was indistinctly there. A flicker under his hand, little more.

He looked down and made out a dim outline, as if his body was made out of glass, a Bret-shaped bottle.

"There's not much *there*, in there—*is* there?" Abnegas observed sympathetically. "But the part of you that can suffer, or feel pleasure, or perceive—*that's* still there. It's something the Authority tucks away in the human brain. We take it out, when you die, and either plug it into a new one, or push it into the outer darkness for recycling—using the contemporary terminology here . . ."

Sage didn't like the confidence this man was literally radiating—it was a soft bluewhite light coming off him. "When you say you 'take it out'—you're talking about a soul?"

"Essentially."

"And . . . my soul will be plugged into a new body? For a new start?"

Abnegas looked at him with surprise. "I hardly think so! You've recently caused the early deaths of several young people! You've been drugging people, lying to them, exploiting them since you found your little hustle in the 1970s, Bret. You've made many hundreds of thousands of dollars off your seminars but you haven't paid your ex-wife a cent of child support. Whenever you had a choice in your life, you chose selfishly. Hence, I'll be taking you right to the outer darkness, where the spiritual ecology will make short work of you. You're pretty low on the food chain, so . . . it won't be pleasant."

Thinking about that, Sage verified he could indeed *feel*. And it was another new feeling—he'd never felt real terror before. "You mean—something's going to eat me?"

"Yes. Not much of a meal. It'll release your light energy as it does so—and that's the part that will be recycled. It'll take time for you to be digested. The outer darkness is not in the sphere of the eternal, see—time exists there. Which is, maybe, the worst part. It'll take a long, long time."

With that, the angelic figure stood up, and stretched out his hands toward Sage.

Sage backed away from him. "No! I have power! I have the power of the warrior! I am a man of mystery! You have no power over me!"

"Oh but I do . . . Come, my child! Take my hand! The sooner you get started, the sooner the centuries of agony will pass—and *you* will pass, like a kidney stone!"

Sage blinked at him. "Like a kidney stone?"

"Ha ha ha, Roy, you idiot, you had him going but you blew it!" This cawing voice came from the kitchen doorway.

Sage turned and saw a man he *did* know standing there—his uncle Rufus. He hadn't known Rufus well. He'd seen him at holiday celebrations, a jolly, usually drunk, flabby chunk of a man—but he knew his big jowly jaw, his gray crew cut, his dark, laughing eyes. "Uncle Rufus!"

"Got that ID right anyway, boyo! It's me, but not in the flesh! Died in 1980 and here I am, floating on the margins, having my fun just like Roy here."

"Rufus, you bastard!" the "angel" grumbled.

Sage looked at the spirit in white. "Your name is *Roy*?"

"I don't care for Roy. Not as classy a sounding name as Abnegas . . ."

Rufus hooted at that. *"Abnegas!* I thought you'd twig to the hoax right there, boyo! What a fake-out name *Abnegas* is!"

Roy, the "angel", shrugged. "Liked the sound of it, what can I say." He grinned. "I almost had him! That Cleansing Authority stuff sounded good!"

Sage looked back and forth between his dead uncle and the spirit named Roy. "So I'm not going to some kind of hell to be eaten alive?"

Rufus snorted. "'course not! What sort of afterlife would that be? But suppose you'd buckled under and passively gone with ol' Roy here? Why, he'd have traded you to some larger, *very* rapacious soul for favors! Would have been quite uncomfortable—slavery, actually."

Roy snorted. "Wouldn't have been that bad. The whole thing was just a kind of hazing, really."

Sage felt giddy with relief. "No . . . judgment? I really don't have to go with him?"

"Hell no! You're a ghost now! You do what ghosts do! You can wander around and enjoy the afterlife!" Rufus laughed. "Judgment! I don't know why people scare each other with that poppycock. Only judgment is, you judge yourself! That's what you're stuck with, yourself!"

"Well—then I judge myself to be . . . to be a great warrior. A man of power! And . . . and a teacher!"

"Right, right, all that stuff, sure, whatever you want, nephew mine! That's why I came, when I sensed you'd died—to tell you not to believe anything you heard. I knew Roy was snooping around and he loves to play these little jokes. Roy there, he's a teacher's aide—or he was. He got fired for hitting on some college girl, got drunk, died in a car accident. Now he drifts around, all bored, and messes with the newly dead. It's his little hustle, do you see . . ."

Sage looked at Roy, who spread his hands ruefully. "Busted!"

Sage tried, out of habit, to scratch his head as he thought it over. Couldn't feel his head well enough to scratch it. In fact, his ectoplasmic fingers penetrated into his mind, and the sensation made him shudder. "I can *feel*, in a way—but is it possible to really, you know, have a good time? I mean, I can't imagine there's sex or drugs for a ghost, or . . ."

Roy yawned. "Not exactly. There's fun though. I make my own fun. I don't miss being mortal. Bodies are overrated, believe me. Think about it—no more having to stuff your face, wipe your behind, no getting sick, no getting tired, no getting old . . ."

Rufus nodded, grinning. "Right! I mean, bodies—ugh!"

Bodies. Making Sage think about the hunched, bloody figure on the front porch. "I was murdered—isn't there any justice for that? I wonder if I should go haunt that guy Cordell."

"He wouldn't know you were there," Rufus said. "You're too insubstantial a spirit. Most are too thin for the living to be aware of. Anyway he's turning himself in to the cops right now. They'll jug him for the killing. Whereas you got away with yours—until today."

"I didn't plan to kill anyone. I was always trying to straighten people's heads out, that's all, and sometimes it goes wrong . . ."

"Sometimes?" Rufus grinned at him, his smile twice as wide as his mouth—which didn't seem possible. "What I heard was, people just wandered off, after you took 'em for their money. A couple of them killed themselves, another one started selling Herbal Life, and one of them is a survivalist in Colorado . . . Then you had your little sweat lodge adventure . . ."

Roy had stepped up close beside Sage. It seemed to Sage that Roy had grown a foot taller. That he was looming over him. "That's what I heard too," Roy said. His voice seemed lower, rougher. "That you never did help anyone at all . . . That you just wasted their time—and sometimes their lives."

Sage drew back from Roy, annoyed. The ghost was trying to yank his chains, so to speak, again. The hell with him. He was going to get out of this depressing house—the scene of his death!—and explore the immortal world, wander around, slip into some women's locker rooms maybe. Oh and maybe expand his consciousness. Or something.

He started to move past Rufus, toward the kitchen, and the back door—

Rufus blocked his way. "Hold on, there, 'Sage.'"

Sage didn't want to hold on—he veered quickly around Rufus, spurred by a rising uneasiness.

Rufus flashed past him—and stood in front of the back door. "I said—wait!"

Seemed like his uncle's head was slowly expanding, like a balloon being gradually blown up. And there was another face, pushing out under the Rufus face, which crumbled apart from the pressure, the outer face becoming powdery, drifting away as smoke, the inner, bigger face something like an enormous hyena's head, but with human eyes, human lips, a subhuman voice, growling: "Bret, you had better stay here with us! We have lovely, lovely plans for you!"

Sage turned and saw Roy looming up, over him—nine feet tall, his face all doughy, collapsing, hardening into a kind of fleshy, semi-human mantis shape. "Sage . . ." The voice coming in a clattering chitter. "Do you like our little joke?"

He turned back to the hyena-headed thing. Realizing, "You were never my uncle . . ."

"No—your Uncle Rufus is in the outer darkness! You may crowd into a demonic gut with him! Say hello for me if you see him . . ."

"You are . . . you're a . . . a *what?*"

The hyena headed thing spread its quite human hands apart—and between its hands expanded a chain of paper angels, exactly the sort that people cut with scissors to amuse children. The angels burst into flame and flew away on wings of ash, to suck into the hyena's mouth, as if he were inhaling dope smoke. "Ahhhh! We are paper angels, for a time! We mix a little truth into the lies. And then we show ourselves to you—as you showed yourself to Muriel Cordell!"

"I was trying to help her!"

"You threw your line into the water, fishing for lonely, lost souls, Sage—and when you hooked them, you reeled them in. You promised them relief from their dilemmas, and took their time and money, and their freedom. And when they realized you could give them nothing, their hope was destroyed . . . and they wandered away, to be lost again, worse than ever. Or to die. You offered them hope, and you took it away. That's how you 'helped' all those people, Bret Sage . . ."

Sage tried to slip off between them, trying to move quickly as the Rufus Thing had—and the Roy Thing blocked him, making a ticky-ticky-tick sound of amusement by rubbing its chitinous front talons together.

Sage froze—and his voice came in a sort of squeak. Not from his mouth. From somewhere in his shriveling soul. "There is . . . judgment?"

"There are—consequences!" the creature snarled gleefully. "Starting with me, and my companion . . . who really is called Abnegas! I am called Krick!"

"Abnegas isn't an angel . . . or Roy . . ."

"He is such as I—who feed on such as you!"

"But however . . . !" Abnegas said.

"Yes however . . . !" Krick chorused.

"However you may run into the side hallway—there! And find a place to hide!"

"I'm a . . . I'm a spirit! You can't hurt me! I don't have to run from you! You're bluffing! You're—"

Abnegas's head darted forward like a striking mantis, and his mandibles dug into Sage's middle. Sage felt his center crushed in chewing jaws, and something worse than pain crackled through him: a sense of vital diminishment, a feeling of an infinitely unheated void, a nothingness aching with entropy, impinging on his innermost being. He felt a shriveling of an inner self he hadn't known was there till that moment . . .

Sage screamed from within himself, silently and with world-shaking loudness, all at once.

He shrank away from Abnegas, seeing shining shreds of himself writhing in the demon's mandibles, each little bit looking like a tiny little image of Sage. As if the thing were eating Bret-Sage-shaped gummy candies . . .

"Just a bite," the hyena-head growled. "There's a lot more of you to consume . . . You'll make thin stuff but a subtle, understated little snack."

Then Sage bolted for the hallway, was rushing, flying through the house, his feet not quite touching the floor, looking for a place to hide. The basement? No. There was a window in the bedroom. He darted into his bedroom, past his neatly made bed, flinging himself toward the window—which went black.

He pulled up short, staring through the glass. It no longer looked on the little succulent garden at the side of the house—it looked into a churning, black space, an uneasy mirror of ink, and Sage knew if he continued to look he would be drawn into it . . .

He turned away—and heard the noises from the hallway. The growling, the chittering. The clicking of claws. Coming closer.

He wailed and threw himself to the floor, tried to push down through it as he'd fallen through the door, but it wouldn't work—it seemed to resist him. He could feel some other *will* there, pushing back. Who was it? It didn't seem friendly, but it didn't seem unfriendly. Just a watching presence. Waiting its turn.

"Help me!" he called out to it. "Let me through!"

The room darkened; a smell came to him then, the reek of a man's kidney ripped open, mixed with blood. The smell of his own death . . . Why now?

He looked under the bed toward the door. Saw the clawed feet there. Poised.

Sage whimpered and crawled under the bed.

"Help me!" he called out to the other presence. "I'm sorry for what I've done! Help me! I'll make up for it, I'll redeem myself!"

You are only lies . . . came a voice from the floors, the walls, the air. *Only lies* . . .

"No, no! I mean it! I—"

A steel-hard, ice-cold grip on his lower limbs—on what passed for legs in a damaged ghost. Something had gripped him hard there, was pulling him back.

"Sage . . ." It was Krick. Pulling him out from under the bed. "You didn't play the game very well . . . nothing to do now but feast . . ."

"It's time," Abnegas said.

"And time goes on and on, for you," Krick said, dragging him into the center of the room. They leaned over him . . .

"Please!" Sage cried out from the very center of his being. "Give me a chance!"

A small tornado of pitch-black was forming in the center of the room, between Abnegas and Krick. In the center of the onyx whirling appeared a point of light. The scintillation grew, and then flashed like a brilliant strobe to fill the room.

A glowing being stood there, arms spread. Its face was an archetype of all angelic beings. It shone with infinite understanding. The two demons, Abnegas and Krick, crouched, recoiling away from it, covering their eyes in frustration and pain and fury.

A feeling of relief rippled through Sage—it was like stepping out of a sleety winter wind into a warm, cozy room. There was hope. There was a chance . . .

The being of light spread its arms; its wings—like a white butterfly's—filled the room with a comforting perfume, which he seemed to remember. Wasn't that his mother's perfume—remembered from his infancy?

"Come, then, Bret," said the being of light; its voice was neither male nor female, just as the voice of a clarinet has no sex. It opened its arms wider, the warm light beckoned—

Sage rose up, weak but eager to go to the angel, to be rescued, and set free . . .

"Give me your trust and I'll give you life," said the white-winged angel.

Sage flung himself headlong into it—and then realized it had been quoting *him*: mocking the slogan subtitling his website. *Give me your trust and I'll give you life.* And he knew it was the same voice that had said, *You are only lies.*

He tried to turn back but it was too late, he was falling through the portal—because that's what it was, it wasn't a real being, it was a mirage, a *doorway* into the sucking heart of the black tornado, which vacuumed him down, with high speed centrifugal intensity, so that he spun helplessly into its depths . . .

Finally emerging in the churning darkness that he'd seen outside the window—where Abnegas and Krick were waiting, with a great many other beings, all of them ravenous.

"Yeah," Krick said, crushing him in its talons, "that was a little more fun at your expense . . . Now . . . And now . . . and *now* . . ."

The ripping began—their hatred was their teeth and claws, tearing him to pieces.

But the pieces drew back together, re-formed wailingly into the nauseating spirit body that was what remained of the man who'd called himself Sage . . .

Which was immediately swallowed by Krick—and all the others, who were, he saw now, all *one creature*: many grotesque heads on one ethereal body.

Down, Sage slipping down into darkness, into its jet-black inner world, where its hate was a digestive acid, reducing him to a shrieking pulp, the grinding pain going on and on . . . and then . . .

A glimmer in the darkness. A living, angelic light.

"Forgive me!" Sage howled, within himself.

"Come to me, and I will forgive you!" the light replied.

Sage rushed to the point of light, weeping, feeling hope blossom . . .

It drew him in . . .

"Just kidding," it said, as it ate him again.

Living pulverization. Unspeakable suffering that went on forever. Then a light gleamed . . . He rushed to it, trembling with relief . . .

It drew him in . . .

THE SPECIAL SON
Jeffrey Hale

"That a boy, Tinkles. You know what I like to see."

Chase smiled, his back to the door. A second ago, Mr. Tinkles had been limp as a noodle. Now, he was long and hard. Like a sausage. A frozen sausage. The kind Chase's father kept outside, in the big chest freezer.

"Wanna play, Tinkles? I bet you do. You're always in the mood for a game."

Shuffling across the room, Chase made sure the blinds were shut tight. He didn't want any of the neighbors to see him without his pants on. The last time someone had seen him naked, a man in a blue uniform had shown up on his parent's doorstep and talked about indecent exposure.

"Indecent exposure," Chase murmured. What a funny sounding phrase.

He didn't understand what "indecent exposure" meant, exactly, but he assumed it wasn't good. His parents had acted mortified while talking to the man in blue.

With a shrug, Chase dropped his pants. The world was a confusing place. Some people did this, and some people did that. Some people preached this, and some people preached that. And some people did the opposite of what they preached.

Oh well. As long as Chase had Mr. Tinkles, he would be happy.

Mr. Tinkles could make a bad day good.

Mr. Tinkles could turn a frown into a smile.

Mr. Tinkles could make all his troubles disappear.

Stepping daintily out of his jeans, Chase appraised himself in the mirror. All things considered, he wasn't a bad-looking specimen. His thighs were chiseled, his shoulders were broad and his hands were muscular. His skin was a bit pale, but that would change in the summer.

"Lookin' good, hotshot," he told himself, striking a pose and flexing his biceps.

He enjoyed seeing himself in the oil-smudged glass. It made him feel important. Unique. Like he was the only person in the whole wide world. But he could only daydream for so long. Mr. Tinkles was getting impatient.

"Okay, okay, Mr. Tinkles. Don't go soft on me."

Pulling down his tighty-whities, Chase let his penis spring to attention. God, he loved Mr. Tinkles.

Granted, he'd never seen another penis in his life, but he was sure that Mr. Tinkles was the best.

Poking out from beneath a mane of curly brown pubic hair, Mr. Tinkles bade him hello, wagging slightly in the cool morning air. His head was purple, full, and supported by a thick, veiny shaft. His posture wasn't perfect—he curved to the left a bit—but that didn't keep him from standing tall.

"Ready for playtime?" Chase snickered, running his index finger along the length of Mr. Tinkle's soft underbelly. "I promise we'll have lots of fun. Remember last time?"

Mr. Tinkles twitched at the memory, and Chase felt his abdomen tighten. Mr. Tinkles wanted to play really bad today. Chase could feel the blood pulsing between his legs, causing his penis to bounce like a Mexican jumping bean.

"Oh, you're bad, Mr. Tinkles. You're bad."

With a wry grin, Chase leapt onto his bed and spread his legs over the sheets. The mattress creaked and groaned beneath him, reminding him of how big he'd gotten. Then, he went to work.

He grasped his penis with both hands and began to pump. Up and down, up and down, until Mr. Tinkles began to salivate. His testicles quivered between his thighs, but he couldn't accommodate them. Not today. Mr. Tinkles was too engorged. His penis wanted to be stroked, petted, pulled, and it wanted it now.

Slowly, Chase began to pump faster. His hands tightened on his shaft, and he heard a moan escape his lips. Mr. Tinkles wasn't the only one enjoying their game.

Shlick, schlick, shlick!

Some of Mr. Tinkle's saliva oozed onto Chase's palms, and Chase responded by pumping harder. He didn't care that Mr. Tinkles was raw and red. The sensation was overwhelming. It made his back arch and his mouth gape. It felt like . . . like . . . like . . .

Like he was about to explode!

"Just . . . a few . . . more . . . seconds . . ."

Chase wet his lips as the pressure built at the base of his penis. He wasn't going to last much longer. Mr. Tinkles was straining, pulsating, like a worm regurgitating its food. Then—

"Oh my god! Chase! Stop that this instant! What the hell do you think you're doing?"

The sound of Mrs. Stuart's voice caused Chase's eyes to snap open, and he released his penis immediately, before it could spew its chunky white sauce onto his stomach.

"M . . . mom," he whimpered, struggling to pull his underwear up from his ankles. "I . . . I didn't realize the door was unlocked."

"Damn right you didn't!" his mother said, averting her eyes. Her face was flushed, and her hand automatically rose to her neck, where she kept her Rosary. "Just you wait until your father hears about this. He's going to give you a tongue lashing you'll never forget!"

"But . . . but I didn't mean to . . . I mean, it was an accident. You weren't supposed to—"

"I wasn't supposed to what, Chase? Barge into the room while you're . . . you're . . . *masturbating?*"

The last word dripped from his mother's lips like molten lead, and Chase felt his erection wither. He didn't like being yelled at. In fact, he preferred eating vegetables and walking home in the rain to being yelled at. And he had a sinking premonition that he was going to get yelled at a lot today.

◆　◆　◆

That night, Chase found himself in the living room, following a virtually silent family dinner. His parents didn't believe in withholding food as a form of punishment, which was fortunate for Chase because he was hungry as a mule, but they had other ways of making life miserable. Namely, one-on-one talks, like the one he was stuck in now.

"Why did you do it, Chase? I just don't understand," his father said, in a voice that was neither hostile nor friendly. "Don't you understand the consequences of your actions? The Bible says that unclean hands are an abomination. And sexual immorality is to be shunned."

"I know, I know," Chase sighed. He was sitting Indian-style on the couch opposite his parents, and was doing everything he could to avoid eye contact. "I just . . . I don't know. Got bored. I . . . forgot it was wrong."

"Oh, you did, did you?" his mother said, with a plastic smile. "Did you hear that, Harold? Chase says he forgot it was wrong. Well, I suppose everything is okay since he forgot it was wrong. Isn't that right, dear?"

"Yes, honey," Mr. Stuart said placidly.

Mrs. Stuart had an annoying habit of talking to Chase indirectly when she was angry.

"I . . . I didn't mean that. I meant—"

"Meant what?" his mother snapped. "You've said sorry a thousand times, but that doesn't change what you've done. You've committed a heinous sin in the sight of the lord. In the sight of your redeemer. Your friend. I thought we'd gotten past these childish sins, Chase. You're thirty years old, for Christ's sake."

"I think what your mother means to say," his father added calmly, "is that you're not a kid anymore. You need to take responsibility for your actions.

You're special, sure, but you know the difference between right and wrong. You know that sexual activities are for married people only. For husbands and wives."

"Then why can't I get married?" Chase said thickly. "Why can't I find a wife and have babies?"

"Because *you're special*," came his mother's patronizing reply. "God doesn't want you to have babies. Special people can play sports. They can have friends. But they can't get married. And they certainly can't partake in sexual activities. We've talked about this a million times. Haven't you been paying attention during Sunday school?"

"Yes," Chase said grudgingly. He was in a deep enough hole already. The last thing he needed was to throw twigs on the fire.

"Good," his father concluded. "Then I think we're done here. You can go back to your room unless you have something else to say. And no comic books, either. I want you to go straight to bed."

"Yes sir," Chase grumbled. He felt like a punching bag, but at least the worst was over. If he was lucky, his parents would forget in a few weeks and things would go back to normal. He just needed to keep a low profile.

Slinking back to his room on a sleeping foot, he closed the door and climbed into bed as quietly as possible. He didn't want to wake his eleven-year-old brother, who slept in the room across the hall. Little Stephen was his best friend in the world. Aside from Mr. Tinkles, of course.

Ten minutes later, the lights went out in the living room, and Chase heard his parents' door shut. Soon, he would hear water rush through the pipes as they brushed their teeth and emptied their bowels. Then, they would crawl into bed and their mattress would squeak. It would squeak, and squeak, and squeak. Some nights, it would squeak for a solid hour.

Chase didn't understand how it could squeak for so long. His bed didn't squeak when he went to sleep. It just groaned a bit when he rolled over. Either his parents' mattress was defective, or they were going to sleep the wrong way. Those were the only two logical explanations.

Sigh.

Chase rolled over and was about to switch off the lights when the door creaked open.

"Hey. You awake?"

"Of course I'm awake," Chase replied, indignant. "The lights are still on, aren't they?"

"Oh. Sorry."

Slowly, the door opened all the way and a diminutive figure waddled inside. It was Chase's little brother, Stephen. He was dressed in Power Ranger pajamas and his eyes were foggy from sleep.

"I heard mom and dad yelling at you and it woke me up."

"Yeah. Sorry about that," Chase said as evenly as possible.

"Well?"

"Well what?"

"What were they so angry about?"

"Oh. It's nothing."

"Didn't sound like nothing." Stephen rubbed his eyes, hopped up on the edge of Chase's bed. "Come on. Tell me what they were angry about. I won't make fun. I promise. Mom and dad have gotten angry at me lots of times."

"Well . . . if you promise not to laugh . . ."

"Cross my heart and hope to die."

Chase rolled his eyes. "Fine. This morning, mom walked into the room while I was—" how had she put it? "—mastur-ba-tating. And she got angry, 'cause I guess it's bad."

"Huh." Stephen's forehead wrinkled. "What's that?"

"Mastur-ba-tation?"

"Yeah."

"It's where you wait 'till your pee-pee gets hard. Then you pull on it 'till stuff comes out."

"Weird."

"You said it. Anyway, I guess only mommies and daddies are supposed to do that."

"Why?"

"I don't know. Because the Bible says so."

"Oh." Stephen nodded, as if that explained everything. "Then you're going to stop?"

"Stop?" Chase snickered. "No way. It feels too good. I'm just gonna be more careful. I forgot to lock the door last time. That's how mom found out."

"But won't she figure out what's happening when she finds the . . . the *stuff* on the floor? I don't know about you, but she cleans my room every week."

Chase smiled. He admired his brother's astuteness. He wished he could've been that smart when he was eleven years old.

"One step ahead of you," he said, pacing across the room. "Last year, I learned that the one place mom doesn't clean is the closet. The top shelf of the closet, actually. So that's where I hide my stash."

"Your stash?"

"Yes. Wanna see it?"

"Sure," Stephen said, and watched his brother toss the closet door open.

A second later, Chase turned around with a dirty glass jar. It was covered in dust and spider webs and, inside, a thick white liquid sloshed. It looked a little like an old vanilla milkshake. But it didn't *smell* like an old vanilla milkshake.

"Pew!" Stephen exclaimed, pinching his nose. "It stinks! What is it?"

"It's my stuff!" Chase said proudly, holding it up, into the light. "The stuff that comes from my pee-pee when I pull on it. I usually squirt it in here so mom doesn't find it. Smart, huh?"

"Sure," Stephen said, a little hesitantly. "But what are you gonna do when it gets full?"

"Good question," Chase murmured. And it was. He couldn't simply throw the jar away. He'd have to dump it down the sink. That way, his parents wouldn't be able to recover it. By dumping it down the sink, though, he'd risk being caught.

"I guess I'll cross that bridge when I come to it," he said after a moment's hesitation.

"That's cool," Stephen said, unsuccessfully repressing a yawn. His small arms rose above his head and he stretched, growing more exhausted by the second. It was well past his bedtime.

"You should get to sleep," Chase advised him, slipping the jar back into the closet and closing the door. "You have school tomorrow, and you don't wanna fall asleep in class."

"No. No, that wouldn't be good at all," Stephen said groggily. He tried to stand, but his knees buckled and he ended up in a pile on the floor. He was done for the day.

With a chuckle, Chase helped his brother to his feet and guided him to the door. "Think you can make it to your bedroom?" he asked.

Stephen's head bobbed like a marionette.

"Okay. Goodnight then."

Releasing his brother's shoulder, Chase retreated back into his room. Finally, he could get some shut-eye. He didn't have early morning classes to attend because his mother insisted on home-schooling him, but he expected a handful of early-morning chores.

Nothing like cleaning the bathroom at seven o' clock in the morning, he thought dismally. Then he sunk into bed and turned out the lights. For a few hours, at least, he could lose himself in dreams and fantasies; in warped kingdoms and strange realities. He could frolic with mythical beasts and mingle with plump, round-faced cherubs. He could immerse himself in a world where he was king. Where only the things he wanted to happen could happen. Where his every whim could come true.

Little did he know what was about to take place in his bedroom closet.

◆　◆　◆

"Oh man. How did this happen?" Chase frowned, the jar of white fluid in his hands.

For the past five minutes he'd watched a fuzzy ball of spider eggs float through his semen, and now he felt sick to his stomach. He didn't like spiders, and he *really* didn't like the idea of spiders crawling all over his jar. Let alone laying eggs in it.

Goosebumps prickled on the back of his arms, and he shoved the jar back into the closet. He couldn't stand the sight of the fuzzy spider sacs any longer.

Mr. Tinkles would just have to wait.

Closing the closet door as quietly as possible, he snuck back to his dresser, where a list of chores lay. It was a long list, as expected, and would take him a majority of the morning to complete.

Oh well, he sighed inwardly. *At least this work will keep my mind off mastur-bi-tation.*

Besides, he'd have plenty of time to play with Mr. Tinkles later, when his mother went to the grocery store.

♦   ♦   ♦

"Chaaa-aaase!"

"Yes, Mom?"

"Dinner's ready!"

"Okay, mom. I'll be there in a minute."

"You better hurry. You don't want it to get cold!"

"Yes, Mom."

Setting aside his stuffed animals, Chase got to his feet. Two weeks had passed since his mother caught him mastur-bi-tating and, thankfully, she seemed to have forgotten all about it.

He smiled at the memory.

Sure, it had been awkward at the time, but now he thought it was funny. The look on his mother's face had been priceless. The way her lips had curled back and her eyes had gone wide made him want to burst out laughing.

Suddenly, he detected movement in the hall.

"Dad says to come eat your dinner right now," Stephen informed him, pirouetting on his heel and nearly crashing into the wall. "He says he wants to talk to you about something."

"Um . . . okay," Chase murmured. He wanted to ask a question or two, so he could figure out what was going on, but common sense stopped him. His father was a secretive man. He liked to keep people in suspense.

"So . . . you comin'?" Stephen asked from the doorway. His hair was disheveled, and in the low light he looked more like a goblin than a boy.

"Yeah. I'm comin'," Chase replied, feeling sick to his stomach.

Had his parents discovered the jar in his bedroom closet?

Had they discovered the knife under his bed?

Had they discovered the Tomb Raider video game in his dresser?

All these questions crossed his mind as he trudged to the dinner table and, by the time he pulled out a chair, he was feeling worse than before. It must have shown on his face, too, because everyone stopped eating when he sat down.

His parents exchanged curious glances.

"Something wrong, sport?" his father asked, absent-mindedly stabbing at a greasy meatball.

"No. I'm just . . . tired," Chase replied. He tried to hide his discomfort by filling his face with spaghetti, but it didn't work.

"You look worried," his mother said. "Is something bothering you?" Her eyebrows turned down into a suspicious V, and Chase redirected his gaze.

"I'm fine," he lied.

"I bet he's upset because we're in the same grade," Stephen chuckled, nudging a chunk of tomato around his plate. But his amusement died when his mother's lips pursed.

"Stephen Alexander!" she exclaimed. "You know you're not supposed to talk like that. Your brother can't help that he's behind. He's . . . special."

Special.

Chase closed his eyes. That word was starting to get on his nerves.

Almost every day, his parents referred to him as "special." But what was so special about him? He couldn't do math, he could barely read, and he wasn't coordinated enough to play sports. In his book, he wasn't special at all.

With a sigh, he leaned back and wiped tomato sauce from his chin.

"Can I go back to my room now?" he asked.

"Actually, your mother and I wanted to talk to you about something," his father said, rolling back his sleeves and revealing a pair of formidable forearms.

"Okay," Chase said timidly. In that moment, his stomach could have doubled as a butterfly net.

"About a week ago," his father began, in a deceptively even voice, "your mother and I started hearing noises late at night. At first, we didn't think anything of it. We figured it was the house, creaking and groaning. But the more we heard it, the more doubtful we became."

"In fact, the noises grew louder and louder each night," his mother added, using her napkin to wipe a spot from the tablecloth. "Do you know what we're talking about?"

Chase swallowed with difficulty. In the back of his mind, he was aware that he said "no," but the rest of his brain spun with anxiety.

This is it, he told himself. *They heard me mastur-bi-tating and now they're going to punish me for it. They're going to lock me in my room for weeks, without toys or movies. They're going to take away my television-watching privileges. And they're going to make me eat broccoli and asparagus every night for a month.*

The mere thought made his head hurt.

Then . . . something surprising happened.

His parents sat back in their chairs and shrugged their shoulders. They weren't mad at all.

"How odd," his mother said. "We were sure you'd heard it. Why, everyone in the house heard it, and it was coming from your bedroom."

"Muh . . . my bedroom?" Chase stuttered, ears burning.

"Yes," his father said. "Your closet, actually. One night your mother and I snuck into your bedroom and located the sound. We didn't open the door, obviously, because we didn't want to wake you, but we're fairly certain that it was coming from the walls."

"The walls?" Chase blinked twice. His head was reeling.

"Yes dear," his mother said softly. "We think a family of rats has come to live in the wall. It's no big deal, really, but we're having a verminator come over early tomorrow to take care of the problem. He's going to spread some poisoned pellets in your closet and in the attic, so we'd like you to stay out of your room for a while, okay? At least until the problem's taken care of."

"Okay," Chase answered dryly. He didn't know what else to say. He felt stupid uttering one and two-word sentences, but his tongue was swollen as a dead cow in the depths of summer.

Sure, he needed to get rid of the jar before the verminator arrived, but for the most part, he was in the clear. His parents were blissfully ignorant of what he did at night. And hopefully, that wouldn't change in the near future.

◆　◆　◆

Breathing a sigh of relief, Chase slipped into his room following a rousing game of slapjack. His family was crazy about card games and, since slapjack was the only game he could play fluently, that's the one they'd settled on.

He massaged his hand as he walked to the closet. The rounds of slapjack had been fun but, now that family game night was over, he had work to do. He had to get rid of his jar before morning.

Rubbing his nose, he grasped the edge of his closet door. It was open slightly, and he could smell a noxious odor flowing between the cracks.

Something was definitely not right.

Tossing the door open as quickly as he could, he gazed up toward the top shelf and—

Found it completely empty.

"What the heck?"

Slowly, he stepped forward and felt along the dusty surface. His fingers glazed back and forth, back and forth, but all he found was cobwebs.

That's when he felt a cold, semi-gelatinous liquid seep through his sock.

"For the love of Mary!" he exclaimed, stooping down to inspect the broken jar at his feet. "So that's what happened to you. Shee-it. The rats must've knocked you off in the night. Dumb rats. Now I have to clean you up before tomorrow morning. What a waste of time."

Grumbling to himself unhappily, he gathered a dustpan and broom from the laundry room and went to work sweeping up the shattered glass. It wasn't an easy task, considering that the smaller shards were buried in the carpet, but he did the best he could and swabbed up the excess fluid with a towel.

After all was said and done, however, he still had the salty, odious aroma to deal with. The room smelled as though a giant had jerked off on the floor and, as an afterthought, had rubbed his sweaty nut sack across the walls.

Fortunately, his mother kept a can of air sanitizer in the kitchen, which he promptly stole and emptied into the closet, until the place smelled like a damned peach orchard. Then, feeling emotionally and physically drained, he collapsed onto his bed and drifted into a deep, dreamless sleep. The likes of which he hadn't experienced in a long, long time.

◆   ◆   ◆

Swoosh, swoosh, swoosh.

Chase swept the broom back and forth over the porch, watching as clouds of dust billowed up from beneath the stiff bristles. Sweeping wasn't his favorite pastime, but he didn't have much choice in the matter. As long as the verminator was inside, spreading his chemicals, Chase was relegated to the front yard.

"Dumb, stupid verminator."

Turning around, Chase spied the bald, forty-year old man through the living room window. He was wearing gray suspenders and big rubber boots. The kind Chase recognized from fishing shops and outdoor magazines. The man held a clipboard in his hand, and every once in a while he made notes on the wrinkled, ink-stained paper.

"Well, that should be it, then," the bald man said as Mrs. Stuart looked on. His voice was low and throaty, muted by the thick pane of glass. "Just sign right here. Once we get this contract taken care of, I'll start working. Vermin infestation is fairly common this time of year. As the weather gets cold, rodents go looking for warmer pastures. I'm surprised you haven't had this problem before, considering how old this house is."

"I suppose you're right," Mrs. Stuart replied, taking the proffered pen and jotting down her name. "This house has seen its fair share of winters. I just can't understand how a family of rodents could get in. We're a very cleanly family."

"Well, those varmints don't require much of an opening," the bald man chuckled. "They can fit through cracks less than an inch high. Most likely, one pregnant female snuck inside, had her babies in the attic, and now you have a whole mess of 'em crawlin' around. Shouldn't be too hard to get rid of, though."

"I hope not," Mrs. Stuart murmured. "They've kept us up at night for a week. And they seem to get louder every day."

"*Oh. Poor me. They get louder every day,*" Chase said in a patronizing tone, setting the broom aside and letting himself slump against the house. He was sick of being outside in the chilly weather. It wasn't snowing, but the wind was howling like a lovesick banshee and his jacket wasn't doing much to banish the cold.

Stiffly, he loped down the front steps. There had to be some way he could get back inside without his mother noticing. Maybe the back door was unlocked. Or maybe his bedroom window was ajar. If that was the case, he could simply remove the screen and climb in.

Unfortunately, both modes of entry were locked tight.

"Ah, fudge," he muttered, standing before his bedroom window. "Now what am I supposed to do?"

His fingers felt numb from the cold, and he could see his breath curl into the brisk morning air.

Great. Just great.

How could things get any worse?

Pressing his palms to the frosty glass, he gazed into his warm bedroom. The verminator was kneeling next to his closet with a bottle of brown pellets in his hand.

Rat poison, Chase thought instinctively. He might've been stupid, but he wasn't that stupid.

Part of him wanted to knock on the glass and tell the bald man to get the heck out of his room, but he knew it wouldn't do any good. The man had a job to do. Besides, his parents would ground him if they found out.

Releasing a deep, unhappy sigh, he stepped back and thrust his hands in his pockets. The only thing he could do was grit his teeth and watch the man work. It was boring as shit, but it beat the hell out of sweeping the front porch.

After about five minutes, the verminator finished spreading pellets around the floor of the closet and stood up thoughtfully. He seemed to be perplexed by something. His brow was wrinkled, and he kept drumming his stubby fingers against his thigh.

Maybe he's wondering which trap he should use, Chase thought.

But that wasn't the case.

Standing on his tip-toes, the verminator reached into the closet and began rapping on the wall. His knuckles sent hollow thuds echoing through the house. Then, suddenly, he stopped, and his expression changed.

Curious, Chase pressed his face to the window. From this angle, he couldn't see much of the closet, but he could see plenty of the verminator. And judging by the man's eyes, something was going horribly wrong.

Chase held his breath as the man edged away from the closet. The man's face had gone from pink and round to pale and gaunt in a matter of seconds. He looked as though he were staring into the bowels of hell itself.

"Oh, no. Oh, no no no no no," he seemed to say, rubber boots bearing him away from the darkened closet.

Before he could reach the door, though, a spiny object shot from the closet and wrapped around his neck, causing his bladder to void. He tried to scream, but the object—the limb—squeezed too tight. Spittle foamed at his lips and dripped down his chin. His face turned purple.

"Help . . . me . . ." he gargled, urine-drenched legs kicking. He tried to pry the thick, spine-covered limb from his neck, but after a minute, he was too weak to struggle. His arms fell to his sides like an oversized rag doll while his pupils, tiny and bloodshot, flickered about the room desperately.

It was the end, Chase realized. The man's life was dangling by a thread, and there was nothing he could do about it.

Wracked with guilt, Chase tried to slip away from the window. His mind was spinning, and he didn't rightly know what to do. He felt like a deer in the headlights.

That's when their eyes met.

Cold, blue, and seconds from death, the man gazed out the window imploringly. His struggling had ceased, and he hung in the thing's grip with a sort of terrified resignation.

"I . . . I'm sorry," Chase stuttered. "I . . . I . . . I . . ."

Thump.

Before Chase could finish his sentence, the man's head drooped forward and hit his chest, sending tendrils of blood and saliva oozing to the carpet. It was not an easy scene to watch. Chase felt his stomach knot.

Then, without warning, the verminator's body disappeared into the closet. It happened so fast that Chase's knees buckled, and he ended up ass-deep in the dry grass.

"Holy cheese and crackers," he sputtered, crawling feverishly away from his bedroom window. He knew he should tell someone about what had transpired, but would anyone believe him? Probably not. Most likely, his parents would call him crazy and ground him for lying.

Halfway around the house, he scrambled to his feet and ran to the front porch. His knees were stiff as cinderblocks and his fingertips ached from the cold, but he didn't pay any attention to them. He needed to verify what he'd seen.

Barreling through the door, he ran straight to his room, heart pounding.

He could hear his mother in the laundry room, humming to herself while the washing machine jostled. She was completely oblivious to what had taken place down the hall.

Then again, had anything happened down the hall?

There was a chance—a small chance—that he'd imagined the whole ordeal. His imagination tended to run away with him sometimes. But it had seemed so real.

Coming to a clumsy halt outside his bedroom, he let his eyes scour the floor. If he'd really seen what he thought he'd seen, there would be evidence. Like in the television show CSI. There would be blood or scraps of clothing or—

Saliva.

With a growing sense of trepidation, Chase knelt down and ran his fingers across the carpet. As he feared, they came back wet.

Now there was no doubt.

Something was living in his closet.

◆   ◆   ◆

"Mom? Can we talk for a minute?"

Chase swallowed nervously. His mother was in the kitchen, making dinner, but he needed to speak with her. There was a throbbing tumor of guilt in his chest, one that had been gnawing at him all day.

"What's that, dear?" his mother asked over her shoulder. She was busy flipping something on the stove.

"I said: can we talk for a minute?" Chase repeated. His mother wasn't the most attentive person when she was in cooking mode.

"Oh. Sure, hon. What is it?" she said, turning briefly and flashing him a plastic smile.

"Well . . ." he stammered. "It has to do with this morning. When the verminator came over."

"Oh, yes," she murmured. "He was a strange character. Nice enough, but he left rather suddenly—and without saying goodbye. Anyway. What about this morning?"

"Well . . ."

Once again, Chase found himself at a loss for words. He couldn't just come out and tell her what he'd seen. He had to take a more roundabout approach.

Taking a deep breath, he started again.

"You know in the Bible, where it says 'do not murder'? Well, I was wondering if that, like, applies to everything. Not just us humans."

"What do you mean, honey?"

His mother retrieved a jar of salt from the cupboard.

"Um . . . well . . . suppose that something killed something else. And that something wasn't a human. Would it be wrong?"

"I don't follow you, dear."

Chase gritted his teeth. This was going to be harder than he expected.

"What I'm saying is . . . would it be wrong for a non-human thing to . . . ah . . . *kill* a human? A human like you or me?"

"You mean like a jaguar or a mountain lion?" His mother adjusted a frying pan over the burner.

"Uh . . . sure. I guess so."

"Well," she began, apron aflutter, "when God made the world, he made it perfect. All the animals got along with each other. There were no wars or famines. There was no death. When Adam and Eve sinned, however, God cursed the earth. His creatures became finite and evil. That's when they began eating one another. So, in a sense, I suppose all killing is wrong. No matter what is being killed. But it's especially wrong for a human to be killed."

"And . . . uh . . . why's that?" Chase asked. Deep inside his heart he knew the answer, but he wanted to be sure.

"Because humans are made in God's image, silly," his mother murmured, not bothering to turn around. "Why, you ought to know that. You were just going over that in Sunday School."

"Oh. Yeah," Chase said morosely. He lowered his eyes.

This conversation was not going according to plan. Instead of banishing his guilt, his mother was heaping on more and more. Every word that escaped from her lips caused another ten pounds to drop on his shoulders.

Finally, he couldn't take it anymore and slipped back to his room. He still didn't know what he should do, but the silence was more agreeable than his mother's convicting voice.

◆　◆　◆

That night, Chase didn't sleep a wink. He just sat on the edge of his bed and watched his closet, the scent of old semen and air sanitizer mixing in his nostrils.

He couldn't rest with the knowledge that something was hiding in the dark corners of his closet, waiting to pounce.

Sure, it probably wouldn't come out seeking new prey for a while as it had the verminator's suspender-clad carcass to nourish it, but that didn't put his mind at ease. If anything, it made him more nervous. The image of the verminator's cold, waxen corpse lying somewhere in the house made the very marrow in his bones shiver.

He didn't like the thought of death. And he liked the thought of dead things even less. Especially when they were in close proximity to him. He couldn't focus on anything else, though.

At seven o' clock in the morning, he rose stiffly, rubbed his eyes, pulled a clean shirt over his sinewy shoulders, and loped to the kitchen. It was Saturday, and the scent of eggs and bacon filled the house.

"Hey there, sport," his father said, sitting cross-legged at the head of the table. "Got any big plans for the day? Gonna go fishin' at the pond, maybe? Or play Frisbee at the park with Stephen?"

"I dunno," Chase answered simply. His throat was dry and his back was sore from slouching all night long. "Maybe I'll go fishing. Catch a fish or two."

"That sounds like a fine idea," his father said. "You look like you could use a break. Your eyes are red as the devil himself."

"Yeah," Chase mumbled. "I guess they are."

He didn't mention the fact that he hadn't slept a wink. Or that something had been rustling around in his closet. Or that the verminator had been killed in his room. Right now, his father didn't need to know those things.

Gathering a plate from the cupboard, Chase shuffled to the stove. There were three pans simmering over low heat, filling the kitchen with mouth-watering scents, but he couldn't bring himself to look at them. Their contents had all been living, breathing creatures once: pigs, cows and chickens. And now . . . they were nothing. They were sizzling lumps of flesh and butter, long dead.

"Something wrong, buddy?" his father said, noticing his discomfort.

Chase turned with a start. "Oh. No. Nothing's wrong," he said, cheeks turning a rich shade of crimson. "I'm just not hungry. That's all. I think I'll head to the pond, if that's okay."

His father shrugged. "That's fine with me. Just be quiet when you leave. Stephen is still asleep. Oh, and Chase?"

"Yes?"

Chase felt his stomach clench.

"Keep up the good work. Your mother and I have seen a change in your attitude over the past few days, and we're very proud of you. You're really show-ing some maturity. You're providing a positive role model for your younger brother. And in this day and age, that's something to be applauded."

"Oh. Um. Thanks," Chase sputtered. Then he fled the kitchen as quickly as he could, trying not to look as guilty as he felt. He couldn't wait to get to the pond, where he could be alone with his thoughts.

◆　◆　◆

Clank!

Mrs. Stuart fit the last of the breakfast dishes into the washing machine and pivoted to survey her handiwork. The sink was clean as a whistle, the counters were freshly dusted and the floor was wet from a thorough mopping.

By all accounts, she should've been done tidying up for the day. But she wasn't.

Every five minutes, a sound like fingernails raking against cement would split the silence. It wasn't loud by any stretch of the imagination, but it was *there*, and it was driving her crazy.

A new rodent family must have invaded the walls.

Unhappily, she drummed her fingers on the counter. She couldn't be certain, but the sound seemed to be coming from above her, in the attic.

Any other day she would have ignored it, called the verminator, scheduled a return visit, and gone about her business, but today she couldn't. Today it plucked the wrong nerve strings and caused her to lose her patience.

With a heavy sigh, she took off her rubber gloves, tossed them beneath the sink, and stormed to the hallway, where the attic door lay. It took several hops to snag the chord, but eventually she was successful, and down came the ladder.

"Pew. What's that smell?" she groaned, brushing dust from her white skirt. Usually, the attic smelled of mold, mildew and mothballs. But this time it didn't. This time it smelled sweet. Sickeningly sweet. As if someone had left a side of beef in the sun for too long.

"Harold, dear, would you bring me a flashlight?" she called, using one hand to plug her nose. "There's something in the attic, and I want to see what it is."

A minute passed without a response.

"Oh Harold, dear. I know you can hear me," she called again. "Be a darling and bring me the flashlight. I just cleaned the kitchen, and I'm in no mood for your shenanigans."

Still, no response.

Then it dawned on her: Harold wasn't home. He'd taken Stephen to the park. And Chase was at the pond, fishing. That meant she was home alone.

"Oh well," she muttered angrily. "That stupid flashlight's probably out of batteries anyway. I'll be fine without it. Besides, it's not like I'm going to be crawling around up there. I'm just going to take a quick look."

Or was she?

Already, she was having second thoughts. The scent alone was enough to make her vomit. It was warm and sticky, and it tasted bitter in her mouth, but she wouldn't let herself be bested by a rodent—one of God's lowliest creatures.

Filling her lungs with fresh air, she took hold of the ladder and marched up the rungs.

"Don't look now," she called as she reached the top and heaved herself into the stifling darkness. "The farmer's wife is coming to get you and cut off your tails with a carving knife! Better run while you still can! You don't want to wake up without tails, do you?"

She snickered at her own wit, but quickly went silent. A melancholy atmosphere had spread through the house.

Deep down, she knew that something bad was about to happen. She knew it with every fiber of her being, but she refused to believe it. She told herself that God would protect her.

She failed to take into account the devil and his wiles.

Allowing her eyes a moment to adjust, she stood and glanced about the room. It was dark, but streams of light managed to enter through the shuttered attic window.

Here and there, old wooden chests were scattered, brimming with old clothes and books. A few plastic totes were piled among them, holding toys and trinkets that Stephen had outgrown, but most containers were ancient and covered in dust—forgotten by the house's previous owners.

Stepping over a dented lampshade, she approached the corner, where a lime-green coffee table sat in solitude. She couldn't tell where the skritch-scratching sound was coming from, but the attic was only so big. It couldn't hide a family of rodents forever.

Getting down on her hands and knees, she made a visual sweep of the room. From this angle, she could see beneath the miscellaneous furniture that cluttered the floor, but it was rather uncomfortable. Dust clogged her nostrils and splinters poked at her legs.

Finally, she tired of stooping and climbed awkwardly to her feet. This was going nowhere. Even if she did find the rodents, what would she do? Trap them? Not likely. Especially if the verminator's traps had failed. She might as well give up now.

Unhappily, she turned in a circle . . . and gasped.

Something had moved along the far wall!

Sucking in her breath, she tiptoed across the room. She was determined not to make a sound and scare the creature—whatever it might be—away.

Perhaps one of the neighborhood cats had found a way into the attic and gotten itself stuck. Or perhaps a curious squirrel had wedged itself between the slats in the attic window and decided to stay for the winter. There were a million possibilities. Just because the creature was making skritch-scratching sounds didn't mean it was a mouse.

With that in mind, she edged forward until she was mere inches from a stack of raggedy, rust-covered mattresses. Then she reached out her hand, touched the edge of a moth-eaten box-spring . . . and recoiled in terror.

The mattresses weren't covered in rust after all. They were covered in blood. Partially congealed blood, that clung to her fingertips like molasses.

Stifling a scream, she backed toward the attic door. Her head was spinning, and the sickly sweet scent summoned bile into her throat. If she didn't recover quickly, there would be regurgitated eggs and bacon all over the place.

Steadying herself against a support beam, she focused on her breathing. She wasn't into that pagan yoga, but she believed wholeheartedly in relaxation techniques.

"Calm down," she told herself anxiously. "Everything is okay. The Lord protects his servants. His Son was in the desert for forty days without food or water, for goodness sake. Compared to that, I'm taking a walk in the park."

"Yes, but didn't the Chrisssssst, the anointed Ssssson of God, die on a crossssss?" a breathy voice said from the darkness.

Mrs. Stuart froze.

"Who's there?" she called. "Harold, is that you? Or . . . or is it Stephen? Shame on you, whoever you are. Now get out here before I decide to whip you to kingdom come."

"Sssssorry. I can't do that," the breathy voice returned, after a moment's pause.

"What?" Mrs. Stuart pursed her lips. Anger was quickly replacing the fear in her veins. "Don't you dare talk to me that way, mister. Either you get out here on the count of three, or I'm going to come back there and drag you out. Understood?"

This time, silence mingled in her ears.

"That's it," she growled. "One . . . two . . . *three.*"

And on the count of three, she stomped forward, grabbed the pile of mattresses, and flung them aside with a fury so righteous, Moses himself would have blushed. Only, it didn't last. As soon as the mattresses hit the floor, her knees went weak.

There, crouched in the corner, was a dark figure. And below the dark figure lay a placid corpse, its eyes milky white and its lips icy blue. The corpse's clothing had been removed, and its chest was opened from sternum to navel, revealing a greasy conglomeration of organs.

"I told you I couldn't come out," the figure hissed. "It's not polite to talk with one'sssss mouth full."

Mrs. Stuart gaped. But before she could look away, the figure turned its head and fixed her with a pearly smile. A length of intestine hung from its lips, and blood spattered its cheeks, giving it the appearance of a deranged circus clown. Except . . . there was something vaguely familiar about it.

Mrs. Stuart struggled to focus her eyes as the creature rose and maneuvered its massive body out from behind the stack of mattresses.

Yes, she was sure she'd seen those two blue eyes before. Not to mention that nose . . . and that doubled chin . . . and those high cheek bones.

My God.

"Ch . . . Chase?" she sputtered, heart throbbing in her chest. "Is . . . is that you?"

She tried to position herself beside the door so that she could flee quickly, if necessary, but the dark figure was too fast. It scuttled across the floor in a blur, blocking her escape route.

"Now, now," it cooed menacingly, broad shoulders tensing, "why don't you ssssssit yourssssself down and relax? I have a few quessssstions to assssk about this . . . *Jeeeeesus* character before you go."

"You . . . you mean you're going to let me . . . live?" Mrs. Stuart stuttered, half falling into the pile of blood-soaked mattresses.

"Why, of courssssse not," the figure chuckled. "What gave you that sss-silly idea? I ssssimply want to talk before you go to the other sssssside. That issss what you Chrisssssstians want, issssn't it? To be with your Lord and Sssssavior?"

"Muh . . . muh . . . muh . . ." Mrs. Stuart whimpered.

It was all she could do to avoid passing out.

◆   ◆   ◆

"Mo-om! I'm ho-ome!" Chase cried as he pushed through the front door. The day at the pond had given him some perspective, and now he felt good as new. He was sure that the whole ordeal in his bedroom had just been a bad dream. Monsters simply didn't exist in the real world. They didn't go around choking people with snake-like appendages, and they certainly didn't live in closets.

With a laugh, he set his fishing gear next to the couch and pranced to the kitchen. His mother's car was in the driveway, so she had to be home. She rarely left the house on the weekend. Between cleaning and doing laundry, she was busy all day.

"Mo-om!" he tried again, tapping his foot on the tile. "Come out, come out wherever you are! I caught a fish, and I need your help guttin' it! I don't want it to go bad."

Only, his mother didn't reply.

Releasing a sigh of exasperation, he trudged to his bedroom.

"Fine," he murmured, reaching his mattress and sitting down heavily. "I don't need her help. I'll just wait for dad to get home. He'll help me clean my fish. Besides, that'll give me time to play with you, Mr. Tinkles."

Blood rushed between his legs at the thought.

Ever since the verminator had disappeared, he hadn't been very playful. He'd been too worried; too wrapped up in his own imagination. Today was a new day, though.

Shutting the door, he began tugging at his belt buckle. Mr. Tinkles was hard as a rock long before he managed to drop his jeans, and he shivered as the fabric rubbed against the head of his penis.

The next moment his hand was in his underwear, and he was sprawled out on the floor, naked legs trembling. The sensation was overwhelming. He had to bite his lip to keep from crying out in pure, unadulterated pleasure. Then . . . something fell on his chest.

He blinked twice.

Was it just his imagination, or was there a dot of blood on his skin?

Slowly, he reached out and touched it.

Yes, it was definitely blood. But where had it come from?

Mr. Tinkles throbbed as he looked up to the ceiling.

"Oh . . . my . . . gosh . . ." he murmured, feeling suddenly cold and vulnerable.

The ceiling above him was completely saturated in blood, as if a large animal's throat had been slashed in the attic.

A second droplet fell on his chest, and he scrambled to his feet in awe. He wasn't scared, exactly. He was more intrigued by the amount of crimson fluid seeping through his ceiling. He'd never seen that much before.

Hiking his jeans up around his waist, he edged toward the closet. There was a faint sound coming from within. It wasn't much more than a *skritch-skritch-skritch*, but it was enough to draw his attention.

"Huh . . . hullo?" he called. The door was shut, and he grasped the knob tentatively. It felt like ice beneath his fingertips. "Is . . . there somebody in there?"

The scratching paused.

"Stephen, is that you? You're not trying to scare me, are you? That wouldn't be very nice."

Chase frowned.

Logically, Stephen had to be in the closet. He was the only one who could fit inside it. Chase's mother and father were far too big. Yet, he couldn't bring himself to open the door. The image of the verminator's cold, trembling body was seared into his memory.

A minute passed without a sound, and Chase took a deep breath. He couldn't be scared of his closet forever. He was a man, and men didn't run away from their problems. They faced them head-on.

Still . . .

He felt a trickle of sweat run down his palm. His fingers were moist, and the coppery scent of blood wafted through his nostrils like a cloud of methane gas. He'd chicken out if he waited much longer.

Gritting his teeth until they ached, he took a step forward, turned the knob, and threw the door open with all his might, prepared to look into the eyes of death itself. Only, the closet was empty.

"What the . . . ?"

Chase furrowed his brow.

Not two minutes ago, something had been inside his closet. He'd *heard* it.

Was this part of a cruel joke after all?

Anxiously, he felt the inside of the closet. There had to be a false wall or a removable shelf somewhere. Not even Houdini could get in and out of a room without a door or a window. He'd learned that by watching the Discovery Channel.

The longer he searched, though, the more discouraged he became. The closet appeared to be impregnable as a fortress . . . until a section of the ceiling gave way, and a dark, malodorous face peered out from the shadows.

"Holy smokes!" Chase cried, falling onto his back in surprise. He wanted to run, but his feet wouldn't cooperate. They felt like lead. "Wha . . . what are you doing in my closet?"

The face licked its lips in amusement. It had blood spattered across its cheeks.

"I wasssss waiting," it said simply.

"W . . . waiting for what?"

Chase couldn't hide the fear from his voice.

"You, of courssssse."

"Why me?"

The face hissed in amusement, revealing two rows of razor-sharp teeth. Its breath stank of rotting fish, mold and decay.

"Issssn't that obvioussss?"

"No," Chase whimpered, fumbling to his knees with all the grace of a two-year old. He was hoping to make a break for the door but, as he summoned up the remains of his courage, the face began to rotate. And as it rotated, it became more than a face.

First, a pair of shoulders emerged from the shadows. Big, broad shoulders, covered in spines. Then, a pair of long, spider-like legs, which it used to lever itself through the hole. But it didn't stop there. Two more legs appeared soon after, followed by another two, and another two—all of which were attached to a bulbous, pus-colored thorax.

Flexing its jaws, the creature cleared the hole and dropped to the floor on eight spiny legs. It was heavy, and when it hit the carpet, it did so with a resounding *thump!* From head to toe, it must have stood five feet tall.

Chase averted his eyes. He didn't want to look at the arachnid freak.

"Just leave me alone!" he cried.

"I'm afraid I can't do that," the creature hissed, crawling forward. Every step made its massive thorax quiver. "I've feasssssted on your mother. Now we can be together. Forever."

"What are you talking about?" Chase returned. Hot tears burned in his eyes, but he refused to let them run down his cheeks. "What makes you th . . . think I want to be near you?"

"Becaussssse," the creature said, laying a spiny appendage on his shoulder,

"I'm your sssssssson."

"What!?" Chase exclaimed, throwing himself back onto his bed. He couldn't believe what he'd been told. "I'm n . . . not your father. I'm nobody's father. This has to be a trick."

But it wasn't a trick.

As the creature moved forward on its massive legs, Chase saw the resemblance. Not only did the creature have his eyes, his nose, his cheek bones and his lips, it had his build, too. It was covered in muscle, from its slightly human shoulders to its distinctly arachnid thorax.

Chase felt as though he was looking in the mirror.

Then, it all made sense.

"Oh my gosh," he whispered.

The thing standing before him really *was* his son. In a way, at least.

Three weeks ago, when the spider eggs fell into his jar of semen, some sort of mutation must have occurred. The arachnid genes must have mixed with his human genes, causing a hybrid to develop. That was the only plausible explanation. But it was still crazy.

Chase frowned.

Humans and insects couldn't reproduce. He'd heard that on television. Unless . . .

Unless that's my special ability! he thought excitedly.

His parents had been telling him that he was special for his entire life, but he hadn't known *how* he was special until now!

Suddenly, he was no longer afraid. Goosebumps stopped prickling up and down his arms. Sweat stopped pooling down his forehead. He felt happy. Genuinely *happy*, for the first time in his life.

Why?

Because he had a *son*. The creature standing opposite him, with blood coating its jaws, was his son. His offspring. The result of his seed. And that filled him with joy. He wouldn't have to be alone for the rest of his life. He could have children. Lots of children. As many children as he wanted, in as many varieties as he wanted.

If his hunch was true, he could have a dog-human son . . . and a cat-human son . . . and a bird-human son . . . and a whale-human son . . . and a zebra-human son. He could have a squirrel-human son . . . and a fish-human son . . . and a fox-human son. Heck, he could have a horse-human daughter too!

The possibilities were endless.

All he had to do was get Mr. Tinkles hard.

ABOUT THE AUTHORS

KURT BACHARD—Kurt Bachard lives in South London, UK, where he was raised as a feral child by stray dogs. He has been nominated for the Pushcart Prize, and his fiction and non-fiction has appeared in numerous publications, notably in the Black Quill nominated *Shroud Magazine*. He also enjoys writing under pseudonyms.

STEPHANIE BEDWELL-GRIME—Stephanie Bedwell-Grime is the author of ten novels and over sixty short stories, novelettes and novellas. She is a five-time finalist for the Aurora, Canada's national award for speculative fiction and has also been an Eppie finalist. Recently, her story "Luck of the Dragon" won best fantasy story in the first annual SWW's from *Strange, Weird and Wonderful Magazine*. Stephanie welcomes visitors to her website at www.feralmartian.com

MICHAEL BOATMAN—Michael Boatman spends his days pretending to be other people, usually better adjusted people. Currently he can be seen as attorney Julius Cain, on the CBS drama, *The Good Wife*. He co-starred on several hit television shows like the ABC sitcom *Spin City,* the HBO original series *ARLISS* and the Vietnam drama, *China Beach*. His horror-comedy novel, *The Revenant Road*, was published in 2009. His fiction has appeared in *Weird Tales, Horror Garage* and *Red Scream* magazines, and in anthologies like *Dark Delicacies 3: Haunted,* and the *Dark Dreams* series.

RANDY CHANDLER—Randy Chandler is the author of the two solo novels *Bad Juju* and *Hellz Bellz*, and authored *Duet for the Devil* with t. Winter-Damon (God rest his soul). Randy has been a magazine editor/publisher, a freelance book reviewer, a mental health worker, a gas-pump jockey, an ambulance attendant, a soldier in Vietnam and a funeral home flunky. He often haunts fields of carnage where angels and devils do battle.

LAWRENCE CONQUEST—Lawrence Conquest is a British author and musician. Lawrence started writing in 2008, and since then his fiction has appeared in magazines (*Black Static, Crossed Genres, A Thousand Faces, Fantastic Horror*), anthologies (*Night Terrors, Inner Fears*), comic books (*FutureQuake, Something Wicked*) and a forthcoming audio for the BBC's *Doctor Who* (Big Finish Productions). A novel is in the works. Full bibliography at www.lawrence-conquest.blogspot.com. Lawrence has also produced numerous albums of exotic electronic noise under the moniker Hate-Male (www.myspace.com/hatemalenoise). He is very busy.

TIM CURRAN—Tim Curran lives in Michigan and is the author of the novels *Skin Medicine, Resurrection* and *The Devil Next Door*. His short stories have appeared in such magazines as *City Slab, Flesh&Blood, Book of Dark Wisdom, and Inhuman*, as well as anthologies such as *Flesh Feast, Shivers IV,* and, *Vile Things*. Find him on the web at: www.corpseking.com.

RALPH GRECO, JR.—Ralph Greco, Jr. is an internationally published author of short stories, plays, essays, button slogans, 800# phone sex scripts, children's songs and SEO copy. Ralph is also an ASCAP licensed songwriter/performer and Internet radio D.J. He lives in the wilds of suburban New Jersey, where he attempts to keep his ever-expanding ego in check.

JEFFREY HALE—Raised alongside genetically altered corn and man-eating carp, Jeffrey Hale is no stranger to suburban horror. He has been accosted by goat-human hybrids, chased by horny, inbred wenches, attacked by giant killer bees, and survived countless hours of prime-time television. When he isn't busy fighting for his life, however, he can be found reading, writing, playing the bass guitar, or otherwise making a damn fool of himself. You can find him online at www.jeffreyhale.wordpress.com.

HARPER HULL—An Englishman by luck, Harper now lives in the Southern US with his Dixie wife penning horror, sci-fi and other writings whenever he can. Inspired by his dad's 'scary bookshelf' as a kid and later by an education in the classics Harper reads like a demon and gets his own ideas from the strange and surreal things that happen in everyday life. His stories have appeared in North America and Europe so far and he currently has several large projects on the go. If you ever read one of his works he just hopes that you enjoy it.

MATT KURTZ—Matt Kurtz writes in his spare time when not working for a small advertising company in Texas. Originally a part-time independent film-maker and screenwriter, Matt decided to narrow down his creative energy to focus more on short stories and future novels. Liberating his imagination—and not having to worry about keeping things within a low budget—he spent the last year writing over three dozen short stories and loved every minute of it. He is currently working on revisions to those shorts while outlining his first novel. "Hunger Pangs" is his first published work.

SEAN LOGAN—Sean Logan's stories have appeared in about twenty publications, including the horror fiction podcast *Pseudopod* and the anthologies *Twisted Legends*, *The Vault of Punk Horror*, and Comet Press's *Vile Things*. He lives in northern California with a wife and Rottweiler who seem to be plotting against him.

AARON POLSON—Aaron Polson was born on the Ides of March: a good day for him, unlucky for Julius Caesar. He currently lives in Lawrence, Kansas with his wife, two sons, and a tattooed rabbit. To pay the bills, Aaron attempts to teach high school students the difference between irony and coincidence. His stories have featured magic goldfish, monstrous beetles, a book of lullabies for baby vampires, and other oddities. *Loathsome, Dark, and Deep*, a historical horror novel, is due from Belfire Press in late 2010.

DANIEL I. RUSSELL—Daniel I. Russell has appeared in various publications such as *Malpractice: Anthology of Bedside Terror, From the Asylum, Dead West, Midnight Echo 3, Pseudopod* and was the featured writer in *Andromeda Spaceways Inflight Magazine* #43. 2010 sees the novel *Samhane* released from Stygian Publications and novella *Come into Darkness* from Skullvines Press, with both books available in German with Voodoo Press. Daniel lives in Western Australia with his partner and three children. Visit him online at www.danielirussell.com.

M. SHAW—M. Shaw has had the easiest life imaginable but still finds itself compelled to whine about the stupidest, most mundane crap imaginable. If it can't find a parking spot or someone spills a drink on the coffee table, its day will be ruined and it will make sure yours is too. You know who you are, people. Blog: mshaw.wordpress.com Twitter: @murdershaw Facebook: Makoto Shaw

JOHN SHIRLEY—John Shirley is the author of numerous novels, story collections, screenplays and teleplays. His novels include the recent *Bleak History* (Simon & Schuster), *Demons* (Del Rey), *Black Glass*, and *Crawlers* (Del Rey). He won the Bram Stoker Award for his story collection *Black Butterflies*.

FRED VENTURINI—Fred Venturini has written in exchange for various treasures, including an MFA fromLindenwood University, contributer's copies, token payments, checks that sometimes do not bounce, and most of all, for the love of the act. His fiction, most of it horrific in nature, has appeared in *The Death Panel* from Comet Press, *Necrotic Tissue, Underground Voices, River Styx, Polluto, Twisted Dreams, Susurrus, Sinister Tales, Morpheus Tales, Writer's Post Journal* and others.

SIMON WOOD—Simon Wood is an ex-racecar driver, a licensed pilot and an occasional private investigator. His short fiction has appeared in a variety of magazines anthologies, such as *Seattle Noir, Thriller 2* and *Woman's World*. He's a frequent contributor to *Writer's Digest*. He's the Anthony Award winning author of *Working Stiffs, Accidents Waiting to Happen, Paying the Piper* and *We All Fall Down*. As Simon Janus, he's the author of *The Scrubs* and *Road Rash*. His latest thriller is *Terminated*. Curious people can learn more at www.simonwood.net

www.ingramcontent.com/pod-product-compliance
Lightning Source LLC
Chambersburg PA
CBHW031401250626
47155CB00004B/1357